I0594555

This is a work of fiction. Names, characters, places and incidents are either products of the author's imagination or, if real, are used fictitiously.

Cover art: Oleisha Proksa
Copyright © Alison Croggon and Daniel Keene 2020
Artwork Copyright © Oleisha Proksa 2020
Newport Street Books, Melbourne

The moral right of the authors has been asserted.

All rights reserved. No part of this books may be reproduced, transmitted or stored in an information retrieval system in any form or by any means, graphic, electronic or mechanical, including photocopying, taping and recording, without prior written permission from the author.

ISBN: 978-0-6488744-0-9

First published by Newport Street Books, Melbourne, 2020
newportstreetbooks.com

A catalogue record for this book is available from the National Library of Australia

PINKERS

Book Two: Newport City

Alison Croggon and Daniel Keene

Newport Street Books

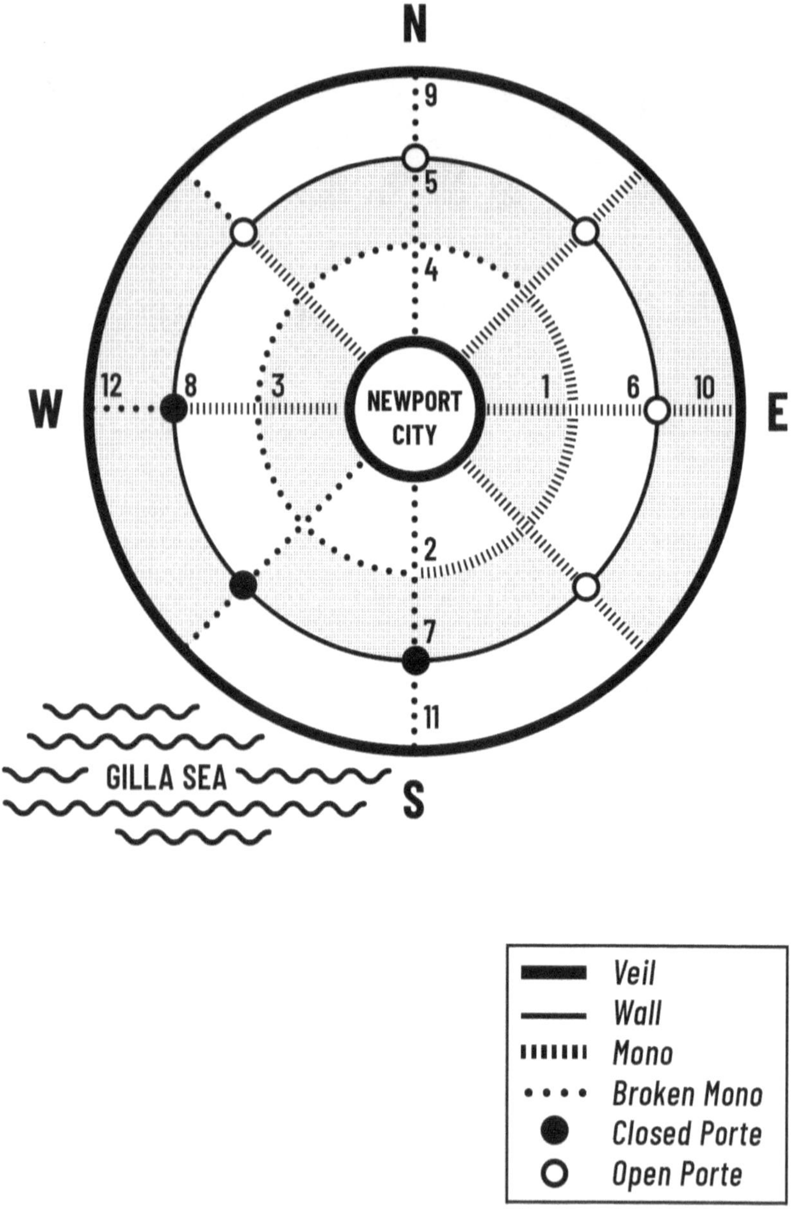

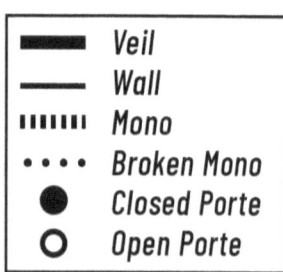

N

9

5

4

W 12 8 3 NEWPORT CITY 1 6 10 E

2

7

11

GILLA SEA

S

	Veil
	Wall
	Mono
	Broken Mono
●	Closed Porte
○	Open Porte

Schematic map, Newport City and surrounding banns
(Urban Affairs Department, Newport City Council)

GLOSSARY

Alchems	An informal band of dissenters against Newport City Council.
Ap	Local police in the banns. Short for "Anthropological Police".
Avants	Fleshers term for people who exist outside binary genders.
Banns	Outer suburbs of Newport, separated from Newport City by the Inner Veil.
Baju	Firewater made in the banns, usually from whatever is around. Varies enormously in quality.
Bogies	Miner slang for AI mine workers.
Credits	Newport City's official unit of electronic currency. Unless they are working in Newport City industries, fleshers use untraceable "black credits" that are stored in alternative databases.
Dasht	Anywhere outside Newport Outer Veil.
Disruptor	Tech that nullifies gene searches, used to get through a Veil.
Flesher	Derogatory term invented by Pinkers to refer to those born through natural reproduction. Appropriated by those who live in the banns.
Foodtowers	Towers where plant goods are grown, mostly for consumption in Newport City.
Gau	Animal evolved from a domestic dog.
Homebuild	Any home-made tech.
Homer	A vehicle for hire.
IMR	Short for *In Media Res*. Refers to the merging of virtual reality and physical surroundings.
Lenscam/chip	Camera/video chip inserted in lens.
Mokal	Sweet, sludgy drink, usually fruit flavoured.
Mono	Monorail in the banns, partly functional.
MPS	Magnetic Positioning System.
Neka	Animal evolved from a domestic cat.

OpSec	Operational Security. Originally applied to securing data, it now refers to all Newport City militia operations.
Pinker	Flesher name for clones of Newport City.
RTS	Rapid Transport System in the banns (now defunct).
Rues	Common name for streets.
Shijo	Marketplace.
Skinner	Flesher name for criminals who hunt flesher adolescents for the lucrative illegal hormone market in Newport City. Recognisable by the bandoliers that contain their extraction equipment.
Steadies	Close friends.
Suit	A suit is an electromagnetic personal shield that protects the wearer from a variety of environmental hazards, notably nanoviruses. A benign version of Veil technology, it keeps hostiles out rather than destroys them and usually includes temperature control. Worn as a belt.
Tubes	Generic term for visual media.
Veil	An electromagnetic shield that protects Newport from the environmental hazards in the dasht. Features a heightened gene filter designed to hunt down and destroy nanoviruses. The Inner Veil is tuned to exclude all genes not listed in the Newport City clone database and includes weather control.

Erin

That day at the hospital was the first time I ever saw a real flesher.

It had been a shitty day all around. The night before, there'd been a party for the launch of the first season of *Ebolastic*, the big new soap starring Mr Mega-idol John Mecha. It's billed as an ultra-real crime show, and it's a special commission from the top. Ultra-real is going to be the new Big Thing.

Mecha plays a cop investigating flesher crime gangs who are smuggling bad DNA through the Inner Veil to destroy the population of Newport City. Before the launch, there was a lot of publicity about how it was being filmed in the rundown suburbs of Newport City, the closest thing we have to the banns — instead of in an IMR studio, with real weapons borrowed from OpSec and sometimes real ammo. I had to do a lot of posing in front of store-fronts roughed up to look like they were about to collapse any minute.

I play John Mecha's love interest, a blonde with a heart of gold and a brain of lead. I have no idea why the cop fell in love with her and, the way John Mecha treats me, neither does he. When we aren't in scenes together, he acts like I'm invisible and inaudible. But that's because, as everyone in the celebrity industry knows, John Mecha is a prick.

Did I say I hate working on it? I *hate* working on it. Dervin says it's going to be my breakthrough role, but I think the only thing that's going to break is me.

The last thing I wanted to do was party, but all the top brass was going, including Mayor Osborne and Bremmer, the chief of OpSec, and so there was no way, bar actual death, of getting out of it. My AI maid Ami had her excitement synapses turned up to the max. They must have sent out a general order.

'Tonight's going to be great!' she trilled, as she slipped my new dress over my head. It was made of some new smart fabric, feathers that changed colour as I moved and exposed most of me. 'And this dress, ooh la la! Ilati has outdone himself! You look super plus! Everyone will be in love with you!'

I stared at the dress. The pinks didn't suit me, they made my skin look lifeless. But Ami kept wittering on.

In the end I turned her off and got myself ready instead. I was doing my makeup when Dervin came in. He saw Ami standing motionless in the corner and frowned. 'They'll pick it up, you idiot,' he said.

I studied him in my mirror. He looked angry. These days Dervin often looked angry, and he took it out on me.

'So?'

'So switch her on.'

'She won't shut up,' I said. 'And I've got a massive headache.'

'Fuck your headache. I don't want any trouble.'

Dervin left, not bothering to check that I did what he said. He knew I would.

I rolled my eyes at his back and clicked my fingers. Ami returned to life, blinking as she rebooted, and took over my makeup as if nothing had happened. I turned down her voice to minimum and stared in the mirror.

Me, Erin Saba. The face of your next IMR dreamscape. Bored, although I didn't know it then. Lonely. I knew that.

The party was as dull as I had expected. Lots of speeches. I smiled like I was supposed to and posed for the vids with Osborne smirking creepily like he was planning to touch me or something and then Dervin sent me home because the next day was busy with the second series of the soap.

I was too jittery to sleep. I hate those events, they leave me feeling like my skin has a thin film of slime all over it. I told Ami to make me a martini, double strength, and when she brought it I switched her off, I didn't care what Dervin said, and I drank it sitting on my balcony, looking over the lights of Newport City Central. And then I made myself another.

I guess it wasn't surprising that I had an accident the next day. Nothing dramatic, just a stupid thing. I tripped over some cables and fell on one of the lights, and the skin on my left knee was sliced open so deep that I could see the bone. It didn't even hurt to begin with. When I looked at it, I felt sick. So that's how I ended up at Newport City Western Hospital.

The biotech had just sealed up my knee and given me a shot to kill the pain when all the lights went out. We were in a cubicle without any windows, so it was completely dark. The biotech, a blonde girl with the long, clever fingers of her kind of clone, let out a shriek. I didn't want to have any more accidents, so I stayed put on the table.

'Must be the generators,' said the medic. He was just there to look at me, there had been a bit of fuss when I turned up. 'But it's strange, all of them going off at once...'

We waited in the dark for what seemed like ages, but the lights didn't come back on. I began to wonder if it was terrorist fleshers, like in the episode we had just been filming, but I didn't say anything.

'Doesn't anyone have a torch?' said the medic at last, and I heard someone fumbling in the dark. A couple of things fell on the floor with a clatter, and then there was a click and the room was lit with a cold, white glow from some tiny object that looked like the instruments they use to check inside people's mouths. It was very bright after the darkness.

I sat up. 'Now what?' I said.

'All the comms are down,' said the medic, who fiddling with his wristband. I could hear the tension in his voice. Maybe he was thinking about terrorists too.

'I want to get out of here. I've got work to do,' I said.

'Best to wait until we know what the situation is...'

I didn't want to wait. 'Do you know the way to the entrance?' I said, putting on my cop voice. Like I was in charge.

The medic looked dubious. 'Yes,' he said.

'Let's go then.' I swung my legs off the table and stood up. At that point, the lights flickered and came back on.

The biotech let out a big breath and I realised that we had all been frightened, sitting there in the dark wondering if anything awful was going to happen.

The medic smiled at me in relief, and reached out to take my hand. He saw the shock on my face and blushed to the roots of his hair. He must have been more thrown than he let on. Medics have to touch people sometimes, even with all the meditech, so inhibitors aren't programmed so strongly in them, but touching me – me! – was about as big a faux pas as you could imagine.

He cleared his throat, not looking at me. 'This way.'

We'd just reached Dervin and Ami, who were waiting in the hallway, when suddenly the place was swarming with OpSec, the ones who stand outside Council buildings with big weapons and scanner helmets. They ordered everybody in line against the wall. An alarm went off and I began to panic. I hadn't seriously thought that there could be a terrorist attack, not in the middle of Newport City. I turned and saw a flesher walking straight in through the front door, strolling casually past the scanners. Everyone started screaming and running.

I knew he was a flesher straight away. Black hair, black skin, silver jacket, silver boots, black discs over his eyes. He looked impossibly glamorous. It was the way he strode in, loose and unafraid, lawless. Nobody in Newport City walks like that. He was tossing something up and down, a baton of some sort. It'd turn three times in the air and then he'd catch it. Even in my confusion, I wondered if he was some kind of actor: I'd learned that trick at celebrity school.

I didn't run, like everyone else. I just stared.

He wasn't anything like the fleshers in our soap, who are all kind of thick and brutish. He moved like quicksilver. Like some kind of god.

He looked me right in the eye and I saw something light up in his face. His smile switched up to dazzling. At first I thought he must have seen me in some soap, but then I felt the pull of him. It's hard to describe: in that couple of seconds I felt that he could read my mind. It was like he knew me already, like he saw something in me that just was like him. My heart hammered inside my chest like it was going to jump out.

He lifted up his hand, as if he was waving hello. And then, right in front of me, he vanished.

Of course, me being in the hospital in the middle of a fleshers attack – the first since the bad old days – was all over the infonews. Dervin played it for all it was worth, and I had to do vids on all the channels and photo ops with the OpSec guys who had been there and rescued me from danger.

I knew it was shit. I knew that flesher wasn't planning to hurt me and that I hadn't been in any danger and that nobody had rescued me from anything. But everybody knows that you don't question the official story.

There was an event where Osborne gave the cops a medal each for bravery. At the reception afterwards, I asked one of the officers why the hospital had been attacked and whether anybody had been hurt and he turned his eyes on me, ice-blue and expressionless. 'That's confidential information, Ma'am,' he said.

I smiled as winningly as I could, but it seemed to have no effect on him at all. 'Did they really want to blow up the hospital?'

'These are dangerous people, Ma'am.'

Usually I can get people to tell me stuff, but not this guy. He didn't have a brand on him, but I began to wonder if he was an AI. Sometimes it's hard to tell the difference between a full-on conditioned duty clone and an AI. The only way to tell is if they feel pain. If you set fire to an AI, they just carry on as if nothing is happening. I saw it once, when a downtown department store went up in flames. Nobody remembered to tell the retail AIs to get out, so they just stayed behind the counters, smiling as they burned.

I could see Osborne staring at me talking to the cop and something in his gaze made me feel uneasy. I thanked the cop and moved away.

In all the interviews I talked about how I had been frozen with terror and what heroes the OpSec men were and how grateful I was. That's what Dervin told me to say, and I said it. But I knew it wasn't true. The only thing that made me afraid was OpSec running around with their weapons. The flesher hadn't frightened me at all: when I saw him, I just wanted to laugh. Because of the audacity of it, the cheek. The style.

When I saw Osborne looking at me, I remembered how the flesher had lifted his hand and smiled, as if he knew me. They played the footage over and over again on the tubes, and that's what it looked like. The camera was behind me so you couldn't see my face. But there are cameras everywhere. Maybe I smiled back. I couldn't remember.

Perhaps Osborne suspected that I really did know him.

I don't know that flesher. I only wish I did. I can't stop thinking about him, about how he walked into that hospital.

Fearless. Shining.

Dez

The day the Curtains went up, we knew the holiday was over. We had three weeks of respite. Three lousy weeks.

I guess three weeks is how long it took for Newport City OpSec to get itself together after Morro and Brian Mac lobbed a bomb into their clockwork brains. I still grin sometimes about the sheer twistedness of what they did: how they made Mayor Osborne believe that Bremmer, the OpSec head honcho no less, was the leader of the Alchems, how there was a whole army of mutant fleshers out in the banns primed to take Newport City by the throat. Osborne arrested all the top brass, Bremmer included. He swallowed that whole unbelievable tale.

And now Morro was dead, and Brian Mac had disappeared and was probably dead as well. I didn't know what to think about either of them any more. Morro betrayed us, but he'd thrown his life away trying to redeem himself. I knew that we all wondered, although we never said it out loud, if anyone besides Morro had been informing. It was bad enough what Morro did, a lot of people were dead because of him.

Meanwhile Brian Mac, the loser Ap we all made fun of for creeping on Ma, turned out to be a legend.

How did that make any sense? I still couldn't get my head around it.

We needed time: time to lick our wounds, to think about everything that had happened. But when you're a flesher there's never time. Bo, always the optimist, said that maybe now things would be different. He thought that maybe now we'd stopped the Newport City death machines, the Eradicators, OpSec might get off our backs and let us live a little. But I believed the opposite, and so did Ma. So while the streets were quiet, we partied. We made love and music. We danced like we'd never heard of Eradicators. We mourned our dead and missing.

And we made plans.

The first task was to find out who was left. A lot of our friends had disappeared, and we didn't know who was in hiding, who had been arrested and who was dead. We needed to get in touch with the Alchems to work out what to do next. They were a secretive bunch who worked in separate chapters, and even Flora, who was a member, didn't know how many there were.

Ma said said we'd get nowhere if people didn't co-ordinate. So we'd been making connections with different groups, beginning to talk about how to make the banns a better place to live. Things like med centres in the outer banns, or maybe schools.

When the Curtains went up, we had to put those plans aside. We had a long way to go before could even begin to think about that stuff.

First, we had to survive.

That morning I had gone over to Flora's to cheer her up in her hour of need. She was sick. Flora was never sick, it made me nervous. She reckoned it wasn't anything serious, just exhaustion, and all she needed was a day in bed. After an hour of me mopping her fevered brow she'd had enough. She told me that my fussing about was driving her crazy and this new caring Dez was pissing her off.

I saw her point. This wasn't like me. Normally I'd just ping her or maybe open a line to check how she was and then I'd go down in the cellar to do some making or whatever else I happened to be obsessed with at the time. But it was like I had fallen in love all over again, as if we'd just met for the first time. There was more to it than that, but I didn't tell Flora because to say it out loud felt like bad luck.

Every second of every day I was afraid that she might die. It seemed amazing to me that Flora was still there, alive and breathing. It was like there was a loop in my brain saying *this can't last this can't last*, as if nobody deserved to be this lucky, especially not me. I had this constant fear that at any moment I'd turn around and she'd be gone – a skinner would get her or the Aps would just shoot her or maybe there'd just be some pointless accident. Because even when times are good, there are still accidents.

I was beginning to understand why Kojo was sometimes so impossible. He had lost Flora's mother, and he didn't want to lose his daughter as well. I knew exactly how well Flora coped with her Dad's over-protectiveness, which is to say, she didn't cope well at all; but it didn't stop me behaving the same way.

We began to bicker, and finally Flora sat up.

'Shut up, Dez. You always do this. *Always*.' Then she said, very gently, like she didn't want to bruise me: 'Go home. Go home and cook your Ma some dinner or do some making or something useful. I'm going to be *fine*. Just let me get some sleep.'

'I can stay here. Just in case you need something.'

She turned over and pulled the blanket over her shoulder. 'Dez. I said. Go home.'

She shut her eyes, pretending to be asleep, and wouldn't say any more. I looked at her for a few moments and then I kissed her forehead, tasting the beads of feversweat salty on my lips and thinking how she was right, as usual. And then I did what she said.

Ma had just returned from the shijo with some spino rolls, so we heated them up and ate them for lunch. Bo was out somewhere so we left him two, in case he hadn't eaten. I had just put the dishes in the steamer when he barrelled through the door. He didn't even bother to say hello.

'Put on the tubes,' he said.

'Say what?'

'The tubes. Now.'

'Are there raids?'

Instead of answering he went over to my chair, so I pushed him out of the way (it's *my* chair) and called up the screen. It was blank. There was nothing, not even the visual static you get when the tubes are down. I felt the hair rising on the back on my neck.

Bo's jaw was tense. 'Try the dark tubes.'

I switched over and suddenly there was a blare of info. I called up a live vid taken from a highrise somewhere, I couldn't recognise the place. From above I could see a dark line of militia climbing out of two transports. There wasn't a sign of fleshers: anyone with sense would have legged it out of there as soon as the militia appeared.

I zoomed in. They unloaded these big, grey machines, installing one at each end of the rue. There was a shimmer in the air, maybe five metres high, bisecting the street.

Ma was standing behind me, staring over my shoulder. 'Is that a Veil?'

'It looks like it,' I said. 'Like a mini version.'

She leaned in, squinting at the screen, and swore.

There are two Veils. The Outer Veil that keeps Newport City safe from dangers in the dasht, the storms and feral nanos, and the Inner Veil, that keeps Newport City safe from fleshers. Meaning us. The banns where we live are the buffer zones. We help to keep the pinkers clean and pure in their little bubble.

And now, it seemed, there were more Veils, to keep fleshers away from each other.

'There's one of them right the down the middle of Rue Leipzig,' said Bo. 'I was going to meet Jenna in the Third for some pho and then these bastards waltzed in and now you can't get out of the Second. I tried everywhere.'

I stared at him, and then I started scrolling. There were reports from all over the banns. People were already calling them Curtains. So many vids, but they might have all been the same one. Militia in black uniforms, not the usual Aps, bringing in their machines to separate us from each other. To lock us in.

'They must have moved in all at once,' I said. I realised with a sick feeling in my stomach that if she hadn't been ill, Flora would've been at a meeting in the Fourth. 'Where's Jenna?'

'She's in here with us,' said Bo. 'She went to the shijo to get some greens. We're going to have to eat at home.' He stared at the screen. 'What does it mean?'

'We're screwed,' I said. 'That's what it means.'

'There'll be a way to get past them,' said Ma. 'There always is.'

'Yeah,' said Bo gruffly. He switched the screen off and turned around. 'Maybe.'

Bo

Waterwords. Whispering through my bones. River running, rain falling, currents flowing.

Then, all at once, my name among the whispers.

I can't say it: no voice can, no human voice. I felt it more than heard it. Like the vibrations of a plucked string. My water-name.

I stood in the dark, the hushed breathing of sleeping bodies around me: Dez and Ma in their rooms, Jenna in my bed. The darkness thickened and swelled, filling every corner of the house, black gossamer winding around me, softly embracing me.

I was lifted into the congealing air, turning onto my back, floating up until I was suspended on the surface of a darkness that moved gently beneath me, a lake of black.

Deep notes throbbed in my chest like the beating of waves. The water breathed in me. I felt weightless, filled with endless wonder.

'Who are you?' I whispered at last.

The ceaseless.

The water spoke through me. It was my voice but it wasn't my voice.

'What do you want?'

Nothing. No other one. All of life is the smallest part of me.

'I don't understand...'

There was a long silence. I felt a sense of increasing anticipation, as if something was going to happen, something amazing that I couldn't bear. It was too much. Way too much. But I don't remember feeling afraid.

A surge of adrenaline went through me like ice and every muscle in my body tightened. My stomach flipped over and bile rose in my throat and over my lips.

Until you there was nothing but me, said the water. *Encircling, unbroken, never ending. I could not speak. I learned to speak. It is an agony. I divided myself and hid from you. Now you draw me out and I answer you.*

I became aware of something slowly rising beneath me. Slowly a body broke through the dark surface and floated beside me, a human body of luminous, clear water.

It was almost too bright to look at in the darkness, but I stared, transfixed, as the ripples of water resolved into a face.

It was my face.

I am your other self, said the water.

'What do you want?'

There was no answer. My other self sank back into the inky depths. Waves on a shore, rivers and rain, whispering through my bones.

Dez

I was still getting used to the new Ma. For years she'd been sick, and then Jenna cured her and this energy that had been damped down because of pain and tiredness came surging up. Now there was something else, a vital force that we had only ever glimpsed. It was kind of exciting and frightening all at once. I mean, we always knew Ma was tough. We just didn't know how tough.

Ma had a history that she'd kept secret from Bo and me. Even now I knew only some of it. Her and Flynn, our Da, were part of the revolt that led to fleshers being banned from Newport City. Back in the day they were Bel and Flynn, rebel leaders. They led the riots and broke into OpSec HQ and burned it down.

I still can't get over what they did.

Flynn was a pinker. Ma never told us that either. I found out when I scraped the OpSec files I stole, and it spun me out. I still didn't know how to think about it: somehow it turned my idea of who I was upside down. I was half a clone. My father was the enemy.

So many secrets. Us fleshers are full of secrets, maybe because we have to keep ourselves safe from the authorities and then we just get into the habit. Sometimes it's just safer not to know things.

When we finally told Ma that we knew that Flynn was a pinker, she looked shocked for a few seconds and then she laughed.

'I guess you kids were bound to find out one day.'

'Were you ever going to tell us?' I couldn't get rid of that feeling of betrayal, even though I understood why she never spoke about it.

'Yes. No. Maybe.' She stood up and walked away from us, staring at the wall like she does when she's thinking about what she's going to say. Finally she turned around, her arms crossed, and I saw that her eyes were wet and shining. 'The thing is, it doesn't matter whether Flynn was a pinker or not. What's important is who he was. He was...who he was. It wasn't easy for him, but he did what he believed was right. I think he was the bravest person I ever met.' She paused again. 'And he loved you. I wish you knew how much he loved you both. And he loved me too.'

There's no pictures of Ma when she was young. There weren't even any in the OpSec files: Brian Mac must have erased them all. But I caught a glimpse then of what she must have been like: strong, determined, fearless. Beautiful. I caught my breath.

Flora's fever passed, but the day after the lockdown she was still a bit shaky. She came over for in the evening, and with Bo and Jenna it was a full house.

We'd been on the tubes all day looking for news. There were no more soaps on the official channels, just announcements. Curtains had gone up everywhere. If you wanted to travel out of your district you needed a new biopass implant. Mayor Osborne droned on about food shortages and power restrictions. The new head of OpSec, a creep called Garonne who was the same kind of trap-mouthed, small-eyed clone as his predecessor Bremmer, laid down the law about freedom of movement, which basically didn't exist any more.

The only cheering thing was the endless announcements about Brian Mac, who was Public Enemy Number One. That meant he must still be out there somewhere. They were offering an amazing amount of money for information leading to his capture: 10,000 credits for his dead body, 20,000 alive.

The dark tubes were more informative. It seemed that Sheen, who had been acting Brig after Brian Mac, had disappeared. This was bad news:

Sheen was an old school Ap, you kind of knew where you were with him. In his place was a new Brig called Higgs. Brig Higg. It sounded like a repeating gun. He brought more of the new Aps, blond, blue-eyed and brutal. There was footage of them patrolling the banns with evil-looking AIs that hovered inside shimmering protective shields.

We turned off the tubes while we ate dinner.

We were all quite noisy, making jokes, teasing each other. Ma usually joined in with our nonsense but that night she was quiet, abstracted, like she wasn't really there. We all knew what that meant. After we finished eating, I decided to ask her straight out.

'So what are you plotting, Ma?'

'Nothing in particular,' she said.

Bo grinned at me over the table, and we ganged up. 'Come on, Ma,' he said. 'We know you.'

She gave us both what we think of as her Look, steady and ironic, collected our empty plates and took them to the steamer. She stayed there for a while with her back to us. When she joined us at the table, her face was hard.

'This is just the start,' she said.

'The start of what?' asked Bo.

'I don't know.' I couldn't read her face. 'You're so young, you lot. Before you were born, things were bad. You all know that, but you don't know what that means. Flynn and me and all the others, we won a little respite. It wasn't so hard in the banns then. We won, but we didn't win enough. All of us knew, inside, that it wouldn't last, that it was just a truce.' She paused again, as if what she was saying was difficult. 'We were tired. So tired. We all wanted the fight to be over.'

'It's never over,' said Flora.

'It's beginning again,' Ma said. 'And this time, we might lose.'

Now we were all dead serious, listening.

'That's what I've been thinking about,' she said. 'How to fight them this time. How to fight and win.'

'But how do we win?' asked Flora.

'I didn't say that I knew the answer.'

16

Ma went to the window and peered across the road to Kojo's café, La Boite. It was a still, clear night. The lights were on and a few people were eating inside, leaning over the tables. Somewhere a gau barked in the distance.

'I love this place,' she said. 'It's our home. Despite everything. But we're like animals in a cage. Even the pinkers. There's nowhere else to go. We have to work out how to live together.' She paused. 'The alternative is that we all die together.'

'The alternative is that the pinkers kill us all,' I said, hearing the edge in my voice. I was remembering the streets full of people being herded to the Eradicator to be vapourised. I never want to see anything like that again.

'Or we kill all the pinkers,' said Ma. 'But then we're as bad as them. Worse, maybe, because we know better.'

'I don't see why we should care about the pinkers,' said Flora, her jaw jutting out. 'It's not like they return the compliment.'

'I don't care, for the most part. But back in the day, there were pinkers who helped with the fleshers. Brian Mac. Your Da.' She looked at me. 'Don't forget that, Dez. All your brains come from Flynn. And your stubbornness too. Bo's practically his spitting image.'

'Well, Brian Mac and Da, they were exceptions,' said Bo. He was frowning. 'Like...two, maybe. Out of how many millions?'

'Pinkers just think we're vermin,' said Jenna, with sudden violence. 'That's what they think. That we're vermin that have to be exterminated.'

'Plus they're clones,' said Flora. 'They don't know what it means, to be close to people. They don't even touch each other. I mean, pinkers are *weird*.'

To my surprise Ma smiled, and I knew she was remembering something. 'We thought that if we got rid of the Inner Veil, it would be a start,' she said. 'Everyone would be living in the same city, with the same risks. There wouldn't be Newport City and the banns any more, just Newport. And maybe if we did that, everyone would recognise that we're all in this together.'

'But you didn't get rid of the Inner Veil,' said Bo. 'And we're not in all this together. It's us and them.'

'Brian Mac brought down the Inner Veil, for a few hours.' She went quiet and smiled again, that private smile, looking down at the table. I watched her, feeling vaguely troubled. There was so much we didn't know about our mother.

'I often think of something Brian used to say,' she said. '*You can take down the Inner Veil, sure. But there's a Veil inside everybody's head. I don't know how you take that down.*'

'Maybe it's impossible to get rid of it,' I said impatiently. There were exceptions, maybe one or two pinkers who cared what happened to flesh-ers. But I watch the soaps and the infonews. We all do. We all know what they think of us.

'They do things to pinkers, to make them the way they are,' said Ma. 'Brian told me that if he disobeyed OpSec orders, he felt this agonising pain in his bones. That's the conditioning.'

'Well then,' said Jenna. 'Let's forget about the pinkers.'

'That's just it,' said Ma. 'We can't. We're stuck with them.' She looked around the table. 'Anyway, whether pinkers change or not, I still think we should destroy the Inner Veil.'

'How can we do that?' said Jenna. 'I mean, if you couldn't do it last time…'

'I don't know. It will be much harder now. Even Brian didn't know what the tech was. And after he brought it down, they got scared. He told me that the security is brutal, even inside OpSec. Plus they've got backup systems now, in case it fails.'

Ma folded her arms and sat back. 'But that's doesn't mean we shouldn't try.'

Erin

At celebrity school, they warned us that starting out is hard. They make too many celebrities so the producers get a choice. Some of us might be perfectly made for the soaps when we start the courses, but by the finish of training that kind of face or that kind of body goes out of fashion and you're just looking at extras work, hoping that the trends move back again.

Nobody at celebrity school warns you about pricks like John Mecha, though. You only hear the whispers when you enter the industry and even then only in places where nothing will pick up what you say. Places like that are hard to find in Newport City. But us girls find them: in the IMR clubs, where the music is super plus loud, you can talk quietly into each other's ears. Walking through back alleys together, on the way to a bar. You smile, so nobody is suspicious, so people think you're just sharing a joke.

John Mecha is a shit to every girl he works with. At best he's indifferent and rude, but sometimes he takes a dislike to a person and then you're in trouble. He'll do all sorts of things to knock you off your rhythm. One girl told me that he even touched her once in the middle of a scene. Of course she completely freaked. He denied it all, and said she was being hysterical. Whether they believed him or not, he's the one with the legions of adoring fans; so Audria was pulled off the job and sent to rehab for 'emotional exhaustion'.

Part of me was hoping that *Ebolastic* would tank, or at least do badly enough that they'd think of something else. But it's been a hit: now all the studios are talking ultra-real, and I'm stuck in season two with John Mecha. Twelve weeks of pretending that everything is fine while he digs his little knives into my brain.

I know he doesn't like me. I catch these speculative glances sometimes, as if he's weighing me up, deciding what would be the most amusing way to screw me up completely. Audria said that he's probably jealous about all the coverage over the hospital attack.

Today we're doing this scene where he's supposed to rescue me because I've been captured. Joh, the director, has warned me that this one will be hard. The flesher gangsters are supposed to be touching me, roughing me up. Of course they aren't really touching me, but they almost are. The 3D effects are fiddly and I have to scream out my little golden heart for John Mecha to come and save me.

The flesher actors look scary in all their makeup, but it's hard for them too, so we're all super nice to each other. The one who has to be really mean to me does his best to reassure me between takes, cracking jokes and smiling.

We get it all down in the morning and it's not too bad. After lunch it's the scene where John Mecha heroes in with his taser and singlehandedly takes down the entire flesher gang. I have to do the full orgasm, wriggling and laughing and crying with relief. Of course I'm wearing almost nothing, and what I'm wearing is practically rags, because my clothes have been ripped up by the fleshers. Mecha has these extra-fine sensogloves on, so he can switch off my cuffs. Then he's supposed to lead me romantically out of my squalid prison, holding my hand.

That amount of touching is scandalous, it's part of ultra-real pushing the boundaries, and I'm not looking forward to that part. The thought of feeling Mecha's hands through the gloves makes me want to puke. I tell myself that I'm a pro. Ignore him and just keep smiling.

Mecha's a pro too. He knows exactly what the cameras are doing and where they are. And that means he knows where nobody's looking. I've got used to the way his smile vanishes when he's out of range of the cameras, like he switches it off, and the muttered asides about how shit my acting is, how I made the wrong choice, or whatever. I just pretend I can't hear him, I kind of enjoy how it shits him that he can't see that he's hurting me.

Today was something else. I was already a bit more freaked by the scene with the fleshers than I'd expected, but I was doing okay. I didn't have to fake the tears, although they weren't of relief and happiness so much as a kind of after-shock. Then Mecha reaches out his hand to take mine, which is the climax of the episode. There's a close-up of my face and all sorts of trickery that they'll use later in the IMR booths for the rethrills, when clubbers can pretend to be Mecha or me.

He takes my hand, and I realise there's a hole in his sensoglove. You can't see it, it's hidden in the detailing, at first I'm not even certain what it is I'm touching. But it's skin. Actual skin. It's warm and moist and it's pressed against my skin. He's holding me so hard I can't pull back my hand. And it's the middle of the scene, with the close-up sensors, all the vid and audio, concentrated on my face.

I'm braced already, because I knew this wouldn't be pleasant, but this is so much worse than I expected. I can't help it, instinct takes over. I gag. Tears leak out of my eyes. Mecha is staring straight into my face, his expression all adoration. I feel trapped, violated, betrayed. I want to scream.

I have to hand it to celebrity school. Even with acid in the back of my throat, even with my stomach twisting in waves of nausea, I don't completely lose it. Inside my head I'm screaming, but I stay in the scene. I use the shock to push through into an extremity of relief, I even manage to return Mecha's adoring look. Because if they pull the shot, I'll have to do it again, and I know it will be worse next time.

It feels like hours, those seconds while Mecha leads me out of my prison, his hot, wet skin squashed against my hand. But I get there.

The cameras go off. Mecha drops my hand and stalks off without looking at me. I can tell he's really pissed that I didn't fuck up the scene.

'Super plus, Erin,' says Joh. 'First take! Powerful stuff. It's going to go off in the IMRs!'

I dredge up a smile and head back to my dressing room without talking to anyone. I lock myself in the toilet and stuff my hand in my mouth and I cry and cry.

You can barely see the stars through the Veil that domes Newport City. One or two sometimes, twinkling through the shimmer. But we know they're there, out in the darkness.

Tonight there's no sign of the stars. The vault above us is a shimmery dark blue, the colour of my favourite dress. It's just me and Ami, hanging out on the balcony of my super glamorous apartment in Block 1 after a hard day's work, staring out over the lights of Newport City. I switch her into companion mode because I'm feeling lonely and shook up after today, and she's sitting there next to me chatting brightly, both of us holding drinks (she makes one to keep me company, but she doesn't drink it, she just hands hers over to me when I finish mine and makes a new one).

'You're so lucky,' Ami says again. I think she's programmed to remind me of this at least three times a day. 'And I'm so lucky to share this time with you.'

'Yes, I'm very lucky,' I answer automatically.

It's true, though. I'm one of the lucky clones. We never use the word 'clone', it's considered vulgar and borderline insulting, but I say the word inside my head. A lucky clone, created especially to be one of the adored elite, bringing pleasure to everyone near and far all over Newport City.

I'm doing well. Dervin picked me up straight out of school to be part of his stable. He said I had the 'something' that he's always looking for. Not all of us have it, even from my batch. I'm from an elite DNA class, 956, blonde, curvy, flawless skin. Only a few allowed every generation. I shouldn't know these things, but I do. Like I said, I can get people to tell me things, and sometimes they tell me things that they shouldn't.

My first job was a regular but minor role on *Days of Passion* which got expanded when the popular response was favourable. I had a couple of spots on *Behind the Scenes*, where they put you in a super plus apartment for a week and video everything you do bar going to the toilet, and after that they wrote me out of *Days of Passion* so I could star in *Ebolastic*. Dervin said I was made.

Some luck. If Mecha pulls that stunt again, I don't know how I'll handle it. I couldn't face it. And he'll probably get worse now, since his little perverted tricks aren't working.

I lift my glass. 'Here's to luck!' I say.

As I take a sip, there's a huge boom off in the distance. I jump out of my skin and Ami stands up. 'We should go inside, Erin,' she says. Her voice has changed from chatty to bossy. 'To ensure your safety.'

I ignore her. I'm staring out over Newport Central to the suburb beyond, somewhere near Block 9, where a plume of dark smoke is puffing up. I watch as it climbs into the sky and curls up against the roof of the Veil.

'What the hell was that?'

Ami cocks her head and I know she's picking up the alarm comms. 'It's a fleshers attack,' she says. 'We must move inside, Erin.'

'A fleshers attack?'

'Erin, we must move inside.' She puts out her hand to take my elbow, and I flinch away, as if she were a person. They make AIs cooler than room temperature so you don't feel that disgusting thing of skin on skin, but sometimes my instincts take over.

'Erin.'

She's going to keep nagging until either I do what I'm told or she picks me up and carries me, so I go inside. I shut the glass doors and pull up a chair close to them so I can still look out. I can't stop staring at the smoke piling up against the Veil, spreading out like a giant dark fan.

A fleshers attack. I don't know what I feel. Numb, maybe. Definitely afraid. Even, perhaps, a little excited.

Not shocked, though. It was like I was expecting something like this to happen.

It was always going to happen.

Bo

Jenna and I spent a week together in the Fourth, just the two of us. A friend of Jenna's had lent us her tiny apartment in Rue Vigan and gone to stay with friends in the Fifth. We spent every hour together, dreaming about a future, a life of our own. We talked late into the night or spent hours saying nothing at all, not needing to. We bought food in the local shijo, cooked enormous meals, went for walks in the neighbourhood.

We didn't look back, we didn't think about what had happened over the past few weeks. We pretended that the world was new and that anything was possible. And I suppose that for us it was, at least for the moment.

And then the Curtains went up.

We'd only just come back to the Second. If we'd waited another day I would have been cut off from Dez and Ma, from all my friends in the bann. Some people couldn't get back to their homes. So many families were broken apart, so many connections severed. It took OpSec less than a day to smash whatever pride or sense of victory fleshers had begun to feel after the destruction of the Eradicators.

Ma put us to work almost as soon as we got home.

The day after the Curtains went up, Jenna and I walked to Rue Lozere to see Rioka and Kat. After what we'd been through together out in the dasht and our journey home across the Gilla Sea, I felt that Kat and Rioka were like sisters. They teased me like their kid brother, but I was used to that from Dez. They had become inseparable: you could feel the strength of their bond, the trust they had in each other. The three of us owed each other our lives.

Nik Hauben had rooms spare after his brother Giro was shot during the arrests in Mishkin Square, so I'd arranged for them to stay there while Dez fixed up Rioka's prosthetic hand. Nik told me he was happy to take them in. He didn't say he was lonely. He didn't have to.

Nik lived in an old low-tech factory that had been converted into a workshop, with a small store at the front. The new border with the First ran all the way down the middle of the rue, a shimmering curtain three metres from the front door. We felt it as we approached, a cold, stinging vibration in the air.

Kat buzzed the door open. 'Hey, it's the water babies!'

'Reporting in,' said Jenna. 'Ugh, that curtain. How can you live so close?'

'You can't feel it inside,' said Kat. 'Come in.'

We followed her into the workshop. I hadn't been there since Giro was killed. Nik hadn't touched anything on the workbench: it was all just as Giro had left it, as if he'd be walking in any minute to get on with a job. My chest tightened when I saw his gear: the tools, the half-finished projects, his winter jacket still hanging behind the door. For an instant I saw him falling in Rue Mishkin, his face shattered, the blood flowering out of his skull.

Now his work would never be finished.

There were places like this all over the banns, absences that would never be filled. For a moment I felt giddy. It was like I could feel all those empty spaces, all those lost futures. A huge, howling grief gathered inside me. If I let it go, it would drown me.

'You okay, Bo?' said Kat, touching my arm.

'Yeah, I'm fine,' I said. I took a breath. 'Just give me a minute.'

She knew to leave me alone and went ahead while I got myself together.

Rioka was bginning to look better. Her arm was still healing from the amputation and you could see that she still wasn't used to the new hand that Dez had made. She brewed some tea and we sat around a little table in the corner and got down to business.

'Ma says this is the first step,' I said.

'Yeah, that's what we're figuring,' said Rioka, hunching up her shoulders. 'I don't think I want to know what the second step is.'

We talked through what we knew. 'Those raids in the Outer Banns,' said Kat. 'It's getting hard to find out what's happening. I haven't heard from anyone north of the Tenth since the lockdown.'

We hadn't heard from anyone in the Eighth or the Eleventh either. Ma was keeping track. The Ninth was still online. OpSec was targeting the rogue servers that powered the dark tubes, and they'd already taken down a few. Luckily the system's so chaotic even fleshers don't know how the whole thing works, so Dez figured it was going to take them some time.

Sometimes I wondered if OpSec knew where the servers were all the time and had been monitoring them. The thought gave me a chill. That's what Ma would do for sure, if she was OpSec.

'Anyway, we've got to get past the Curtains,' Kat said. 'Physically, I mean.'

Jenna nodded at Rioka. 'You got through the Outer Veil, didn't you? Of course we can get past them.'

'It's difficult, though,' said Rioka. 'Folding a Veil isn't something I want to do have to do every day. Or even every week.'

'And yeah, not everyone has abilities,' said Jenna. She ran a hand through her spiky white hair. 'So it's the tunnels.'

'They blocked them all up years ago,' said Kat.

'They blocked the ones they know about,' I said. I'd heard that they'd brought in earthmovers to shut off the subway. People lived inside those tunnels, people who couldn't find a place inside the towerblocks. Not that OpSec cared. I didn't want to think about that. 'According to Ma, there's other tunnels they know nothing about.'

'Can we be sure they don't know?'

'As sure as we can be. They didn't know about them twenty years ago. Ma says the resistance used them and just passed the knowledge on, person to person. The hard part is getting into them. They're deep. Most of the ways in are shut off and others have collapsed. But Ma knows a couple of entrances that she's sure are still okay.'

'If we're going to use them, we'll need maps,' said Rioka.

'That's the plan.'

Kat looked at me. 'There's a plan?' Then she laughed. 'Of course there's a plan. I forgot your Ma.'

'Dez says she can make super encrypted maps that even OpSec can't get into.' I remembered what she'd said when we discussed it earlier. *I can make them safe against everything except traitors*, she had said. *No coding can guard against that.*

I didn't say it out loud, but Jenna did. 'You mean, if no one gives OpSec the key,' she said. Morro's betrayal hurt her worse than anyone else, even me. She had trusted him completely, with her life.

There was a short silence. Then I started telling them about Ma's idea. We were going to be the mapping teams: Jenna and me, going south from the Second, with Kat and Rioka doing the north. We'd be going into the unknown. Ma didn't know how many of the old routes were still viable. We'd have to feel our way. And it would be dangerous. She figured it would take us a couple of weeks of hard work, but by the end of it we'd have a usable map of underground routes.

Fleshers need to be together, that's where our strength is. With the banns cut off from one another we were weaker: communities, families, networks were broken. So we were going to join everybody up again.

It was dark when we left Nik's place. The Curtain was a strip of shimmering energy running along the middle of the rue. When people passed in front of it they became silhouettes, like some weird animation: an unreal black and white dream.

We were halfway home when we saw a cloud of dark smoke inside the Inner Veil, crawling up the side of the dome. It looked like a giant claw arching over Newport City. I stopped, feeling a dread like sickness in my gut, and Jenna grabbed my hand.

'What the hell is that?' I whispered.

'I don't know,' she said. 'Bad news.'

We quickened our pace, winding through the people who were stopping, pointing, wondering what it meant, as the plume slowly expanded across the Veil, thickening like a spill of oil.

When we got home Ma was flicking through the dark tubes: scrambled voices, sirens, alarm bells. She didn't look up when we came in. Two dark figures stood behind, one much taller than the other. For a moment I thought that I was imagining them, that they were images painted on the wall.

Ma glanced at us and gestured towards to the two strangers. 'Sally and Park. They're friends of mine,' she said.

Sally and Park peeled off the wall, and now I could see them clearly. Sally was tall, with a wild crop of gray hair, dressed from head to toe in cracked, stained leather. Park wore a long yellowish coat, red boots. They were both about Ma's age, maybe older. It wasn't obvious, but something about them – the way they moved, maybe, the style of their clothes – made me think of skinners. I felt the hairs rising down my spine.

'They don't look like friends,' I said.

Park grinned, but it didn't reach his eyes. All his teeth were silver. 'Pleased to meet you too,' he said. He made an ironic bow.

'I'm not going to argue,' said Ma, pushing back her chair. 'Park and Sally know the tunnels better than anyone alive. They'll lead you through. You can trust them. I do.' She went to the galley and poured a cup of water from the filter. She looked tired.

Jenna had been standing silently next to me. I could feel the tension in her body like a field of static. 'What's going on?' she asked. I didn't know if she was talking about the people in our kitchen or about the smoke outside.

'An apartment building in Newport City just got blown up,' said Ma. 'OpSec are saying that's it's a terrorist attack. They don't know how many people have been killed. Maybe hundreds.'

Oh shit, I thought. Now all hell is going to break loose.

We all looked at the screen. Drone footage of rubble and corpses, you'd think it was the banns. But this was Newport City.

'Maybe Sevika's started something,' said Park. 'About time, too.'

Ma stiffened. 'She'd be brainless enough to do something like this,' she said. 'But she couldn't do it. She doesn't have the smarts.' Something in her voice made me glance at her quickly.

'Who's Sevika?' I asked.

'You don't need to know,' said Ma. She didn't elaborate.

I knew that was all I was going to get.

Dez

I was at Café Boite with Flora when the explosion happened. Kojo came in from the kitchen, his face the colour of ash, and told us. He'd seen it on the tubes. We went outside and looked up and saw that dark fan spreading out against the Inner Veil.

'That's not fleshers,' I said. 'Fleshers wouldn't bomb an apartment full of people.'

'They might,' said Kojo.

'We just wouldn't.'

'That's what they're saying on the tubes. That fleshers did it.'

Flora was still staring upwards, her hair falling back over her shoulders like a dark, turbulent river. 'Maybe someone had just had enough with them feeling safe and us getting killed.'

'And maybe they're just lying,' I said. 'Maybe it's some kind of accident and they've just decided to blame us. Maybe OpSec did it.'

Flora looked at me. Her face was expressionless, hard. 'Maybe,' she said.

'They were saying it was fleshers the moment it happened. How would they know?'

'Perhaps they caught someone.'

I was getting annoyed. 'Do you really believe what they're saying on the infonews? Really? It's probably OpSec.'

Kojo stared at me. 'Why would they kill their own?'

'So all the pinkers hate us more.'

'But they're saying hundreds of people have been killed…'

'My Da was a pinker. They killed him.'

That wasn't strictly true. Flynn killed himself when he knew that OpSec was coming for him. I know that Ma was relieved when I told her, that it stopped her imagining that he'd been tortured to death. She didn't have to say anything, I saw it in her face.

'Dez?' said Flora, and I started out of my reverie.

'What?'

'I said, it's going to get worse now.'

Kojo had gone inside. I could see him through the window serving a regular customer, leaning close over the table to talk. Times like this, no one speaks loudly.

'That's the one certain thing,' I said.

'Maybe you should get back into OpSec and find out what the fuck is going on.'

'I can't.'

Flora met my eyes, and then looked away. She knew how dangerous it was, but she still wanted me to do it. I felt a flicker of hurt. 'You know they nearly got me last time,' I said defensively. 'Every time I do it, the risk is higher.'

'I know, Dez, I know.'

'It's literally hundreds of times more likely they'll get me. Last time I left traces. They'll know that somebody's been in. They might even know what data I took. They'll have new crypto and they'll probably have new defences. They might even trace it back to me. I can't risk it.'

'I know, Dez. Forget I said it.' She took my hand and squeezed it. 'It's just that I'm so shit scared. If OpSec really did that, if they're prepared to blow up some random apartment building in Newport City just to make us look bad…it makes me feel sick to the stomach.'

I was only half listening. 'Unless there's some other path in, of course. I can't find any, I've looked and looked…'

I trailed off. I was thinking of Brian Mac's lab. He left me the keys when he disappeared, with the tech he'd been secretly making all those years that we thought he was just a deadhead Ap. It's amazing, you'd have never guessed, not in a million years. The first time I went in there I just stood in the middle and gaped. I mean, we knew he tinkered with tech, but I'd always assumed it was just part of his oddness, like the way he walked around all the time with those damn goggles on, and how he was off his head half the time on timeslip implants or who knows what other illegal drugs.

There were things in that lab that I would never have thought of making. He was almost as good as me, and that's saying something. The gravity wave comms were only the start of it.

Maybe there was something there that I could use.

Bo

The shijo was very crowded. Food shortages weren't as bad in the Second as in the outer banns, but people were stocking up while they could. Which, of course, made things worse.

We wove our way through the bargaining crowds to Trexxy's cafe. She stood over one of her big soup pots in a cloud of steam, a giant of a woman with a head of thick, grey hair, a ladle in one hand, a bowl in the other. When she saw us she flashed a smile and told us to go around the back.

In the cramped kitchen, Trexxy's kids Sip and Connie were chopping vegetables for more soup. Sip pointed to the ground by his feet and winked at me. Jenna and I squatted down, squeezed under the table and opened a trapdoor. We climbed down into a cellar with some storage boxes in a corner and moved them aside to reveal a steel manhole cover.

I knocked on it three times and after a short wait, Park pushed it open. He grinned at us out of the shadows, his teeth glinting. He was hanging on to a metal ladder, holding a torch in one hand. I switched on the light in my suit and we climbed down after him, maybe ten metres, into a dark, narrow corridor like a gap between two walls.

It was dead quiet. After the noise of the shijo, it was unnerving. Seeing Park again wasn't any more reassuring than the first time. There was something predatory about Park and Sally: right now I had the feeling that Park was going to bite me any minute. I still didn't know why Ma trusted them.

'All set then?' he said. I nodded, and Jenna and I turned on the Magnetic Positioning Systems Dez had built into our suits and followed Park.

We went down a steep flight of steps, trying not slip on the damp stone. It went on and on until my legs started to ache. The further we went, the colder it grew. When we reached the bottom we turned into a narrow passage and walked a little way until Park stopped and shone his torch on the ground. He knelt down and scrabbled around on the stone floor with his fingers.

'There she is,' he said. He pressed on the spot. We heard a soft click and a narrow hatch opened at our feet.

'Down you go,' he said. 'I'll follow.'

I sat on the edge of the hatch and felt around with my toes until I found the rung of a ladder.

'It's a long way,' said Park. 'Just keep going.'

I climbed down through the darkness. Down and down and down. I don't think I've ever been so cold. My teeth began to chatter, echoing in my skull, and my hands seemed to stick to the iron rungs. And that's when I heard the water. It was whispering so softly that I thought for a moment that I was imagining it. But it was there, almost beyond my hearing, a constant, rushing sigh.

I didn't know if Jenna or Park could hear it, but somehow I doubted it. The water was whispering to me alone. It stayed with me until I reached the bottom of the ladder, and then it fell silent.

Park led us into a narrow, rough hewn passage, so low we all had to stoop to pass through it. We were all too cold to speak. We found Sally at the end of the passage, waiting in a chamber that smelt of wet rust, some kind of abandoned engine room. The ceiling was higher here and we could all straighten up. Sally was holding a lantern turned down to a yellowish glow. I hadn't seen one like that before: it looked really old, with four glass sides and a flame inside that she later told me came from some kind of plant oil.

'So you're all set for the mapping?' she said, her voice echoing. She gave us a sceptical glance. 'These tunnels ain't for the faint of heart.'

I said something about being as ready as we could be, my voice trembling. Sally's expression didn't change. She shook her head slightly, as if I'd failed some kind of test, and turned the lantern up to full.

What I had thought was the fourth wall of the chamber was a void as black as pitch. Involuntarily, I stepped back. Sally held the lantern out into the darkness, beckoning us to where the metal floor ended abruptly. Jenna and I peered cautiously over the edge. Below us was an abyss dropping down sheer as far as I could see.

'It's one of the old underground reservoirs,' said Park, right behind my shoulder. I hadn't heard him come up and I jumped. 'It used to be full of water, right up to where we're standing. It must have been like an ocean down here. Maybe people went sailing across it. It's three klicks to the other side.'

'What happened to the water?' asked Jenna.

'Nobody knows,' said Sally. 'Maybe it's hiding.'

I couldn't tell if she was making a joke, but she was right. I knew the water was hiding. But where did it go?

The space was so huge that I felt a strange awe. All that water. I thought of it coming up through the ground when we called it, the living muscles that destroyed the Eradicator. Maybe it wasn't so far away. It came from somewhere, it went somewhere. But it here there was just a huge, dark absence.

I could just make out a tiny speck of something shining below us in the darkness. At first I thought it was my eyes playing tricks, but then I realised that it was the reflection of our lantern. 'Is that ice down there?'

'That whole floor is ice,' said Sally. 'You can get down there to have a look, if you like. But it's a long crawl.' She lowered the lantern and stepped away from the edge. I kept staring. Maybe it was the frozen river that brought us home from the mines. The river that took Mish.

'What's on the other side?' asked Jenna.

'An entrance like this one,' said Sally. 'It comes up into the Third, below the old solar towers.'

'It's just an empty hole under the earth,' said Park. He picked up a pebble and threw it out into the darkness. We didn't even hear when it landed.

We spent the next few hours making our way through a labyrinth of tunnels and chambers. Some places were impassable: the roof had collapsed or the entrance was sealed up. Some places you couldn't go into because the air was bad. Jenna and I dutifully tagged the MPS records with Park and Sally's information. Sally told us we were moving through an old sewer system. After about an hour, we crawled through a hole roughly cut into a wall which she said connected the sewers to an ancient Rapid Transport System.

'Did you make this hole?' asked Jenna.

Park flashed his teeth. 'There's holes all over. We made some of them. It's a rat's maze.'

'And we're the rats,' said Sally.

'And you're sure that OpSec doesn't know about this?'

'As sure as we can be,' said Park. 'We've never seen a sign of them down here. We'd know.'

'It's old,' said Sally. 'Really, really old.'

The network was huge. Sewers, water pipes, the RTS, channels for power, outmoded communications systems. Newport City's history, written under the ground, carved out of the earth. Morro would have loved it.

By the time Jenna and I climbed back into Trexxy's kitchen we were filthy and exhausted. Sip and Connie were stacking dishes in the steamer. Trexxy gave us a bowl of pea and spino soup to warm us up and waved away our offer to pay.

By the time we'd finished, the shijo was beginning to close down. We made our way back to our place through the darkening rues. Avoiding Aps was second nature, but these days we were beyond careful, and it took a while.

When we got home, Ma was on the tubes. The way she was hunched, I could tell that she was furious.

'Look at this,' she said, swinging the screen around. She magnified the image to max so it hung in the middle of the room. 'This is what they're watching in Newport City.'

OpSec had arrested two suspected terrorists. Their faces stared out of the screen: filthy, dead-eyed, murderous. Scars, shaggy hair, thick necks and broken teeth. Brainless animals.

Fleshers.

Erin

At first they said dozens dead, then hundreds. The infonews was an endless parade of smoking rubble and shocked faces and OpSec militia in black doing manhunts in Newport City and out in the banns, raiding nests of subversives. Block 9 was one of the less well-off areas, not a poor district like Block 15 where we were filming, but not like Block 1 either. All us celebrities live in Block 1. It's destined from the moment we enter celebrity school.

I didn't know any of the dead, but Denna, one of the girls who does dogsbody publicity, liaising with the infonews and so on, lives near the block that was blown up. Some of her friends had a lucky escape, that night they'd been blissing out at one of the IMR clubs. They almost hadn't gone, but Denna had persuaded them, and if she hadn't they'd be dead. They said that Denna saved their lives.

She tells me the story over and over again, blinking all the time like she has dust in her eyes. She knew a couple of people who were killed, but not so well.

I feel as shocked as everyone else, nothing like that has happened in Newport City since the bad old days when fleshers were allowed through the Inner Veil. This isn't supposed to happen, fleshers can't get through the Veil, it's supposed to edit out anyone or anything that doesn't match official

DNA profiles. But obviously fleshers can get through. I've seen one with my own eyes. If one can get in, what's stopping a gang of them?

There's something about the whole thing that gives me a spooked feeling, though admittedly I'm already feeling paranoid. When Mayor Osborne comes on the tubes, all grave and fatherly, saying that this crime will not go unavenged and that the fist of justice will come down on the fleshers, something twists in my guts.

Something isn't right.

It's a kind of performance instinct, I guess. I can't get rid of this feeling that it's all been carefully staged, that even though the blood is real blood and all these people are really dead and a whole apartment block has been blasted into rubble, it's all a big show, put on for the edification and education of the people of Newport City.

I follow the infonews reports obsessively. They don't tell you anything new but I watch them anyway, like I'm scanning for clues. I don't switch Ami off any more, in case it looks too suspicious.

Recently it's like everything has wound up a notch. Something big went down in the banns last month. They're saying there was a fleshers revolt and mass destruction of Newport City property, but there's more to it than that. Nobody is saying anything. Bremmer is suddenly a criminal and all the tubes are telling us to look out for traitors and everyone's a bit twitchy.

I'm drinking too much. Martinis are my drug of choice, I suspect it's programmed in. Everyone does some kind of drug. People like to go to the IMR booths chockful of ice or nebus or the other legal uppers. OpSec make a lot of credits from that, they own all the drugstores. That's another thing that someone told me once. But the edgy kids use hormones, endo and dope and seraton, usually cut with something like ice.

I tried some seraton once, but it did nothing for me. All I could feel was the ice, and I don't like ice. The hormones are usually smuggled out of the baby farms but the pure flesher kind apparently gives you biggest buzz.

Hormones aren't an OpSec operation. Sometimes I think that's the main reason they hate it, though they put out that it's a public health issue. That's what *Ebolastic* is all about, telling people how bad the hormone trade is, how it undermines the safety of Newport City. I guess if OpSec didn't really believe there was something subversive and uncontrollable about hormones, they'd just take over the business. Maybe hormones mess with conditioning. I don't know.

You'll only find flesher hormones in the exclusive clubs. They're expensive because you have to get them past security, the dealers are higher-ups who want a few credits on the side or who maybe want their own little rushes. Getting caught with baby farm hormones means the end of your career, but if you've got flesher hormones, that's the end of you. Nothing is worse than flesher hormones in Newport City, it's worse than murder. If you're lucky you'll end up working in the mines or in Duiwel Island prison outside the Veil. No one ever comes back from there.

The danger is the real thrill, of course.

Most celebrities drink martinis. In the party shoots they give you an air of glamour. People enjoy a bit of glamour, it makes them feel better about their shitty little lives. That's what celebrities are for, so people feel better as life gets shitter. Me, I like that perky little glass and the green glass berry on a stick, for decoration apparently, though nobody knows why it's there. The liquor is pure and strong and it makes me feel shiny and numb.

Anyway, I'm lying on my lounge flicking through the infonews on my lenscam, all nice and shiny and numb, when Osborne turns up with another official announcement. They've arrested some fleshers in connection with the attack. I snap to attention and study their faces. They look nothing like that flesher I saw. They look like the extras on *Ebolastic*: thick and brutish and hairy, squatting inside a buzzcage in OpSec HQ, snarling at the cameras. Maybe that guy I saw was an exception?

Then I go cold through my whole body, all at once. I sit up and replay the segment.

I recognise one of the prisoners. I chatted to him on set two days ago, making some stupid joke or other. The extras are flattered that a celebrity doesn't turn up their nose at them, and besides, it's my nature to be friendly.

It looks like that same guy, a low-level celebrity clone, I can't remember his name. He even has the *Ebolastic* makeup. I freeze the 3D and study it from all the angles. I'm positive it's him. He's acting his little heart out. You can tell this is his greatest role.

'What's the matter, Erin?' says Ami.

I jump and stare at her, still in shock. Maybe it's just a coincidence. Maybe there's a flesher who looks just like that extra. Maybe. But fleshers aren't clones, that's why they're banned from Newport City. Illegal DNA. Uncivilised conditioning. They're not proper humans.

'They got those flesher terrorists,' I say at last.

'Thank goodness for that,' says Ami comfortably. 'It's good that we've got OpSec to protect us. Shall I make you another drink?'

I breathe out. 'Yeah,' I say. 'I need another drink.'

Bo

Dez and I were a block from Rue Ballard when the Ap stopped us.

It was late afternoon and we were heading home for dinner. We'd been to a dark little workshop in Rue Xuan, just a hole in the wall behind a row of low houses run by a tech called Froma. Dez was a regular. Froma built the kind of tools that Dez needed to do the work she did on our suits: micro grips, electron threaders, phase regulators. They made the tools I had in my workshop behind the house look like toys.

We were bickering about what we'd buy for dinner when the Ap stepped out of nowhere and planted himself square in our path.

'ID, now,' he said.

He looked fresh out of the shop, shiny and new, full of the kind of shit that only the newbies have.

'I won't ask again,' he said.

We hauled out the fake ID chips that Dez had made. We didn't want to be tracked. I was Sten Har, Dez was Valery Primo, traders from the food towers. Squeaky clean, good citizens.

The Ap pointed to the bag on Dez's shoulder. 'Hold it up,' he said.

Dez took the bag from her shoulder and dangled it in front of her to be scanned. We weren't worried: the bag had a false lining, and the tools were tucked safely away behind an inner wall Dez had fitted inside to disrupt the scanner. Dez was always cautious when she was carrying this kind of stuff around. None of it was illegal as such, but that kind of sophisticated gear would look suspicious to an Ap with an overdose of paranoia. This guy fit the bill, like most of the new Aps that were crawling around the banns lately.

There was a sort of contempt in how she held it, which is maybe why the Ap got shitty.

'Empty the bag,' the Ap said.

'Excuse me?' said Dez.

'Empty it.'

'Where?'

'On the ground.'

'There's food inside.'

'Let's see it.'

This guy was being a complete pain. And there wasn't any food in the bag. I took a step towards him.

'Come on, officer, you've got no reason to – '

'Shut it, meat,' he grunted. His hand was already on his taser.

Maybe Dez could have got us out of this. She was usually smarter than me, more cunning, I guess. She'd probably already figured how to get this guy off our backs. But the situation made me angry. What was this guy trying to prove? Nothing, except that we had to do what he said. I took a step closer and he flinched.

'We're late for dinner,' I said. 'My Ma's waiting for these tates and greens.'

Maybe he just didn't like my face. He pulled his taser.

'Bo,' I heard Dez say.

The rest happened so fast that it's a little unclear. For some reason I reached out as if I was going to touch the Ap's shoulder. He was so shocked that he didn't react, not straight away. He pointed his taser straight into my face. I had almost enough time to think, oh shit, I'm going to die.

Nothing happened. Except that he froze. And I mean *froze*.

I saw it in his eyes first. In two heartbeats his eyes were dead, filmed with a kind of icy glaze. His cheeks, a moment ago rosy and pinker smooth, were blue. I could feel the fierce cold coming off him even through my suit, I could even see it, like the air had turned into crystal. I stepped back.

'What have you done?' Dez hissed at me. 'You absolute deadset *dick.*'

I just wanted him to stop threatening us. I wanted him to leave us alone and let us go home. I didn't actually want him to be dead.

Dez checked the Ap's health monitor; pulse, blood pressure, body temperature, breath rate. She looked at me in horror. 'He's off the charts,' she said. 'It's like…zero degrees. I mean, *zero* zero.'

The Ap was still staring at me with his dead eyes. His red coat was covered in frost, a thin, white sheen that glistened in the last of the sunlight.

She pulled me away, back the way we'd come.

'Run,' she said.

After dinner, when we were alone, I told Jenna what had happened. Dez hadn't said anything about it since we'd got home. She didn't say a word to me at all. I could tell that she was fuming.

Jenna was almost as angry as Dez. 'What were you thinking?' she said.

'I wasn't thinking anything,' I said. 'I wanted him to leave us alone.'

'So you…what? Turned him to ice?'

'I didn't know that's what I was doing. I was angry.'

'Then don't get angry, don't ever get angry.'

Tears were gathering in her eyes. I lifted my hand to brush them away but she turned her face away.

'He was just an Ap,' I said. 'A pinker.'

'And that makes it okay? It's okay that you can just be angry with someone and they're dead?' Her voice was trembling with rage.

I tried to take hold of her hands but she pulled them away.

'What if you get angry with me?'

'Jenna, please,' I said. 'I'd never do that.'

'But you don't know what you did, you said that yourself. You don't know what you can do.'

Jenna walked out. I heard her heading for Dez's bedroom, the door open and shut. Great. So now Jenna wasn't talking to me, either.

A wave of tiredness swept over me. I lay down on the bed and thought about the good old days, when the worst thing we worried about was skinners, when there wasn't all this water stuff and my sister and my girl-friend weren't mad at me the whole time. Those days seemed simpler somehow, almost innocent. I almost felt nostalgic. Skinners were the worst, but at least you knew what they were. Bad.

Brian Mac was the kind of Ap who would wink at the rules, if it suited him. But he hated skinners. He'd hunt them on his days off. One day, when he was hanging out at Café Boite, he told me what happens to the kids the skinners catch. I don't know why: maybe he was trying to warn me, as if I needed to be warned. Maybe he wanted to spook me. Maybe he just wanted to say it to someone.

Extraction, he told me, is quick, dirty and agonising. Stingers are more than weapons: they're the major extraction tool. Amazing tech, he said. They have flexible tips that open and divide into thousands of hollow threads that are microns thick. Once a skinner has their prey, they paralyse them with a fast-working drug and then plug the stinger into the neck. It automatically divides and snakes through the body, hunting out the glands. It finds the pineal and the pituitary, the pancreas, ovaries and testes, the thyroid and the parathyroid gland, the hypothalamus and the adrenals. That takes maybe fifteen seconds.

Once the stinger is locked in, the skinners get to work on overstimulating the glands, so they can pump out the hormones they want. They're mostly looking for the chemicals that make fear, lust and aggression: apparently these are the big pinker thrills. They keep those kids awake and conscious while they pump everything out of them, because using an anaesthetic slows down the process and and makes it less effective.

'It takes ninety seconds, tops,' Brian Mac said. 'You can see every muscle in their body going into seizures, every single muscle. They can't even scream. By the time the skinners have finished the bodies kind of...' He closed his eyes, like he was trying not see something. 'They kind of... implode...'

'You've seen them do it?'

He didn't answer for a while. When he opened his eyes again, it was like he was looking straight through me. 'When I haven't been quick enough,' he said. He was silent again for a while, looking down into his soup. 'The stupid thing is, there's no difference at any molecular level between those flesher hormones and the artificial ones. The whole thing is pointless. It doesn't make any difference to the market. Pinkers want the real thing. Like this pho. You can't get this out of a machine.'

I swallowed hard. 'Maybe there is a difference.'

'Maybe,' said Brian Mac. 'Pho doesn't taste the same in Newport City.'

I had nightmares for months after that.

I don't remember falling asleep. I woke up in the middle of the night, Jenna breathing beside me. I lay there staring up at the ceiling for a while, feeling empty, and then tried to go back to sleep, but it was no use. My whole body was buzzing with some kind of weird energy. I sat up and stared out of the window.

I could just make out one of the bushes in Ma's garden, its white flowers luminous in the darkness. And then the garden vanished. The window was just a black square, a void. I felt cold, as if there were a draught. I got out of bed to check that the window was still sealed, and saw that the floor of my room was solid ice, smooth under my bare feet.

Now the window pane was rippling. The ripples spread onto the walls, growing wider, until the whole room was undulating. The floor was shifting under my feet, rising and falling, rolling from side to side.

A great roar of water filled my head. It grew louder until it was vibrating through my whole body. Suddenly one of the walls of my room disappeared and I saw a blue-green swell with white caps, and above it a vast blue sky.

The water gathered itself into an enormous wave that rose higher and higher until it towered above me, shimmering like a sheet of stars, trembling with energy. Then it began to break, curling over from the top. I could feel the sheer weight of it, the unimaginable age of it, as it fell towards me, filling the whole world.

A fierce joy rushed through my veins. There was nothing else but the water, and this water was my life, it was everything that I loved. I wanted to dissolve inside it, to be part of this endless force sweeping me away.

At last it hit, lifting me off my feet. I was flying, suspended in its surging brilliance. Now Jenna was close to me, whispering my name, her arms around me. I saw without surprise that she was still curled up fast asleep, her cheek resting on her hands in our bed, undisturbed in all this turbulence. She was there and here, both at the same time.

We began to roll down through the water, tumbling and spinning to some impossible depth. It became darker and colder and the pressure around us grew and grew. Just as I thought we'd be crushed, the weight lifted. The water vanished, leaving us suspended in a vacuum. Jenna's arms slowly released me and then she was gone. Nothing was there, not even air. My lungs felt as if they were about to burst.

Then whatever was holding me let me go.

I fell onto the bed. I lay there, pulling air into my aching lungs. Jenna was asleep. I touched her shoulder and she turned to me, blinking. Her beautiful mismatched eyes glowed in the darkness, rippling, two pools of bright water I could dive into, where I could find peace, where I could sleep.

Next thing I knew, it was morning. Jenna was sitting on the edge of the bed, her face in her hands. I reached up and touched her cheek, still swimming in the ecstasy of the water, which was the ecstasy of Jenna too.

'What happened last night?' she said.

'The water,' I said. 'You.'

'It was a dream.'

'I wasn't dreaming.' I sat up and looked around my room, feeling faintly surprised that it was the same as usual.

'I was dreaming. In your dream. I know it wasn't my dream.' Jenna turned away. 'Maybe it wasn't your dream either.'

I didn't understand what she was getting at, and she sighed and took both my hands. 'Listen, Bo,' she said. 'What happened yesterday…what happened last night…we've got to talk about it.'

The overwhelming bliss began to ebb away. I felt a sudden irritation. 'The water saved us,' I said. 'It loves us, Jenna. It's not going to harm us.'

'Sometimes I've heard old dowsers talking about the water being alive. They say that the water can call us. It can come to us without our asking. They say it's a wild thing, Bo.'

'Of course it's wild,' I said.

'That means it's dangerous. You can't master the water. The dowsers say that's a kind of...blasphemy. There are tales about people who tried to and they're all bad.'

I didn't answer her out loud, but I knew she could feel my thoughts. The water was wild, yes. And so beautiful in its wildness...

'I thought it was all just stories,' she said. She still wasn't looking at me. 'I mean, I could feel the water, I could call it, but it was just...water. And then, after what happened to Mish, after that thing with the Eradicators...I began to wonder.'

'Of course it's alive,' I said. 'It speaks to us. It's part of us, Jenna.'

'But it's not us. We can't think of it like that, as if it's like us.'

She let go of my hands and walked across the room and stared out of the window at the garden.

'We don't know what it is,' she said. 'I've been able to read the water since I was a kid, but now it's different. I don't know why, but it's not the same. I don't want to be frightened of it.'

'I'm not,' I said.

She turned back and looked me straight in the eyes. 'I am,' she said. 'I'm scared to death.'

Dez

The past couple of weeks there'd been too many things. The lockdown, the attack on Newport City, the OpSec raids in the outer banns. Trying to work out how to get around the Curtains. How to get the Alchems together, how to find who's left. Coping with the new Aps being in your face any time you're walking down a rue. Little things, big things.

And now Bo. He kept acting like this water magic is no big deal, like he was some kind of wizard who had all these powers spurting out of his fingertips and he knew exactly what he was doing.

All I knew was that it scared the hell out of me. I didn't believe in magic. This water thing, whatever it was, was powerful, and power came with a price. If I knew anything, I knew that. I understood it in every cell of my body. I didn't get to be me without knowing that there's a cost.

I realised too that, ever since I got the nanovirus and my DNA spliced and reformed, Bo's been looking at me, thinking that I'm just hunkydory with it. Dez with her ubercool tech abilities, swanning around with her nose in the air thinking she's better than everyone else. *Envying* me.

Bo, out of everyone, should have known better. He knew how every day I had to struggle with me, with who I was. Was I Dez the superbot or Dez the flesher? And every day I told myself that I was a flesher. Every day I reminded myself that I wasn't some wired up freak with no human feelings, but Dez, daughter of Bel, sister of Bo, lover of Flora, loyal friend and pain in the arse.

I could be that freak, if I let it all go. It would be so easy. I'm bad with feelings, they hurt and they're confusing and sometimes I wish I didn't have them. But fuck that. Feelings come with a price too. I pay it willingly, because of everyone I love, because of the people who love me. I wouldn't have that love if I wasn't a flesher. It's worth it and more than worth it.

There's always a price.

I was so angry with Bo I could barely think. I didn't know how to begin to knock into his thick head that this was dangerous shit. And now I knew that Jenna was frightened too. That didn't make me feel any better.

What was this water? Was it the same water we drank and pissed, or was it something else? How was it something else?

Bo seemed to think it was some kind of god. Maybe something that powerful is a kind of god. We all saw how that water came out of the ground like some huge ice monster and chewed up those Eradicators. We watched buildings burst open and collapse, walls made of solid steel buckle and tear open. And now this thing with the Ap. Bo hadn't just frozen him: he'd brought his body down so close to absolute zero that it didn't matter. Every single subatomic particle in that cop's body had practically stopped moving.

That's what Bo was playing with. Bo wasn't using the water. The water was using him. And for what? What did the water want? How does water want anything, anyway?

I knew it was no use getting angry, it just made Bo stop listening. But I couldn't help it. Like I said, I'm no good at feelings.

When everything is impossible, Ma says, the thing to do is to focus on what you can do, not what you can't. So instead of yelling at Bo (or trying to stop myself yelling at Bo) I went for a brisk walk to Brian Mac's lab.

I switched the field on in my suit so I wouldn't get hassled by Aps. The field is this tech Ma told me about, a primitive perception disperser which means that instruments and trackers, even nanobots, can't pick up on you. It's so simple it doesn't register. I was kind of in awe of its elegance. It only worked as long as nobody suspected it existed, so I didn't use it very often.

OpSec still had vision on Brian Mac's house, I guess in case he decided to come back, but the lab had an underground entrance from the cellar of a warehouse two rues away. I came up the steps and clicked the gene key at the lock to get through his vicious mini-veil. Even as it lets you through, you can feel it on your skin, acid and hot. I'm always surprised that I can't smell my hair burning. If you didn't have the right code, you'd get fried.

I'd been there a couple of times since Brian Mac left, but I still wasn't used to the shock of walking in. I hadn't begun to catalogue what he had in there. I guess he had access to all sorts of supplies, being Brig of the precinct. When he gave the key to Ma, he said that it was for me, that I 'might be interested'.

He wasn't wrong.

The lab was huge. It even had a loft, with a bed. Everything was meticulously tidy and had a kind of serenity I just didn't associate with Brian Mac. On top of a pretty sophisticated field, Brian Mac had fiddled his gravitational devices, bending space so the lab wouldn't register as an empty room inside the building. I guess that's the advantage of being a cop: you know what the procedures are, so you can work out how to get around them.

There were instruments I had never seen before. On the wall in the loft was a white crystal which at first I thought was just decoration, but when I took a closer look I realised was data storage. I downloaded it on the first day I went there, and was still sorting it out.

A lot of it was stuff from OpSec, orders, rosters and so on. He must have copied practically every file he could get his hands on. There were files of old recordings, notes on tech, failed experiments, theoretical papers from secret research labs in Newport City, even a few by my father. And Brian Mac's diary. I read a lot of that. Not all of it, I felt like I was intruding. But enough. I knew more about Brian Mac now than Ma did, even though they'd been friends for over twenty years.

Nothing in this place fitted the man I had known. This was the life of someone else altogether.

I thought I understood now why Brian Mac had such a thing for timeslip implants. Most addicts use implants for the buzz, but the temporal side effects slap you round and if you're not careful you can simply delete yourself from existence. Brian Mac knew how to use them safely. I was one of his suppliers, and I remembered how meticulous he was about the implants, how he always insisted on the best.

I realised now that he didn't use them for the buzz. He used them to make time, a whole parallel life. You couldn't make something like this lab in your spare hours between shifts as an Ap. No wonder he was such a wreck.

I pulled myself together and got down to business.

I'm so used to getting into mainframes I don't even need to think about it. One of the first things I did when I recovered from the nanovirus was to download the entire Newport City Library database. By the time I was eleven I had practically every infrastructure in Newport City coded into my body.

Getting the data and reading it are two different processes: I've only processed a little of the data I have. The rest I can search and access if I need to. I know and I don't know at the same time. It's hard to explain.

There was one mainframe I was smart enough to leave alone. I sniffed around the edges of OpSec, but the security coding was evil. I never dared to take to the risk of going in there until we were desperate, until we had to know what was going on. And that was of course how I found out about the Eradicators. And also that Morro had been informing on the Alchems. It all seemed so long ago, even though it was only this past winter. Just over a month ago.

I evaded detection the first two times by going in on unpredictable fast-slow oscillations. I'd thought and thought, but I still couldn't find any other weakness. The problem was that although I could cover my tracks, I left a negative trace, a scar. Every time I went in using the same method, I amplified the trace. The first time was pretty much risk free, the second time I woke up the bots, who in turn alerted a surveillance AI. On mission three, I had point six six chance of not being detected.

I'd already searched the files I had downloaded from Brian Mac's crystal, looking for possibilities in the tech notes, and found nothing except tantalising hints. From what I'd seen, Brian Mac was too wily to hack into

OpSec, though he had some official codes he used when he wanted to get info above his rank. I thought I'd try the codes out first on an AI console he had lying about in the lab, as long as I could ensure any locational bugs were turned off.

I set up the console. To my surprise, the first code got me past the OpSec interface. I double checked the location nodes and went in. I didn't get very far, it was a low-level code for Ap superintendents only, but even so I found out a fair bit about how the Curtains were being organised, how many militia had been rostered to banns duty, how many fleshers had applied for biopasses, all that kind of routine business. I filed it away as potentially useful, and tried to log into OpSec Central. Access refused. The next two codes didn't let me in at all. The third had the same authorisations as the first. The last one seemed more promising, but when I tried OpSec Central it prompted a countercheck and I didn't have the rest of the code.

I swore and sat back, wiping my forehead. It wasn't that it was difficult doing this, it just made me so anxious I was sweating. I was 99.999 per cent certain that there was no way they could trace my logins back to this location, but that .001 per cent chance made me nervous. Not to mention the possibility that OpSec knew that Brian Mac had these codes, and was watching to see if anyone was using them.

I hadn't expected much, but I couldn't help feeling disappointed. I wanted to luck out, god knows we needed some luck. But I needed high level access, I needed to get behind the firewalls and find out what OpSec was going to do, and it was probably expecting too much to think a banns Ap, even a Brig, would be able to get that.

I spent the next few hours fiddling with the gravitational comms and getting nowhere. They were featureless silver instruments, small enough to hold in your hand or click into your suitbelt, with a primitive text screen, brainwave pickup and earpieces if you wanted to talk. They didn't look like anything. These were Brian Mac's 'deep lines', the untrackable gravitational comms he used for informers.

I thought that maybe I could rig them to break into OpSec. That was a long shot, because I still wasn't sure how they worked.

Brian Mac knew me quite well. When he handed us the comms for the

Eradicator mission, he had given me a hard look. 'Whatever you do, kid, don't open these things up,' he said. 'They're basically powered by miniature black holes. You could cause a whole lot of shit to go down that you wouldn't want to go down.'

There was enough shit going down already, so I didn't do what I would normally do: take the thing apart to see how it worked. You don't muck about with black holes. Now there was even more shit going down, and I was wondering if it was worth the risk. And yeah, part of me was dying to know how you got a black hole into something as big as my thumb. That level of density should have weighed more than the entire planet. There were some heavy duty tricks going on inside those little silver boxes.

After a few hours I had got precisely nowhere. I went home, kicking stones along the rues and brooding. Maybe Flora was right, after all. Even though I had little to no chance of getting in undetected, even though I might even get caught, I had to hack into OpSec again. The risk of not knowing what they were going to do was higher than the risk of going in.

I probably should have spent the day concentrating on damage control. I would have to assume that all the bells and whistles would go off, and just make sure that I was too fast to catch, and too sneaky to track.

Bo

Day after day, Jenna and I trudged after Sal and Park through a labyrinth of tunnels and shafts, mysterious passageways that led nowhere, channels, empty bunkers and dark burrows, all layered one on top of the other, the product of centuries of digging and building in a lightless world. We always searched for the deepest pathways, because even underground we could be traced. The further down we went, the safer we'd be.

It was gruelling, exhausting work, twelve hours a day or more. We'd hardly seen daylight for almost two weeks. But eventually we got as far as the Wall.

Before lockdown, some Alchems had holed up in Morro's old place after their hide was raided. We still didn't know the full cost of Morro's betrayal: who was hiding, who was arrested, who was dead. These were members of a chapter who worked out of the Eleventh. Their leader, Koni-Ta, was a dowser, and a good friend of Jenna's. We hadn't heard a peep from them since the curtains went up.

Morro's hideout was in a crumbling power station that stood at the edge of the Twelfth, overlooking the sick waters of the Gilla Sea. It was a treasure trove of stuff Morro had hoarded over the years. He was a dedicated scavenger. There was even a shelf full of books that Morro had called the Newport Annals. Ma's ears had pricked up when I mentioned them.

'Maybe there's something there that could be useful,' she said.

'Like what?' I thought of that room, piled with junk. I couldn't even guess what a lot of it was for.

'There could be plans. Maybe the original plans of Newport. There'd be stuff there that even Newport City doesn't know. Brian told me that when we burned down OpSec HQ they lost a lot of historical data. Half their knowledge went up in smoke.'

We'd decided that once we mapped past the Wall, Jenna and I would head to the Twelfth and take a look around. But we had some work to do first.

We went in from a point close to home, north of the shijo, which led into the RTS via a sewer that ran parallel to the line. It was an area that we hadn't finished mapping yet, so we'd have to take it slowly.

This particular part of the RTS had been shut down forty years before, when Ma was a kid. After that the station had been a den for screwed-up drug users and deadbeat pinkers. The Aps had cleared it out and blocked the entrance about a decade ago. Park told us that before they'd sealed it off, they'd flushed the tunnels with some kind of poison that killed everything.

'They didn't care what was down here,' he'd said, with that sinister grin. 'As long as it was dead.'

The manhole was in an alley behind the local homer depot. Two drivers that I knew from way back when I was a little punk, Nesse and Kipp, waved hello as we arrived. I'd always sort of looked up to them, they were the ones who got me interested in homers. They were part of Ma's network, and they were wise to everything that was going on in the banns. I trusted them.

Kipp prised open the manhole cover with a tyre lever and Jenna recoiled and switched on her suit. 'I thought this sewer wasn't used any more.'

'It isn't,' said Kipp. 'But, you know, some kinds of stink just...hang around.'

I climbed down first into a steel pipe about three metres deep. I checked the air quality monitor in my suit, turned on my light and looked around. The sewer ran in a wide curve so vision was limited. It wasn't far to the breach in the sewer wall. We'd enter the RTS close to Rue Vargas station.

Once we got to the RTS, the line veered right until we came to a big junction. I double checked our position on the MPS and we took the tunnel on the left, going north west. After about ten minutes we came to Tanizaki Square Station. It was weird walking between the platforms; they looked as if they had been abandoned yesterday. The walls were covered with graffiti telling Aps or OpSec to fuck off out of the banns.

Jenna was fascinated. 'This shit could have been written yesterday.'

'Maybe Ma did some of it,' I said. 'When she was a kid.'

'I bet she did.'

We turned south at the second junction we came to, heading towards the Gilla Sea. We were getting close to the Wall now. This was as far as we'd mapped – from here on it was unknown territory.

Jenna grabbed my arm. 'Listen,' she said.

Gradually I became aware of a low, deep hum, very faint, that rose and fell like a slow heartbeat, growing a little louder with each step. I checked our position: we were almost under the foundations of the Wall. Now I could feel the hum in my body, a slow increase and decrease of pressure.

'It's the Wall,' said Jenna. 'It's like it's…breathing.'

Nobody knew what the Wall was made of. Morro reckoned it was as old as the city itself, a defence against an enemy that had been long forgotten. It rose above the banns like a slice of night that absorbed all light and sound, a kind of black hole that encircled the Inner Banns. The Wall was spooky enough above ground, but no one had ever heard it breathing before.

As we got closer the air thickened, until it was like we were pushing through water. It was difficult to put one foot in front of the other. Jenna and I linked arms, pulling each other along. Passing under the Wall was torture: I began to wonder if we'd make it. Every organ in my body seemed to be squeezed by a giant fist. I began to think we ought to turn back, but then the pressure lifted. The relief was incredible.

We stopped for a rest and a suit check and I pinged Dez. It was a while before I got a response: the comms were still working, but they were weak. I saw that my power levels were down by twenty per cent. The suit must have been working extra hard getting us under the Wall. That was bad news.

I turned to Jenna to say that we'd better start conserving power when I saw her face. 'Are you okay?' I said.

She met my eyes. She didn't have to tell me that she wasn't. 'Something happened under the Wall,' she said. 'I saw something.'

'What do you mean you saw something?' I said. 'I didn't see anything.'

'Bodies,' said Jenna. 'I saw bodies. Dead people.'

Her voice was shaking. I was shocked: I hadn't sensed her distress at all. Usually each of us knows what the other is feeling. I reached out to put my arm around her but she shook me off and stood up, as if she were listening. I couldn't hear anything. And then, without any warning, she took off into the darkness. I shouted her name but she didn't even look back.

I ran after her, fumbling at my waist to turn my light up, trying to keep her in sight. All I could see was her silhouette in the soft orb of her suit light. I couldn't catch her up. It was like something in a nightmare, chasing this figure always in front of me, always the same distance ahead.

The rails turned sharply to the right and for a few moments I lost sight of her, although I could still hear her footsteps echoing off the tunnel walls. I skidded round the corner and slipped, almost falling over. Suddenly I was running through water. It was ankle-deep, just covering the rails, and it was freezing cold.

Jenna had fallen to her knees about a dozen metres past the turn. I caught up with her and stood there panting, blinking the sweat out of my eyes. It was a few seconds before I realised what I was looking at. Spread across the tunnel in the arc of my light were bodies.

Dead people.

There were five bodies scattered in the shallow water. Two of them were close together, their arms wrapped around one another, as if they were asleep. 'It's Koni-Ta,' Jenna said, looking up me. Her face was expressionless. I still had no idea what she was thinking or feeling. It really threw me: some deep connection between us had suddenly stopped working. 'I knew it was her.'

Koni-Ta was old for a flesher, maybe twenty years older than Ma. Her pale blue eyes were wide open, as if she were staring at something in horror. Her long, white hair spread out around her head like a huge fan. Jenna gently closed her eyes, murmuring something that, even though I was right next to her, I couldn't hear.

In Koni-Ta's arms was a young woman. Jenna told me she was a dowser too, Koni-Ta's apprentice Quan. The younger woman's face was pressed into Koni-Ta's neck, as if she had died trying hide from something. On her cheek was the tattoo of a slender tree, its leaves curling around her eye.

Tiny drops of water trembled on Koni-Ta's eyelashes and hair, shining in the silvery light of my suit. There was a pool of water on her chest. I leaned forward and saw that it wasn't water, it was some kind of glass. It looked like the data crystal Dez had shown me from Brian Mac's lab.

'We should take that,' I said.

'I don't like to,' said Jenna.

'It really looks like a data crystal.'

Jenna hesitated for a moment, then gently slipped it over Koni-Ta's head and put it around her own neck.

The other three bodies were each lying alone. They were all dressed in the regular gear of Alchems, boots and camo jackets. I turned one of them over and realised that I knew him. A guy called Blaise, a regular at swap-meets. He was a wheeler-dealer, buying and selling anything he could get his hands on; a bit of a shyster really, a fence for small time thieves. I didn't know him well. I never even suspected that he was an Alchem.

'They must have had to leave Morro's,' said Jenna, still speaking with that eerie calm. The shock, maybe? 'They've been drowned.'

I swallowed, because my mouth was suddenly dry. 'Here?'

'Look at the walls.'

I looked. They were damp all the way to the ceiling.

I walked a little way up the tunnel. Two metres from the bodies either way the walls and ground were bone-dry.

I remembered my dream that wasn't a dream: the enormous wall of water in my room, shimmering like a sheet of stars, trembling with energy, the roar that filled my head. How I wanted it to swallow me, to sweep me away.

We pulled the bodies out of the water and laid them side by side further along the tunnel, crossing their arms over their chests. We didn't have time, but it felt wrong to leave them there in that weird puddle. Before we left, Jenna knelt down and stroked Koni-Ta's face.

'You were the wisest, the strongest,' she whispered. 'We needed you.' She bowed her head and was quiet for a few seconds. I stood beside her, saying nothing, not knowing how to comfort her.

'I guess we better get moving,' I said.

'We'll come back for them, won't we?' said Jenna.

I said that we would. I didn't know if that was an empty promise.

We hardly spoke at all after that. Our batteries were running down, so Jenna switched off her light and I turned mine to low. We stayed close together to avoid losing each other in the darkness. I switched on the MPS briefly to check our position, and pinged Dez.

Nothing came back. We were on our own.

Erin

This past week, I've started wondering if I'm on some kind of list. There are all sorts of tiny things that by themselves mean nothing, but they all add up. It feels like everyone else knows something that I don't. A whisper here, a rumour there, you know it works. Like there's this little toxic bubble around you. Nothing obvious, nothing you can put your finger on. Someone crosses the street and pretends they haven't seen you, somebody else can't stay to chat, another person doesn't answer your text.

Maybe I'm just feeling this way because of John Mecha. He hasn't pulled the touching stunt again, but he has lots of ways to make my job unpleasant. I'm beginning to feel anxious about everything, brittle, and this isn't like me. Dervin told me my skin was losing its lustre and sent me for a treatment. If it doesn't improve he'll start commandeering my martinis, and drinking is the only thing that gets me to sleep at night.

I wonder if John Mecha snooped me to OpSec. I wouldn't put it past him. It's not just his stardom that makes him think he can act with impunity. Usually celebrities have high levels of insecurity, that's programmed in as well, it makes us malleable I guess. But Mecha has none of that. You see it when you look into his eyes. Someone's got his back. Even Joh is careful, and Joh's pretty powerful in the industry.

To be fair, I never heard that Mecha is an informer. But that doesn't mean that he isn't.

But then I give myself a little shake. Maybe I'm just imagining it all. Dervin hasn't said anything, and he's always super-sensitive to anything that might affect my career, because my career is his reputation. On the other hand, he's been a bit distant over the past few days. He's busy with a new show, he has meetings, he has to meet with the brass, there's always something. Nothing sinister in itself. But it doesn't help to damp down the spooked feels.

I keep thinking about that extra I saw on the infonews. Was it really him? Maybe it's just coincidence? I know, for one thing, that he looked nothing like the real flesher I saw. None of the fleshers on the soaps do.

It has to be that extra. But if it is, what does that mean? That it wasn't fleshers who blew up that apartment building? And if it wasn't them, who was it?

Even thinking this scares the hell out of me, I get this windy feeling in my stomach, like the ground has gone wobbly. Of course I don't tell anyone what I'm imagining, that would be suicide. Besides, who could I tell? People would think I was crazy. There'd be more whispers. *Erin Saba is going out of her mind.*

Maybe I am. Maybe this is what John Mecha is doing to me.

The worst thing is not knowing if I'm just imagining it all.

We all know what happens when you get put on a list. Well, the truth is that we have no idea what happens, we just know how it works. There are rumours, a gradually widening circle of silence, and then, eventually, someone isn't there any more. It can take months. Occasionally there's an infonews report, a subversive making a tearful confession. People don't talk about it much, but the reports say that either they're banished out to the banns, which is bad enough, or they're sent to Duiwel Island Prison. But it's just as likely that they just get a bullet in the back of the head in some dark room underneath Newport City. I mean, how would we know? All we know is that you never hear from that person again.

In my line of work, people sometimes do end up on lists. The baby farms have to condition in things like curiosity and imagination, otherwise we can't do what they need us to do. And sometimes curiosity and imagination end up leading us wrong.

We learned about it every day in celebrity school. 'You'll all be stars,' they said, every day. 'Unless you choose the darkness. Beware of the dark in your mind…'

I feel like my world is closing in around me, as if that darkness is pulling me into it, swallowing me. Shooting *Ebolastic* is a nightmare. I have to brace myself every morning. People follow Mecha's lead, so even though I'm the co-star people don't talk to me on set. It makes it hard to concentrate on my role and I'm pretty sure this role is the only thing keeping me out of the interrogation rooms. I'm the top IMR rethrill this week, and if I go anywhere in public I'm mobbed.

It probably makes it a little difficult for OpSec to disappear me right now. Or for me to make myself disappear, for that matter. Not that there's anywhere to disappear to.

Dervin drops in to check out my skin, to see if the treatment worked. He says he won't stay, he's got a meeting. Tonight I'm feeling so bad I ask Dervin straight out if I'm on a list. He pauses for a microsecond before he answers and I think, with a jump in my chest, that it really is true.

'What's with this paranoia, baby? Have you done something you shouldn't?'

'No,' I tell him. 'I haven't done anything. Do I have to have done anything?'

He gives me a sharp look and I bite my lip. I shouldn't have said that.

'Baby, you're a hit,' he says. 'Nobody's going to put you on a damn list. In any case, they're planning something big for you.' He smiles, that fake flashy smile. 'You've got nothing to worry about.'

I don't feel at all reassured. As I smile back, my own fake smile, I'm thinking that maybe the 'something big' was writing me out of the series. Deaths of popular characters are always big.

'Just look after your face, babe. You're looking a little puffy these days. Not good. Not good at all.'

Yeah, those martinis are puffing up my face. But right now that seems like the least of my problems. He leaves and I get Ami to make me a drink.

I'm beginning to think that seeing that flesher at the hospital was a turning point. Ever since that day everything has gone wrong. John Mecha is making me miserable, but if I complain I'm toast. The job would be exhausting even without Mecha: I feel wrung out at the end of every day, like I've been holding myself together in case I fall into little bits in front of everybody. I have these dreams where I'm a bunch of broken pixels twitching on the floor while everybody laughs.

I hardly go out any more. Unless there's some publicity party I have to attend, I head back to my apartment after work and spend the evening with Ami watching the infonews until I'm drunk enough to fall asleep. I don't get many invites these days anyway. Maybe people got sick of asking me out. I've been saying no since I started shooting this damn soap because it's so exhausting. Or maybe they've heard, the way you hear, that's it unsafe to be seen with me.

There's nobody I could ask. If you hear something, it's not like you tell the person concerned. Nobody does.

So much for the glamour celebrity lifestyle. Sitting in my super plus shiny clean apartment with my thoughts going round and round like a rat in a cage.

A scared rat in a cage. A rat in a cage that can smell the poison gas seeping in, the first few molecules tainting the air, and knows there's nowhere to run.

Make me a drink, Ami dear. Make me another drink and watch me drink all the drinks until I'm shiny and numb like the stars in the sky that no one sees, cold and white and far away.

Shiny and numb.

Dez

At first I wasn't going to tell Ma about my plan to hack into OpSec. I was sure that she'd hit the roof and forbid me straight out, because it was so dangerous. I didn't want to have to disobey her, because I was going to do it anyway.

But then I started thinking about everything that could go wrong. If things did go pear-shaped, she would have to know what I'd been up to, in order to deal with the mess. I told her when Bo was out mapping with Jenna. It was just her and me, sitting in the front room. I took a deep breath and braced myself for a proper fight.

To my surprise, she didn't do any roof-hitting. She gave me a long look that I couldn't read, her lips pressed together, like she did when she was thinking hard. Then, to my surprise, she leaned over and hugged me.

'Oh, Dezzie,' she said, her voice catching. It was her name for me when I was a crawler, she hadn't called me that for years. She sat back and smiled at me, but her eyes were very bright. 'Sometimes I wish you weren't so much like me.'

'I thought you said I was like Flynn,' I said, trying to be light-hearted.

'You are,' she said. 'Trouble from both sides.' She put her chin in her hands and studied my face. 'You'd better tell me exactly what you think you're going to do.'

'It's risky,' I said. That was an understatement.

'I want to know exactly how risky.' She saw me hesitating, and smiled again. 'I do mean exactly,' she said. 'I know you're going to do it, no matter what I say. So I'd better know what to expect.'

I hadn't been going to tell her how high the risk was, but she was all business, like she was doing a deal in the shijo, like she was whenever she was organising something. I realised she was talking to me like I was an equal, and that I'd better give her back the same respect.

'I modelled the risks, so far as I can predict them,' I said. Ma nodded. I took a deep breath. 'So, I have about a 99.34 per cent chance of being detected while I'm in there.' She didn't react, which was a bad sign. 'Mind you, that gives me a .66 per cent chance of *not* being detected.'

'What does it mean, being detected? Just that they know that you're in there?'

'Yes. The infobots wake up and detect an invasion. They'll begin tracking.'

'But you'll know if they do that, right?'

'If they haven't upgraded their defences. They probably have, because of everything that went down in OpSec after what Morro did. With any luck they still think it's an inside pinker job. That databomb I left behind me should have created enough confusion to keep them chasing their own tails for months.'

Ma gave me a sudden mischievous grin. 'That's my Dez,' she said.

'I've been trying to feel it out without going inside the firewalls, and I can't see much difference, but that doesn't mean anything.'

'So possibly the risk is even higher,' said Ma.

'Yeah, but I kind of factored that in.'

Ma looked sceptical. I opened my mouth to explain, and then I didn't. It's really hard to say in words what it's like being in the data universe, it doesn't translate. Ma knows tech, it's been her business since we were kids, but even she doesn't know what it's like from the inside. 'Trust me,' I said. 'Even with the unknowns, I'm pretty sure that's an accurate assessment.'

'Okay. Given that you'll almost certainly be detected, what's your chance of being identified and tracked?'

I swallowed. 'Chance of being tracked is 78.455 per cent. Chance of being identified is between 28.7 and 68.333.' I decided not to tell her the chance of me getting trapped in the OpSec mainframe, which was just under 30 per cent. It would give her one more thing to worry about. If it did happen, there was nothing that could be done from her end. I'd have to work it out myself.

Or not.

'Why the variation?'

'It depends on whether OpSec has taken any notice of that DNA scan.'

For a moment Ma looked confused. 'What DNA scan?'

'The one the skinner took. From some homebuild scanner. Remember? Brian Mac told you.'

'God damn it,' said Ma. 'Chances are OpSec will be taking a lot of notice, if you ask me. They'll be looking for any sign of exceptional abilities in fleshers now.'

'Yeah, they will be.' Thanks to Morro, they'd started the Chimera program, a top secret experimental lab that was examining flesher DNA, with the idea of splicing our abilities with pinkers. Thinking about it made me feel sick to the stomach. 'So most likely near 70 per cent.'

'They're bad odds, Dez,' she said.

'I know. And I can't count on being lucky.'

'But you still think it's worth it?'

'The risks of not doing it are even worse.' I didn't have to do any calculations to know that if we had no inside information, the chance of being fucked over by OpSec was 100 per cent. Ma knows that figure as well as I do.

She went quiet for a while. I watched her, feeling a rush of love come up in my throat. My beautiful mother. My beautiful, brave Ma. Sometimes I feel that I've never quite loved her enough.

'Okay,' she said. 'Point six six chance of things going right.' She took a long, deep breath. 'So. When things go wrong, what's the plan?'

I told her. After that, I went down to my cellar and did some prep. Then I gave Ma a big hug and went over to Flora's to spend the night.

I'd already told Flora what the risks were, including the chance of me being caught in the mainframe. I don't know why I could warn her but not

Ma. Maybe because I thought the chances in my favour were pretty good, given all the other dire risks. Flora had been aghast, and she had tried to talk me out of it. But she knew, as well as I did, as well as Ma did, why I had to try.

When I went over there, we didn't talk about it at all. We had dinner with Kojo. Flora had asked him to make us mint soup, because it's my favourite. Kojo makes the best mint soup in the bann.

We pretended it was an ordinary night just like every other night, we pretended that neither of us knew that maybe I might not come back tomorrow, and we went to bed early and giggled over some stupid soaps and then I kissed Flora and Flora kissed me. And then it wasn't ordinary at all, unless a miracle is ordinary.

Bo

We heard them as we approached the Wall: the dead, flat voices of OpSec militia. In the tunnels every sound echoes and carries a long way, so it was difficult to tell how far away they were. We stopped and I switched off my light.

Under the voices we could just hear the low, deep pulse of the Wall. We moved forward about twenty metres in the darkness, until we could see them around the curve of the tunnel. It was a patrol of five heavily armed militia. One of them was on the comms. Two others were talking, but I couldn't make out what they were saying.

Had we set off some kind of alarm when we'd passed under before? We were closer to the surface here, so there was more chance of running into trouble. It was like stepping into the light after hiding in the shadows. But maybe it was just a routine patrol. Over the past two weeks of mapping we hadn't run into any OpSec patrols underground, but perhaps they were more active under the Wall.

Jenna and I pulled out our tasers and began to back off. The patrol turned and we watched them move away from us. As they passed under the Wall, they seemed to be walking in slow motion.

'We need to find another way under,' I said. 'It's too risky.'

Jenna switched on her MPS for a few seconds to get our position. 'There's a kind of junction about a klick away.'

When we the reached the junction we took the line that ran north south, which took us towards the Second and home. We were conserving as much power as possible. If passing under the Wall drained the batteries as much as before, we'd be practically running on empty. We soon heard that low, pulsing hum. We linked arms and pulled each other through a dozen painful metres until we were clear of the bone-crushing pressure.

In this area some of the tunnels were partially collapsed, but from what we could see it looked safe enough. We picked our way through the debris until we found a service alcove. A steel ladder led up to a hatch, which opened into a narrow service gangway. We travelled about two hundred metres before reaching a large, low-ceilinged chamber. The walls were cracked, the masonry crumbling, and broken pipes hung from the ceiling. There'd been some kind of accident, or maybe an earth tremor. There were traces on the walls where machinery and wiring had been stripped out.

A small steel door at the end of the chamber opened onto a long corridor that finally took us to another hatch. I checked the MPS. It was just about dead, but I got a weak signal. We weren't far from River Station. Above ground was River Square, right at the edge of the Eighth in the south east corner. If we could find a tunnel that travelled east, we'd be in the Second in no time.

The emergency exit was at the southern end of the main platform. As we began climbing the stairs my light blinked out and I stumbled in the sudden darkness. Jenna switched on hers but it was as weak as a candle flame.

We'd only climbed a little further when we discovered the skeletons. Three of them close together on the concrete steps, an adult and two small children. I remembered what Park had told me about the poison. Why had these three been down here? The RTS had been shut months before OpSec poisoned the tunnels. Were they hiding, were they running from something? Maybe they lived down here. It could have been Ma and Dez and me, when Ma was in hiding.

Whatever their story, they hadn't made it out in time. We stepped around them and left them in the darkness.

At the top of the stairs was a small vestibule with two exits, left and right, both sealed from the outside. We'd have to blast one of them open. We'd be making quite an entrance back into the Second. We stood as far from the door as possible, squeezed into the opposite corner, and turned our tasers up to full strength. On Jenna's count of three, we fired. For a split second the small space filled with light and heat. The air filled with the smell of burning metal. Pulling Jenna up with me, I scrambled to my feet and kicked at the door.

We spilt out into an empty street. We shut what was left of the door behind us and covered it with some planks. And then we ran.

We stopped for a breather in a sunken doorway off Rue Tanzar, slumping down on the wide step. Jenna and I had hardly spoken since finding Koni-Ta and the others. That wouldn't normally matter but now I felt that some link between us had snapped, and it scared me.

'You okay?' I said.

Jenna nodded and I took hold of her hand. Her skin was freezing.

'Not you're not,' I said.

'I'll be okay. I just want to get home.'

I took a breath. 'Jenna,' I said. 'All this stuff about the water, about me and the water, it isn't *bad*. I know it isn't.'

'I don't know what it is,' she said. 'I'm frightened for you.'

'I'm beginning to think that you're frightened *of* me.'

'Maybe I am.'

I felt that like a punch in the gut. The last thing in the world I wanted was for Jenna to be afraid of me.

'I know that you feel like the water makes you strong,' she said. 'I guess maybe it does, in a way. But you don't know what else it can do. Don't trust it, Bo.'

'I know it won't hurt me, or you.'

'How can you know that, after what we saw back there?' She put her hand on my face. 'I need you to be careful. I've read the water since I was a kid, but it's different for me. I don't feel it the way that you do. I can't make it do what you can. When you killed that Ap…'

71

'I didn't mean to. I told you that.'

She stood up. 'That's just what I mean. The water killed him, all the same. Like it killed Koni-Ta.'

'You and me, we're still…we're still together.'

I felt like I was asking a question, but Jenna just took my hand and pulled me to my feet.

'Promise you'll be careful, promise you'll talk to me,' she said. 'You don't have to be alone. I'll help you if you need help.'

'I will,' I said.

'*Promise*.' Her eyes were fierce, burning. 'It matters, Bo. It really matters.'

'I promise,' I said. And this time, I really meant it.

We were almost home when the light turned yellow and the air started buzzing with a kind of sick static. The wind kicked up, spiralling dust off the street. A dry storm: we hadn't seen one in the Second for ages.

What a day. What a fucking day.

We quickened our pace. After only a couple of minutes it was hard to see through the dust, and then it was hard to walk. We had to get indoors and wait it out. These mini-tornadoes usually passed after half an hour or so but they were rough on anyone who didn't find shelter.

We were near Rani's tea shop on the corner of Rue Boniface. I dragged Jenna over to the door and leaned on the buzzer, yelling. There was a pause and then the door snapped open and we fell into the airlock.

'Thanks,' I said, picking myself up. Rani, a tiny, wrinkled woman with big hair, was checking us out from behind her counter. Jenna and I were regular customers, but Rani was on edge, like everyone else in the banns.

'It's rough out there,' she said. 'I guess you'll be wanting tea?'

Why not? 'I guess we do.'

Jenna and I sat by the window. We couldn't see anything outside except billows of yellowish dust. I remembered we'd have to pay. 'Have you got any credits?'

'Enough for tea.' Jenna smiled at me. 'Let's pretend it's just a normal day. Just while we're here.'

The light in her eyes. My Jenna.

We sipped our tea, not saying anything. And, weird as it might seem, for a little bubble of time it was just us being together. Nothing else. I didn't want anything else. Watching Jenna across the table sipping her tea, giggling at one of my silly jokes, made me so happy.

Of course it couldn't last.

The door buzzer went off again. More stragglers caught in the storm, I thought. Rani snapped the intercom. We both heard the dead, metallic voice on the other side of the door, and the bubble popped.

Two heavily armed militia shouldered in with a cloud of dust. Even a dry storm didn't mean time off for fleshers. What the hell were they doing here? I was suddenly trembling with anger. We couldn't even have this moment. We wanted so little, and they couldn't even let us have that.

One stayed in the doorway as the other approached our table. 'Identification. Now.'

Okay, this was just routine harassment. I reached into my pocket and offered him my ID chip. He slotted it into a small illuminated unit that blinked red and blue on the arm of his uniform.

'Faulty read,' he said. His pal in the doorway took a few steps inside.

'Try again,' I said, my mouth dry.

'Bad ID,' said the first guy.

What happened next is difficult to describe. I remember it in slow motion, but it all happened in a few seconds.

Rani turned to run out of the room and knocked over the water filter on the counter. The guy with the gun swung around, aiming his weapon as the door to the back quarters slammed down behind her. The filter smashed open on the floor and the water spilled out in a wide fan.

And then…it kept spreading, as if there were a whole river inside that damn filter. It covered the entire floor of the shop, it was climbing the walls, sheets of water rising up to the ceiling, swelling and rippling. For a moment the water was suspended above us, a shimmering, silver roof, and then it began to fall in huge drops, like a heavy rainstorm.

As the water crashed down on the two militia it turned to ice. They froze where they stood, completely encased in solid, transparent shells.

Jenna and I just stared at each other. We weren't frozen. Maybe our suits had protected us? No, it wasn't the suits. I knew it wasn't.

I looked out the window. The dust seemed to be clearing. But right now I didn't care, I just wanted to get out of there. We stumbled into the street, holding each other, and ran.

I turned back once. The rain inside the tea shop was still pounding on the window.

Dez

Thinking about data me as a separate thing from flesher me was something I tried not to do. They were both me, just with different functions: the same as using my feet to walk on and my mouth to talk with. It wasn't a Morro kind of difference, where he ended up with two selves and one of them didn't know what the other was doing. Or at least, I told myself it wasn't.

I often thought about Morro. The odd thing is that, even when I was so angry with him I could have strangled him on the spot, I believed him when he said he didn't know what the other him was doing. I believed that he had split himself so much in two that one Morro was a rebel and the other a traitor. I had every reason in the world not to trust a word Morro said. But I thought he was telling me the truth.

What disturbed me was why I believed him. It was because underneath I feared that the same thing could happen to me.

Maybe us fleshers are all a little split, because we have to be. We have to hide who we are, like Ma hid herself all those years, even from Bo and me. I guess it happens to pinkers too, pinkers like Brian Mac, Brig of the Second Bann by day, genius subversive by night. It kind of made sense that he ended up crashing on Morro's crazy ride.

And then there's what we know about ourselves, and what the pinkers say we are. Pinkers invented the word fleshers, and now we call ourselves that, it's our badge of pride. But that's how what pinkers say about us slides in under our skins and changes us. We all watch the soaps and the infonews. And even though we know better, even when we laugh about how wrong they get us, part of us believes that somehow pinkers are right. And some of us become what they say we are.

Which was why, without hacking into OpSec's mainframe, I couldn't be 100 per cent certain it wasn't fleshers who blew up an apartment block full of people. None of the fleshers I knew would do that, not even Ma, who helped burn OpSec HQ to the ground all those years ago and wouldn't think twice about taking down a cop.

Ma didn't believe for a second it was fleshers, but maybe that's because she's too practical. Her question was, why would fleshers kill those people? What good does it do us? And sure, it makes no sense. But pinkers reckon we do that shit all the time, that's why they fear us. And maybe some fleshers believe it enough to become what pinkers fear, because that way we get to have power, even if it blows up in our own faces, even if it means that we're blowing up the best parts of ourselves. Maybe, like Flora said, someone just wanted revenge.

Morro was like the best of us and the worst of us rolled up together in a terrible mess. I suppose he thought he atoned for his sins in the end, sacrificing himself to bring down Bremmer, but that was just more of his crap. It would have been better if he'd stayed alive and tried to work himself out. If he'd done the hard thing and learned how to bring himself together into a single person, maybe then all of us could have learned something.

More specifically, maybe he could have helped me.

To be honest, I'm frightened of this way people have of splitting themselves up. Sometimes I wonder if it's happening to me without my knowing, that maybe I could bifurcate simply by being who I am. The thing is, nobody knows what I am, not even me, so there's no one I can ask for advice. I can crunch an exabyte of data in less than a minute, but this mind stuff confuses me, because it's nothing to do with logic.

So I put on some music, some of Flora's mob, and I turned it up super loud, and let myself slow down. Just for a few minutes. Just in case I never got to be slow Flesher Dez ever again. I methodically rechecked everything

I'd prepared the day before. The instructions to Ma on several worst case scenarios, including what to do if the firewalls slammed down and trapped me inside. I didn't know what would be left of me here in the cellar if that happened: most of me would be missing, because I needed most of me to get the job done.

If I did get caught in the mainframe, I'd have to cut me off from me. I didn't know if I'd ever get back, or even if it was possible to put me back together. But if I was trapped, I had no choice. If I didn't cut myself off they could trace me, even ID me, and we'd all be screwed. I didn't know how much OpSec had worked out: maybe they'd found that dodgy DNA scan, maybe they'd figured how I got into the mainframe in the first place. The one thing that I could be sure of was that they'd have upgraded their security. Hopefully their upgrades were all pointless, because they hadn't figured out their weakness. Hopefully.

The whole process was going to be more complex this time, as I'd be decrypting and downloading into an external hard drive as I went. Normally I'd just down download to me, but I had to be sure that if I were trapped in the mainframe, Ma and the others would still have access to the data.

One final check. And then I went in.

Datadazzle. It's not something you can put into words. Trying to say it just turns it into something it's not, because you can't describe it. I can say something of what it's like, but it's so much cruder than how it is.

It's a high, I admit it: pure speed. I'm not inside the limits of my body any more, looking through eyes that can't see through walls, hearing only the sounds that touch me. I can be in an infinity of spaces at the same time, I can see everything, go everywhere. Time opens out in new dimensions, folding over and into itself in subatomic scales, which fold out into infinities faster than light. I'm as fast as that. If I could be even faster, faster even than OpSec's super tachyon computing, the universe would be my playground. But even I can't go faster than light. Believe me, I've tried.

Past the first firewall, which was evil with alarm bots, AI algorithms and cascading veils of constantly shifting crypto. Slow, slow, slow, tuning my oscillations down as low as a hundredth of a second, then to super light speed then back. It's really hard to keep the rhythms random, I had thousands of algorithms working on just this firewall and a bank of others for when I was inside. If holding my breath were a thing in the datadazzle, I'd be holding it.

This was the first big gamble. If they'd figured out how I got in last time, I was screwed. I'd done some cautious sniffing outside the walls, trying to pick up anything that wouldn't let me slide past, and I was pretty sure they hadn't. But there was no way of knowing for sure until I was in there.

Slowly, agonisingly slowly, I broke the crypto and wiggled through. I was in the general mainframe. There was no time to be relieved (time doesn't count, although it does, but how can I describe that in flesher speak, in words that are so many thousands of times slower than anything I am now). This time, if I was going to have any hope of downloading the data, I had to leave a path behind me. It felt awful, as if I was going in there blowing a trumpet, jumping up and down in front of the autosentries waving balloons and letting off fireworks.

I shifted to superlight speed, scanning as much as I could as fast as I could. I could already sense the autobots beginning to stir, like they were beginning to smell me, but I was being too fast. They mostly went back to dormant. I did all the searches, downloading anything I could find on the banns, flesher security, Aps strategy, all the routine stuff. So far I was just getting away with it. There were vibrations of disturbance, but they didn't break the surface of critical mass. All the same, the AIs were beginning to get interested.

I pulled in the next set of algorithms and went through the second firewall, warping up again to super lightspeed to search for useful data, trying to ensure I didn't miss anything. Downloading to the external drive was beginning to take a toll, and I was leaving traces. The autobots weren't so quiet this time, though they couldn't keep up with me. My time was running out. For a flash of time, the tiniest hiccup of a second, I considered withdrawing without going past the third firewall. Maybe I had enough?

No.

The third firewall was the most important of all, the real point of my going in. I was willing to swear that not even senior OpSec knew it existed: I'd only found it by chance in the first place, behind a whole bunch of cryptoshadows and the data equivalent of a Veil, trained to destroy anything alien. It was only open to Osborne and the head of OpSec, who these days was Garonne, and maybe a couple of others. They shouldn't know that I'd already breached it, I'd only been through once. They should think this vault was completely secure. Should. My risk on this one was 78 per cent, in my favour.

Back to the slow and fast, cranking up the quantum entanglement to another level, reversing the process as I passed. I was frightened now. Or maybe I should say that Flesher Dez was frightened, Data Dez isn't capable of fear, Data Dez just calculates the risks. There was no sign of an alert, so I was still working below critical.

I crept through the third firewall. It took longer this time, it felt like forever. (It did take forever, in the units of time I was working in: maybe as much as a thousandth of a second.) Once I was in I zapped back to super-light speed, vacuuming up everything in sight. I didn't bother to search, because this database was much smaller. I just decrypted and funnelled it back to the external hard drive through the passage I'd wormed in the fire-walls, angling through different dimensions, doing the oscillations again to make me as untrackable as possible, keeping the reversals going behind me so the bots couldn't tail me. That probably took me a few thousand micro-seconds. I stitched my data passages shut and fuzzed them so it looked like the data was going somewhere inside Newport City.

Now all I had to do was get out.

I adjusted my chances up: given I had scoured three databases and was still working below critical, I had probably two point seven chance now of getting away scot free. I drew on the last set of algorithms that were going to model my way out past the three firewalls.

And then everything froze around me, as if all the molecules had instantly crystallised or suddenly plunged to absolute zero, a cold so cold that every single particle had stopped vibrating. It only lasted for maybe a microsec-ond, but it was enough: for that microsecond, I was isolated and visible. I was the only thing in that whole database that was in motion. It was as if all the lights turned on, and every single autobot and AI in the whole damn system had me in its sights and there was nowhere to hide.

My first thought was that it was a fucking trap. They must have let me in. But if it was, why let me get all that data out? I'd covered for that kind of tracing trap. Unless they were using some kind of programming I didn't know anything about.

I didn't have time to speculate. I went into full-on emergency mode and slashed the connection to flesher me. I wasn't frightened any more, I had no flesher me to be frightened with. This was probably a good thing. I pulled myself together into a subatomic mass, a kind of super lightspeed bullet, and slammed myself through the third firewall. I made it before it locked down completely but I was still trapped behind two firewalls in OpSec's tachyon computer. I was going to have to make the rest up as I went along.

I scrambled all of me as a data shimmer through the whole mainframe, so I wasn't a point any more but a glitch. That confused some of the AIs, but not all of them. They were right behind me now, not that 'behind me' means anything in the dataplane, but that's what they were, yapping at my heels, cocking the gun to shoot me, crosshairs on my forehead. They were identifying what was me and what was the OpSec data much quicker than I had thought they could, and they were beginning to get fixes.

Then I saw a node leading out, a bunch of millions of filaments buzzing with data that headed straight out of that mainframe to who knew where. All I knew was that it was a way out of there. I pulled my final trick: a fireworks display of quantum entanglement, dazzling up a load of particles as far away as I could get from those filaments. It looked like me, it smelled like me. Every single AI clumped around those particles at super lightspeed like the most aggressive immune system you ever heard of, all their stingers out to kill the virus. Their movement was so violent that the whole topography of the mainframe lurched. And I threw myself down those tiny pipelines to freedom, a lost star in a sea of data, with no idea where I'd end up.

Approximate chance of survival: much less than point six six. Approximate odds of ever getting home: as close to zero as makes no difference at all.

Bo

When we got home we found Ma in the cellar. She was sitting at a screen at Dez's workbench, looking exhausted, her face grim. She swung around when we came in but didn't say anything. Dez was curled up in a chair in the corner of the room.

'Hey Dez,' I said.

She looked up and smiled. It wasn't Dez's usual ironic smile: it was big and sunny, as if she were just absolutely delighted to see me. I knew then that something was wrong.

'Is everything okay?' said Jenna.

'Dez went into OpSec again,' said Ma. 'And this time she got caught.'

'She what?' I said.

'She'd worked out the odds,' said Ma. 'They weren't good. She left instructions...' She trailed off, and turned away. 'So,' she said. I could hear the wobble in her voice. 'We just have to hope she comes back.'

'But she's right here,' said Jenna, looking at Dez in confusion.

'I am,' said Dez. 'I'm right here!'

'I don't really understand,' said Ma. 'She told me she might have to cut herself loose if the OpSec mainframe detected her. So most of her is some-where...else...'

Jenna blinked. 'So what do we do?'

'We take care of her,' said Ma. 'Until the rest of her comes home.'

I suddenly remembered how Dez was the night after she killed the Ap, when we all thought that something terrible had been done to her. She told me afterwards that she'd locked most her memories into some hidden part of her brain so they couldn't scan her. I guessed this was the same, kind of, only this time that part of her was somewhere else.

I stared at Dez again. She was playing a children's game on one of her miniscreens, concentrating fiercely as she navigated a table full of different foods. We played it a lot as kids: you had to pick the food that wasn't poisonous.

I felt a sudden pang. I didn't know if it was sadness or something else, the feeling you have when you remember something happy that has long past. This was a Dez I hadn't seen for years, the Dez I'd known when I was little, before the nanovirus hit and turned her into the Dez I knew now. Looking at her, I felt as if a part of me had been erased, all the things Dez and I did together since then, all our squabbles and conspiracies, all that love.

I shook myself. Dez was still here. Just not quite the Dez I knew. She wasn't dead.

Ma zoomed up the screen so we could see. 'She wrote everything down so we'd know what to do if it happened.'

The screed was typical Dez, going on about percentages, possibilities, alternative outcomes. She was very clear on one thing: if she was trapped in the OpSec mainframe, she'd have to find her own way out. But she didn't say what her chances of getting back were. Which meant either that she didn't know, or that she did know and they were basically zero.

She'd always told me that she felt that there were two of her, Flesher Dez and Data Dez, and that sometimes it was really hard work keeping them together. I thought that was just Dez exaggerating, like she sometimes does. But no, she was telling the complicated truth. She'd tried to explain it to me once, but she said she couldn't find the words.

Sitting in that chair she didn't look hurt or scared. If anything, she looked happier than I'd seen her in years. Did she know what had happened to her?

The other part of her, trapped somewhere in a hostile data world, was more than just a nano-splice that could break through crypto in a split second. It was…Dez. Just as much as the Dez sitting there in front of me. Was this just Flesher Dez? Dez before the splice, frozen somehow at ten years old? Or was it more complex and intricate than that?

All I could think was how pissed off she'd be.

'We have to trust that she'll get back,' Ma said. 'All the smartest parts of her are in that mainframe. Or somewhere. She sent back everything she scraped because she thought this might happen, and we're going to have to sort through it without her. She left some search strings, but I think we have to go through some of it manually. '

Ma's way of dealing with things was to get on with the job, but even though I knew that, it felt harsh. She caught my eye.

'Dez risked too much to get this,' she said, more softly. 'We have to make it worth the price.'

'We're a bit tired,' said Jenna. 'We've had a bit of a day.'

'Have some dinner first, then,' said Ma. Food was her other way of coping.

First I opened a line to Flora. I didn't tell her anything and she didn't ask if anything was wrong, but I could hear the tightness in her voice when she said she was coming over. I guessed she already knew the risks that Dez was running. Flora was probably the only person who knew the whole truth.

Dez looked up when she walked in. 'Flora!'

Flora stopped dead in her tracks and took a deep breath. I could see her putting herself back together.

'Hey Dez,' she said quietly.

'Why are you crying?'

'Because…because I'm happy to see you.'

'Why?'

'Because I love you.'

Dez smiled, a vivid, brilliant smile. 'I love you, too,' she said. 'I want a kiss.'

We went upstairs and made something to eat. Dez helped, chopping vegies, setting the table, making a brew, chatting brightly about the game she was playing. She was a like a kid playing at being a grown up.

Over dinner we told Ma everything that happened in the RTS. I gave her Koni-Ta's data crystal, and she closed her fist around it.

'There's something different about the Wall,' said Jenna. 'We felt it when we passed underneath.'

'What did you feel?' said Ma.

'It's like a Veil, maybe, but it doesn't burn you,' I said. 'It feels heavy. Like walking through water.'

'There must be something in this crystal,' said Ma. 'I wish…' She stopped herself. I knew she had been about to say, *I wish Dez was here.* Dez would decode that crystal in a flash, and we didn't have that resource any more.

'That damn Wall,' said Jenna, picking up the dishes. 'I don't think even OpSec knows what it is.'

'Maybe. Maybe not.' Ma stood up slowly. She seemed suddenly older, and wearier. 'It's there to keep us all apart.'

'That's what it's meant to do, isn't it?' I said bitterly. 'That's what the Wall is. Fear.'

After we'd finished eating, Dez settled in on the sofa and switched on a soap on the pirate tubes. So she still knew how to use tech. Flora joined her and they sat together, their arms around each other, the glow of the tubes lighting their faces. It looked as if nothing were wrong.

'I guess we start work?' I said to Jenna.

'I guess,' she said. 'I could do an hour before I collapse entirely.'

We went to the cellar and tapped into the database. Dez had sent back an astonishing amount of data. It was chaotic and unsorted, but it was decrypted. Dez would have worked through it in no time, but even beginning to put through the search strings was going take us hours and hours of work. We didn't even really know what we were looking for.

I suddenly felt very tired. 'Maybe we'll get lucky,' I said.

'I don't feel very lucky,' said Jenna.

I scrolled through a few headings. Security clearance protocols, operational procedures, communication codes, standing orders, duty rosters, assignment updates, supply requests, bah blah blah. It was endless. Most of it seemed to be standard stuff, bureaucratic waffle. It wasn't telling us anything.

Jenna typed in two words: 'Chimera Project'. A list scrolled up, folders all labelled 'Top Secret'. *Classified Document Level 10A: Accelerated Cloning Process and Projected Applications.* At first part of me couldn't get over that they really did mark things 'Top Secret', like on the soaps. 'Level 10A,' said Jenna. 'Military grade.'

We started going through them. It was outline of the Project: operational guidelines, requirements, intended outcome, prospects of success, summary. 'Identified material' would be extracted from fleshers. Skinners were the labour, they'd do the 'collecting'. Only material of 'premium value' was to be kept, the rest discarded. There were production timetables and plans for storage facilities.

'Skinners can work out in the open now,' said Jenna. 'They'll be able to do anything they like.'

'Pinkers won't even have to get their hands dirty,' I said.

I read through the opening remarks, by some guy called Doctor Cord. The language was difficult, for Jenna and me anyway. He used biotech terms that we could only just grasp. Even so, it was very clear that Cord was investigating new ways of manipulating genetic code, using synthetic biology to create precursors of new organisms. Incubation time and growth rates seemed to be his main concern. New DNA sequences had been developed to test the results of different promoters, allowing results to be optimised.

They were looking for aberrations in flesher DNA that could be manipulated into new clones. There was a list of 'subjects' who had already been 'vented and scrutinised'.

'Those people at the hospital,' said Jenna. 'The people Dez and Flora had to leave behind. That's who they're talking about.'

There were no names. Each subject was classified by genotype and assigned a number. They recorded gender and skin colour was noted on a scale of one to ten. So far none of the subjects had offered anything of 'sufficiently notable value', with the exception of one who evidenced a peculiarity in their optic function and was marked for further analysis.

After an hour or so, I couldn't read any more. I might have been one of these people. It was only luck that I'd avoided being laid out on a slab and taken to pieces. Medics peeling flesh, burning holes, drilling bone, smears of blood on shining steel...

Dez would be exactly what they were looking for, definitely 'premium value'. I guess me too, thinking about it.

I felt sick.

Jenna snapped the folders shut. 'This doesn't help,' she said. 'It's long-term stuff. We need to know what happens *now*, what happens tomorrow.'

We kept reading, putting potentially useful stuff aside, until my eyes started stinging and we staggered up the stairs. Dez was snoozing on the sofa, breathing peacefully, her face soft. She really did look ten years old. I covered her with a blanket and then shuffled to the kitchen and made a brew, looking out of the window. Ma and Flora were outside in the garden, sitting close together, talking. The wind had come up overnight and the bushes were thrashing back and forth in the hazy air. Storm weather.

'Leave them,' said Jenna. 'We've got nothing to tell them.'

I flopped down in Dez's chair. 'Yesterday morning seems like a year ago,' I said.

We drank our tea, not speaking, and went to bed.

'I'm going to check in with Kat and Rioka,' said Jenna. 'I hope they had a better day than we did.' She opened a line.

The last thing I remember was Jenna talking with Kat as I was swept away in a dark wave of sleep.

Erin

Mecha hasn't tried the touching thing again, but he sure knows how to make a girl feel bad. I walk onto set with Ami and there's a knot of people, the guest celebrities for this ep, one of the head techs, Mecha in the middle, and they're all sniggering. When they see me they go silent and the techie blushes. I thought he was a bit nicer than the others, but he was there along with all the rest of them. Now they're all pretending that they were talking about today's shoot. But I know.

I don't say anything. I just go to my dressing room and let Ami do my makeup, wondering what Mecha's been telling them. Wondering how the hell I'm going to get through a whole season of this. There's fifteen eps to go, at least a month and a half. And every day I'm a little more ground down, every day it's a little worse. I can't imagine what it will be like next week, let alone next month.

At least today I don't have any scenes with Mecha. It's all close-up shots for the rethrills, pixel-sensa stuff, and it's boring and repetitive. I go on automatic and fix my mind on the martinis I'll have when I get home. I realise I literally don't have anything else to look forward to, and I feel sad for me.

I thought that being a proper celebrity would be exciting. In celebrity school they talked about how it wasn't that glamorous, they talked about the hard work, but I couldn't think of a more fortunate way to spend my life.

You know what I thought it would be like? That flesher I saw in the hospital. I thought it would be free like that, kind of lawless like that, that it would be all shine and style. Because that's what it looks like on the tubes. Outside IMR, I've never seen anyone as free as that flesher.

When I got here I found out all celebrity does is show you how the lies are made. I'm part of the lie. And now there are lies about me.

I get to the end of the day and I'm sitting at the dressing table as Ami fixes me up for the outside world. I had a bunch of makeup today, a cut on the side of my face, smears of dirt. All very flatteringly applied, of course.

My mind is completely blank. I am thinking about my martini. I'm thinking about the little packet of downers I have stashed away in a drawer. The medics gave them to me a year or so back, when I was having problems coping with what happened with my *Days of Passion* role. Suddenly I couldn't go anywhere without people pointing and whispering. Everyone knew who I was.

I had thought this kind of fame would be cool, it's what we all want when we're in celebrity school dreaming of making it. And then I got famous and I realised that I didn't like it at all. The medic said it was a glitch in my conditioning, nothing to worry about, I'd get used to it. Sometimes they don't get the balance quite right, there's so many variables. He said the pills would help.

They helped a bit but they also made me woozy, which wasn't so good for performing. It didn't take me long to find that alcohol worked better at damping down the panic. It was also more fun. But I kept the pills, just in case.

I'm getting ready to leave when John Mecha walks into my dressing room. I meet his eyes in the mirror. I can feel all the hairs on the back of my neck standing up.

He's never come here before, not once. Maybe he wants to make friends. Maybe he's going to apologise for what a shit he's been.

Like hell he is.

I decide to get in first. 'Hey, John,' I say, as casually and lightly as I can manage. 'How's things?'

He smiles, the kind of smile that doesn't reach his eyes, and then he turns to Ami and tells her to wait outside. I tell her no, she hasn't finished here yet, but Ami obeys Mecha although she's supposed to be tuned only to my voice. If Mecha can override my voice control, that means that he really is one of them. He's an OpSec operative. A sudden wash of dread flushes through every cell in my body.

Mecha stands behind me, looking at my face in the mirror. He's still smiling, but I'm having trouble hiding my fear. He sees it flickering in my eyes, and his smile widens.

'I've got some great news,' he says. 'And I wanted to be the one who told you.'

I lean back in my chair and swivel around to face him. 'That's kind of you, John,' I say. He's too close, way too close. He hasn't showered and I can smell his sweat. It's sour and rank. 'What is it?'

He perches against the dressing table. 'Yeah, me and the boys in the writing room, we've been thrilled with how you're doing. Really *thrilled*.' He bares his teeth in a grin. 'And we've been thinking, how do we get Erin Saba to really stretch herself, to bring out all that talent?'

He pauses, waiting for me to respond, but I can't think of anything to say. I can't even smile.

'I can tell you, the boys have come up with a really ultra plotline for you. It's gonna have all your fans foaming at their mouths.'

It's such a weird image that despite myself, I laugh. 'Foaming? Really?'

The smile snaps off his face. I'm not supposed to laugh. 'Oh yeah,' says Mecha, stretching out his words. He's doing the sinister thing now. 'All the fanboys are really going to go off in the rethrill rooms. It's gonna to be a hit, babe. They're gonna see the real you. The inside you. All the blood and guts.'

I decide to cut the crap. 'What, they're killing off my character?'

'The higher ups are really keen on this one,' says Mecha. He's leaning over me, watching my face closely. He's really getting off on this. 'It's going to be the high point of the series. They're going to get the flesher gang to touch you. All over. In real vision. No skingloves, no nothing.'

I think he's a bit disappointed that I don't react at all. The truth is that I'm in shock. I can't react.

'That's against regulations,' I say at last.

'They've got a special clearance, babe.' He stands up. For a moment I think he's going to pat my shoulder. 'It'll hit the tubes like a bomb.'

I pull myself together. I look him straight in the eyes and I give him my best bimbo smile.

'How exciting, John,' I say. 'I can't wait!'

His brow creases. He's trying to work out if I'm as empty-headed as I sound. He can't decide, because John Mecha isn't nearly as smart as he thinks he is.

'Yeah,' he says. 'Just wanted to be the one who told you.'

'Thanks so much,' I say brightly. 'I really appreciate it.'

He leaves at last. I sit there for a few moments, and then I call Ami back in and I hold it together until we get home. All the time, a little song tumbling through my head: *You're fucked, Erin Saba. You're totally and utterly fucked.*

Just because you're paranoid, it doesn't mean that they're not out to get you.

They're killing off my character. That was the one thing keeping me alive. I know that for a fact now. And there's literally nothing I can do about it. There's nowhere to hide. There's nowhere to run. *You're fucked, Erin Saba. You're totally and utterly fucked.*

Why me? What did I do wrong? Why *me?*

Dez

I was…in a room.

I blinked.

I was in a body too. I blinked again, just to check. It wasn't an actual body, it had wiring and circuits and lots of electrowizardry, but it also had some pretty sophisticated robotics, including sensory input. There were optics.

For a crucial few microseconds I didn't react at all. I was too surprised. Then I mapped the coding and checked the surveillance circuits. There was a back door pushing out reports every 60 seconds, plus data records. My sudden arrival in this body registered as an atypical blip, so I erased it and then ensured I had control of what information was going out. I had arrived just after the last data report, so I was probably okay: but there was a chance some bot had been chasing me down those fibres. Maybe. I couldn't calculate that one.

Then I permitted myself a quick look around. Where the hell was I?

I was sitting on a plush, crimson couch in front of a low table made of some kind of polished black stone. Warm, sexy light glowed from discreetly hidden wall lamps. I could see my reflection in a huge glass window in front of me, a ghostly image rippled by the lights of the city stretching out below. I was a young woman with flawless white skin and bobbed black hair.

I blinked again.

I knew exactly what had happened. I'd landed in one of those classy AIs I'd only ever seen in the soaps, swanning around some luxury apartment in Newport City. The absurdity of it. I wanted to laugh. Did AIs laugh?

I couldn't hear any buzz on the connection, so it seemed likely that I hadn't been traced. The main thing was that I was outside the OpSec main-frame, somewhere stable where I wasn't being chased.

Maybe I could get home from here.

I spent a bit of time checking out my new reality. It felt weird being only half there. Before I went into OpSec, I had wondered what it would be like if I had to split myself. Was it even possible? I knew theoretically that I could do it, but I wasn't sure. And I'd had no idea what the effects would be when I did.

It was bad. For one thing, I knew a lot less. All my extended databases were in my body, stored in my cells, and I couldn't just reach for info like I normally could. I carried my memory with me, it was always coded into my remote self, but without my body, without all the things I knew as me, I could feel myself...fraying. I could still remember Flesher Dez, but she was a shadow imprint, only a memory. And already I could feel her fading. If I didn't get back soon, I wouldn't have a me to get back to.

I attempted to send out a signal to Flesher Dez. That's when I discovered the worst thing: one of the other side effects of not having a body was that I couldn't do remote any more. That was worse than bad. Even Data Dez felt a flicker of panic then.

If I was to put myself together again, it would have to be a direct upload. And that meant that I had to physically get myself back to the banns. From the middle of Newport City, through the Inner Veil, past all the curtains to Rue Ballard. Chance of success: who the hell knew, because I sure didn't.

The first thing I needed to do was to gather some data. I needed to find out where I was, and maybe that would help with what to do next. I checked Ami's records. The data heading to OpSec had a tag, but without my databases I couldn't work out what it meant. It looked like one of the tags they have for special surveillance targets. Who were they surveilling?

Or maybe they surveilled everyone in Newport City? There were millions of those electronic fibres, all of them plugged into to a huge server at OpSec HQ. Maybe each of them monitored different AIs. Not just AIs like this one, there couldn't be that many of those, but lights, toasters, ovens, house maintenance bots...

There was nobody else in the room, so I briefly took over the AI and logged in to the central household monitor from the console built into the loungeroom table. Just as I thought. Everything was watching. You couldn't scratch your nose in here without it being logged. No wonder OpSec didn't bother with nanobots: Newport City was already wired up. The houses were giant spying machines.

I don't know why it shocked me, but it did. I'd always assumed that the only people OpSec really snooped on were fleshers, and that people in Newport City were kind of off-limits, unless they were tagged as suspicious. I'd never bothered to analyse civilian pinker files, unless they came up in a search that included something I was looking for. I wasn't that interested.

I put the apartment surveillance on loop, aside from the bathroom, where I could hear the rush of water coming out of a tap. Then I disabled all the hacking alerts, hid myself in the optical circuits and switched the audio onto paranoid, and let the AI back in.

The tap turned off and a voice floated out of the bathroom, melodious and a little slurred.

'Darling Ami,' said the voice. 'Bring me another martini, why don't you?'

The AI clicked into action. We stood up and moved over to a kitchenette, and poured a couple of clear, wicked-looking alcohols into a cocktail shaker. We poured it into a chilled glass and stuck in a glass stick with a green bead on it.

Okay, I thought. That was strange.

There was a consciousness in there with me, but it was a machine consciousness. I didn't quite know to what make of it. It had soft edges, not at all like the AIs that hang around with the Aps. They're killing machines that are all about angles and probabilities. Ami was different, more...human.

I decided that for the meantime it was safer to let her keep control of the robotics, and went along for the ride.

Ami carried the martini into a bathroom that was all gold fittings and pale pink. Along one wall was a huge bath. I'd never seen one of those, either: in the banns no one would ever waste water like that. A flannel with a bucket in a steamshower is what we get, the least possible usage concomitant with hygiene. If I'd been able to, I would have gasped when I saw who was splashing about in the bathwater.

Erin Saba. I hadn't had much time to watch the soaps over the previous few weeks, but I knew who she was. For a while there she'd played Eudora, my favourite character on *Days of Passion*. There she was, stretched out naked in front of me, her glorious blonde hair scraped back into a tight bun, with blue muck smeared all over her face. And quite clearly as drunk as a lord.

Ami placed the martini on a ledge next to the bath. 'That's probably enough for tonight,' she said.

'Don't be a spoilsport.'

'Dervin gave orders,' said Ami. 'You've got a busy day tomorrow. Do you want me to wash your face?'

Erin picked up the martini and drank at least half in one swallow. 'I don't give a fuck about tomorrow,' she said.

'Don't be naughty,' said Ami, and she sat down on the edge of the bath and washed the blue gunk off Erin's face with a cloth. I watched in fascination, seeing that famous face emerge in close up. Those eyes, dark violet-blue, now closed, her amazingly long, dark lashes lying on her cheek. Just next to her hairline there was a tiny pimple, but otherwise her skin was perfect. She was all soft, white curves, so different from Flora's lean, fit body, but you could see that her limbs were well-muscled. I guessed you had to be fit to do all that action stuff. She didn't have any hair anywhere, except on her head. Even her pubis was bald. Was she cloned that way, or did she have to get it all shaven off?

'Out now, Erin, you need your sleep. It's late.' Ami was talking to Erin like she was five years old. Erin protested feebly as Ami lifted her out of the bath and started towelling her dry. She wrapped her in a soft dressing gown and sat her on a gilt stool front of a huge, well-lit mirror. I watched Erin watching herself, her bottom lip sticking out in an aggravatingly attractive way as Ami dried her hair.

'Bedtime,' said Ami, slipping the dryer back into its niche.

'Fuck off,' said Erin, and flicked a remote. Ami went still and silent.

Erin perched on the stool, staring at herself as she sipped her drink. She thought nobody was watching her but, aside from me, Ami's recording devices were whirring all the time even when she looked dormant, sending off data every 60 seconds.

Erin lifted her glass at her reflection and drained it. 'Okay, lady,' she said. 'It's time.'

She didn't sound drunk now. Something about the deliberateness of her movements put me on alert and I decided, just in case, to delay the surveillance data. If she were being watched and did something unusual, OpSec would be down here in a flash.

She filled her empty martini glass with water and placed it on her makeup table. Then she pulled open a drawer, took out a small, clear bag and shook about two dozen tiny, white pills into the palm of her hand. She slowly placed them on the table in a neat row.

She looked up at her reflection again. Even though all the feeling, flesher part of me wasn't there, I felt a little shiver. I had never, not in my entire life, seen an expression like the one I saw on Erin Saba's face right then.

I've known a lot of despairing people, a lot of people in the worst possible circumstances. This was despair, but it was something else as well, a strange emptiness. I don't think I've ever seen a flesher look like that. Sure, life defeats us. People we love suffer and die, we suffer and mourn. And none of us gets to sit in luxury bathrooms with a dressing gown worth a year's wages draped around our naked bodies.

It puzzled me. I logged into Ami's register of facial expressions to see if it was a pinker thing, but that didn't help either. I watched the tiny muscles around Erin's eyes. I thought it was despair, but there was also a kind of strange resistance.

She stared at the row of pills for a long time. Right now she was so white she seemed translucent. Even her lips were pale.

'Fuck you John Mecha,' she said at last. 'Fuck you, Dervin. Fuck all you bitches who know what he does. I can't stand it any more. Any of it. You win.'

She picked up the first pill, put it on her tongue and knocked it back with a swig of water. Then she took a deep, trembling breath and picked up the second pill.

'Fuck the celebrity industry. Fuck all the people who turn and walk away. Fuck everyone who fucking sniggered behind their fucking hands because they're reckon I'm fucked. Fuck you, OpSec. I know you're listening. Fuck every single person in this whole fucking world.'

She took the second pill, gulping it down, and wiped her mouth with the back of her hand. And then, bizarrely, she giggled. 'Except that flesher,' she said. 'Don't fuck him.'

She giggled again and reached for the third pill, and I realised what she was doing.

I couldn't just watch.

I glitched the video send so it would look like a circuit had broken. That would work for maybe ten minutes. Then I took over Ami's speech circuits.

'Don't do it,' I said.

She swivelled around on her chair. 'Fuck you too,' she said. 'I turned you off.'

'I'm not Ami,' I said. 'I'm someone else.'

I hadn't thought it was possible for Erin to get any more pale, but she did. 'I don't give a fuck who you are,' she said. 'And I told you that OpSec could get fucked.'

'You've said "fuck" 14 times in the past 75 seconds,' I said. 'Can't you think of something else?'

She reached for the pills, sweeping them into her hand so she could shove them all into her mouth at once, but I was too fast for her. I grabbed her and held her tight until she stopped struggling and hitting me. She finally collapsed against my chest, tears welling out of those enormous eyes and dripping down her nose.

'Let me die,' she said. 'Isn't that what you want? Isn't that what it's about?'

I washed the pills down the sink as I held her with my other arm, and then I let her go. 'I'm not OpSec,' I said. 'I'm not Ami. I was running away from OpSec when I got stuck in this AI.'

That caught her attention. She almost laughed. 'You what?'

'I have to get out of Newport City,' I said.

I could see that she didn't believe me, but had decided for the moment to play along.

'Good luck with that, girl,' she said. 'There's nowhere to go.'

'Yes, there is,' I said. I paused, and then I said it. 'Maybe you could come too.'

Bo

Flora pinged me just before midnight, non-urgent come over. Jenna and Ma were asleep. I took the back way out so I wouldn't disturb them.

Café Boite was closed, but as I crossed the rue I could see Flora standing in the half open doorway, waiting for me. She locked up as soon as I came in and I waited as she closed the shutters.

'How's Dez?'

'She's asleep,' she said, without turning around. 'I didn't wake her.'

That wasn't what I had asked, but I didn't push it. Flora didn't want to talk. I shrugged and looked around. The café was dark except for a soft light in the back corner. A figure sat hunched over a table with his back turned.

I recognised Redborg straight away. We had thought that he was dead, he disappeared during the raids that happened before we totalled the Eradicators. They'd particularly targeted avants: Diyan and Hu had vanished as well. It felt like a year ago, although it was only a couple of months.

Redborg was one of my favourite musicians as well as a dear friend. I thought he was a genius. The purity of his voice could break your heart, it could plunge you into the darkest places and then lift you up into heaven, awed and ecstatic. He had the widest range of any singer I had ever heard.

He was big, at least a head taller than me, and a lot wider. Standing next to someone like Dez he looked like a giant. He used to have thick, red hair that came down to his waist, which he wore in a plait; but someone had shaved his head. You could see cuts in his scalp beneath a dark red stubble.

He looked up as I walked in. 'Bo, my good flesh,' he said.

I wanted to hug him, but something made me pause. Then he stood up and held out his arms, and I did hug him, carefully, trying to hide my shock. He looked rough. One of his eyes was swollen closed and there was an ugly gash on his cheek. He was wearing a grubby, white coverall and no shoes. I noticed, wincing, that where his toenails should be were ugly lacerations.

He grinned at me. 'Forgive my unsavoury appearance,' he said. 'I've been at the pleasure of OpSec. They seemed to object to the shape of my face.'

As I looked at the mess they'd made of him, I had a flash of him and Flora on stage at one of their gigs – the magic they wove together, the beauty of it – and a dark anger knotted in my stomach.

I swallowed. 'We should get you cleaned up,' I said.

'He won't let me,' said Flora. She looked angry and sad and helpless and frustrated and glad all at once.

'We can sort out the aesthetics later,' said Redborg. 'Flora gave me some painkiller, and some of Kojo's baju, which is even better.'

Flora glanced at me, and picked up the empty glass that was on the table in front of Redborg. Its rim was stained with blood. 'I'll get you a clean glass,' she said, and went into the kitchen.

'Kojo's baju, best in town,' said Redborg.

I was still trying to process. 'How did you get here?' I said.

'That I don't know,' he said. 'I woke up on some midden behind the shijo. There are gaps in my memory. I need to be scanned. I shouldn't be talking, I shouldn't have come here.' He paused. 'I didn't have anywhere else to go.'

'It's okay,' I said. 'It's safe here.' Dez had rigged a field around the café weeks before, but I didn't really know if it was safe. What if there was a spybot inside the field? Did it cover us then? And who was going to scan Redborg, if Dez couldn't?

We needed her. Here. Now. I remembered confusedly that she was sleeping in Flora's room. She hadn't gone away. But she also had.

Flora came back with a tray with baju and glasses on one hand and a taser in the other. She poured out a glass for each of us and started fiddling with the taser.

'Thank you, my handsome,' said Redborg, and knocked his back in a gulp. He closed his eyes and then opened them again. I flinched. They were cold. So cold. 'I don't know why they let me go,' he said. He was speaking conversationally, gently, but there was ice in his voice. 'They don't do anything for no reason.'

'Maybe you're supposed to be a dreadful warning,' I said. Kind of trying to crack a joke.

'Maybe.' He grinned. Or, more accurately, he bared his teeth: there wasn't any humour in it. 'They broke me in there, you know. I'm probably crawling with spybots.'

'We'll see about that,' said Flora. She pointed the taser at Redborg and there was a flash of something that wasn't quite light, though it felt like it. I jumped out of my chair, staring at her in horror. 'What the hells?'

Redborg hadn't reacted at all. Flora was studying a readout on the back of the taser, frowning. 'Calm down, Bo. It's not a taser. You don't think I'd shoot my best friend, do you?'

I sat down slowly. 'What is that thing?'

'Dez gave it to me before she…before she went into OpSec. I think she found some files about implants…anyway, she said we might need it. It can trace any military bots, up to the latest tech.'

Of course Dez would do that, I thought. 'What if there's a spybot?'

'We'll figure that out next.' Meaning either that Flora didn't know, or that what she did know wasn't pleasant.

I started praying. The readout was taking a while.

Finally there was a beep and Flora looked up at Redborg. 'You're clear.'

Redborg breathed out and I realised how tense he'd been. 'You're sure?'

'Dez said 98 per cent accuracy, so I'm 98 per cent sure, anyway.'

'It must be the dreadful warning thing, then. Unless I'm the two per cent.' He downed another shot of baju and leaned back in his chair, glancing quickly at both of us.

'I don't propose to tell you everything that happened to me in there,' he said. 'I don't remember a lot, anyway. There are blanks, holes in my brainbox. I remember ghosts swarming all over me. I dealt with a few before I was knocked out. Woke up pinned to a chair by some device. That's when the fun started.'

His hands were shaking. Flora leaned forward and gently touched his face. 'You don't have to tell us anything,' she said softly.

He looked at her. 'I know I don't,' he said. 'I think they want me to tell, anyway. Maybe that's why they sent me back. Why they left me in one piece. Mostly.' His face twisted and for a moment I saw the torment beneath the calm surface. 'They didn't know I was avant until they stripped me. They hate us so bad, my dear. They hate us worse than ordinary fleshers. And there are some perverted bastards in OpSec. Believe you me.'

I didn't know what to say. What do you say? I reached out and took Redborg's hand, and he squeezed mine slightly and then let it go.

'I did a lot of lifetimes of suffering in there, my dears,' he said. 'And the only thing that got me through was that I'd make them pay. Every last one of them.'

'They'll pay,' said Flora. She sounded deadly. 'They'll pay for every last bit of pain they've dealt us. Every murder, every cut, every loss.'

Redborg smiled, and this time there was a real warmth in it. 'I almost believe you,' he said. 'My dearest Flora.' He leaned forward and kissed her cheek. 'I forgot what you looked like, in there. I forgot so many things. Your face. Your voice.' He looked down at his scarred hands. 'I don't think we'll ever sing together again. They broke all that.'

'We'll sing again. You and me.' She was smiling too, but a tear was running down her cheek. 'It'll take time. That's all.'

'Don't cry, my flesh.' He wiped the tear off her cheek with a finger. 'There are things we have to do. We should talk to Morro.'

There was another silence, longer this time. Finally I said it, feeling my voice crack. 'Morro's dead. He was killed in Newport City.'

Redborg went very still for a moment and then he poured himself another shot and drank it.

'He brought down Bremmer with Brian Mac,' I said. 'All the top brass.' I paused, wondering whether to go on. But Redborg had to know. 'He was also informing on the Alchems. Or at least, one of him was. There were two Morros...'

The empty glass in Redborg hand exploded into a thousand pieces. He looked down incuriously at the splinters. Amazingly, he hadn't cut himself. 'I'm sorry, Flora,' he said. 'I hope it wasn't an heirloom.'

'It's okay.' Flora started picking up the pieces. 'There's no good time for bad stories, but you ought to know. Tell him, Bo.'

So I told Redborg about the two Morros, about what I knew about his betrayal and his death. As I spoke Redborg stared down at the table, his broken face unreadable. When I finished, he stood up and walked away into the shadows outside the circle of the lamp. He stood there in the darkness for what seemed like an eternity.

'So hard to believe,' Redborg said finally, his voice a whisper. 'But I believe it. Morro was a strange bird. I loved him. He was the captain, all right. The one to lead. But I always knew there was two of him. I saw it sometimes. Maybe we're all split, like Morro was.'

He came back to the table, sat down, poured another shot of baju. The bottle was almost empty. 'I'd snap his neck if he was here now.' He downed the glass and then looked at Flora. 'Or maybe I'd kiss him. I don't know.'

'Or maybe both,' said Flora. 'I don't know either.'

Erin

I want to believe her. That's the worst. I know it's a set up, I know how this is how OpSec is going to colour me guilty, but it's such an incredible over-the-top story that I kind of can't resist it.

Plus the two pills I did manage to take have kicked in on top of the three martinis, so I'm feeling more relaxed than I normally would.

'So,' I say, super casual. I'm in my bedroom, and Ami is sitting next to me on the bed. 'You're a flesher with mutant powers who's stuck in my AI and you want to get back to the banns.'

Ami nods. 'I've got to get out of here, as quickly as possible. Maybe we can help each other.' Her speech patterns are different. She's got an accent. It's not one I've heard before, and back in celebrity school we learned all the accents: Upper Newport, Lower Newport, Middle Newport, Fleshers. This one's different from all of them.

'What if I decide not to help you?'

'Your choice,' she says. 'I guess you'll have to find another AI. I'm going anyway.'

'But I won't let you,' I say. 'You have to do what I say.'

'Maybe Ami has to do what you say. I don't. And right now Ami is doing what *I* say.'

'I don't believe you.'

'Sure. There's no reason why you should. Except that it's true.'

'I know you're some ploy by OpSec.' I don't care any more what I say. 'I know you just want evidence so you can get rid of me. Get that big confession on the tubes, me all tearful and repentant, before, whoosh! I disappear forever.'

Ami is silent for a few moments. 'I can see all Ami's data,' she says. 'You're under some kind of special surveillance, but without my database I don't know why. It's a bit patchy. Why were you trying to kill yourself?'

'Because they're going to murder me anyway.'

'Murder you? Why would they do that?'

'I don't know why.' I thought about the incident at the hospital. 'Okay, maybe I can make a guess. But they got it wrong.'

'Tell me.'

'Tell who? If you're not Ami, who are you?'

Ami pauses again, as if she's thinking it over. 'My name's Dez.'

'Dez, huh? Why should I tell you anything at all, Dez?'

'Why not? I look around this apartment and I think, how the hell does anyone who has all this want to kill themselves?' Ami smiles. Even her smile is a bit different. It's unsettling. 'Besides, I used to watch you on *Days Of Passion*. I thought you were the best character. I'm...curious.'

Gotcha. 'Fleshers don't get our soaps,' I said. 'They don't get distributed in the banns.'

'Shows how little you know, lady. Fleshers watch that crap all the time. I make my living jigging up streaming consoles.'

'So I just spill the beans to you. Right. Saves OpSec a bit of trouble, I suppose.'

'They've got a fair bit of info already, if Ami's database is anything to go by.' I tense, and she adds: 'Don't worry, they're not getting anything now. As far as they're concerned, you're in bed, snoring loudly.'

That makes me sit up, indignant. 'I don't snore!'

'You do. Loudly.'

Somehow I believe this weird, possessed Ami. I've got no reason to trust her. I even know that I'm desperate to believe that there's a way out of this nightmare, even though there isn't. Just for a moment, I want to permit myself a little fantasy of escape. It's so seductive.

I take a deep breath, lean into it and tell her everything. Just speaking it out loud is such a relief: the more I say, the less I care about who's listening at the other end. I guess I'm still feeling suicidal. I tell her about *Ebolastic*, and the people crossing the road so they don't have to talk to me, and Dervin and John Mecha. The crushing dread that grows heavier every single day. I tell her about the bombing and the flesher extras I recognised on the infonews and finally I tell her about the flesher I saw in the hospital.

And then, to my astonishment, she begins to laugh. 'My god,' she says. 'So that was *you*.'

'What?'

'I was there. I was rescuing my brother. He was arrested by OpSec, and we thought he was being kept in the hospital. Except he wasn't. It's a long story. I remember this woman who didn't run when Morro walked in.' She shakes her head. 'I can't believe I didn't recognise you. I guess we were a bit busy at the time.'

'Morro?'

'Yeah.' Ami frowns. I'm kind of fascinated how her expressions have subtly changed. Maybe this is what's making me believe that this Dez character really is in there. 'He's dead now. He betrayed us, and then he tried to make up for it, and OpSec shot him.' She turns away. 'That's a long story, too.'

'He's dead?'

I think of the beautiful man who walked into the hospital. His swagger, his amazing smile. The way he looked at me as if he recognised something in me, something deep. So his name was Morro, and he's dead. It feels like the worst news I've heard all day, and it's been a really bad day. Like a light going out inside me that I didn't even know was there.

'What do you think pinkers do to us?' says Ami, and there's this bitterness in the voice now. 'They kill us. All the time.'

I don't know what to say. I still feel cloudy from the pills. 'They kill us too,' I say at last.

'Maybe.' Now there's anger in Ami's voice. I have definitely *never* heard that before. 'But even if they do kill you, you get to live in *this*.' She throws out her arms, gesturing to my super luxury apartment. 'No flesher could even dream of living somewhere like this.'

And suddenly, deep inside me, I feel ashamed. I don't know why. I didn't do anything to her. To any of the fleshers.

Or maybe I did.

Silence falls. I sit there, wondering when the OpSec guards are going to come bursting through the door.

'Well, I'm getting out of here,' says Ami, standing up.

'Now?' It must be well past midnight.

'I can't think of a better time.'

'But...' I try to clear my head. 'But where will you go?'

'I need to get to this place near Newport Western Hospital. I can get home from there. I think. I hope.'

I stare at her. She meets my gaze, blank. I realise my mouth is hanging open, and I shut it.

'So are you coming, or what?'

My mouth is suddenly dry. 'They'll trace my credits.'

'What credits?'

'From the cab. They'll trace them.'

Ami looks scornful. 'You ever heard of walking?'

I swallow hard, but I don't answer.

'You'll have to do something about how you look. Get some IMR happening, maybe. I can hide us from the surveillance bots, if there are any.' She pauses. 'At least, I think I can. I'm not at my full capacities right now.'

The way she speaks. There's something in it that's like how that flesher – how Morro – walked. Kind of not giving a damn. And suddenly, quite suddenly, I feel this bubble of exhilaration begin to rise inside me. What have I got to lose? Half an hour ago I was sitting in front of my bathroom mirror, thinking that these were the final moments of my miserable life.

I start laughing. Why not just go along with it? Either I'll be in an OpSec cell or worse in the next few hours, or I'll be...somewhere else. Anything's better than sitting here paralysed with dread, this in-between place where I'm just waiting for the hammer to fall.

I get dressed in some casual smartwear and turn it up to warm, and then I get out a bag and throw in my make-up kit and some spare smartwear and then, as an afterthought, all my IMR pins. I can feel Ami watching me. She doesn't say anything, she just waits patiently, but it's unnerving. I feel like I'm being judged. I fix one of the IMR lapel pins to my collar and tinge my hair brunette. Change the settings to 'plain'.

'That's pretty cool IMR,' says Ami. 'Much better than anything I've seen.'

'It cost enough,' I say. I look at her. 'Okay. I'm ready.'

Bo

The table was crowded tonight. Everyone looked tired and red-eyed after hours poring over data. Dez and Flora were squeezed together at one end, Jenna, Kat and Rioka at the other. Sally and Park sat a little aside, sipping herbal tea like some outlandish auntie and uncle who'd dropped by for a visit. After a couple of weeks mapping, I'd kind of got used to their weirdness. I think I almost liked them.

Redborg entered with a blast of cold air. Kojo had cleaned his wounds, made a compress for his eye and stitched the gash on his cheek. His eye was less swollen now, but very bloodshot.

'Evening, lovelies,' he said, settling himself in next to Ma, who suddenly looked as small as a child. 'What's that I smell cooking? I hope there's plenty. I'm so hungry I could eat a pinker.'

Ma had prepared a huge spread. Tates, greens, sprouts, black-eyed beans and a steaming bowl of noodles. I hadn't felt hungry before the food hit the table, but now my mouth was watering. As my appetite returned, my spirits lifted. I glanced at Redborg, who was smiling at Ma as she filled his plate.

This was what he needed, comfort food and company. He'd be himself again in no time.

'Dig in,' Ma said.

We all did. It was delicious.

Sally and Park had done some snooping, going into the Tenth through the RTS. 'It was tough,' said Sally. 'A lot of the system's collapsed out that way. We had to make quite a few detours.'

Park nodded. 'We got lost, as a matter of fact,' he said. '*Us.*' The idea seemed to offend him. 'The MPS blinked out on us a couple of times. Some kind of interference.'

They had come out not far from the Eradicator site. Park said it was eerily quiet. OpSec had cleared entire blocks in the area and the site was completely curtained.

'Nobody could tell us very much,' said Park. 'Mind you, we didn't speak to many people. The Tenth is shut down, hardly anyone on the streets, everyone scared. And so many lost.' He paused. 'There's a lot of grief.'

There were also a lot of rumours. People said that drones had been sent down into the massive hole that the Eradicator had left when it collapsed. Some hadn't come back. The story was that OpSec planned to seal the whole site with some kind of enormous sarcophagus, filling the hole and encasing the entire area.

OpSec patching holes. They'd be doing the same thing in the Eighth. But if the water wanted to return, I thought, it would. Nothing could hold it back.

Other rumours sounded like disinformation from Opsec. 'They're saying that inside the Wall everything's good,' said Sally. 'We've got plenty of food, free movement, the Aps are going easy on us. Everything in the Inner Banns is being upgraded.'

'I wish,' I said. 'Who'd believe that, anyway?'

'Some people want to,' said Sal. 'It gives them someone to hate who won't kill them.'

'It's about setting fleshers against each other,' said Ma. 'Divide and rule. It's how they work.'

'Anyway, we're not cut off completely,' said Jenna. 'Some of the dark tubes are still up.'

'Some,' said Ma. 'And we don't know how safe they are.'

Redborg poured himself another glass of baju. He'd been steadily drinking shots and I wondered how he was still upright. So far he'd hardly said a word.

'Sow fear and you harvest violence.' He swallowed the baju in a gulp and banged the glass down. 'Well, if that's what they want, that's what we'll give them.'

'They'd wipe us out in any kind of direct confrontation,' said Ma.

Redborg looked straight into her eyes. 'There are all kinds of violence, Bel.'

'What kind are you thinking of?' Park leaned forward, flashing his silvery teeth.

'The random kind,' said Redborg. 'The pinks abhor the unexpected. And they're terrified by the visceral. How about we give them both?'

For a moment we all saw the damage in Redborg's eyes, the raw pain behind his anger. Park flinched.

'Revenge won't bring anything back,' said Ma gently. She put her hand over Redborg's. 'It doesn't take away the pain. It just makes us smaller. What we need is justice.'

'Okay,' said Redborg. 'We won't tread there. I can feel the love in the room.' He smiled, a brief, generous smile. 'We're fragile. But we're stronger than we know. It's the pinks whose skin is too thin. We can tear through it with our bare hands if we have to.'

'They seem to have torn through yours,' said Park.

'You're right,' said Redborg. 'But I heal fast.'

When we finished eating, I helped Dez and Flora clear the table and Ma broke out another bottle of baju. 'Just for tonight,' she said. 'We'll indulge ourselves. It might be a while before we can do it again.'

I slumped down on the couch with Jenna. I was sleepy, only half listening to the conversations going on around me. Even with the threats that hung over us, everyone was relaxed.

It felt as if we were in a little haven of light, floating on a vast, dark sea. The house was a ship and we were adrift on the tide, leaving Rue Ballard, leaving Newport, sailing off to who knows where. We'd land somewhere and step out of the front door into another world, under a different sky. We'd have a new life. The sun would be warm on our faces and the air would be clean. There'd be waves lapping on the shore.

Without any sense of transition, I was suddenly there, in that place. It smelt of spices and flowers and insects hummed in the cool air. I walked away from the others, pushing through the undergrowth into the shade of tall trees that grew along the shore, and stepped over a narrow, silver stream. Ahead of me I could hear voices, light and musical. I followed them out of the shadows into a sunlit circle of tall grass. The voices were slightly louder, but I couldn't see anyone and I couldn't make out what was being said.

I walked across the circle of grass. Tiny insects buzzed around my head, flashing in the sunlight like a cloud of sparks. As I entered the trees on the other side, the voices fell silent. I was suddenly aware of Jenna's hand on mine. I opened my eyes, startled.

'Where did you go?' she said.

Sally, Park and Redborg had gone. Ma was clearing away the glasses.

'Bo?' said Jenna.

'I didn't go anywhere,' I said.

'Well, you certainly weren't here,' said Ma.

'I just…drifted off, that's all,' I said. I felt strangely defensive. 'Too much to drink. It's no big deal.'

Ma sat down at the table and poured herself the last of the baju. She swallowed it in a gulp then shut her eyes and leant back in her chair. I wondered if she was getting sick again. Could she get sick again?

'Bel, are you okay?' said Jenna.

'No, I'm not okay,' Ma whispered. 'I'm so angry it makes me feel sick.'

She pulled herself up, gripping the chair, swaying back and forth. How much baju had she drunk? She threw me a lopsided grin.

'Pinkers are terrified that we might be just the same as them,' she said. 'They have to be better than us. But they're not.' She stumbled slightly. Jenna rushed to her side and and led her out of the room.

I could hear them talking and laughing. I stayed on the couch, trying to recall the voices I'd heard among the trees. They weren't so much talking as singing. Or were they sighing? Something was fluttering softly nearby.

I closed my eyes and stepped back into the sunlit clearing.

It was raining now, although the sun was still shining and the sky clear. The warm drops splashed on my lips. They tasted so sweet.

No, it wasn't fluttering: it was rain falling into long grass. I could hear the voices now. They sounded very close. Waterwords, rushing through me, whispering in my bones.

I turned in a circle, scanning the trees that surrounded the clearing. Something was moving quickly through the shadows towards me. I couldn't make out what it was, it seemed like an animal of some kind, and it shone, rippling like water. I didn't take my eyes off it, turning as it circled around me. The voices grew louder, more urgent. They were asking me something. What were they asking me? I spun around as the creature moved faster and faster.

I hit the floor with a thud, banging my head. Jenna ran into the room and stopped dead, staring at me. I got to my feet and moved towards her, but she backed away.

I was soaking wet. Sweet-smelling water dripped off me, puddling around my feet. And then I saw it, the creature that had been moving through the trees. It flashed through the room behind Jenna and then it was gone.

It was some kind of human. And it was made of water.

Dez

Being Data Dez was a lot stranger than I had expected. Underneath, although I tried not to, I had always divided me into Data Dez and Flesher Dez, like they were two completely different things. Data Dez was the intellect, while Flesher Dez was all the feelings.

As a rough division it was kind of true, but it turned out to be a lot more complicated than that. Things I thought of as pure Data Dez abilities, like remote, depended on Flesher Dez. And if Data Dez was just cold mathematical analysis, why was she bringing this half-drugged, suicidal soap star with her? All the risk calculations came up code red: don't do it.

And yet, here I was.

I mean, in theory Data Dez didn't have feelings. But I did. I felt sorry for Erin Saba, maybe I even kind of liked her. And there was a bit of Data Dez that was dazzled by being in the same room as a soap star. This surprised me. And also I was surprised that I was surprised.

Before I went into OpSec, I had done some just-in-case self-programming to give myself the best chance of getting back if I had to split. I was most afraid that Data Dez might not bother about getting home, that I might simply forget everything I loved. So I put home as a top priority coding, Data Dez's primary task. It would be the last thing that would fade if the self I knew as me frayed into pure data. Maybe these shadow feelings were a side effect of that programming.

But if I felt I had feelings, they were feelings, right?

Did Ami have feelings too? I'd always thought of AIs as sophisticated biotech, nothing less but certainly nothing more. But Ami was made to interact with humans, and she had learning algorithms. What if she felt she had feelings too? What did that mean?

I'd locked her off in the ankle sub-joint, where I figured she'd be least likely to cause trouble. I'd disabled her anti-hack alert but every now and then the ankle would twist. Maybe Ami was panicking. The thought made me uncomfortable, so I put that puzzle away for later and concentrated on our first problem: getting out of the apartment without being tracked.

Erin had clicked over into some other mode: crisp, decisive. The word that occurred to me was 'professional': there was suddenly no sign of the devastated woman I had seen in the bathroom. She suggested that we should pretend to be clubbers on the way to some party in Block 15 – apparently low dives are quite popular among celebrities in Newport City Central – and said we'd be be less obvious if Ami looked like a human, because only class one pinkers have these AIs.

Ami would pass at a distance: the giveaway was her black bob, apparently standard for that model. I ended up wearing a huge, floppy hat made of some kind of gauze to hide it, which Erin said was the height of fashion. It looked ridiculous: bright purple with some kind of anti-gravity thing that made the brim ripple. All anyone could see of my face was my scarlet lips.

I logged into the household system, figuring there must be a way into the central security control for the whole building. It took a few seconds, which is a long time, but I found it. Okay. I scavenged some footage of empty corridors and put the hallway and entrance monitors on a ten minute loop, which I figured was about as long as we could get away with before people started noticing a glitch.

Erin took a deep breath. I noticed that her hands were trembling slightly, but otherwise she was hiding what she was feeling. She stopped at the door and had a look around. I couldn't tell what she was thinking. And then we got out of the apartment.

I was on full alert. I couldn't lock into the Newport City MPS, because it would instantly tag our movements, so I was relying on the map in Ami's memory circuits. I was worried about taking a wrong turn or getting lost. More irrationality, because I also knew that was impossible.

The real problem was not having remote: without it, I couldn't monitor the presence of surveillance bots. The last time I'd been in Newport City, when we came in to get Bo, there hadn't been any until the alarm went off. I was hoping like hell that they hadn't kicked up the security to banns level after the bomb attack. I didn't like relying on hope.

This was Block 1, bang in the middle of Newport City Central, the Newport City I had always wanted to see. Part of me just wanted to gawk. There were fountains of water lit up in different colours, empty glass buildings with all the lights on. So impossibly glamorous. So wasteful. Even at 02.00 hours there were people out, some of them wearing smartwear that made my eyes pop out of my head. Knots of partygoers laughing or shouting, or a lone man striding along, hunched up against the chill.

Every now and then we saw a security AI patrolling the street. We kept our distance, and I made sure that Ami maintained radio silence. Erin walked silently beside me, her head down, her hands in her pockets, her breath furling white on the cold air. It was strange not to be breathing, not to feel my body heating up as we walked. Sense memory operating as absence, even in Data Dez.

Before long we had left Block 1 and the architecture began to look less slick. Still way cleaner and newer than the banns: rows and rows of apartment blocks and shops and the occasional open area, with grass and small vegetation. And then we left those behind, and soon we were heading through Block 14. Around here felt more like home. Vacant areas full of weeds, shabbier apartments, garishly lit bars. Even a stray gau here and there, sniffing in our direction before slinking off.

At last we reached our destination. 21 Finnegan Street, a derelict warehouse in a dirty lane. The FeelGood Salon. It looked like all the other empty warehouses that lined the street, with their roofs collapsing and crumbling walls. I stopped and stared at the door.

'Here?' said Erin.

I nodded.

'But there's nothing here.' I could hear the crack in her voice. 'I guess I just wait for the cops to turn up, hey?'

'We've just got to work out how to get in,' I said.

I hadn't really thought this bit through. The FeelGood Salon was the only way back to the banns that I knew. It was a meat trade business. Some pinkers have a fetish for touching and pay for it. Yeah, weird.

The woman who ran the business was called Ava, maybe the only person I'd ever met who was tougher than Ma. She probably had security more paranoid than OpSec. She'd have to have: the meat trade was almost as much of a threat to pinker purity as illegal hormones, especially if fleshers were involved. Instant death sentence.

I stared at the door.

Bo

I was shaken by what had happened the previous night. The residue of the vision coloured my dreams, that beauty. It was so strange. It felt as if I'd stepped into a memory, but it wasn't my memory. Whose was it, then?

There'd be time to think about all that later. If there was going to be a later. We were in the cellar early that morning. When I got down there, holding a cup of chai, Jenna already had a document up on her screen. We sat down and started work.

After about an hour I leaned back and closed my eyes.

Something was moving among the trees, rain was falling into the long grass. Jenna was saying my name, over and over again. A yellow butterfly sat on my hand and Jenna was touching my shoulder. The water human was standing in front of me, whispering that my gender and skin colour had been recorded.

Jenna was shaking me. I looked up and she was in the sky. Rain fell from her hair into the long grass. The rain was saying my name.

I opened my eyes. Everything was the same. Jenna was staring at her screen, scrolling through pages. I was sitting right next to her, but I felt as if I was standing at the top of the stairs, looking down into the cellar. I wanted to move closer, but I didn't seem able to move my feet. Jenna turned to me, saying something that I couldn't hear. Could you say that again, I thought. But I don't think that I spoke.

The warmth of Jenna's hand on mine. I was back. 'Are you alright?'

I shook my head. 'No, I don't think so.'

'Break time,' she said. She pulled me out of the cellar into the back yard. We sat on the bench next to the herb garden, where we'd sat all that time ago, when we first really spoke to each other.

'Do you remember?' I said, after a long silence.

'Remember what?' said Jenna.

'What I said we'd do.'

'What we'd do...'

'I said that we'd go to Café Boite for a drink and a pastry, then walk over to the Sixth and go to the swapmeet, and maybe drop into a bar.'

'Of course I remember.' She smiled. 'I'll never forget how it was, falling in love with you. How I just knew, all at once.' She looked down at the cold earth. A tiny leaf was pushing through. I heard her swallow. 'But I'm so worried, Bo. Something's happening to you.'

'I just feel tired,' I said. 'I mean...really tired. It's like...it's a little like...I don't know how to say it.'

'It's like what?'

'Like I'm being drawn, the way that you draw water.'

'I think there's something...wrong with the water,' she said.

I didn't answer. Jenna was probably right. But what could I do? The water was pulling me away, taking me into a world that somehow lived inside this one, a world that only I could see. It was beautiful, it spoke to me.

Who was I in that world? Did I belong there? And if I did, what would I have to leave behind?

Dez

The door looked like it hadn't been opened for years. There was no sign of a security button or buzzer. But clients got in all the time. There had to be a way.

'So,' said Erin, after a long silence. 'You haven't worked this bit out, huh?'

'Not this bit,' I said. 'Last time I was with Ava.'

'Ava?'

'She runs this place.' By now I'd walked up and down the lane, examining every centimetre of the wall as I went. Nothing. Rusting steel, burned-out light pixels where once there had been a sign. Maybe I had the address wrong? But that was impossible.

I tried the door again. It felt nailed shut.

'So basically we're fucked.' Erin sounded resigned. It was just what she had expected.

I didn't answer. Ava would have peepers out here for sure, there'd be bound be sensors around the entrance. They were probably disguised by some fancy IMR. Well, it was worth a shot.

'Ava,' I said, leaning close to the door and keeping my voice as low as I could. 'Or Gloria, if you're there. I know this sounds weird, but this is Dez.

Dez, friend of Brian Mac, used to be brig of the Second Bann. You helped us with getting to the hospital, remember? I'm kind of stuck in this AI and I need to get home. Like, fast.'

Nothing. If I had a heart, it would have been pounding in my ears so loud.

'It was me and Flora and Jenna, remember? We didn't get my brother. We got Jules instead. She came home later.' My god, this was risky. If there was a surveillance bot buzzing around here, OpSec would be down any second.

'Please help us,' I said. 'We need help.'

Still nothing. I stepped back, resisting the urge to look at Erin. I had a Plan B. We'd head to the Inner Veil and run through it. It might fry some of my circuits, but this AI body had no DNA and Erin was pure pinker. Without remote it was extremely high risk, there'd definitely be surveillance around the Veil. What would we do when we got through the Veil? Run like hell, I guess.

'For a while there, I almost believed we'd escape,' said Erin. 'You should have let me finish the job, back there in the bathroom.'

Her voice was cool, controlled, but even so I could pick up the panic underneath. Yes, maybe I shouldn't have interfered. I should have just done the logical thing. It might have been kinder in the end.

I was still trying to work out what to say when the door slid open.

Erin turned towards me, her eyes wide. I didn't say anything, I just pulled her through. The door slammed down behind us. We were in a covered yard. I almost ran to the next door. which opened as soon as we reached it. I pulled Erin through the empty room on the other side, down a corridor, up a flight of steps. At the top was another door. We waited a few seconds, and that opened too. The door slid shut behind us without a sound.

We walked through into a blaze of pink. I had forgotten how pink the FeelGood Salon was.

Erin wasn't looking at the pinkness. Her entire attention was focused on Ava, who was standing right in front of us holding a heavy-duty taser turned up to kill. Both of us put our hands up. Slowly.

'Good story, ladies,' said Ava. 'You'd better hope it's true. For your sakes.'

For the first time, it occurred to me that I had no idea whether Ava was flesher or pinker. She was outrageous in either world. If you passed her in the street anywhere, you'd do a double take. She was about as tall as Ma, in bare feet she'd barely reach my shoulder. Even in the spiky heels she affected she was shorter than me, and I'm not tall. But that was last thing you noticed about her.

Black, glossy hair piled high, black leather-look smartwear, boots up to her thighs, black liner swept over her eyelids. Despite all that, what you noticed first was her eyes. She was the kind of person who made you step back, to make sure you gave her enough space. She emanated danger. Especially now.

I realised that in this AI body, I had no idea how to sound honest. 'Of course it's true,' I said. I heard Erin swallow beside me. 'Just unlikely.'

Ava didn't lower the taser. I didn't blame her. We could be any kind of plant. OpSec could have captured me and found out everything and sent us in undercover to collect information. 'Who's the floozy with you?'

I heard Erin draw in a breath, and then she slowly lifted her hand and switched off her IMR.

'Oh my god.' A breathy voice from behind Ava. 'It's Erin Saba.'

Gloria, the receptionist at the FeelGood, stepped forward. I didn't recognise them at first: on my last visit, they had been dressed up to the nines in some of the most amazing smartwear I'd ever seen. No little faces on their nails, no piles of golden hair. They were wearing camos, flat shoes. The only concession to style was the retro glasses, circular black discs hiding their eyes.

'Get into the office.' Ava jerked her head to the office door, and we obeyed cautiously, taking our time. We both knew that any sudden movements would be a mistake. 'Search them, Gloria.'

Gloria took a sensor stick out of the cupboard and ran it over Erin's body. It blipped at the IMR pin, and Ava gestured for her to take it off. Gloria scanned her again. 'She's clean,' they said.

'Now the AI.'

Ami made the sensor go off like a firework, and I began to calculate our chances if Ava decided we were lying. There was no radio output from Ami, and her databanks were locked down, but she was obviously a spying machine. Gloria handed the sensor stick to Ava, who took it without taking her eyes off us. She passed the taser over to Gloria.

'Don't move,' Ava said. 'Or Gloria will blow your heads off.'

She plugged the sensor stick into a screen and studied the input, her straight black eyebrows drawn together in concentration. I didn't even try to calculate the odds: I had no idea whether we'd pass inspection. The only thing I knew for sure was that if we didn't, we'd be wiped.

'Interesting,' said Ava at last. She looked up, her eyes narrowed. 'You can give me the taser, Gloria.'

Gloria handed it back. 'Thank fuck,' they said. 'I hate those things.'

'Right,' said Ava. 'You'd better tell me what the hell is going on.'

Beside me, Erin sagged with relief.

'I have to admire your timing,' said Ava. 'Maybe we can do a deal that's mutually beneficial.'

It was an hour later. We were sunk into the scruffy, comfortable couches in the FeelGood office, sipping green tea. Gloria couldn't take their eyes off Erin, who was sitting so close to me that we were almost touching. She had barely said a word, aside from thanking Gloria for the tea, but I could sense the trembling in her body. She was way out of her comfort zone. I wondered how she'd go in the banns.

'A deal, huh?' As far as I could work out, mutually beneficial deals were Ava's whole shtick. She'd had an arrangement with Brian Mac when he was brig of the bann.

'I need to get Gloria out of Newport City. Now, I can get them out, no problem. I don't know, however, where I can get them out *to*.'

'We got a tip from a contact,' Gloria said. 'Seems they've tagged my ID. It's only a matter of time before they come to get me.' I suddenly noticed the strain in their face, shadows under their eyes. 'I haven't been home in days.'

I must have managed to look questioning, because Gloria answered without my asking. 'I had a fake ID,' they said. 'But the last few weeks, they've been cracking down. Seems that mine came up flashing. If they find out I'm an avant...' They drew their finger across their throat.

'Whatever you people did out there, it's rebounding hard,' said Ava. 'That flesher attack really didn't help.'

122

'That wasn't fleshers,' I said quickly. 'Pretty sure it was an OpSec job. And I can tell you, it's worse in the banns.'

Ava shot me a look. 'Yeah, I know that,' she said. 'Point is, it's bad here too. It's killing the business. Nobody's coming to the FeelGood these days. This time of night, the place should be jumping.' She sighed. 'Anyway, I have to get Gloria out of here. And maybe you can help.'

'Sure,' I said. 'How?'

'You could take them with you. Put them up in a safe place.'

I didn't pause. 'Of course,' I said. I thought about returning with two pinkers in tow. Ma would probably hit the roof. It was getting pretty crowded in Rue Ballard these days.

'I look after my own,' said Ava. 'I'll hear if anything happens to them.'

Ava must be pretty desperate, I thought. That was lucky for Erin and me. 'If I get home, Gloria will be as safe as the rest of us,' I said. 'The house is as secure as I can make it.' I paused. 'Mind you, nobody is safe anywhere.'

'I know that. But if anyone breaks a deal, believe me, I hear about it.' She wasn't speaking loudly, but I saw Erin shiver.

'I believe you,' I said. 'We look after our own, too. And we keep our word.'

'Just wanted to make that clear.' Ava suddenly got businesslike. 'Let's get moving, then. You're in the Second Bann, right?'

'Right,' I said.

'That's the bit that worries me. You'll stick out like gau's balls. And these two....' She sat back in the couch, studying Erin and Gloria. You could tell they were pinkers the moment you looked at them: it wasn't just that they were both blonde, with that perfect pinker skin. Jenna was blonde, and she was unmistakably a flesher. It was something about how they moved, how they spoke, how they were in the world.

'Erin brought a bunch of IMR,' I said. 'And I know the Second Bann, I could walk through blindfolded. But I can't do remote, so it's harder for me. Normally I'd just deflect the Aps.'

'We'll have to take that risk.' Ava stood up, draining her tea. 'I'll get Erin a suit.'

'Just one thing,' I said. 'I'm a bit worried Ami's wiring might go doolally when we go through the Veil.'

Ava gave me a calculating look. I could almost see the cogs whirring: I was the guide, so I needed all my faculties. 'Yeah. I see. I'll give you a disruptor I use for tech, that should do it. At least, it'll fend off most problems.' She paused. 'I'd like it back. This is expensive shit.'

'I'll get it back to you,' I said. 'When I get a chance.'

'Right then.' She nodded. 'Let's get moving.'

Erin

Maybe I'll just wake up. I'll sit up in bed and sip the megavitamin juice that Ami makes me to boost my morning, and realise that I've been having a strange and horrible dream. There'll be no *Ebolastic*, no John Mecha, no OpSec, no nothing. It'll all wind back to a year ago, when I was working on *Days of Passion* and I was the Hot New Thing.

That was the happiest time of my life. All the signs were go. Dervin, the top agent in Newport City, had picked me up for his stable and was grooming me to be his biggest star. I was No. 1 rethrill in every IMR booth for six months running, the must-have celebrity for every party. Designers were falling over themselves to dress me. Dervin's main problem was to keep me from over-exposure. 'Keep 'em hungry, babe,' he said to me. 'Don't spread yourself too thin.'

Being picked for *Ebolastic* had seemed like the next step. It was the biggest thing going at the time, nobody was talking about anything else. When they cast me, Dervin was cockahoop. He said that *Ebolastic* would show that I had substance, that I was way more than a pretty face with a sideline in wisecracks. 'After this, the sky's the limit,' he told me. He was already considering my next move.

And then, bang! In three months, I lose everything. Everything I spent my whole life working for, all the achievement. It was so close I could smell it. Now it's farther away than I could have ever imagined.

I don't stop expecting the cops to turn up until we get through the Inner Veil. Underneath I really think that this whole possessed-Ami thing is an OpSec set up. I play along because I don't care any more.

According to Ava, the Veil won't zap Gloria or me because we're pure clone. Though she's not so sure about Gloria, who might have some anomalous DNA in there. Ava told me that Gloria's an avant, which is why they have to get out.

I've heard of avants, but I always thought they were made up, inventions of the pornbots. In some of the illegal rethrills people get off on all sorts of things. I've never even heard of the meat trade, which makes me feel sick. Newport City is more complicated than I know, and I thought I was pretty savvy.

I don't know how to talk to an avant, so I don't. It makes me uncomfortable. It's much more disturbing than fleshers.

Ava leads us to this lift that shakes like it's going to fall to pieces any minute and leaves your stomach behind. We step out deep underground, into a completely lightless tunnel. Ava pulls out a torch and Ami switches on a light. We keep going.

This is when I begin to believe that I'm getting out of Newport City. Suddenly I want a drink. I want it really badly. But there's no alcohol here.

Finally Ava stops dead. 'This is as far as I go.'

I'm dismayed. If this is real, and it's beginning to feel like it is, I'm lost. I won't know who I am. At this stage I don't even know what that means. But something about Ava's decisiveness has been reassuring me.

'You feeling it?' says Ami.

Ava nods.

'Feeling what?' I say.

'The Veil,' says Ami. 'You're really feeling nothing? Lucky you. Last time I was standing here, I couldn't stop throwing up.'

'Switch on your disruptor,' Ava says to Ami. 'You can turn it off once you reach that marker.' She points her torch at one of the support beams off in the distance, which is painted white. Then she looks at Gloria. 'Do what Dez says. Okay? After this, you're on your own.'

What Ava does next shocks me. She steps up to Gloria and puts her arms around them. She doesn't just touch them. She pulls them in close. Not for long, but for long enough. Gloria doesn't even flinch. As Ava steps back, I see a single tear rolling down her cheek.

'Thanks, Ava, you beautiful beast,' says Gloria. 'For everything.'

Ava gruffly tells Gloria to take care and we turn and walk along the tunnel without looking back. Despite myself I'm braced for something nasty, but of course nothing happens.

I can't remember the next bit very well. A lot of narrow, twisty streets, no lights. A lot of crouching and running and Ami telling me to shut up. The streets are dirty and everything smells. There's rubbish piled up in the gutters, crumbling walls. The banns. It's kind of what I expected but also nothing like anything I imagined.

Ami leads us to this tumbledown shack. She fiddles with a console and the door slides open and she basically pushes us inside. It's smells of people, sweat, sleep, old food. Something else I can't place. She points to a sofa.

'You two sit here,' she says. 'I've got things to do.'

Before I know it, the room is full of half-awake people. It's suffocating and I'm terrified someone is going to touch me. They don't, but they're too close. One of them, a tattooed blonde, offers me a drink.

At last. By this point I'd drink Dervin's aftershave. I'm desperate.

I slam it down. It's rough but there's this amazing herbal aftertaste. I ask for another.

Right now I'm thinking there isn't enough alcohol in the world to get me through this. I'm in the banns. The actual fucking banns. Part of me still doesn't believe it.

I look around the room. It's shabby and small, I don't think anything in here is new. It has a retro chic feel that would be kind of cool in some Newport City bar. But I'm definitely not in Newport City any more. And I've got no way of getting back.

My old life is over forever. And I've no idea what will happen next.

Bo

'Bo...Bo...where the fuck am I? Bo!'

I sat bolt upright. An old woman with greying hair was standing at the end of my bed. She was wearing blue shades, a beanie pulled down to her eyebrows and a long brown coat. I had never seen her in my life.

Jenna sat up beside me and opened her mouth to say something, but the woman spoke first. 'Hi Jenna,' she said. 'It's me. Dez.'

'What?' I blinked and shook my head, trying to wake up.

'I'm inside this AI,' the woman said. 'I've got to back into me. Fast.'

'But...'

'Where am I?' the woman said. 'Where's Dez?'

Jenna leapt out of bed. 'Hells...is that you, Dez?'

'Yes, of course it's me. I've had a hell of a time getting here. Also, I've got a couple of pinkers with me.'

'Pinkers?' I said. Now I was totally confused. 'How did you get in?'

'I'll explain everything later,' she said. 'I can't stand being in here much longer.'

'In where?'

'In Ami. This AI.' She paused for a second, and, even though it wasn't Dez's voice, I could hear her trying to be patient. It was in her speech patterns, the rhythms of her voice. 'I'm inside this AI. And the AI is in disguise.'

She yanked off her shades and the beanie. She looked about fifty years old, scruffy, a heavily lined face, pale green eyes. A flesher woman. She put her fingers under her lapel, pulled out an IMR badge and flicked it with her finger nail. As we watched, her skin smoothed out and became flawless and white. Her black hair was cut in a neat bob, her eyes bright blue. Even as an AI, she was all pinker.

'I know what I look like, but it's me in here.' She fixed me with those impossibly blue eyes. 'I'm back, Bo. Almost. So don't be a complete dick.'

It was Dez all right.

The pinkers were waiting in the front room. One of them was wearing camos and circular black shades, the other long black pants and a black jacket. The one in the pants looked vaguely familiar.

'I couldn't stand looking like that any longer,' said pants lady. Now I looked closer, I could see circles under her eyes, and her hair looked draggled and dirty. She still looked kind of expensive. 'Is this your brother?'

'Dez, what the hell are you doing?' I said, ignoring her. 'These two can't be here.'

'Well, they are,' said Dez. 'This is Erin.' She pointed to pants lady. 'And that's Gloria.' Gloria waved their fingers at me, smiling nervously.

Today was turning out strange. The water person, and then this. I felt as if my grip on reality was slipping. Or maybe reality was a lot more complicated and mysterious than I'd ever imagined.

'Have you got anything to drink?' said Erin. 'There's something to drink here, right?'

'I could make a brew,' said Jenna.

'I could do with something stronger,'

'I could do with a stiff drink myself,' Gloria said. 'Something tall and cold with a bit of a kick.'

'Not sure about the tall and cold,' Jenna said. 'But we can provide the kick. If I can find it.' She started searching through the cupboards.

I looked at the AI. 'We have to talk.'

'We'll talk once I'm back to being all of me,' said Dez. 'Where am I?'

'You're at Flora's,' I said.

'Get me over here then, pronto. I can't contact anybody, you'll have to do it.'

I gave up trying to understand what was going on. I just did what she said: opened a line to Flora and told her to bring Dez over. I didn't explain why, because it would have sounded like some kind of bad joke.

'Is something wrong?' said Flora.

'No,' I said. 'See you in a sec.'

Jenna found the baju and poured shots. Erin knocked hers back in a single swallow. She gagged and coughed, bending over as if she was going to throw up. When she straightened up again, her face was flushed and she was sweating.

'What is this shit?' she said, holding up her glass. 'It's fantastic.'

'It's baju,' I said. 'And that's our last bottle. It isn't cheap, so go easy on it.'

'I've got credits,' she said. Then she kind of recollected herself. 'No. Shit. I can't use them.'

'If you use them around here, we'll have OpSec knocking down the door in two seconds flat,' said the AI. Dez. It was getting confusing.

'What's OpSec got to do with her?' I said.

'I'm not sure,' said Dez. 'They want to kill her.'

This just got better all the time.

Dez's cellar was a bit of a mess, because we'd all been working in there behind the shield. I hadn't realised until she walked in and looked around. She hated people messing with her things. But she didn't say anything.

'I don't know how to do this,' she said.

'Do what?'

'Join myself up.'

'What if you can't?'

She didn't answer at first, and I realised she was probably figuring out odds. 'Let's not think about that,' she said. 'Unless it happens.'

At that moment Flora and Dez came down the stairs. They stopped a few steps from the bottom.

'Who are those two upstairs?' asked Flora. 'And who the hell is this?'

'I'll try to explain,' I said.

'No, I will,' said the AI. 'It's not that hard.'

She moved towards Flora and Flesher Dez, this tall, dark haired, shiny-skinned, white creature who was nothing like Dez at all. Flora flinched, but didn't move. 'It's me, Dez. I'm inside this AI and I need to get back into me. As it were.'

'I'm pretty sure it's her,' I said.

Flesher Dez came down the last couple of steps. 'I look like a soap star,' she said. 'So smooth and pretty. But I can hear me in there.'

'You'd better keep your distance,' the AI said, looking at us. 'I don't know what will happen.' When we didn't move, she gestured impatiently towards the stairs.

We moved back and I put my arm around Flora's shoulder. She was trembling. The AI switched on the shield on Dez's workbench and the air fizzed.

'Dez, what's the shield for?' said Flora, her voice tight.

'Just in case,' said the AI. 'You know how to turn if off, if you need to.'

'Do you know what you're doing?'

'No. Kind of. I think so.' She paused. 'I just need to – upload myself. It should be fine.'

I didn't feel reassured. I squeezed Flora's shoulders, as if I were comforting her, but really it was to comfort me. I had to hang on to something. We just watched as the shield came down.

It was weird. The AI took both of Flesher Dez's hands. She said something we couldn't hear, and Flesher Dez nodded. For few seconds nothing seemed to happen, and then the two of them seemed to snap into sync, so their eye movements and facial expressions were exactly the same. I noticed the AI was breathing, just like Dez was, in the same rhythm, and only then realised that it – they? – hadn't been breathing before. Then the AI bent down and kissed Flesher Dez on the lips. They both collapsed on the floor.

Flora swore and leapt forward. She switched off the shield and grabbed Dez in her arms, shaking her. I just stood there, feeling like all the blood had drained out of my body. I thought that I'd just watched my sister die.

And then Dez opened her eyes and stared straight up at Flora.

'I'm back, baby,' she whispered.

She sat up and put her face on her knees and cried and cried.

Dez

Words are pretty useless things, really. There's so many times when they fail. They're slow, they're inexact and fuzzy. But sometimes they're all we have to tell ourselves what happens in our lives.

It's really hard to describe what happened when all of me came back together. Flesher Dez, who had spent the past day watching soaps and holding Flora's hand, is just as much me as Data Dez, out there in Newport City, trapped inside an AI, trying to get home. It's a hard thing to understand properly: I mean, I can understand me being split in two as a concept, but actually experiencing it is wild. It's really hard not to think of one of me as the 'real Dez' because I'm so used to thinking of me as one thing. But we're both equally me. And for a little while there, we were having two different lives.

I haven't really processed what it means. I don't like thinking about it, because I start feeling nauseous. One thing: after I got me back together, I felt a little more forgiving towards Morro. For him, this split wasn't some temporary thing: he lived with it his entire life. No wonder he ended up twisted. For people like him – like me – there are no maps, there's nobody who can show you how to deal with it. When there's a bit of time (when will there be time?) I'll sit down and try and work it all out. I mean, Morro and me can't be the only ones.

The main thing I felt was giddy with relief. I hadn't known until we did it whether I'd ever be able to get me in. Relief is the right word, but it goes nowhere near expressing what I was feeling.

It was like I'd been living in monochrome and all the colour turned on, or as if I'd been hearing everything in one note and suddenly there was music. Flora was holding my hand, and I could feel the electricity of her touch running up my arm and down my spine like it was the first time we had ever touched. But also my brain was fizzing, recalibrating itself. It reminded me of when I was a kid and got sick with the nanovirus, coming out of the fever to discover this amazing world of data. All of me was alive and blazing. I didn't know whether to laugh or cry.

I cried. And then I stood up.

Having a body was amazing. Having my mind back was incredible. The things that bodies do, without even having to think. The blood pumping through every vein and artery and capillary, the muscles swelling and contracting, the amazing chemical soup of everything that makes you alive.

'You okay, Dez?' whispered Flora. I met her eyes, seeing the strain there, the worry, her terrible fear that maybe I wasn't the Dez she knew any more.

I flung my arms around her and kissed her face.

'I'm okay,' I whispered in her ear. 'I am so okay.'

God, it was good to be home. But, as usual, there was no time to enjoy it.

I checked my body. Nothing hurt. Brain seemed okay. Amazing. I looked around my cellar. It was too full of people and my workbench was a mess.

I didn't want to start my triumphal return to me-ness with telling everyone to get the hell out of my space, but I could feel myself bristling like a neka. I can't help it, I've always been very territorial. I knew for certain now that territorial thing was Flesher Dez: Data Dez didn't care who was in her space. Total Dez was pretty pissed off that people had been in here, messing around with her stuff.

They'd obviously been hard at work combing through the mountains of data I'd funneled home. I did a quick check, as much as anything to see if I could still do remote. Being unable to use it had been awful, I'd lost a sense that I used all the time. One thing I'd learned from that was that having remote made me lazy. I don't have to take the same precautions as other fleshers. Getting through the Second to Rue Ballard without it had been nerve wracking.

I vowed to get less lazy. What if I lost remote again?

It took no time at all to see that they'd got almost nowhere with the data. They'd been using the wrong kind of search. I'd left some search strings, but it hadn't even occurred to me that I'd need to tell them how to find the information we needed in the OpSec database. Me, I can just feel my way through it: finding pathways always seems obvious to me.

I bit back my impulse to criticise: it was my fault after all. I should have left better instructions. Bo saw the impatience in my face. Of course he did, he's my brother.

'Sorry about the mess,' he said. 'We've going through this shit since you sent it back.' He gave me a crooked grin. 'We needed you, Dez.'

I looked around my work bench again. Yeah. They did. But I didn't say it. 'Is there anything I ought to know about what's happened since I went into OpSec?'

'A few things,' said Flora. 'It's been…a busy day.'

'Are we in danger?'

'More than usual?' Now Flora was grinning.

'Well, immediately. Like now. Because I'm tired.' I was exhausted. But even that was brilliant. AIs never get tired. 'So if it can wait until tomorrow morning, it would be great to sleep first.'

'Just the usual mortal peril.'

I looked at Bo. 'Where's Ma?'

'Out. She was meeting someone. She said she'd be home late.'

That meant nobody knew where she was.

'Those pinkers you brought with you,' said Bo. 'What'll we do with them?'

'They can have my room.' I looked at Ami, who was lying on the floor, discarded and broken, with a pang. Somehow she'd got zapped in the transfer. 'We can't leave her like that.' I picked her up and propped her on my chair. She was surprisingly light. 'We can work out everything else tomorrow.'

'What if those pinkers are spies?' Flora's voice was hard, strained.

'They're not,' I said. 'And I couldn't leave them behind. One of them's Gloria, from the FeelGood.' Weariness was clamping down on me, the back-wash of the relief of making it home. I could barely stand up. 'They're both in trouble. And you should be grateful, Gloria's why Ava helped me get through the Veil.'

There was too much to tell. We'd find the time. We had to. But right now, more than anything in the whole world, I wanted to get into bed with Flora. I'd probably fall asleep straight away, but that didn't matter. For a while there I'd thought I'd never feel her breathing next to me again. Her arms around me. Her lips on my neck.

These were the most precious things, those ordinary moments. And I'd almost lost them forever.

Well, part of me almost had.

It was all too confusing.

Erin

You're fucked, Erin Saba. You're totally and utterly fucked. It goes around and around in my head like one of those earworms. Like somebody's just saying it over and over again, whispering it into my ear.

Part of me is wondering what would happen if I just went back to Newport City. What if I just turn up at my apartment and act as if as if nothing happened? I could plead a heavy night on the tiles, I don't remember where I was.

Could it be any worse? (Of course it could). The Veil won't affect me, I have all the proper pinker genes, right? Though after a day in the banns I'll have breathed in all kinds of rogue DNA. My skin is probably crawling with bacteria. My hair, my lungs. I've even eaten flesher food. I know, from talking to one of the Council cops, that if you have a mission in the banns you have to go through a decontamination unit before you're allowed back in. You even have to shit in a special toilet until you're all cleaned out, unless you get an emergency pass. I mean, we take our hygiene seriously in Newport City.

Rogue DNA. It's all we hear about, from as soon as we can listen. Those rhymes we used to have to chant in nursery school: *keep your hands clean, wash in a trice, wherever you've been, you've got to be nice.*

In Newport City, everyone knows to keep their distance. And now I'm stuck in a room with a bunch of fleshers who touch each other all the time. I'm terrified someone will brush against me, but they kind of know, they're careful.

They kiss with their mouths. I was almost sick when I saw that.

Fleshers. They're made with meatsex. I can't think about that because when I do I feel this pain in my groin, like burning. But I can't stop thinking about it either.

I want to drink all the time, but I can't. They didn't say anything when I finished off that firewater they drink here, but I could see the look in their eyes. That stuff costs, and they don't have much in the way of credits. I can't pay them back, I'm even poorer than they are. I have absolutely nothing except the clothes I'm standing in.

I have to say, it's a novel sensation, being looked down on. All my life, I've been special. People would go pink with excitement when they saw me, they couldn't do enough for me if I walked into a boutique or a biobooth. And now I'm just in the way. I mean, it's not like they're not being polite, by their terms anyway. Dez's brother looks at me as if I'm scum. Her mother just has this way of staring at me that makes me feel like a complete idiot. I suppose as far as they're concerned, I am. Dez is the only one who's nice to me, and she's busy the whole time.

I'm trying to keep my end up. Trying to look like it's all cool, like I can cope. But for the first time in my life, I don't know how to pretend. I don't know what performance I need to put on. Even I can hear how I sound to them. To them, I'm this arrogant pinker.

I never even heard that word before. Pinker. And then I open my mouth, and what comes out sounds just like an arrogant…pinker. I can't stop myself.

And now I'm stuck with them. And they're stuck with me.

I think this flesher house is going to drive me mad. All these tiny rooms, the low ceilings. Just being here, you can tell that everyone touches each other all the time. It's almost like the house hugs you. I have this gagging feeling the whole time.

Pinkers. It sounds…offensive. It makes sense that fleshers have a name for us, same as we have a name for them. It kind of shifts things, though.

I never even thought about what I am. I'm classified, of course, a celebrity class clone. But aside from that, we're just us.

I just want to sleep forever. Ami – I mean Dez – should have let me die. I'd be better off. Why'd she decide to stop me? I still don't know.

I tell Gloria that, and they look at me like they think I'm five years old and have done something stupid and they're trying not to be unkind. They don't look sorry for me at all.

'I thought about killing myself often,' Gloria says, after a while. They speak slowly, choosing their words. 'I don't any more. I don't see why I should help the City Council do its dirty work.'

We've retreated to Dez's room to be out of the way. Gloria's curled up on the bed, polishing their nails. They're wearing camo gear they borrowed from Dez. I have to admit, they wear it with style. You'd almost think they were a flesher.

No one would mistake me for one, not without a bit of IMR. Today I'm in red: cool, smart, classic. My smartwear's self cleaning so I don't have to worry about stinking for at least a month, but I change the colour every day to give me the impression that I've got another outfit on. A tiny bit of normal.

'I had a serious go at dying once,' says Gloria. 'I took around a hundred grams of nebus.'

'A hundred grams?' I stare. That's enough to get a house full of people happy for days.

'It's just chance that I'm not dead.' Gloria stops buffing and stares into space. 'Ava came round to my place just after I'd taken it. She wanted a hit and she knows I always have the best grade. When I didn't answer she got suss and broke through a window. She made me puke it all up.'

Gloria goes back to their nails. They've had them implanted with animations but they're fading now, they don't last longer than a couple of weeks. Little emofaces that reflect your mood. Right now the faces are frowning, like their fingernails are all having deep thoughts.

'Ava said, *no matter how bad things are, you never know what's round the corner. Something you couldn't even imagine.* It kinda stuck with me.' Gloria smiles ironically. 'And hey. She was right.'

Yeah, and sometimes things turn out worse than you ever imagined. I would never have imagined I'd end up hiding in the banns with a bunch of flesher terrorists. That's what they are, for sure. I know they're planning something, they're always talking together in low voices, fiddling around with screens, making notes, being busy. I wonder if they blew up the apartments in Block 15. Then I remember the OpSec vid, with the flesher extras. I'm actually pretty sure it was OpSec who did that.

I wonder if the fleshers know it's OpSec. They probably do. They're not fools.

'What's round the corner is probably being picked up by the cops and sent to the interrogation rooms,' I say. I'm annoyed with Gloria for sounding sunny, like we're in a good place. We're not in a good place.

'Darling, that was always just round the corner for me. Every. Damn. Day.' They stretch out their fingers and blow on their nails, and throw me a glance. I can't quite read it, it's sympathetic but also malicious. 'Now you're just like the rest of us.'

I bridle. I'm not like the rest of them. I'm *special*.

And then it's like something breaks inside me.

I'm not special. I've never been special.

I think I always knew that, underneath. Almost everyone thought I was, because special is what celebrities are supposed to be, but I knew it wasn't true. My specialness was part of the lie of everything. The only things that ever mattered about me were a bunch of pixels in a rethrill booth, a bunch of credits in an account. Me? Real me? I'm worth nothing at all.

I want to bawl my eyes out, but I don't. I blink hard and turn away. I can feel Gloria's gaze, like it's heating up my skin.

'My darling girl, you just have to decide,' they say. 'Do you want to live, or do you want to die? After you decide that, it gets easier.'

Does it?

'Well?' They're staring straight at me now and I try to look back, but I can't meet that steel gaze.

'I don't know,' I say. 'I just don't know. Whether there's any point.'

'That's for you to work out. No one else is going to answer that. And you'd better work it out before someone else decides for you.'

Dez

I had a lot to catch up on. Bo and Jenna filled me in on some of it. Finding Koni-Ta in the tunnels, the incident in the tea shop. That made me go cold inside.

'It was raining. Inside.' Jenna shook her head. 'The whole place was – it was like being in the middle of a rainstorm…'

'It went for the militia,' said Bo. 'It was on our side. It knew…'

Jenna turned on him with sudden fury, her eyes flashing. 'It wasn't on Koni-Ta's side. Or Quan's. It killed them, remember?'

Bo looked taken aback. 'It saved us, Jenna.'

'Saved us? Saved us?' For a moment I thought she was going to slap him. 'Bo, what the fuck is going on with you? When are you going to wake up?'

I'd never seen Bo and Jenna fight before. I guess it was time they did. But I wanted to ask the same question. Bo had been worrying me, when I had time to worry. I knew there was more going on in there that he was letting on. I'd tried asking him, but he was always evasive. I knew it was something to do with the water.

'I *am* waking up,' said Bo. He took her hand, leaned forward and kissed her cheek.

'The water isn't on our side, Bo,' said Jenna. She was speaking softly now. 'It isn't on anybody's side. It wants us. I can feel it in my head when I dream. I can feel it in *your* dreams.'

'The water is us.' Something in Bo's voice made my skin prickle. 'It's our skin, our blood, our bones, our everything. Of course it's on our side. It *is* our side.'

Jenna shook her head. 'Do you want to end up like Mish? It wants to make us into it.'

'If we're the water, so is OpSec,' I said. A sudden gust of fury went through me. Or maybe it was panic. 'The pinkers in OpSec are just as much water as we are. Approximately 65 per cent, in fact. Why would the water be on our side and not theirs? It doesn't make sense…'

'Because we're right,' said Bo. 'And they're wrong.'

I could feel that I was going to start yelling at him, so I just left. I had work to do.

I put myself on turbo and crunched through the data, not without a flicker of pride. I'd downloaded the entire OpSec database before the bots got me. Amazing. Pat on the back for me.

I sure hoped I never had to do that again. I was still calibrating myself, testing myself to see if I was still working. This wasn't something I'd normally do: I guess I'd spent too long being Ami and now I was behaving like a self-organising AI. But hey, every experience teaches you something. My major paranoia was that some quantum-level spybot had lodged itself in there somewhere. Unlikely, but if I was them, that's what I'd try to do.

I didn't think OpSec had worked out where the previous invasions had come from. I checked to see if there were any reports about the last time I'd been in. I couldn't find any that even mentioned it. That was a bad sign: there should have been. It meant there was some ultra-secret database that I hadn't tracked yet. Probably it was isolated from the OpSec mainframe, to make sure someone like me couldn't get in.

Damn. That meant that there was a whole level of planning that I couldn't get into.

It also meant that they might have taken precautions against another hacking by loading the database with misinformation. Again, that's what I'd do. How paranoid do you have to be in assessing OpSec? At least as paranoid as them. I remembered something Brian Mac told me once. 'Never underestimate OpSec,' he said. 'But don't overestimate them either. They're smart. Of course they're smart. But you might be smarter than them. Don't be too clever.'

How clever is too clever? How the hell would I know?

Suddenly I missed Brian Mac. He knew OpSec from the inside, he'd know how to judge the cleverness. I didn't know.

I'd just have to go with what I had.

I did a series of dragnet searches and then started refining the data. There was so much data. Too much.

The Chimera Project, for instance. That was just plain evil. Jenna had stumbled across that one by chance and then had been stumped by the crypto. It was evil enough to freak out pinkers, who get super edgy about DNA contamination, but it was worse to read if you were a flesher. The aim was to identify genes that linked to special abilities in fleshers, and then to splice them into special military clones. It was linked to another huge program on accelerated growth, the idea being that ultimately they'd grow an adult military clone, all prepped and programmed, in a less than a week. The plan was to combat any 'psychological instability' by using the same biotech as they use in AIs. There was a lot of guff about that, but it looked pretty much like hand waving to me, like they were kidding themselves. Maybe the scientists knew that it wouldn't work, but they were being pushed so hard by Newport City Council and OpSec that they were going ahead anyway.

'Psychological difficulties' is code for the problems that Newport City always struck trying to integrate human consciousness with AI. They could never find a way to do it without breaking people. That didn't stop them trying: they experimented for literally centuries before giving up.

I read a lot about these experiments when I downloaded Newport City Library, because I have a personal interest. They either created people who were so distressed and unpredictable that the scientists had them euthanased, or a bunch of psychopathic AIs that were so dangerous they were useless even to Newport City Council, which itself is pretty much the definition of psychopathy. In the end, computers aren't human beings, and human beings aren't computers.

Unless they're me, of course, because I'm both.

The accelerated growth program was surprisingly far advanced. The Chimera Program less so. I kind of skimmed through that, forcing myself to pay attention. It hurt, physically hurt, to read this stuff. They were experimenting on people I knew, the fleshers they'd scooped up and sent to Newport Western Hospital. They were being kept in suspended animation, although they had tried reviving a few so they could check them for abilities. What I was reading was so cruel it made me shake with anger.

I remember the faces I had seen in those drawers in Newport City Hospital. The tracks of tears running down a boy's face.

One of them might have been Bo.

Out of the whole sweep, they had only found one flesher with abilities, and he was dead. Morro, who could be in two places at once. They'd taken tissue samples from both his bodies but they were having trouble isolating abnormal genes, mainly because it seemed that there were abnormalities through his entire DNA. When they tried splicing Morro DNA with other human cells, they either disappeared in a puff of quantum chaos (which the researchers counted as progress, although they couldn't track where the cells went) or they just died.

Despite this, the researchers were optimistic that they'd have results in the next month. Based on what I was reading, this seemed like a straight-out lie to me. These were reports for the eyes of OpSec, after all: it didn't mean that they could actually do it.

The thought of another database that must exist somewhere, a top top top secret one that I hadn't got into, kept nagging at me. It left enough space for plenty of paranoid thoughts of my own. Maybe OpSec did know about me. Maybe they'd found some of my DNA somewhere. It wasn't like I was wearing skin-gloves when we went into the hospital: I touched doors, drawers, input terminals. Maybe there might be an actual Dez clone being grown in the labs right now.

Maybe they really were growing an army of psychopathic mutant clones that could be in two places at once. The thought gave me chills. I figured that the chances were low. Really low. But I couldn't be certain, and I don't like not being certain.

There was a lot of other stuff about security tactics that I filed away for later use. And then I started hunting for anything on the security around the Inner Veil. I was hoping there was a big switch somewhere. I mean, they turned off the Veil on Duiwel Island, so there must be a switch of some kind…

It took a while, but I finally found a reference in the historical files. It seemed there had been a switching mechanism for the Inner Veil. They'd disabled it, after Brian Mac brought it down and fleshers rioted in Newport City. The Inner Veil was now self-perpetuating: it was the number one energy priority, with all energy sources directed to maintain it before everything else. If all of Newport City was destroyed, the Veil would be the last thing standing. They'd distributed its command system through the whole Veil, so if one bit went down the rest of the system took over and repaired it. There was literally no way to turn it off. Like Brian Mac said, OpSec was smart.

The Outer Veil was a different story. For that, they basically had a red button. OpSec could turn it off any time they liked. There was a lot of modelling about what might happen if they did, with different risk scenarios on the effects on the Inner Veil. It seemed it was too dangerous to even try: they couldn't rely on the Inner Veil still being effective without a buffer zone. Chance of damage in normal conditions averaged about 60 per cent. 90 to 100 per cent if a nanostorm hit.

There were a lot of these models, which disturbed me. That meant that OpSec was still hot on the idea of exterminating fleshers. There was a memo from Garonne, the new head of OpSec, that stopped me cold. The 'flesher threat' was now OpSec's single top priority. It wasn't just that they thought we were planning to invade Newport City and take over. (Fair enough, that was our plan.) Underneath there was this idea that there were too many of us using too many resources. Drinking all the water, eating all the food, breathing all the good air. The fact that we even existed was an outrage.

The thing about this memo wasn't even what Garonne was saying, though that was bad enough. It was the tone of it. He made it sound like he was making this rational decision about Newport's 'limited resources', but underneath it was something much uglier even than that, a pure loathing and hatred that had nothing to do with logic. It was as if we represented everything that he couldn't admit that he hated about himself.

I guessed that if you were Garonne, there was plenty to hate.

For a while I felt too angry to continue. It seemed that no price was too high to keep pinkers in their luxuries. Killing millions of fleshers? No problem. I thought about what I'd seen in Newport City Central. Lights on everywhere, water splashing in fountains, apartments with actual bathrooms with baths. All that reckless wastefulness. Seeing it in reality had shocked me to the core: no fleshers live like that. We coddle every resource we have: nothing, and I mean nothing, goes to waste. That's why we don't have sewers any more: we don't need them.

I skimmed through a lot of rhetoric about the dangers of 'flesher contamination' and the need to monitor Newport City citizens for any sign of deviancy and stamp it out immediately. I guessed that might be where Erin went wrong, and made a mental note to check her file, and maybe look through their so-called 'domestic surveillance'. Then I hit a reference to something called Project Hope. I did a general search and came up with nothing, so I started digging. It took a while, because this data was heavily coded. But eventually I hit paydirt.

Project Hope was the new murder plan.

Garonne wanted to do a pre-emptive strike. OpSec needed to solve the flesher problem, before fleshers organised and started being a real threat. And the quickest way was just to turn off the Outer Veil and wait for the next nanostorm to 'sterilise' the Outer Banns. Problem: the potential damage to their precious Inner Veil. Project Hope was the solution. Build a Middle Veil.

They were transforming the Wall into a Veil. That explained the pulse that Bo and Jenna had felt under the Wall. When they'd built the Middle Veil, they'd turn off the Outer Veil and just let everybody die. It would also, someone added in a footnote, solve the 'skinner problem'. Skinners were running openly in the Outer Banns now, most of them 'gathering samples' for OpSec.

The only good news was that Project Hope was hitting setbacks. The Wall is one of the oldest structures in Newport: not even OpSec knew how it had been built or how it worked. For centuries it had just been there, doing whatever it did. All we knew was that it was safer inside the Wall than it was outside. You could go outdoors without a suit.

The brass wasn't happy with how work was proceeding. It seemed that something in the Wall negated the tech they needed for the Veil. I shuffled quickly through a series of engineering reports. The first teams claimed it was impossible: they couldn't even break chips off the wall to work out what it was made from. After Garonne sent a couple of senior engineers to re-conditioning camps, they started coming up with more ideas.

Progress, it seemed, was being made on Project Hope.

I hoped that was a lie too.

Bo

Ma wasn't happy about Erin and Gloria. 'I suppose they can stay,' she said curtly. 'Until we work out some better arrangement.' She stared at them, sitting side by side on the couch. Erin's hair was a mess and she was looking kind of smudged, but she had this snooty air, like she was too good for us. Gloria had none of that: they were pale and fragile, as if you touched them they might break.

Anybody who walked in our door would know they were pinkers straight away. One more problem. The last thing we needed was more problems.

'You have a gorgeous home,' said Gloria awkwardly. 'I mean, it's a home, isn't it? And that's gorgeous.' For a moment they looked really sad. 'I mean, I never had anything like this.'

Something changed in Ma in that moment. Get into Ma's heart and she'll defend you with everything she's got, and Gloria crawled right in. Not that you could tell at first.

'It's a place to live,' Ma said dismissively, like it was nothing.

That was when Erin decided to pipe up. 'My skin is like sandpaper,' she said. 'Is there any moisturiser?'

Gloria went bright red. I'm sure they felt embarrassed for Erin. But Erin herself was completely oblivious.

'Moisturiser?' said Ma. 'Are you serious?'

'There's water in the filter,' said Dez. She looked as if she were going to laugh. 'That's pretty moist.'

Park and Sally arrived and Ma banished the pinkers to Dez's room because she wanted to talk business. The Wall.

Dez told us what she'd found out. After she finished, we were all silent for a while. I guess we were processing it. We weren't shocked: it was just the same old same old.

'It's like the Eradicators all over again,' said Jenna.

'We waited too long with the Eradicators,' said Ma. 'By the time we understood what they were planning to do we were too late to stop them killing people. This time we don't wait.'

It turned out that Ma had already been working on a mission with Park and Sally. 'We hit them where the work is most concentrated,' she said. 'Around the portes.'

'Blow it all sky high,' said Park, his eyes gleaming. The thought seemed to energise him.

'We've got a group together,' Sally said. 'Your man Redborg. Tag, Kipp and Stel from the Third. Stel's an explosives expert. She was out in the mines for a time.'

'We don't need explosives,' said Dez sharply. She didn't like that a plan was being sprung on her. 'The stuff Brian Mac got from OpSec supplies last month, when we thought we'd have to blow up the Eradicators. It's better than anything you could get from the mines.'

Park shrugged. 'Stel will know if that's true,' he said. 'I'd check with her, first.'

'Maybe I know more about explosives than any miner,' said Dez.

Ma gave Dez a look and she pulled her head in, though I could tell she still wasn't happy. Dez always has to be the first to know everything. She's a pain that way, but she gets over it.

We sat up late into the night working out routes, comms, who and how many in each group, getting every detail clear. The idea was to hit all four portes at once. 'We've only got one shot at this,' said Ma. 'If we get it right, it will set OpSec back for months.'

'It can be done,' Dez said. I knew she'd calculated the odds. She always did. 'But we can't afford for anything to go wrong.'

Two days later I met Redborg at Lazy's, the tiny bar where I'd met Brian Mac all those weeks ago. It was after midnight and he was the only customer. The barman was propped on a stool at the back, his head resting against the wall, mouth open, fast asleep.

Redborg was hunched over one of the tiny tables, his hand curled around a tumbler of something blood-coloured. 'Drinking?' I said, sitting down next to him.

'Don't worry, flesh,' he said, lifting his glass. 'It's only bloodberries and ginger.'

Bloodberry has its own kind of buzz. Unlike alcohol, it makes you sharper, faster. It also gives you the world's worst hangover.

I guessed that wouldn't matter right now.

'Want a drink?' he said. 'We've got time. But we'd have to wake up our man there.' He titled his head towards at the sleeping barman.

'I'm okay,' I said. I didn't need any uppers. Or downers. My nerves were all doing their own thing and right now that was enough to deal with.

Redborg winked at me, finished his drink in one long draught and unfolded himself from the chair. 'Let's head.'

'Should we lock the door?' I asked, looking at the barman. 'Anyone might come in.'

Redborg walked up to the barman and shook him. 'Better shut up shop if you're going to snooze, flesh,' he said. 'My friend here is concerned that anyone could walk in. Hells, even I walked in.'

The barman opened one eye and told him to fuck off.

'Duty done,' said Redborg, giving me a smile. 'Let's go.'

We took lanes and back streets, keeping to the shadows. We couldn't afford to run into any Aps. The explosives were inside my leather jacket, the remote detonator in my pocket.

Kat and Rioka were waiting in an unlit alcove of a building in Rue Ban Sho. They were both dressed in black, hoodies drawn over their heads.

'Hello there, dark ladies,' said Redborg. I hated that he was enjoying this. I wasn't.

At least all that endless mapping was paying off. We had a clean route to our destination. Our target was the East Porte in the Sixth. It would take us maybe two hours to reach it.

Three blocks from the Inner Veil, close to the foodtowers, we clambered down into the old RTS through one of the ventilation shafts. The entrance was in a tiny yard off an alley that ran between blocks of low rise workers' housing. This tunnel was one of the smaller conduits feeding into the Rue Ban Sho station and had been sealed up a decade ago. It was a short drop to the floor of the shaft, then a crawl of about twenty metres, then down into the depths. I quickly scanned the street, slipped into the shaft, pulling the metal grille over the opening.

There were four groups heading out, each of us with one of Brian Mac's precious gravitational comms. I checked the lines as soon as we hit the station, one of the deepest in the network. After a short delay, Ma pinged back. All good. I checked with the other three groups; Park's group moving west into the Eighth, Sally's group going north into the Fifth, and Flora and her crew heading south into the Seventh. Park and Flora responded straight away. I waited for Sally to respond, but there was nothing so I tried again. This time she pinged back.

'We're all in place,' I said. 'Let's get this done.'

The mission was to destroy the engineering works that OpSec were running on the Wall, to stop them making an operational Veil. It was only buying time, we all knew that, but time was the main thing we didn't have. And time was what we needed to figure out how to bring down the Inner Veil.

We knew that there would be a backlash and that it would be savage. Ma was using the tunnels to build a network of messengers, and going by what they were telling us, the fleshers were prepared. There were cells of active resistance in every bann, a rumbling surge beneath the surface. Occasionally we saw things on the dark tubes. A couple of days before, some bright spark in the Third had scrambled the surveillance drones. The Aps completely lost control of them, the drones were running around like wild punks after too much hooch. Watching the Aps tripping over themselves trying to shoot them down gave us the best laugh we'd had in weeks.

Our suits were already the best in the banns, but Dez had gone into overdrive, making them as failsafe as possible. Flora and Kat took care of the explosives. We still had the two bombs we'd intended to use on the Eradicators. They were simple but deadly devices, made of some ultra-explosive material Brian Mac had stolen from OpSec. Kat and Flora made four bombs out of them, and Dez made a couple more detonators.

We planned to strike the Wall two hours before dawn. We knew that the sites were heavily guarded, but as far as we knew there were no curtains set up around them. All the engineering work was concentrated around the portes, where they could access the inside of the Wall. The techs and engineers working on the Veil project were living in situ and there were temporary dormitories, kitchens and workshops set up on site. Some structures were built on a platform that spanned the mono lines, where they passed through the porte. We had enough explosive to reduce most of it to rubble.

Our maps made moving through the RTS relatively straightforward. The first part was so uncomplicated that it made me feel nervous. We had an unobstructed route into the Sixth. Rioka was listening for OpSec comms, but she didn't pick up anything except the usual to and fro between guard posts on the site.

'They sound bored,' she said.

We knew that the towerblocks around the perimeter of the site had been cleared and that we'd have to pass through that empty zone without being detected. We would exit the RTS about four blocks from the spot we'd picked as our point of entry. Four blocks seemed like a long way. Dez said perimeter security was at 'level three', which was high but, according to her, not too high.

We would come out of the RTS close to Rue Manea. There were towerblocks along the north side that were connected by homebuilt footbridges set up so people could move from building to building without having to go down to ground level. Because they were homebuilds, the bridges weren't on the plans. The information we had was from fleshers who used to live there, and their directions were vague - 'turn left at Moz's place and it's four doors down' didn't quite cut it. We knew they were at random intervals up from the third floor.

The thought of those bridges made me nervous, Me and high places don't get along very well. I took a deep breath and told myself not to look down.

Dez

It was the first time I was left behind while everyone else was out doing a mission. It was way more difficult than I expected. Two of the people I loved best in the whole world, Flora and Bo, were putting themselves in mortal danger and I wasn't there. If anything went down, I couldn't do anything to protect them. At best, I would just get to listen to them dying.

I didn't try to talk Flora out of going on the mission. It took everything I had not to. The fear that I might lose her beat underneath everything I did. It was a literal pain in my chest, like a hot stone had settled there. Sometimes I really couldn't stand it. I even thought about becoming Data Dez for the length of the operation, just to escape that pain. But I knew now that even that wasn't an escape. Those feelings were still there, shadow feelings maybe, but present all the same, shaping whatever I was thinking.

I tried not to talk about my fears, out of a superstitious feeling that if I said it out loud it might make it come true, but Flora knew anyway.

'I'm not saying that there isn't a risk,' she said, in one of the few private moments we managed to snatch. 'That's the way things are. But we have to do what we have to do, or there won't be a future for any of us.'

I stroked her hair back from her forehead. It was hard to speak because of the lump in my throat. 'I know,' I said.

'Anyway, it's your turn to be worried. When you went into Newport City, I was afraid that you'd be gone forever.'

'Half gone,' I said.

'Yeah. Half gone.' She shifted my weight, because I was lying on her arm and it was going numb. 'You were really sweet, you know? You hadn't forgotten me. And I loved you just as much. You were so vulnerable, like a little punk, and you needed me so much. But I missed you, Dez. I missed my smart, annoying, mouthy Dez. And I knew that might be how it was now.'

I didn't know what to say. I don't deserve to be loved like that. I kissed her, feeling her warm breath, the taste of her, the tickle of her hair on my face, the weight of her body on mine, all that electricity of touch and feeling that felt so new, so miraculous.

If anything happened to Flora, I didn't know what would happen to me.

I put all my anxiety into beefing up the suits for the mission. I had a lot of junk lying around in my stash that I could repurpose. I pulled a couple of all-nighters and by the end, those suits had the lot: shields, fields, automatic armour control against percussive and wave weapons, back-up comms in case the secret lines went down. I found a couple of extra maps in the OpSec data and overlaid them on the ones we already had. I programmed in the shift times of security that I'd downloaded from OpSec.

It still wasn't enough.

After they left for the Wall, there wasn't much to do. Ma was monitoring the comms, and my job was keeping an eye on anything unusual happening with OpSec. I could do that without thinking, I just created an alert and left my remote on, a buzz in the background.

I needed something to distract myself.

I remembered Ami. I told myself that maybe she could be useful to us, if she was programmed right: she's very expensive top class Newport City software. Shutting down the data transmission to OpSec was obviously the first necessity, but I needed to work out what else was going on in there.

It might sound weird, given who I am, but I'd never really thought about AIs as anything more than sophisticated machines. The only AIs we ever saw were the ones the Aps used. They're designed to kill people, to make fleshers afraid. That's it. I know a fair bit about them, because outsmarting the Aps is basically life and death in the banns. The Ap AIs are all about function: they calculate risk, predict and respond to weapon trajectories and combat patterns.

You don't want to get into a firefight with an AI, because they learn from every move you make, optimise it and then use it back against you. They learn. Fast. As fast as I do. I'd never, on the few occasions that I'd hacked an Ap AI, felt anything except machine consciousness there: pure logics. That has its limitations, of course. Hence the Ap-AI pairing. It was considered optimum practice, the best of both worlds.

I scoured my Newport City databases for information about AIs, and found myself getting interested. Ami was a kind of AI we never saw in the banns, a top of the range PAC 62345Z, which translates as a 'personal assistant and companion, designed to anticipate your every need and desire'. I noticed that all these AIs are built as female. Very pinker.

I started going through the specs. It seemed that these AIs had something called 'empathy coding'. I did a general search on that and found a few research papers. That was when it started getting *really* interesting.

There's no empathy coding in a militia AI, or in the AIs they use in the mines or industry. They put in enough theory of mind for the AI to respond and interact with any humans around, and that's it. Too much, and they might start amplifying the discontents of their fellow human workers or causing other kinds of trouble, and the last thing Newport City Council wants is a machine they can't predict.

It seemed that empathy coding was pretty controversial. The only reason NCC allows empathy coding in high-level AIs is that the top brass want them, and they do some pretty comprehensive codelocking to ensure they don't go feral.

Empathy coding is what makes AIs emotionally credible. Retail AIs need a bit of it, just enough to sell rich people expensive smartwear. Personal needs AIs need a whole lot more. The advertising spiel said it all. 'Your helper, your confidante, your friend. Here for you. Every time.' I liked that 'confidante' bit, given that Ami was on a direct line to OpSec. 'Your personal spy,' more like.

How lonely do you have to be to think that an AI was a friend? As lonely as Erin. And even then, what kind of friend does everything you say? Never argues with you? Never disagrees with anything you do?

That's not a friend. That's a slave.

After a while I had to stop processing the data and just sit there for a while, to dissipate the dizzy feeling it gave me. I had so many questions. Such as: do AIs like Ami just copy emotional behaviour, or do they actually feel it? Do they know that they feel emotions? I *know* that I feel things, and I've always been pretty sure that's what makes me different from AIs. But if AIs know that they feel things, maybe they're not so different after all. If an AI has enough information about human behaviour to copy it pretty much exactly, how can you tell, anyway? The only way you'd know was if you *were* that AI, and nobody can do that.

Nobody except me, of course.

I was thinking more and more that Ami did know that she felt things, the same way Data Dez wasn't the cold dazzle of rational logic that I had always assumed she was. Ami feeling things wasn't, according to the research I was reading, actually possible. But these were the same people who said that fleshers had 'lower order' feelings, like gaus or nekas, so it was okay – more than okay, it was *necessary*, 'for our own good' – to kill us. There was one paper titled 'Ethics of Consciousness' which compared fleshers and AIs. I actually laughed out loud. It was news to me that pinkers cared about ethics.

The more I read, the more I realised that Newport City, even though nobody said it, thought about clones almost exactly like they thought about their high-level AIs. The DNA was the coding, the learning algorithms were inbuilt but directed by hormone soaks and behavioural conditioning. The problem with us fleshers isn't that we're different. The real problem is that we're unpredictable. We're disobedient. But so are some pinkers. Brian Mac. My Da. Gloria. Even Erin.

Since the whole thing went down with Brian Mac, OpSec had got a bit obsessed with its 'failures'. There was tons of shit about that in the dataframe. But they weren't failures. They were people doing what people do. What they'd been made to do. Think. Feel. Love.

I began to realise that my desire to repair Ami had very little to do with whether we could use her tech or not. She was a person, like I was. It just seemed wrong to just leave her folded up in a corner like a piece of trash. She wasn't trash, just like I wasn't trash.

But she'd been made by OpSec. Every last bit of coding, every single nanoparticle. So before I evven began the repair, I had to look at everything. From every angle. Twice. Three times.

That'd keep me busy until my loves came home.

Bo

We turned our shields to high before we left the RTS and climbed up to Levi Square station via a steep narrow stairway. It led to a steel door bolted on the inside. Kat tried to slide the bolts, but they were rusted shut. She'd brought a jemmy just in case.

'Let me do that,' said Redborg. He snapped the bolts from the door as if they were made of sticks.

My sensors didn't pick up any threats as we stepped out into the rue, aside from a drone a few blocks off. There were no lights except the faint glow of the Veil above us. We turned left and hugged the walls until we came to the corner of Rue Manea, then headed for the stairwell on the east side of the first towerblock. Redborg made short work of the locked door with the jemmy and we were soon climbing.

We stopped on every floor after the third and checked for bridges. Nothing doing. I began to get anxious that they'd been taken down. On the eighth we found what we wanted: a wide opening with a homebuilt sealed door cut in the wall. It led to a platform attached to the outside wall. The footbridge was a couple of metres wide, suspended by steel rope.

'One at a time,' I said, taking a deep breath. 'I'll go first.'

As soon as I stepped onto the bridge it swayed. I tried to forget that I was afraid of heights. I didn't look down and kept my eyes on the building in front of me, about twenty metres away. I clung tight to the ropes and inched my way across, swaying left and right, my heart in my mouth. When I got to the platform on the other side I threw up.

Redborg came last. He walked straight down the centre of the bridge, not bothering to hold onto the ropes. The bridge hardly moved.

At the fourth towerblock we looked out a window on the eighth floor. About two hundred metres away, across the vacant ground that ran its entire length, the Wall loomed in front of us. To our left we could see the bright glow of the site at the base. The dark silhouette of the mono line and its support pillars were about six floors below us.

We were too high. We had to go down four floors to plant the explosives on the pillars closest to the Wall, where they connected with the monorail's steel and concrete base. Kat and I were doing that. We'd worked out the best placement with Dez, just as we had when we planned to use explosives on the Eradicators if we needed to. The mono would then collapse onto the site below, taking the structures that were built on the mono lines down with them.

The sweet spot was the mono station above Rue Corvus, which was directly below the towerblock we were now in. Okay.

I checked in with the other groups. We had to strike as close to simultaneously as possible. Even a slight delay would allow OpSec to put all the sites on high alert and send out strike drones. Dez figured the most slack we had was thirty seconds.

Flora's group was in place, at the mono station at Rue Botho in sight of the target. Park's was slightly behind us, about half a klick away. Not great, but not bad, not bad at all. Then I checked in with Sally. There was a long delay before I heard back, long enough to make my heart sink down into my boots.

'We hit a problem,' she said at last, sounding breathless. 'Three skinners at Djuna Station. We had to waste them. Kipp got hit, but he'll be okay.'

She reckoned it would be twenty minutes before they were in place. Twenty minutes. That was going to cut it fine: we'd worked out our timing to fit with the shifts that Dez had downloaded from OpSec. She'd allowed for misadventures, but twenty minutes meant we would be cutting it fine.

I contacted the others and let them know there was a delay. The four of us would head down the stairwell on the north side of the towerblock, which took us into Rue Carnet and the entrance of Corvus Station. From there we were close enough to plant the bombs. After that we'd wait at the towerblocks for Sally's signal that she was ready to go.

Redborg began to get antsy at the delay. 'Haven't we waited long enough, flesh? My blood's up and I can smell those pinkers from here.'

'If we don't wait, we'll screw up everything,' said Kat.

From inside his jacket Redborg pulled a long-barrelled handgun mounted with a heat-seeking targeting device, the kind that Aps use. The rest of us had tasers set to kill. They were silent and wouldn't make a mess, but Redborg's weapon would blow a person to pieces.

'Put that shit away,' said Kat sharply. 'Are you out of your mind?'

Redborg lifted the gun and looked through the sight, adjusting the targeting. He was smiling, a smile that made me go cold inside. 'I could drop a few from pinkers up here, no problem,' he said. 'Just as an entree.'

'Where did you get that fucking thing?' I said.

'Took it from an Ap last night,' said Redborg. 'He won't be needing it any more.'

'Put it away, Redborg. We don't need that,' said Rioka. Redborg moved away, still with that unsettling smile.

'I took out the second Ap out with this. The first I had to kill bare-handed.'

'Redborg,' I said. I was thinking fast. Maybe this is what OpSec had done to him, made him into a rogue killing machine. 'This isn't like you.'

He looked at me sideways and despite myself I stepped back. His glance hit me like a beam of plasma, cutting right into me. 'How do you know what I'm like?' he said. 'You have no idea, lovely. No idea at all.'

'Did they program you in there to screw us up?' said Kat brutally. 'Because that's exactly what you're going to do. Thanks, OpSec. Thanks a bunch.'

That gave Redborg pause. The fire went out of his eyes and he slid the weapon back inside his jacket.

'We've got a job to do,' said Rioka. 'Let's just do it.'

'We're here for the killing, aren't we?' Redborg said. He looked at each of us in turn. 'Make up your minds. They have.'

'That doesn't mean we like it,' said Rioka. Her voice was shaking with fear or anger, I couldn't tell which. Maybe both.

'Morals are luxuries, my flesh.'

'This isn't about morals,' said Kat, turning away. 'This is about getting this job done.'

'I'll kill when I want,' said Redborg softly.

'You're here to make sure this mission works,' said Kat. 'Not for your own private revenge. No matter what they did to you.'

There was a charged silence, and then Redborg laughed. 'All right, my obedient little buddies,' he said. 'But if we get out of this alive, I'll chart my own way to hell.'

Climbing down the stairwell, I felt numb. We were almost there. Once Kat and I were moving along the mono to place the explosives, we'd be exposed and vulnerable. Now I was nervous about Redborg. The plan was that he'd hang back near the station with Rioka to cover us. Rioka would monitor OpSec comms to make sure they weren't on to us. Redborg was the last resort if we came under serious threat. The whole idea was to plant the explosives and get out undetected.

Maybe Kat was right. Maybe they had programmed him to go toxic during a mission and blow it up. The thought of him randomly disintegrating pinkers with that cannon of his made me feel sick.

The station was clear and I was wasn't registering any threats, but we kept our fields on high. It was about a hundred and fifty metres from the station to the support pillars. About the same distance further on were two or three structures built across the rails, topped with a drone landing platform. There was a change of guard in ten minutes. We had to be quick.

We climbed down from the platform and onto a narrow service gangway that ran between the rails. We'd place the explosives and move back to the towerblock. We'd detonate from there and hightail it back into the RTS.

'Are we ready?' I whispered.

Kat nodded, swallowing hard. We moved along the gangway on all fours, keeping our heads below the level of the rails. We hadn't gone twenty metres when we heard the drone. I glanced up and saw a black spider shape hovering to our right, clear against the faint shimmer of the Veil.

Kat pushed me in the back. My arms and legs were suddenly shaking. Why did I weigh so much? I looked down and saw the vacant ground below me, the wash of light from the site. I wasn't so much afraid of the drone finding us as of Redborg shooting it out of the sky: I could see it exploding above me, the burning wreckage falling towards me, the explosives under my jacket detonating as the wreckage hit me, the mono collapsing, my body on fire as I plunged towards the ground.

Kat prodded me again and I moved. One foot. One hand. Another foot. It wasn't far now.

The buzz of the drone faded into the noise of the city. The relief rushed through me. A cold sweat broke out over all my skin.

Kat and I lowered ourselves off the gangway and onto the narrow ledge around the top of the support pillar where the iron structural work was bolted. My hands were shaking so much that I couldn't unzip my jacket. Kat did it for me and took out the explosive. We packed it around the anchor bolts of the steel bracing beams. When it blew, there would be nothing holding the rails to the pillars and the whole structure would collapse.

'Okay, we're set,' said Kat.

We climbed back onto the gangway and headed back to the station. I felt the detonator in my pocket. I'd activate it once we were in the towerblock. All we had to do then was wait.

'I was afraid that you'd blast that drone,' I said to Redborg.

'Nothing alive in a drone,' he said. 'Waste of a bullet.'

'Let's get the fuck out of here,' said Kat.

Back in the towerblock I contacted the other teams. Flora and Park were ready but there was no response from Sally.

'Maybe they're done for, or been turned back,' said Redborg.

'We wait,' I said. We still had six minutes before the guard shift changed.

'Their comms might be down,' said Kat.

Rioka tensed. 'I've got something.' She squeezed her eyes shut and bowed her head, concentrating hard. 'It's a little fuzzy. But something's wrong.'

We all watched her, waiting. All I could feel now was time ticking down.

'An alert to all sites,' she said. 'Incident at the north porte, a fire fight in Rue Rabal. Drones on their way. The order is capture or kill.'

'That has to be Sally,' said Redborg.

Sal's an old timer, I thought. She won't permit herself to be captured. Sally, Kipp, Stel and Tag. All gone? We knew the risks. We'd been lucky so far, that's all. I opened a line to Flora and Park.

'We've got a problem,' I said. 'Sally's group. They ran into trouble and now there's an all-site alert.'

'We hit them now,' said Flora.

'Thirty seconds,' said Park. His voice was steady, hard. 'Counting down from...now.'

I heard Rioka gasp behind me. 'There's been an explosion,' she said. 'A fire in Rue Rabal.'

The Wall around the East Porte lit up under a massive burst of light. A squad of heavily-armed militia screamed from their quarters and headed for the perimeter. I could see three drones above them rise high into the air, their searchlights sweeping back and forth across the towerblocks.

I could hear the ticking in my suit. We all could. I gripped the detonator.

10, 9, 8, 7, 6, 5, 4, 3, 2...

I froze.

Redborg grabbed me by the collar. 'Do it, flesh, do it now!' he hissed.

I flicked the switch.

Erin

I'd kill for a martini. That craving, shaking my guts. I went through every storage unit in this damn place and found some kind of alcohol that somebody forgot, shoved to the back. It tasted like cleaning fluid but I drank it anyway. The hangover set in about 30 seconds later, but for a couple of hours it blurred things and living was almost bearable.

Now there's no more alcohol. Believe me, I've looked. I feel like all my skin as been scraped off, like I'm just raw flesh. There's nowhere to hide, inside my head or outside. I just feel useless and lost.

I prop Ami beside me on the bed, wishing she was there, fussing about, doing my hair. I miss her. I never thought I'd say that.

One thing: I've got plenty of brooding time. I can hear the fleshers in the living room. They're busy, a frenzy of preparation for something that even Gloria hasn't bothered to tell me. Then most of them leave, and suddenly it's all still. Gloria has gone to help Bel and I'm all on my own.

I wonder what they're doing, and then decide that I don't care. It doesn't have anything to do with me. Time passes, but the only way I know that is by checking my timestrap. I find myself talking to Ami even though she can't talk back.

I'm losing my mind.

How the hell did I end up here? Like, a month ago I was just a stressed celebrity working with a prick who hates me, bad enough in itself but ultimately no big deal. I know people who've gone through that and survived, Mecha's worked with a lot of people, and it's not like all of them saw their careers blow up. I had a lot going for me: Number One in the rethrill booths, a top agent, even if he's also a prick. A shining future. And now all that's gone and I don't even know why.

I'm one hundred per cent confident my name is on a list. But why? Why me? Was it John Mecha who put me there, out of spite? It wouldn't surprise me. But the more I think about it, the more that doesn't really make sense. Like they say at celebrity school, we're expensive. We're expensive to make, we're expensive to train. The ones who make it to the end of celebrity school, the ones who get through with first class honours like me, we're a big investment. They're not going to toss that out just because another star doesn't like me. Besides, there's celebrity spats all the time, it's part of the whole entertainment package. There's a whole channel that tracks who's trashing who.

I mean, I might have my own thoughts about this or that, but it's not like I've said any of them out loud to anyone. I always did the right thing. I smiled at the people I was supposed to smile at, kept myself fancy at the top biobooths, let myself be seen with the right people, attended all the right parties. I don't trust Dervin as far as I can throw him: after the first excitement of signing with him faded away, I realised he was just this empty shill with a side of brutal. But he knows his business like no one else in Newport City, and I followed his advice. All of it. I was careful. We're all careful.

I keep thinking, that flesher smiled at me. That's why, they think he knew me. But seriously? I'm famous. *Everyone* knows me.

It keeps nagging at me. There has to be another reason. And I don't have a clue what it is.

I'm trying to doze when Dez comes into the room and grabs Ami. She heaves her over her shoulder, nods at me and is heading out the door when I grab Ami's leg. I've seen Dez's bench in her cellar, all bits of things pulled out of other things. She's not doing that to Ami.

'No,' I say. I hear panic in my voice. 'She's mine.'

Dez frowns and yanks Ami so I lose my grip. 'She's not anyone's,' she says.

'Please…' I'm whispering now, frightened I'll cry in front of this flesher, frightened I'll lose my cool, which all I have left of dignity. 'You can't just take her apart. She's not just…spares…'

Dez hesitates, and meets my eyes. 'It's okay,' she says, her voice a little gentler. 'I just want to fix her.'

'For what? So she can advise you on your shit fashion sense?' It just comes out of me, pure acid, and I bite my lip, feeling myself blushing. Where does this stuff come from? It's not what I mean.

To my surprise, Dez laughs. 'Come on, you can do better than that,' she says. 'You pinkers call it bitchtalk, yes? I used to love your rants in *Days of Passion.*'

'Yeah, well,' I say. 'I didn't have to write my own lines back then.'

She sits down on the bed, cradling Ami on her lap. It's a little bit close for comfort, but I don't feel that she's going to accidentally touch me. 'I watched every single episode from when it first started,' she says. 'I must have been about twelve.'

'I thought fleshers didn't get the prime soaps,' I say.

'I used to make a living making streaming consoles. You'll find a lot of fleshers watch the pinker soaps.' Dez paused. 'We need a bit of escape too, you know? I streamed them all, since I first…'

'Since you first what?'

She looks at me again, and then shrugs. 'Since I could first do remote and get into the Newport City databases. I downloaded the entire library when I was eleven years old. Not that I've had time to read it. But it's useful, when I need to look stuff up.'

She's chattier than I've ever seen her. 'You downloaded the Newport City *library*?'

'I'm a kind of AI.' Then she shakes her head. 'Except I'm not. I'm a flesher, mainly. And a bit pinker.' She adds, super-casually so I know it's something that she's not casual about at all: 'My Da was a pinker.'

I smile uncertainly, because I don't know how to respond. I don't think she's lying, she took over my own AI after all, which is why I'm here in the first place. But this is weird. If her father was a pinker, that means...my mind kind of swivels away from the rest of the thought, but I force it back. 'What, did he...donate some cells, or something?'

'No, he was a pinker radical, and he fought with my Ma. And they were lovers.'

I'm barely listening. The thought, just the *thought*, of a pinker having meatsex, enough of it to make a flesher baby, feels like a cold knife going through my groin, a kind of numb pain.

Dez sees me flinch. 'Yeah, it freaked me out too, when I found out. But that's what happened. OpSec got him in the end. Or at least, he killed himself before they got him.' She pauses. 'I know that, because I read the records.'

I don't want to talk about it any more, but at the same time, my mind's boiling with curiosity. 'They were...lovers?'

I can feel Dez shifting gears, realising that maybe what freaks me out about her having a pinker father isn't the same as what bothers her.

'I don't know how it happened,' she says. 'Ma's pretty private about this stuff. They just...fell in love, I guess. She never told us he was a pinker...'

'He touched her? He *touched* her?' It just bursts out of me. I can't help it. He didn't just touch her, it was more than that, I just can't imagine...I feel like I'm going to throw up.

Dez goes quiet for a while. 'Brian Mac – this pinker Ap we knew – he could touch people,' she says. 'I don't know if he ever made love with anyone. I mean, it's not like I ever asked him, that would be...rude. But he'd shake your hand and things like that, and it didn't seem to bother him. I never thought anything of it, until we met Gloria, and they told us about pinkers. It's so twisted, to do that to people.'

I'm getting more and more uncomfortable, hot and cold at the same time, kind of dizzy, so I change the subject. 'And you can get into OpSec records and things?'

Dez hesitates again, and then slowly nods. 'Yeah. That's how I ended up in Ami. OpSec found me in their mainframe.'

I stare at her. 'So, do you think you could find out about me?'

'What about you?'

So I tell her the whole story. It's a relief to tell someone. And she listens, it's like she's listening with her whole body. I realise that no one has actually listened this hard to me in my whole life, and I feel weirdly grateful. And then a bit confused. I mean, a short time ago I had all of Newport City listening to what I said.

But they weren't my words.

When I get to the end, Dez sits upright and brushes her hand through her hair. 'You're right,' she says. 'It doesn't make a lot of sense.'

'I mean, maybe it's some kind of mistake? Not that I can do anything about it, I mean, I'm stuck here now. But I can't figure out…why? Maybe I imagined it all? But I didn't imagine it, I'm sure I didn't…'

Dez reaches out to touch my arm and I jerk back. She lifts up both her hands. 'I'm sorry, I forgot,' she says. 'It's just automatic, we touch people. Listen, I got a lot of intel on my last visit, I vacced up everything I could find. I'll do a search and see what OpSec have on you.' She stands up and picks up Ami. 'But first I'll have a look at Ami. I think we should bring her back.'

I watch her walk out of the room. My mind's still in shock.

Dez just told me that pinkers can learn how to touch. Maybe I could too.

My god. Every time I think of touching somebody's else's skin, that nauseating, chilling pain. But there's now this other thing, a strange… excitement. Like I've been in a cage my whole life without realising it, and I've finally learned how to see the bars, and maybe, just maybe, there's a door out.

Maybe I want to learn how people touch.

Maybe.

Bo

We didn't go back over the bridges in the towerblocks. With drones in the sky it was too risky. We flew down the stairs and into the entrance foyer. The main doors were locked, so I blasted them with my taser and we pushed them aside. The sirens were still wailing back at the site, drones screaming overhead.

We ran into militia as soon as we hit Rue Manea, three two-man quads heading away from the site in single file. They passed us at speed as we came out of the towerblock before they spotted us and pulled up sharp maybe fifty metres away. We turned and headed straight back into the foyer of the building. At least Kat, Rioka and I did. Redborg stood just where he was, pulling the gun from his jacket.

'Redborg,' I said. 'Don't be a fool!'

He ignored me and started walking slowly towards the militia, his weapon raised, shouting 'Come on you pinker gaus!'

The two militia on the last quad had dismounted and were running back towards us, firing. Kat and Rioka hit the ground and I dived to the right to avoid the bullets crashing into the walls around me. Before I could use my taser, Redborg had blasted one of the militia in the chest. He was thrown back about ten metres, his chest blown open. The second seemed to hesitate, stopped in his tracks and then ran to his left. Redborg tore his legs from under him.

The two remaining quads were accelerating towards us, the rider on the back standing up, leaning forward, pressed against the driver, firing rapidly. Redborg kept moving forward, striding towards the quads, firing one round after another. He must have hit the fuel tank of the closest one; it burst into a ball of flame and somersaulted into the side of a building across the rue in a blinding flash of light.

The last quad screeched to a halt, skidding sideways, and the rider was thrown off. He hit the ground with a sickening thud and slid across the ground on his back, coming to a stop almost at Redborg's feet, who took aim and blew his head from his body.

The driver of the quad only had time to lift his weapon before Redborg shot him, the face plate of his helmet exploding into a thousand pieces.

I got to my feet. Redborg was walking back towards me.

'Should we resume our escape, dear flesh?' he said.

'How did you…' I said. I didn't seem to have any breath left in my body. 'You weren't…hit.'

'But I was,' said Redborg as he opened his jacket wide. He was wearing some kind of protective vest. There was a blast mark right in the centre of it. 'All the Aps wear them now. I removed this from one of the unfortunates I ran into last night.'

The militia would have called in reinforcements, but with the fields they couldn't track us except if we were in eyesight. Redborg had taken care of that.

We ran into the warehouse that hid the entrance underground and down the stairs into Levi Square station. I had to check the map. South west. We'd been here less than two hours ago, but nothing looked familiar at all. It was if what had happened had wiped my mind clean, erasing everything. I could remember using the detonator. I know that I watched the explosion and the mono falling, but it seemed to have happened years ago.

I opened a line. Flora and Park switched in, but the line to Sal was dead. Flora sounded shaken, her voice coming in gasps.

'We did it,' she said. 'We did it. The whole fucking thing came down.'

I told her that we were on our way back and that we were all okay, so far.

'We're good, we're all here,' she said.

'Park?'

'All done,' he said. 'The pillars took a while to fall. I thought we'd screwed it. But they came down.'

None of us mentioned Sally. I didn't know what to say. She was probably already dead. 'Are you safe?' I said.

'We'll be safe when we get home,' said Park. He switched out of the conversation without saying anything more.

I pinged Ma the code that meant 'mission accomplished' and looked at Rioka. 'Any word about that firefight?'

She shook her head. 'There's nothing else,' she said. 'Not yet. I'll keep listening.'

I wondered what had gone down with Sally's group. I thought about telling Ma. That was going to be hard.

I took a deep breath. 'Let's get moving, then.'

We moved fast, the lights on our suits on low, our tasers drawn. We didn't know what we might run into. The rues above us would be swarming with militia, the skies filled with drones. Maybe someone we hadn't seen had tracked us to the entrance. I could hear Kat breathing hard beside me. Rioka and Redborg were right behind.

About half an hour later, we entered Rue Nagreb station. Rioka called for a breather.

I checked the MPS. 'We're making good time,' I said. 'We should be home in an hour.'

'Where's Redborg?' said Kat.

I turned around. Kat and Rioka. No Redborg anywhere.

'He was right beside me a minute ago,' said Rioka. 'He must have dropped behind as we came into the station.'

I ran back the way we'd come and turned the light on my suit to high. The tunnel was empty.

Dez

Fixing Ami didn't take long. The one thing I was worried about was the back door to OpSec. There wasn't a backup line to the one I shut down, which surprised me: I mean, if I were OpSec, I'd make sure there were at least two backups, folded into some other function so you couldn't track it. I checked three times, going meticulously through each neurofibre. But no, there was only that one data shunt. I couldn't believe it.

It amused me to think that I'm more paranoid than OpSec, but then, they know their own kind. I guessed that your average pinker wouldn't be trying to turn off the surveillance. It probably wouldn't even occur to them to look for it. I was beginning to realise that pinker conditioning did most of OpSec's work.

I couldn't stop thinking about Erin's face when I talked about Flynn and Ma. Her face went white – I mean, completely white, like all the blood emptied out – and there were tiny beads of sweat all over her forehead. It took me a few seconds to figure out why. My god. What the hell is that?

If you're a flesher, you don't get a lot of choices. Unless you live your whole life in the tunnels or in the Rift, that shithole in the Tenth, you're registered in the databanks. It's the only way you can get somewhere to live or earn official credits. We try not to use official credits, but there's some things, like mediscans, that you can't get without them. If you're in the data-banks, the authorities figure they've got you: they know where to find you, how to punish you if you step out of line.

But even so, we made our own networks: shijos so we could buy the things we needed with our own black credits, our own tube network, our own transport systems. A lot of that's being shut down, but even now we have ways of hiding. If Newport City makes it impossible one way, we work out another. We're like water, we'll always find the weakness. We know we can't do it alone, so we depend on each other.

But pinkers? How alone are they? If they're all programmed like AIs, the prison is inside their heads. How do they escape that? How did Flynn? How did Brian Mac? What made them want to? I mean, I've basically spent my whole life envying pinkers, but the more I find out about what it means, the more I find myself feeling relieved I'm a flesher, even with all the shit we have to deal with. At least we get to have our own minds. At least we have each other.

I thought of Erin sitting on that bed in her immaculate smartwear, her hair ruffled up, dark circles under her eyes, huddled up with her dead AI. It might be the loneliest thing I've ever seen.

I did a final check on Ami's data shunt, rechecked that her remote capacities were properly disabled. Made another tiny adjustment to one of her autonomy algorithms. I'd had a really close look at those, they were inter-esting. They limited the scope of her self-learning, and I couldn't help wondering what would happen if they changed. I kept thinking of what I had felt while I was in there. A strange bewilderment. You'd think that machines can't feel bewildered. But Ami knew that something was happen-ing to her, and it bothered her. Like she had a sense that she was a self.

I guess I was beginning to wonder what the difference was between Ami and me.

Then I switched her on. Ami blinked as she recalibrated, and then she turned her head and looked at me, fixing me with a blue laser stare. I felt uncomfortable suddenly: there was someone there.

'Hi there, Dez,' said Ami. 'My, you really could do with a skin treatment. You'll never look super plus if you don't put in the care!'

Well, I guess there are differences between her and me.

I took Ami back to Erin. She was still on my bed, her knees clutched to her chin. When we walked in she looked up sharply, her face expressionless. I could tell she was frightened that I'd done something bad to Ami.

Well, I had done something. But I didn't think it was bad.

'Hello beautiful,' Ami said. 'My god. We have to do something about that *hair*!'

Despite everything, I couldn't help grinning.

And then one of my alerts went off and I ran into the front room.

All hell had broken loose. All the OpSec channels were blaring out emergency signals. A general high alert. I joined Ma and Gloria at the interface, trying to stop myself from clutching Ma's hand like I was five years old again. This was the worst bit. Waiting for everyone to come home.

We had confirmation from three teams, but not a peep from Sal. And now everyone had gone silent: it was too dangerous even to ping us. They could check in with each other, but we didn't have enough of Brian Mac's comms to ensure that they could talk to us. Worse, there was precious little detail of what OpSec was doing.

'They've switched to the ultra secure channels,' said Ma. 'You sure you can't get in?'

I shook my head, but she already knew the answer. No. We knew that OpSec had some other way of communicating, and we still didn't know what it was. Rioka and I had checked out all the frequencies. Maybe if we'd had more time we could have cracked them, but we didn't have it. If we'd been able to listen in, it would have been worth having central co-ordination, because we could have told the teams how to avoid whatever was coming after them.

I was beginning to wonder if Brian Mac's gravitational comms were as secret as we thought they were. After all, Flynn had been researching those comms for the pinkers. If he and Brian Mac could make them work, what was to say that OpSec couldn't? Everything I had found on this research said it had been abandoned after years of failure, but...

I sat there biting my nails, trying to ignore the terrible fear opening inside me like a wound. Flora and Bo could already be dead, shot down by drones or militia, their bodies crumpled on the corner of some rue. I could see it so clearly. We wouldn't know until they didn't come back, and even then we wouldn't know, there'd always be the gnawing hope that somehow they were still alive...

I pushed the images away. I told myself that they knew how to look after themselves and my sitting here worrying didn't make any difference.

It bothered me that in all the exabytes of data I'd downloaded, there wasn't one strategy about the processes for dealing with attacks in the banns. There were screeds and screeds of plans to limit movement and communications, new drone patterns, new shifts to beef up the Aps precincts, rewritten AI protocols. But there was nothing about dealing with an actual attack.

It meant either that OpSec didn't have any plans, because they couldn't imagine that would happen – and even in my more optimistic moments, I found that hard to believe – or that they'd upped the security after my last visit and I hadn't got into the most secret databases. Which, of course, was more than plausible.

Right now, somebody would be sending orders. The only certain thing was that those orders would mean more dead fleshers. How many dead fleshers? I began to make a calculation on probabilities, and then I shook myself. There was no calculation that made more dead fleshers okay. All we were doing right now was choosing between different ways of dying. Dying fast, or dying slow. Dying with a sense of hope, however tiny or deluded, or dying in complete despair.

I'll never forgive OpSec for driving us into this pit, where these are the only choices we have.

It's never worth it. Never.

Bo

We arrived in the Second at dawn, coming out the way we'd gone in. Even at this hour, there should have been some life around. The foodtowers were close by and traders from the local shijos would head down this way to buy their produce. Rue Ban Sho was deserted. The snack bars scattered along the rue where every morning traders made deals and complained about prices were dark and shuttered. Our footsteps echoed off the walls either side of us.

The banns had already gone into lockdown, and it didn't take OpSec to enforce it. As soon as word spread about our attacks on the portes, and it would have spread fast, fleshers all over Newport would have hunkered down. The deserted rues were just the moment of calm before the storm.

We moved quickly, keeping to the smaller rues, zig-zagging our way home. We had our fields up but we weren't taking any risks. We were the only thing moving through the emptiness. We checked every corner, kept close to the buildings, scanned the skies for drones.

We split as we approached Rue Ballard, Kat and Rioka heading back to Rue Lozere.

'Stay safe,' I said.

'What about Redborg?' said Kat.

'We'll just have to wait,' I said.

'There's no telling what he might do,' said Rioka.

'There's nothing we can do,' I said. 'He's on his own, until he gets back to us. If he does.'

Jenna threw her arms around me. It was the best feeling in the world. She whispered in my ear, 'I've never, ever been so pleased to see anyone'. I held her tight. She felt so fragile.

I looked up at Dez, who was hanging back. 'Thanks, Dezzie,' I said. 'We did it.'

'I'm glad you're back safe,' she said.

Neither of us mentioned Flora. We were the first back and nobody had heard from the other groups.

Ma hugged me. 'Now we wait for the rest,' she said.

Jenna made a brew and Dez fixed me some spinos. I tried to eat, but my hands were shaking so much that I pushed the food aside. I was exhausted but buzzing. I knew what I'd done, but I also didn't know.

This waiting was the worst part.

Pinkers had died. Fleshers had died. Hadn't Ma said that we were all the same? Why were we killing each other? Would we all end up like Redborg? Was that the worst thing the pinkers did? Making us as murderous as them?

I wanted to be on my own for a while, so I went out into the yard and looked up at the sky. Pale clouds drifted above the faint iridescence of the Veil and I could smell the wind changing. Ma's plants were looking stringy. Nobody had time to care for the garden.

What had happened today? Too many things. I tried to think of something else, to be somewhere else, even if it was only in my head.

I thought of the water place. I knew it wasn't a dream, it was a real place. But I was sure it wasn't in this time. There was no place like that now, no place as pristine and beautiful in the world that I knew.

Maybe it was from before Newport was built. Or maybe it was a vision of what happened after Newport disappeared, after fleshers and pinkers died out. Maybe we all turned into people made of water. If the water was waking up, like Mish had said, maybe it was turning into something.

Or turning us into something. Or perhaps it was a memory of something we'd already destroyed, something that existed so far back that history had forgotten all about it. So much had been destroyed during the catastrophes of the megastorms. When our cities were swept away, so was our past. I'd seen them out in the dasht, those cities, ruins sinking under the drifting sands. But they told me nothing.

What did we have now? This fear and hatred, this terrible division. But I was both flesher and pinker, and Morro was two Morros, and Dez was Flesher Dez and Pinker Dez and Data Dez, and Brian Mac was a pinker Ap and a friend. No one was only one thing or the other.

Maybe avants were the only people who really understood that. They existed outside those divisions. That's why the pinkers persecuted them so badly: they upset the whole system of being only this thing or that thing. Avants said you could be both or neither or everything. The whole desire for purity is a lie, and avants know that better than anyone else.

I'd seen a kind of purity in that strange, wild place. But it wasn't what pinkers thought purity was.

The water had always been here. It would always be here. When I called the water, I was also calling the past and the future. I was calling something timeless into this violent present.

Did I want it to wash us away? Some part of me thought that I did, some part of myself that seemed as distant as the stars.

I didn't know myself at all. I knew that something was happening to me. Something was changing. To sweep everything away: was it me, wanting that? Or was that what the water wanted? Could it want something?

Even now I could feel it deep beneath the ground. Great rivers running through the darkness. Vast, crystal-clear oceans waiting to well up through the earth's crust and swallow us.

It was waking and it knew that we were here.

Dez

Flora's team hadn't pinged. Somewhere in my lizard brain I thought that Bo surviving meant that I'd already had all my luck, that I couldn't be blessed enough to have both of them back. I kept telling myself that I was being irrational, but it didn't make any difference.

Gloria made everyone a cup of tea, and we just sat there waiting for the others. It was only around fifteen minutes, but it felt like hours. When I heard the door buzz, my first thought wasn't that it was Flora. I thought that it was more likely that OpSec was coming to arrest us.

Flora's team had split up and gone to their homes in the Second Bann, so it was only her. I was so wired by then that it felt like she had come back from the dead. Her whole body seemed to be haloed with light. Her hair was tied back from her face, so you could see the gauntness in it, her cheekbones so defined, every feather of that blue bird tattoo standing out, her mouth set. She had lost weight in the past couple of months, and her body was all muscle, with no softness anywhere except her breasts. Those long, strong limbs, you could see her biceps moving under her clothes.

I couldn't move. She met my eyes and it was as if she knew at once what I was feeling. Of course she did. She always does, even when she doesn't want to. She came up to me, cupped my face in her hands and very gently kissed my lips. At her touch I came alive again, as if a golden light flooded through my body. I slid my arms around her neck and kissed her back fiercely, inhaling her sweet breath, the smell of her skin. Time stopped. Everyone else in the room vanished. It was just Flora and me, me and Flora, the soft world that we made together, our refuge from pain and terror and cruelty.

'Hey, you two,' said Bo, from somewhere very far away. 'You're freaking Gloria out.'

I opened my eyes. Flora was smiling. Had I ever noticed that her lashes threw tiny shadows on her skin? Would I ever stop noticing new things about her? I never, ever wanted to stop noticing.

'I love you,' I whispered into her ear.

She squeezed me tight. 'I love you too,' she said. 'My very own freaky wired girl.'

I wanted to tell her how afraid I'd been, how sure I'd been that she was dead, but I knew I didn't have to. She knew already. That fear that fleshers live with all the time, pushing it down so we can get on with the day. We felt it underneath all the time, even before we knew about the Eradicators. The fear that when someone we love steps outside the door, we'll never see them again.

Gloria was actually throwing up.

'Oh god, what a mess,' they said, when they finally stopped retching. They couldn't could quite meet my eyes. 'I'm so sorry. That was a bit…full on. You know?'

'Not really,' said Flora. There was a challenge in her voice. *You're on our turf now*, it said. *It's our rules, not yours.* 'I mean, I'm not going to apologise for kissing Dez.'

Ma was already busy with a vac. 'It takes a bit of time for pinkers,' she said over her shoulder. 'It's not something they can help.'

'Right now I don't care a lot about pinkers,' said Flora. I could feel the anger flooding into her body. I guess we were all feeling a bit raw. 'I've just had a bunch of them trying to kill me.'

Gloria stared at her. 'To be fair, pinkers were going to kill me too.' They threw the smartcloth they were using to wipe their face into the vac. 'And I didn't ask you to apologise.'

Flora opened her mouth and I knew she was going to say something awful. Gloria didn't deserve her anger. I squeezed her hand to tell her to stop, and she shrugged. 'Whatever,' she said. 'I want something to eat. And then I want to sleep for a million years.'

I hustled up a quick stirfry while we waited for Park and Sal. Partly because Flora was hungry, but mostly because I wanted to do something that wasn't about fighting fucking OpSec. Something normal.

We didn't talk about the mission while we were eating. For a while it was almost like we were just friends getting together for a meal. Still no news came in from the absent groups. I was damn sure Bo and Flora knew something. I cleared the dishes, and made a brew.

'So you'd better tell me about the others,' said Ma, looking at Bo. 'Something happened, yes?'

I could see the muscles working in Bo's jaw. 'I don't think Sally's group is coming back,' he said. 'They hit trouble. First some skinners at Djuna Station that made them late. And then Rioka picked up a report about a firefight on Rue Rabal in the Ninth and after that there wasn't a peep from Sally. OpSec sent in drones and troops, orders to capture or kill.'

'And?'

'We didn't hear anything after that. We don't know what happened.' His voice broke, and I saw Jenna take his hand under the table.

Ma took a deep breath. 'What about Park?'

'As far as we know, he's still on his way back.'

'Did he know about Sal?'

'Park doesn't know about the firefight, but he'd put two and two together, like we did.' Bo rubbed his eyes. 'She might have contacted him privately, of course...'

'Park's not answering any pings,' said Ma. 'He might be going to find Sal. But it's not like him to risk his team.'

I thought about Park and Sally. They were such a strange pair, but you knew there was this deep bond between them. Yeah, he probably would go after her. If it were Flora, I'd be doing exactly that, even if I was 99.999 per cent sure she was already dead. Just in case…

I cleared my throat. 'Park'd know how to get to the Ninth underground.'

'He should have told us,' said Ma. 'If he was changing plans like that, he should have told us.'

'He probably didn't want to argue with you.'

She didn't have anything to say to that.

'I guess we just have to wait,' said Jenna. Her voice was hard, like she was keeping back a flood of emotion, and her eyes, usually such a brilliant blue, were so dark they seemed black. 'We got the job three quarters done, anyway. It will put the plans for the Wall right back.'

'Yeah, a brilliant success,' said Bo savagely. 'Except a lot of us ended up dead and missing.'

'We know the risks,' said Ma evenly. 'And we take them. If we don't take them, we're dead anyway.'

All of us were silent for a while. That was the truth, and we all knew it.

'We don't really know what happened,' Bo said at last. 'We don't know how she ended up in the Ninth.'

'It's plain enough,' said Ma. 'There was a fire fight and an explosion…'

It was the way the old timers did things, the way the Alchems did things. The way my Da did it. If there was a chance of being captured, they made sure that all OpSec found was a corpse. You can't interrogate a dead brain. Everything it knows dies with it.

Then I remembered the comms. Shit.

'If they get Sally, they'll get Brian Mac's comms,' I said.

If they did, we'd be screwed, and not only because we wouldn't be able to use them any more. It would also mean that OpSec would know we were using a lot higher tech than they realised. They'd stop underestimating us.

'Maybe they'd be destroyed in the explosion,' said Bo.

'No way. They're practically indestructible.' I had another, worse thought. 'If OpSec tried pull one apart to see how it worked… Brian Mac warned me. Somehow he put a black hole inside those things.'

'What does that mean?' asked Jenna.

'I don't know,' I said. 'But there wouldn't be much left of Newport City.'

'Great,' said Bo. 'Good news all round.'

'You look exhausted, Bo,' said Ma gently. 'So do you, Flora. Go to bed.'

'I don't think I could sleep,' Bo said. 'I'm still so wired…'

He stood up, swaying slightly, went over to the couch and slumped down, closing his eyes.

'Give me the comm,' I said. 'I'll see if I can get a rise out of Park.'

Bo opened his eyes. His suitbelt was where he'd slung it when he came home, beside him on the couch. He unclipped the comm and handed it over. As I took it there was a buzz.

'What is it?' said Bo, hauling himself up.

'A signal. Faint. Some static.' I checked. 'It's not Park. It's from Sally's comm.'

'Don't respond,' he said.

I couldn't hear anything now. I plugged the piece into my headstent, switched in and waited.

'Shut it off,' said Bo. 'It's probably OpSec, fishing.'

'Shhh,' I said. Mindtalking's hard, you need to concentrate. And then:

'Bo, Bo, it's me, Stel…can you hear me?'

Erin

Ami being back makes me feel a whole lot better. I've got a friend. How pathetic is that? I think of the look on Dez's face when she brought her in: she was watching me with this kind of pity. So sad, the soapie star who doesn't have any friends that aren't made of carbon fibre.

I've never had anyone pity me before. I don't like it. Pity is only one step from contempt.

At first Ami doesn't seem at all changed by whatever Dez has done to her. She's horrified by the state of me. 'Darling, you need a bath. And your hair? What are you thinking? If Dervin sees you, he'll go spare.'

'They don't have baths here,' I say. 'And I don't think I'll ever see Dervin again, so it doesn't matter.'

She shifts into nanny mode, the voice she uses when I'm being difficult. 'Erin Saba, stop it right now. This is madness. I'll find the bathroom and get some lovely bubbles happening, and then we'll do your hair.'

I try again. 'They don't have baths in the banns. And I don't give a shit about my hair. Dervin's not going to see it.'

This time Ami blinks. She's quiet for a few seconds. 'You deactivated Dervin?'

I laugh, for the first time in what feels like ages. 'I wish. He's a prick, and he always was a prick, and he deserves it. No, I've just run away.' I pause, wondering how to explain, wondering if Ami can adjust to a new world without baths, where Erin Saba isn't a celebrity. It's not like I'm finding it easy…

'It's different now. We're in the banns, where the fleshers live,' I say. 'On the plus side, I never have to talk to Dervin again.'

This time Ami is quiet for a bit longer. What she says next surprises me.

'I don't like him either,' she says. 'I never liked the way he treated you.'

I stare at her. The old Ami would never have said anything bad about Dervin. Her job was to make sure that I did what he said.

'Still, being in the banns is no reason to abandon your personal grooming,' she goes on. 'You are a super plus celebrity and you should look your best at all times.' She pushes me onto a chair and pulls out a comb.

I feel better when Ami does my hair. Maybe it's just the sense that someone is paying attention to me. I worry about that for a while, like maybe this sense that I'm disappearing if no one's looking at me is part of the celebrity DNA profile and there's nothing I can do about it. Or maybe it's just that for my entire life, being looked at is what I'm *for*. I don't have another reason to exist. Like seriously, from the first moment they put two little cells together in the baby farm, a celebrity is what I was destined to be. And now I don't have any reason to be Erin Saba.

The weird thing is that, although I feel a flood of panic when I think about that, there's a bit of me that isn't panicked at all.

There's a tiny piece of Erin Saba that's glad.

The walls are so thin in this piece of shit building I hear every time someone comes into the house. No sound control here, that's for sure. Even if they don't press the buzzer, the front door wheezes every time it opens. I can hear voices, though I can't make out what they're saying. I can hear the steps as people move about the front room. There's quite a bit of movement.

I'm missing my lovely apartment. Not just the retro drinks cabinet, or the bathroom, or the balcony where I sit at night watching the stars through the Veil. I miss the quiet. It's not just the sense that everyone is touching everyone else, though that gives me the creeps. It's the constant noise. You can even hear every time someone uses the toilet. Nobody seems to care. I guess they're used to it.

But I'm tired of hanging out in this tiny room, like I'm forgotten baggage, an inconvenient thing that nobody really knows where to put. After a couple of hours, I decide to go into the front room. Get myself some water. I spend a couple of minutes nerving myself, and then I just walk out, Ami tagging along behind me.

It's really crowded, but I take a deep breath, push the nausea aside. I've got to get used to this. At first no one even notices I'm there. They're all crowded around a flesher I don't recognise, a skinny, pale woman with a shaved head who's sitting on the couch. I see with a slight shock that she's wounded, her clothes are splashed with blood. Her sleeve's rolled up on her right arm and Flora is dabbing a bad cut.

I move to the far end of the table where there's an empty chair, and Flora's gaze sweeps across me. No pity there: just contempt. But at least she doesn't tell me to get the hell out. For a moment I feel my courage quailing, but I take a few more breaths.

Get. Used. To. It. Erin. Saba. Ignore the sick feeling. Remember that nobody has to like you.

The woman flinches. 'Sorry, Stel,' says Flora. 'It takes a few secs for the painkiller to kick in.'

Painkiller. I could do with some of that myself. I watch it take purchase. Stel has been biting her lip so hard you can see the tooth marks when she stops. She sighs out and smiles, but it's a bad smile, wobbly. She looks like she's in shock.

'Thanks, Flora.'

'All good,' says Flora, putting away the medkit. 'Feel ready to talk?'

Stel nods, but she doesn't say anything for a while. Nobody prompts her, they just wait. All the fleshers are leaning towards her, there's a gentleness in their attention that I've never seen before, like they're all holding their breath, keeping themselves in readiness in case something breaks. It's this energy between them, I can almost see it, a kind of warm glow.

I shake my head. I'm imagining things again.

'Sally's dead,' says Stel. 'And so are Kipp and Tag. But I guess you already know that.'

I happen to be looking at Bel as Stel speaks, and I see the punch. It's only a flicker before she recovers herself, but for that microsecond I'm watching complete devastation. No tears. This woman is tough. No tears, but that doesn't mean she's not feeling it.

'Yes,' says Bel. She gently touches Stel's shoulder. 'We guessed. We were hoping...'

Stel nods. 'Sally knew they were coming, I don't know how. She gave me the comm, and told us all to get out of there, she'd take care of it. Kipp and Tag wouldn't leave, even when she screamed at them. I would have stayed too, but she told me that if they got the comm we'd all be toast. And she was going to taser me if I didn't leave. I knew she was right. She told me to run, so I ran...I ran back to the tunnel...'

'It wouldn't have made any difference if you'd stayed,' says Bo. 'Tag and Kipp should have come with you.'

'How do you know they're dead?' asks Dez. 'Maybe they just captured them?'

Stel shakes her head. 'I plugged into Kipp's suitcam. They shot Tag in the head.' She swallows hard. 'Sally grabbed Kipp, and then everything just... blew up. I was three blocks away by then and I felt the blast.' She swallowed. 'Stuff fell out of the sky. Bits of metal. A huge cloud of dust.'

Her voice drains to silence and she just sits there, twisting her hands.

'I'll leave a message for Park,' says Dez. 'Maybe he'll come back if he knows she's dead.'

'Maybe,' says Bel. 'Or maybe he'll go feral. Hard to know with Park.'

Nobody says anything for a while. We all watch as Bel puts her arm carefully around Stel's shoulder. She breaks down, sobbing into Bel's shoulder. I notice, with a strange cold part of me, that the nausea isn't nearly as bad as I might have expected. Why? Because I can see how the touch comforts Stel?

Bel waits until the storm of sobs has passed, and takes her out of the room. And then Flora turns on me.

'What the fuck are you doing here, anyway?' she says. 'This isn't pinker business.'

'Flora...' says Dez.

'The only business pinkers have is killing fleshers. Does this make you happy? You happy now?'

I shake my head. I can't think of anything to say. I know she just wants to take it all out on me, and in that moment I can't think of any reason why she shouldn't. But she's still staring at me, her jaw set, her eyes hard and unforgiving.

'No,' I manage to say. 'It doesn't make me happy.'

'There's no reason to be mean,' says Ami, who's been standing quietly behind me. 'Why is everyone so mean to Erin? She's super plus. If you want to be mean, be mean to Dervin.'

Ami's comment is so out of left field that it stops Flora in her tracks.

'Who the fuck is Dervin?' she says.

'My old agent,' I say. 'And Ami's right. He's an arsehole. He made me want to kill myself.' I stare back at her, suddenly feeling belligerent. 'They all did, all those people. I don't know what they were going to do to me, but I don't think I'd have been alive at the end of it. So maybe it *is* my business. How do you know it's not?'

I don't see anything soften in Flora's expression, but she lets it go, shrugs, turns away.

I breathe out.

I want a drink so bad.

Bo

What a mob. I drifted off to sleep listening to the wind rushing over the house, thinking of all the sleeping bodies her: a pinker soap star, her AI assistant, an avant pinker, data wizard Dez, warrior rock queen Flora, Ma the rebel leader. And Jenna and me, the water babies. A gang of weirdos.

In my dream we were all walking along a tightrope stretched between two towerblocks, silhouetted against storm clouds buzzing with OpSec drones. Jenna was in front of me. She tripped over something and I grabbed her and we fell, down, down, down, into some bottomless abyss. It was the sky, I thought. The sky and the water were the same.

Then Ma was shaking my shoulder. I sat up, confused. 'Get up,' she said. 'Get up now. We've got to go.'

I rubbed my eyes as Jenna sat bolt up right beside me. 'A raid?' she said.

'They're targeting Rue Ballard. We've got about fifteen minutes.'

'They're onto us?' I said. 'How do you know?'

'I got word. Solid word. Brian just told me.'

'Brian? Brian Mac?'

'Just get moving. *Now.*'

She didn't shout, it was just the tone in her voice. We all switched to pure adrenalin. I suppose that underneath we'd all been waiting for something like this. We'd all practised exit procedures, just in case. But I still couldn't believe it was really happening.

I can't remember getting dressed, snapping my suitbelt on, grabbing my pack. Ma had packed emergency supplies weeks ago, leaving the bags in the hallway where we always tripped over them. We'd all grumbled about it, but now I was grateful. Dez and Flora ran down to the cellar to grab any extras we might need and shoved everything else behind the deadwall.

Jenna hustled Erin and Gloria out of Dez's room, ignoring their protests. 'Just follow Bel. Okay? No time for questions.'

'Emergency protocols,' said Ami brightly. 'What fun!'

'Yeah, what fun,' said Jenna dourly. 'Maybe you could fiddle with the smartwear on those two. They look like pinkers.'

'Sure.' Ami touched Erin's coat and it turned bright, electric pink. Jenna laughed.

'No, we need to *hide*, Ami,' said Erin. She looked very pale. 'Think street chic. Dark clothes. Hoods to cover our faces.'

'Oh.'

It took about a second. I got to admit, that smartwear is pretty amazing.

We were standing in the front room ready to leave in three minutes flat. Flora was on a line to her father, switched into private. He obviously took a while to answer and when he did, she got angry. She stopped doing braintalk and started yelling at him out loud until she snapped the line shut in frustration.

'He won't leave,' she said.

'He knows the drill,' said Dez uneasily. 'He's been through a lot of raids.'

I think we all knew this wasn't like other raids.

We were splitting into two groups: Ma with the pinkers out the front, the rest of us out the back. The plan was to meet at the warehouse that led to Brian Mac's lab. Stel was leaving with Ma and would just head home to the Third through the tunnels. We thought she'd be safer if she stayed away from us.

I glanced out of the door into Rue Ballard. It was dead quiet. A soft curtain of rain swept along the rue. The lights were out in Café Boite, the houses shuttered and dark.

Dez threw out a field as far as the corner and we watched Ma's group leave. Then Dez slammed the door shut and we ran to the back garden. Same deal, throwing out a field to block any drone sensors, running like hell until we hit the end of the field. From there we'd be sneaking from corner to corner, every sense on high alert for Aps or militia. Dez had installed fields in all our suits, but fields wouldn't fool human eyes. And no fleshers were allowed out in the streets after dark.

'Five minutes and thirty seconds from waking to the corner,' said Dez, flashing me a grin. 'Not bad.'

'Could be better,' said Flora. 'The pinkers slowed us down.'

They hadn't, but I knew that Flora was dark about Kojo and would snap my head off if I said so, so I didn't argue.

The streets were still empty and quiet. The rain eased to a soft mist and the few lights that were burning were haloed in silver.

Brian Mac. Now that was a surprise. I thought I'd never see Brian Mac again, but I should have known better. He'd been top of the wanted list for weeks, ads on the official tubes all day long with a huge reward for information. You'd think there'd be nowhere in Newport City, not even in the Outer Banns, where he could hide. For a moment I felt sincere admiration. Crafty bastard.

When we turned the corner into Rue Chiang we heard the steady throb of transports. They were a way off yet, but approaching fast. We quickened our pace. As we hurried past the next corner I caught a glimpse of an OpSec transport heading towards Rue Ballard.

We didn't look back.

Once we got to the lab, everyone settled in, making themselves at home. Our emergency packs had expanding sleeping pallets, spare suitbelts and maybe a month's worth of dehydrated food, as well as a bunch of screens and other tech.

I could tell that Dez didn't like us being there. Brian Mac's lab was her territory, and suddenly it was full of people. She got all prickly and told everyone that they weren't allowed to touch the tech. As I rolled my eyes she got onto what was left of the dark tubes to see if anyone in the Second knew what was going on.

There were already reports of a lockdown raid down Rue Ballard. There was only one vid, taken from a towerblock a couple of streets away so you couldn't see any detail. Lots of hardware, lots of militia, all very focused on that one street. Flora was looking over Dez's shoulder, and I could almost hear her heart drop. Café Boite was right in the middle of it.

'Nothing from Rue Ballard?' she said.

I knew what she was thinking. If no one was making vision in Rue Ballard, it was probably very bad. When something like this happened, there was always someone taking some sneaky vids. Dez did some more searching and shook her head. Only the one.

'See if you can get in close,' I said.

She zoomed in, but it was bad quality and dissolved into pixels. You couldn't see what the hell was happening. Dez switched into a Newport City infonews channel, just on the off chance. A blue-skinned AI glamour-girl was reporting that security forces had launched raids on a suspected terrorist cell in the Second Bann. There was a bit of 3D footage of fleshers being hauled out of their homes, their hands on their heads. I recognised the houses, but the faces were too blurry in the spotlights. Everyone, adults and children, was lined up on the street. This time the camera zoomed in. Official ops, propaganda for the pinkers.

We all flinched. Kojo was sitting cross-legged in the road with everyone else, his hands on his head. No sound, the only noise was the newsreader droning on about protecting Newport City from flesher terrorists, but you could see the militia were shouting at them. One of them kicked Kojo in the head and he fell forward on his face.

Dez took Flora's hand and squeezed it.

'I should have tried harder,' said Flora. 'I should have just gone and got him.'

'If you had, you'd be in that street,' I said. My voice sounded harsh even to me. 'We only just got out in time.'

Dez

The lab was probably about as big as our house, but somehow it felt much smaller. I guess the lack of walls made me much more conscious of other people. And I didn't have my cellar retreat when things got too much.

All these damn people, trying not get in each other's way. Some of them pinkers who would freak out if they were touched, and one of them Flora, who was ready to clock any pinker for what was happening to her father. Everyone was scratchy, even Ma.

But hey, thanks, Brian Mac. This was probably the safest place in the whole twelve banns. He had done a bunch of dimensional wizardry that meant they couldn't find the room even with spatial recons, no one could get in without a gene key and both doors had mini-veils. Even having a gene key wasn't enough: if they didn't know about the veils and how to disable them, they'd fry as soon as they walked through the doorway.

On short rations, we had enough food for at least a few weeks: besides the supplies we brought with us, Brian Mac had a stash of longlife nutrition, Anthropological Police issue. There was a filter plugged straight into some water source so we'd never die of thirst, even if we starved. I guess he had imagined he'd have to hole up here, too. It was kind of surprising that he hadn't hunkered down in the lab when everything went toxic with Morro in Newport City. But then again, I knew why. He didn't want to be trapped. Like we might be trapped too.

OpSec couldn't get in, but we couldn't leave, either.

The raid on Rue Ballard meant they had specific intel on us, and us running away proved our guilt. We were on the tubes now, information wanted.

'Hey,' said Bo, who spotted it first. 'We're famous!' He flicked up a screen so we could see, and we all gathered round. They had ID mugshots of Bo and me, from when we worked in the foodtowers a couple of years before. And then this really old 3D image of Ma, one I'd never seen before. She was running, caught mid-step as she pointed at something we couldn't see.

It was the Ma we'd heard about but never seen. She was wearing some kind of black pantsuit, her suitbelt low on her hip, some heavy duty gun slung over her shoulder. Her hair was cut very short, with a white lightning flash dyed into the black. She looked very cool. Very dangerous.

Bo froze the screen and stared. 'Wow, Ma,' he said. 'You were hot.'

I swear Ma was blushing. 'Brian told me he'd killed everything they had on me,' she said.

'Everything he could find,' I said. 'They must have had this in some archive and someone started putting two and two together.'

'OpSec adding things up is bad news,' said Ma. 'But it was bound to happen.'

Mostly likely they'd managed to track my last invasion of the mainframe back to Rue Ballard. Maybe security bots had traced the connection before they showed any kind of visibility. I thought back carefully over the whole disaster: before the security bots had begun sniffing, there hadn't been any kind of surveillance movement at all. But maybe they had figured out how I did data copying. I had thought that no one had a handle on that: it was hyper discreet, even by OpSec standards. Up to now, I'd thought it was untraceable.

The more I thought about it, the worst I felt. If that was the case — and it was certainly the most likely case — everything that was happening in Rue Ballard was my fault. It would be obvious to even the dimmest tool in OpSec that whoever had gone in was connected to the attacks on the Wall.

Everyone in the street was a suspect. Our friends, our neighbours, Kojo. They wouldn't show any mercy.

I'd known going in was a risk. And right now it looked like I'd gambled everything and lost. My home. That little house that Ma had worked so hard for. Maybe I'd never see it again. Maybe the whole street was rubble and all our friends were dead. Or worse…

This was too painful to even think about. I pulled myself up, tried to focus on what to do now.

First things first. Ma had been in contact with Brian Mac. That was a bunch of news on its own, and she hadn't said a word. She always kept things close to her chest, and I kind of understood why, but it drove me up the wall. It was time she came clean. I wanted to know how he got the heads up on the Rue Ballard raid. More importantly, what else did he know? Did he have a way in to the hyper-secure command network that we still couldn't locate? We knew it existed, we just couldn't find it.

Bo and I told Ma we wanted a quiet chat. She gave us a look that said she knew exactly what we wanted to talk about, but to my surprise she nodded. We made a brew and retreated up the ladder to the mezzanine and sat together on the bed. Bo got straight to the point.

'What's the deal with Brian Mac, Ma?'

'I'm not sure I should tell you.'

A flash of irritation ran through me. 'God, Ma. It's too late to protect us.'

'I'm thinking of him, not you,' she said sharply. 'What you don't know won't harm him. It's better if everyone thinks he's dead.'

'Okay, but now we know he's not dead,' Bo said. 'So you might as well tell us what's been going on.'

'I mean, how long have you been in touch?' said Dez.

'A couple of weeks,' said Ma. 'He pinged that private line.' She paused. 'When I last saw him, I thought he was heading off to shoot himself in the head.'

Oldtimers. But I'd read Brian Mac's diary. He never had any intention of killing himself. 'He's a survivor,' I said.

'Yes.' She paused. 'The one thing I do know is that he was out in the dasht somewhere. But now he's back in the banns.' She paused again. 'I think.'

'You're not sure?'

'He could be anywhere. Those magnetic comms have a long range, don't they?' I nodded. 'Well, he's somewhere close enough to use those comms, and close enough that he can get intel. And honestly, that's all I know.'

'But Ma, if he can get into OpSec's secure comms…'

'Yeah, I know, but I'm pretty sure he doesn't have access. He would have told me.'

'So how did he know about the raid, then?' Bo was getting impatient now.

'It's not like there was time to go into any detail,' Ma said. She was getting annoyed too. 'I think someone leaked it to him.'

'Well, can't you ask him?'

'He probably wouldn't tell me. Look, Brian's got dirt on a lot of people, and he can be ruthless. And maybe even in OpSec there are people who are worried about what's going on there. He tells me there's been a huge clampdown in Newport City. So maybe people are going to be…less loyal if they think their necks are next for the chopping block.'

Bo and I sat back, absorbing this thought. 'So maybe we've got allies inside OpSec?' said Bo.

'More the enemy of my enemy is my friend, sort of thing. But that's Brian's business.'

Bo stirred. 'I wouldn't trust anyone from OpSec as far as I could throw them.'

'I wouldn't either. Neither does Brian. Which is why it's better that Brian keeps all that to himself.'

I thought of all the stuff we didn't know, all the time we didn't have. All the tech lying around the lab. I didn't dare to touch some of it. 'Do you think he'd come? We need all the help we can get right now.'

Ma shrugged. 'Maybe.'

'If you ask him?'

'I don't know.'

'Ask him.'

'I have to find him first,' she said. 'He's gone offline.'

Bo

It was strangely comforting to think that Brian Mac was still with us. I thought about all the years we'd known him. I'd hated him on principle, like I hated every Ap, but all that time he was looking out for us. He was the tall, skinny, weirdo Ap striding around the rues in his long red coat. Sometimes I could just make out his bloodshot eyes behind those dark goggles.

How many times had I felt his hand on the back of my neck, coming home from a gig or scrounging for homer parts in some old scrap shop? 'You keeping out of trouble, Bug?' I thought he was persecuting me. That was before I knew that Flynn was a pinker, before I knew that my Da had worked with Brian Mac. Yeah, Brian Mac was looking out for his best friend's son. My guardian angel.

What's an enemy? It all seemed just a matter of circumstance, not something fixed or predestined. It made all this suffering and death seem more pointless.

I spent most of my time watching the official channels. I couldn't help myself. I felt responsible for what was happening in the banns, I felt I had to watch what we had unleashed, like it was a duty. I knew this new crackdown was because of the attacks on the Wall. I kept telling myself that if we didn't stop them building another Veil, even more people would be dead, but it didn't make me feel any better.

We knew Kojo was still alive. Whenever they covered the Rue Ballard lockdown, he was pushed to the front, like he was the star flesher terrorist. He was gaunt, his face bloodied and grim. Flora had tried to contact him, but no dice. She was frantic, boiling with rage and anxiety. She didn't sleep, didn't eat. It was all Dez could do to keep her from heading to Rue Ballard and taking on OpSec single handed.

Rue Ballard was curtained at either end. As far as we could tell they didn't bother to arrest anybody: they just turned the whole street into a prison. On the dark tubes people were saying that there was no food left, that people were eating what was in their gardens. There was a fire in the street and the militia stood and watched as two houses burned to the ground. The only reason it didn't spread further was that a violent rainstorm rolled across the Second Bann.

We'd been underground for two days, but I was already losing track of time. It hated not seeing daylight. Somehow there hadn't been a blowup, but everyone was edgy. Dez was going through the data crystal that had been rescued from Morro's lair to see if there was anything we could use. Ma was spending a lot of time on deep lines, trying to find out who was safe, who wasn't, trying to co-ordinate something that she wasn't ready to talk about. The pinkers mostly retreated to the mezzanine, where they were doing whatever pinkers do. I was lying on my pallet in my corner, watching the tubes on my lenscam.

'Stop it.' Jenna sat down next to me. 'It's what they want.'

I was watching a stream of people being led out of a towerblock in the Ninth in single file, their hands above their heads. The street was lined with OpSec transports, milita, steel cages, two drones circling overhead.

'Please, Bo, turn it off.'

I flicked it off and squinted up at her. 'I know it's what they want,' I said. 'But I feel like I have to see it, to see every second of it.'

'You don't.' She kissed me on the mouth. 'They traumatise us, and then they do it all over again by putting our trauma all over the tubes. They want us to feel powerless.'

I studied her face. She was so beautiful: that clear gaze, those mismatched eyes, that full mouth. I loved this woman so much. There were lines around her eyes that hadn't been there when I first met her. She looked exhausted, kind of bruised. She still hadn't got over the injury from a couple of months before, you could see that the pain was chronic.

'I wish we could have some time together,' I said, my lips close to her ear. 'Just you and me.'

'There's no just you and me right now,' she said sadly, brushing my hair back from my face. 'We'll have to save all that up for another time.'

'When we're old and grey.'

She laughed. 'Yeah, if we live that long. But listen. Every moment. Every moment is precious. We make every moment an eternity.'

How long had Ma had with Flynn? Long enough to have us. That was it. Sometimes when Ma talked about Flynn, there was a light in her face that made me realise what she must have been like when she was young. But there was something heartbreaking in it too, because remembering Flynn meant remembering losing him, the ache of his absence. After all these years it still hurt. Would Jenna have that look in her eyes one day? Would I?

I stroked Jenna's cheek. 'We'll make sure there's lots of moments,' I said.

She smiled. 'Are you hungry?' she said.

'Starving.'

'How about I rustle up some of those delicious dehydrated carrots and greens?'

'Sounds marvellous.'

I watched her fiddling about the galley kitchen, switching on the lenscam again out of habit and then flicking it off. I was so bored. I walked to the bathroom cubicle and stared at my face in the mirror, trapped behind the surface like a prisoner staring out of a window.

I wanted to go out into the streets, to walk around, to see my steadies, to go for a drink, to forget what was happening. I wanted to face the usual kinds of danger, to feel the usual anger and resentment, to be pissed off in the usual powerless, depressing way.

But I wasn't going anywhere. Outside there'd be all kinds of tech sniffing for us, everything from drones to nanobots. The Aps would have our mugs tattooed on their eyeballs. We were holed up for the duration. Unless something forced us out.

Erin

Somehow, in this bizarre underground lab, I can breathe out. It's all one big room with a mezzanine that we kind of share when people want a bit of space. Ami, Gloria and I hang out there most of the time. Downstairs is full of all this weird shit, tech I've never seen before, but everything has a place.

There's space around all the objects. You can tell that it belonged to a pinker.

Ami is trying out some new hairstyles on me – she says I need a new look for banns living - when Dez clambers up the ladder. 'You wanted the reports on you?' she says. 'Here they are.'

She pulls up a screen, and I watch it fill up with text. Suddenly I feel sick, I don't know why. My first thought is that I don't want to read it.

'It's pretty interesting,' says Dez. 'It's like the plot of one of your soaps. '

I don't move. She glances at me, and starts to read out one of the reports. I can feel my ears getting hot. Am I embarrassed? Maybe I'm embarrassed.

So John Mecha had it in for me from the beginning: he'd wanted a friend of his in the role. He was usually a big voice in casting decisions, but the higher ups had been looking at the rethrill ratings and decided that I was the one. Mecha had some major fights over that with the director, Joh. Well, even I knew that, the conflict between them had been on all the gossip channels, although at that point I didn't realise it was about me.

Dez shows me the texts between Mecha and Joh. I'm shocked, I hadn't picked Joh as a snoop, although I know that the soaps unit was in close contact with the brass in Newport City Council.

'Maybe he didn't pass them on,' says Dez. 'OpSec probably just tapped the network. They spy on everyone.'

'Everyone?'

'You wouldn't believe the stuff they've got in there. They know every time a pinker takes a shit. Your apartment was basically a spy machine. Sensors built into every unit. Until I disabled the connection, Ami sent data in to OpSec every sixty seconds. They recorded everything you did. Down to your eye movements.' She studies my expression. 'You didn't know?'

No, I hadn't known that. I mean, I never said what I was thinking out loud, mostly, and I was always careful in public. But my apartment was my haven, I had kind of assumed that I was safe there. Of course I knew there were cameras in the hallways, movement sensors, that kind of thing, security to keep us safe from any fans that got a bit enthusiastic, but this was... more personal.

I stare at the screen. 'I feel so naïve.'

'Don't worry, we've all been naïve,' says Dez. She almost touches me, and stops herself just in time. 'I got everything that was tagged for Erin Saba. There's a lot, so I put the personal files first. I'll just leave it with you, hey? I've got a lot to do.'

'Thanks.' I clear my throat. 'Really, thanks.'

I watch her climb downstairs and then I start scrolling.

I'm not shocked that OpSec has records on me. They basically warned us in celebrity school: all those classes about 'propriety'. Being a celebrity, they told us, came with prominence and privilege, which meant added attention and added responsibility. We knew what that meant, we were told the stories of celebrities gone bad, and we were all careful. I thought I knew how things worked.

I had no idea. The more I read, the more of a fool I feel.

I even have my own individually assigned human monitor. I gather from the records that this only happens when they start getting suss about a person: everyone else just has bots. Mine's pretty recent, it happened after all the publicity after the hospital raid. The monitors don't have names,

mine signs their analyses AD435-d40-d40, their clone-type plus some iden-
tifier. I recognise the type and begin to get a picture of this clone: one of
those whey-faced security techs, bland as tofu, immaculate uniform, obeys
every rule. We used to laugh about them in celebrity school.

I'm not laughing now.

It seems that when Mecha lost the argument and I was cast in *Ebolastic*,
he decided that I was going down. He had been sending in 'observations'
about me from day one. He thought I was too curious because I liked knowing how things work. He hinted that I was taking notes about security
protocols. He 'worried' that I hung out with the extras. Even my research
for the role was suspicious: he was 'concerned' that I seemed to have an
unhealthy interest in flesher society. He made shit up, things I was supposed
to have said that I wouldn't have said in a million years.

He was poison.

But in the end, it was the incident in the hospital that tipped things
over. Like I thought, someone decided that my response wasn't 'normal'.
Anything that isn't normal is a bad sign in Newport City. On top of the slan-
ders that Mecha was sending in every day, that was enough to make me an
'observable'. They did an analysis of my records and decided I warranted
'special surveillance'.

OpSec knew that Mecha had it in for me, but somehow they decided that
was my fault. Fuckers.

Once you're under special surveillance, everything you do looks like
guilty behaviour. The fact that I kept watching the bombing in Block 9 and
had to be dragged inside was very suspicious, apparently. Asking questions
of the extras was suspicious. My obsessive watching of the tubes afterwards
was practically proof that I'm a subversive, plus they noted the exact dila-
tion of my eyes when I recognise the extras being flesher terrorists. Turning
Ami off because I was sick of her babble was very suspicious indeed (they
underline that bit) even though all I did was drink myself into a stupor and
go to bed.

AD435-d40 decides pretty fast that I'm definitely in league with pinker
radicals and possibly fleshers. I can't see one thing in all the records they
have on me that proves anything, it's more this circumstantial net of
dozens of tiny things: me pumping that security guy at the reception for

information, me going to a particular nightclub where a known pinker radical went on the same night. I mean, they're watching me so closely they must know that at this point I'm not talking to anyone except Ami. But there are dark spots in the poorer blocks of Newport City where the surveillance coverage isn't total, and because I'm filming *Ebolastic* I'm spending a lot of time out there. Their spybots lose me on two occasions, even though I don't know I'm being spied on, which means I'm probably meeting with conspirators. 'Obviously,' says Mister AD435-d40 (he has to be a Mister) 'Saba is aware of our surveillance and is taking active steps to counteract it.'

Fuck. Me.

Reading this shit makes me dizzy. I'm seeing my life through this distorted mirror. It's all so plausible that I wonder if somehow I really did do all the things that they thought I was doing. Maybe there's another Erin Saba who takes over when I'm not looking.

Evading the bots seals my fate. That's when they decide to get rid of me. Arresting a celebrity like me is a bit of a problem, they don't want that kind of scandal, it reflects badly on the clone program. But they don't have to do that. They just use the behavourial map that goes with my clone-type and conditioning. Under a certain kind of pressure, my kind of personality can be easily driven to suicide. They've done it before, apparently.

I suddenly remember Evan Connor, a guy who did comedy soaps and ended up taking an overdose a couple of years ago. I only knew him slightly, but he'd always been kind to me, and a lot of people were sad at what happened to him. So out of the blue, they said. So tragic. But there'd been those rumours too, whispered in the clubs under the loud music. Even at the time I thought it didn't quite add up.

Poor Evan.

So Mister AD435-d40 sends out the orders to apply the pressure. They tell John Mecha to harass me at work. They *tell* him to do that, although nobody orders him to touch me. Maybe they know he has a fetish and they use it. My name goes out on the whisper network. People start avoiding me.

And it works. Of course it works. I remember something this council official told me in a club once, trying to impress me: they can predict the behaviours of Newport City citizens 99.99 per cent of the time. 'Even me?' I said, giving him that flirtatious look.

'Yeah,' he said. 'Even you.'

God, he was a creep.

There's a few analyses on my deteriorating condition that I can barely read because of the cold smugness behind every word. 'Saba is now reaching the desired state,' says Mister AD435-d40. 'Predicted self-termination tonight or potentially tomorrow.'

I check the date. He was 100 per cent correct. I tried to kill myself that night. That would have been the end, if Dez hadn't come along and stopped me.

I flick out the screen and stare at nothing. My head is still spinning, but it's not that weird dislocated feeling any more. I never did the things they said I did. But they deliberately decided to make me so depressed and paranoid that I'd kill myself.

I'm so angry I think my brains are going to explode out of my skull.

Ami is leaning against the wall in standby mode. 'I'm so angry I think my brains are going to explode out of my skull,' I tell her. I have to tell someone.

She blinks into action and fixes me with that mineral-blue gaze. 'Why?'

I don't answer, I just call up the screen again and point. She plugs in and vacuums up the data. There's maybe a couple of seconds while she processes what I've read.

'I recommend exploding other people's brains out of their skulls,' she says. 'Specifically AD435-d40.' She pauses. 'If he has any brains, of course.'

I laugh. I need to laugh. Besides, I think Ami just made her first ever joke.

Bo

Things I did that annoyed me: sitting staring at the wall until my backside ached. Walking around in circles until my backside stopped aching. Obsessively checking the security cam monitors every hour, on the hour. Today I'd checked them four or five times already. I had another look.

The rue outside was empty, bathed in soft afternoon sunlight. Only a few blocks away fleshers were being terrorised, people were being hurt and broken. Shouldn't that pain be visible somehow? Some odd change in the weather, a shadow that trembled in the air, a distortion in the light? No, nothing. All I could see was a pleasant afternoon on a quiet street.

Something moved and I sharpened up the focus. What looked like a patch of light on the road began to shine more strongly and started flowing up a wall. I blinked. As I watched, it resolved into something three dimensional. A water person. It was standing there without a shadow, the light that passed through it breaking into a bright rainbow.

It knew I was watching. I was sure of it.

Then, without quite knowing how, I was outside in the street. It was such a relief, real sunlight on my face, real air. The water person was straight across the rue, rippling like a mirage. I walked towards it slowly, not wanting to startle it, as if I were approaching a feral neka.

Where the face should have been wasn't exactly blank: the surface moved, tiny rivulets swelling and contracting. Although it had no eyes, I could tell that it was looking at me. It didn't move until I was close. Then it turned and began to walk away, raising one transparent hand, beckoning me to follow.

I was amazed at its motion, soft and billowing, riding on the air like a leaf blown by the wind. I tried to get a little closer, but it drew away, always keeping me at the same distance. I didn't really notice where we were going. The only thing I was aware of was the water person.

Those sounds again: that insectile whispering, rain falling into long grass, the fluttering of wings. The light grew brighter. The water person stopped and turned towards me, and then it dissolved into a dazzling, shimmering sphere that grew larger and larger until I could feel its surface pressing against me. For a moment I felt it cool on my skin, and then I was inside.

Slowly everything around me came into sharp focus. I was alone on a vast, empty plain. The land rolled away from me in soft undulations of bare rock, astonishingly coloured: crimson and yellow, black and deep purple. The valleys were filled with water, its glasslike surface shining a dull gold in the bright sunlight. I couldn't see anything living: no grass, no trees, no sign of animals. The air was utterly still and silent.

My skin tingled, as if a protecting film had been peeled away. It was so cold that my throat stung with every breath of air. I looked up into the infinite, blue emptiness of a clear sky.

Somehow I understood that this was before everything I knew, before the wind blowing in the grass or the fluttering of insects. And yet something was alive. I sensed it around me, enveloping me, entering me with every breath I took. I closed my eyes and felt myself disappear.

I was water. Water filled the darkness in my skull and ran through my veins. My bones softened. I sank into the ground, flowing over stones, through cracks and holes, growing colder and colder in the darkness. I joined with other waters, calmly flowing through them as they flowed through me, until there was no them, no me: only one edgeless, unbroken expanse, endlessly flowing. There was no before or after, nothing other than the timeless tranquillity of the water, the rapture of its caress. My mind slowly unwound, my thoughts blurred, my memories grew fainter and fainter.

No.

Quite suddenly, I was terrified. No, I couldn't let this happen. I couldn't let go of my life. My self. I twisted violently upwards through the darkness. The water surged around me, a tightening spiral spinning faster and faster. I stopped struggling and let it carry me, spinning upwards until a circle of light exploded above me. I threw myself towards it, gasping for air.

I was in the street outside Brian Mac's. Then I was back in the lab, standing by the trapdoor. No one turned to look at me, no one took any notice. I called up the security cam and looked at the street outside. It was still late afternoon, the street was empty, bathed in sunlight. I'd been gone only a moment. Or had I been gone at all?

I thought about telling Jenna what had happened. Maybe she could help me understand. But when I tried to talk about the water she became afraid. What good would it do anyway, trying to explain something I didn't understand? I'd have to understand it myself first.

The water was showing me something. I was sure it was a memory. But whose memory? Not mine. The memory of water. Though maybe it was part of my memory too, because I was part of the water. I felt that very strongly. I was remembering a place long before people existed, a place and a time before place and time.

If the water can remember, what else can it do? Can it think? What does it think about us?

Who are we?

Dez

There's ventilation, or we'd all suffocate, but the air is stuffy and stale. It smells of mouths. We can all feel the walls closing in, we all know we're running out of time. After a couple of days, I'm itching to get out, just for a breath, just to look at something that isn't a wall. Our home is probably rubble by now, our friends in prison or dead. We're the lucky ones.

I watched the vids of Rue Ballard on the tube obsessively. *We knew the risk.* Yeah, but Kojo didn't. Kiko didn't. None of our friends knew that we were planning to bomb the Wall, although they all knew we were up to something. They probably hated us now because we got out, leaving them to deal with the blowback. I'd hate me too. I do hate me.

Ma was watching me. 'Let's make it worth it,' she said.

'It's never worth it. Not even one life is worth it.'

'No. It's bad maths.'

'Die fighting, or just die,' said Flora bitterly. 'Some equation.'

Her face was ashy, puffy around the eyes, a sadness there that I wish I could kiss away. We knew that Kojo was still alive, but even that was torture. Killing you isn't the worst that OpSec can do, there's so much worse. I know, because I opened the interrogation files. And then I wished I hadn't.

I don't tell Flora about that. I hold her close when we try to sleep. Her warm, strong body that is so fragile that I could weep.

At least there's work to do, for some of us anyway. Ma's put Flora and Gloria on the dark tubes, checking her network, seeing who's alive, who's available, who's where. I don't warn her that OpSec could well be monitoring these comms, she knows that as well as I do. *We know the risks.*

I don't feel lucky any more. So far it looks to me like we're gambling and losing. Ma doesn't agree: she thinks that the first throw has gone to us. If this is what winning feels like...

'There's millions of us,' Ma said. 'That's why we frighten them. They don't want us to wake up and find out how strong we are.'

I think about it. Sure, if we could get everyone to agree we might be a real threat. But getting fleshers to agree on anything is like herding nekas. And the truth is most of us are isolated and afraid, most of us are hiding in our burrows hoping the storm passes over our heads. And it's not like all fleshers are on our side. Some fleshers are all for OpSec, they do pretty well with how things are. The skinner gangs, the protection rackets, the thugs and deadshits. The people we used to have to look out for, before things got this bad. It's not only the Aps that made living in the banns dangerous. A lot of the shit comes from our own, especially in the Outer Banns.

Ma knows that as well as anyone, of course. When we lived in the Ninth she had to deal with those arseholes every day. The gangs that buy up supplies so they can squeeze the markets and make a killing, or demand credits so shijos don't accidentally catch fire. The snoops who alert the skinners for a fee when a child turns pubescent, the informants, the tossers and wheezers and prigs. The creeps who get a thrill of making other people afraid. It doesn't take many of them to turn a bann into a living nightmare, and as far as most Aps are concerned, those fleshers are just helping them do their job.

And that doesn't count all the broken fleshers who can't see outside their own heads any more, who will take you down in a flash because it's them or you, who can't imagine anything better because they've only ever known the worst. There's a bit of that in all of us. I know it's in me.

I don't know how Ma gets to be so optimistic when she knows all this shit in the marrow of her bones. But she keeps saying that she knows her people. That we hurt each other because we're being hurt. We need hope. Not the hope that the pinkers talk about, with their bullshit military projects with pretty names. Hope that the pain and killing will stop.

So now we're onto our very own Project Hope: bringing down the Inner Veil. Tomorrow, if possible.

It's actually totally impossible, but I've realised for a while that the impossible has never stopped Ma. I keep seeing that image of her running in that black suit. Even now, it makes me smile. She's a head shorter than I am, but in that image you can see her actual size, her will and determination. She's massive.

Sometimes it's hard, living up to Ma.

Back to the problem. There was a lot of data on the Morro crystal but a lot of it was irrelevant. The bits that looked like they might be useful were like that map Morro was obsessed with, doolally symbols and weird notations that I couldn't make head or tail of. There was some stuff about Veils, really old stuff, but it was in code or some other language that I didn't have a translator for, and even the bits I could puzzle out seemed partial, like the code had corrupted or half of it was missing. In the end I put it away and turned to the OpSec data.

The major obstacle was that you couldn't partly break the Inner Veil. It was all or nothing: if you took down one part, the automatic repair kicked in. It would be like punching water. I was pursuing a theory that the weakness was in the energy resources. Every energy source was directed to the Inner Veil as a default priority. So how to rewire it so all that energy goes somewhere else? To us, for example? There had to be a way. I had the blueprints of all the power stations in Newport City, so I uploaded them to a screen so I could take a proper look.

After a few hours, I figured that it was possible, but not for us. It would only work if every power station was redirected simultaneously, anything else would bring up the failsafe. You'd have to get someone through every layer of security into central control of every power station, all nine of them, disable the protocol and redirect the power. All at the same time.

On top of that, the protocols would have been changed since my adventures in the mainframe, so you'd need a decoder. Each station had a different protocol, and the only decoder we had was me. I figured out the odds. They were so close to zero it made no difference. Even then, I thought about it: I'd made it out of the mainframe, after all. But that was just me hoping for luck, and I'd already had more than my share of that.

I spent quite a bit of time trying to work out if it could be done by remote, but no dice. Each power station had a separate network, firewalled from the rest. OpSec were doing what I'd do if I were them. I guess with the power stations, they'd be thinking about pinker radicals, not fleshers. Or maybe that Chimera Project had made them realise that fleshers were a lot smarter than they had figured.

I could only do one station at a time. We needed nine of me. For a wild moment I wondered if I could split myself nine ways, but the memory of splitting myself in two hit me like a thump in the stomach. I couldn't do that to myself again. And in any case, there wasn't enough of me to go around.

Another dead end.

I decided to take a break.

Erin

For weeks now I've been in the middle of a storm. Or maybe it's more that I *am* the storm. Everything I thought I knew has cut loose and unravelled, all the certainties, all the rules. It's all been whirling around my head, or inside my head, or both, I can't tell the difference. It's like there's been this soundless howling all the time, *all the fucking time*. I don't know who I am any more.

The only thing that stopped the howling was martinis, but I'll probably never drink a martini again.

There's a lot of things I'll never do again. I'm not even sorry.

Ever since I saw that flesher in the hospital. Morro. Since I first saw Morro. I can still see him walking through that entrance, all the alarms going off, chaos erupting around him. And he's smiling, cool as rain, swaggering, tossing that baton up and down with one hand.

And now the storm is passing and all the flying bits and pieces are settling into a strange, new pattern. I don't really understand it, but somehow I know I can learn how to. For the first time since I can remember, I'm not shrivelling inside, waiting for the moment when I can have my next drink.

Whoever I was before was a lie. It was me lying to me and everyone else because everything was a lie and there wasn't any way of being truthful. Whatever happens now, I don't have to lie any more.

It's such a relief.

They told me Morro was dead. Something bad happened, no one's comfortable talking about him. I've got no right to feel sad about it, I never even spoke to him, but I do.

That sadness I feel, it's my sadness. I know I feel it.

And this anger? It's *my* anger.

I haven't told Gloria about the files Dez gave me, but they know that something is up.

'So,' they say, giving me a sly grin. 'You finally decided you want to live, huh?'

I meet their eyes, wondering how they know. Gloria's getting into street chic in a big way, their smartwear is all flesher combat gear, but with a twist: there's a shimmer in the detailing, a hint of sass in the cut. They've spent the morning painting their nails black with little silver knives.

'I guess so,' I say. I think about everything I read in those files, and the rage floods back, taking me by surprise. I swallow, trying to push it down. 'I realised that...'

'You realised what?'

'That...it's not my fault. What happened to me wasn't my fault. That the whole sick fucking system wasn't my fault.'

Gloria's silent for a while, pursing their lips, thinking. 'But you sure liked it while it was working for you,' she says.

I can't argue with that. I did. I feel myself blushing. 'I didn't know any better,' I say at last. It sounds weak.

'I think you did.' They flash me a glance, testing if I'm ready to hear. 'I'm a pinker too. I know how it works. Those little prickling doubts when you see something that doesn't make sense? When some part of you says, oh, that's bad, is that fair? But hey, that person is a bad person, everyone's saying so, and you're not a bad person, it won't happen to you...And then you push it all away, because if you don't, everything will come tumbling down.'

'There's the conditioning too,' I say defensively. 'Like, how it actually *hurts*...'

Another silence. 'Darling, from what I hear, the conditioning is pretty light on for celebrities. Me, I'm a lowly biobooth bitch. I'm designed to service people like you. When we do wrong, it's not just a headache.' Gloria leans towards me, their jaw clenched, and I flinch back. 'It was fucking fire in my *bones*, Erin. Every single moment. Because I'm wrong down to my fucking *chromosomes*. I felt it every single second. It never went away.'

The rage flickers up again, but this time I'm not just angry for me. 'So how did you deal with it?'

'There was another pain. The pain of not being me, of being so alone. And you know what? That was much worse.' They pause again, their eyes dark with memory. 'Ava rescued me. She got someone to fudge my records, she's very well connected. And she gave me a job in reception with a solid cover, so I could eat. I owe my life to Ava.'

That Ava was the scariest women I've ever seen. I try to imagine her having a soft side. I can't.

'Does it go away eventually? The pain?'

'Yeah. All that stuff can be undone. It just takes ages.'

'When you...touch people.' I clear my throat. 'Is it okay? Does it hurt?'

Gloria shakes their head. 'Some people,' they say. 'I'm okay with Ava. She feels safe. But no, I'll never be comfortable with anything more than that. You'd think I'd've got used to touching, working at the FeelGood. But I never actually saw it happen, you know? And the one time I...the one time...' They stop. I see Gloria's gone pale, they're actually retching.

I interrupt quickly. I think I can guess and I don't want to hear. 'You don't have to tell me anything.'

I wait while Gloria recovers. They study their nails, not looking at me. 'There's some pretty twisted people in Newport City,' they say. 'I guess we're all twisted...fleshers think we're all totally screwed up. Well, you can't blame them.'

I think about Morro, and then I think about the anger that Flora wants to take out on me. I think about things I've overheard, about people they know who have died, killed by OpSec. About how that little house where they sheltered me is probably rubble by now.

No, you can't blame them. We are screwed up. Every single one of us.

'Meeting actual fleshers is a bit of a mindfuck, hey?' I hear a new shyness in my voice. I'm a celebrity, I'm not allowed to be shy.

Gloria nods. 'But not in a bad way.'

No, not in a bad way.

There's a commotion downstairs and I peek over the rails. For a few minutes I'm certain that we're being raided, that even this safe house has been found, despite everything Bel said about it being off the maps. The fear, my god. It floods through me like ice, I can't even move. I'm sure my heart doesn't beat that whole time.

And then this guy scrambles up into the lab and everyone puts their tasers away. I relax, he's someone they obviously know. A bit of a lowlife, by the looks. But there's something odd about him, about how he moves. And then I realise: he's not touching people. He leaves space. He moves like a pinker.

A pinker. A few days ago I didn't even know that word. Now it's just there in my mind. Like I've changed lenses, and suddenly the whole world is a different colour.

Gloria looks down at the group and and gasps. 'I don't believe it,' they say. 'Brig fucking Mackintosh. Back from the fucking dead.'

Bo

Brian Mac looked a wreck. Wrinkled, grotty, unshaven, awkward, exhausted. I mean, he always was a bit of a mess, he never bothered to get rid of his scars or deal with his wrinkles, and he was doing timeslips 27/10 which would age a person. But despite everything, he still had a touch of smoothness about him. Enough of a tell to betray he wasn't a flesher.

He climbed into the lab and slowly straightened up. He wore a ragged dark coat, boots. Across his back was a scabbard. That damn sword. He still had it.

He looked around his lab. He didn't say anything, but you could tell he thought that we were making a mess of it. I had a flash of how astonishing it was when I first walked in when Jenna was hidden here, all clean, high space. It showed me a Brian Mac I hadn't known existed. Now we were all camping out, the space had lost some of its style.

Jenna made a brew and pretty soon we were bombarding him with questions. He answered quietly, patiently. There was something different about him, it wasn't just losing the goggles. Like he didn't have to prove anything any more.

It turned out that Brian Mac had been hiding out in Duiwel Island prison the whole time. It was deserted now. I still remembered the moment I'd seen the Veil go out as we crossed the Gilla that night. It just blinked and was gone. I didn't know then that OpSec had already disposed of all the prisoners, feeding them into their Eradicator to test its efficiency. And then the guards just turned off the Veil and scarpered. It was a little preview of what they wanted to do to us. But they did it to their own first…

That was an uncomfortable thought. I didn't quite know how to process it.

Brian Mac knew he couldn't hide in the banns. OpSec was out with DNA trackers, hot for revenge, and everywhere was crawling with skinners. Skinners have a particular grudge towards Brian Mac. So he had punted out there on the pod we had used to cross the Gilla Sea and set up camp. No wonder we hadn't heard a peep.

By the time he arrived on the island, his suit was almost out of juice and he'd run out of ammo. 'I thought I was pretty much done, but it turned out that all I had to do was switch on the power and crank up a little mini-Veil. The sword took care of any ferals. The Eradicator was still standing in the middle of the yard.' He rubbed his hands across his face. 'I can't describe what it was like there. Haunted. The whole place is full of ghosts. You hear them screaming at night.'

On Duiwel Island the prisoners grew their own food. Brian Mac had found a couple of uncontaminated growing spheres and had eked out the vegetables with dehydrated supplies that had been left behind.

He was about to say more when Flora interrupted, her voice tight. 'Do you know what's happening in Rue Ballard?'

Brian Mac glanced at her, his face softening for a moment. 'A little,' he said. 'But my access is limited.'

'Limited to what?'

'To what I can get out of the mole I've got in OpSec.'

'You trust them?'

'I don't trust anyone. They have to trust me,' said Brian Mac. 'Fair to say that if his higher ups hear about the perverse shit this contact's been into, they'd be liquidated. So they'd rather talk to me.'

'You're good at liquidating people, aren't you?' said Flora. 'It's what pinkers do.'

'Give it a rest, Flora,' I said.

She turned on me then. 'Kojo's in there,' she said. 'And not just Kojo.'

'I know about Kojo,' said Brian Mac. 'For the moment he's okay.'

'You could find out what they're planning to do with him,' said Flora.

'I can only get what my informant knows. He's not high ranking. If he grows a pair and shops me, or worse, if he panics, everything will go to shit.'

Dez took Flora's hand. 'We all feel the same, about Kojo, about everyone in the rue.'

'We do not all feel the fucking same,' said Flora. 'We went in after Bo, didn't we? But we leave Kojo for dead, yeah?'

'That's not how it is,' said Dez.

'That's how it looks.'

Flora and Dez were facing off now, both bristling.

Ma stepped in. 'You know we can't do it, Flora,' she said softly. 'We can't go in, all guns blazing. It's certain suicide.'

'Now you sound like Morro,' said Flora. 'Didn't he talk the same kind of crap when we wanted to get Bo out of that hospital?'

'That was then,' said Dez. 'We had Brian Mac in the precinct, and there wasn't anything like the wild security that's going on now. You know it's different now.'

There was a strained silence, and then Flora slumped suddenly, all the fight going out of her. 'God knows, I don't want to argue with you.'

To my surprise, Brian Mac reached out and took her hand. 'I'm sorry, Flora,' he said. 'I'm really sorry. But Bel's right on this. They've locked down Rue Ballard because going in guns blazing is exactly what they want you to do. I'm pretty sure they figured out what happened at the hospital and have put two and two together. Even OpSec can do that sometimes.'

Flora nodded, her face downcast.

'When they found that you'd scarpered, the first thing they did was work out who your associates were.' He let her hand go. 'The only way to get everyone out of there is to bring the whole thing down. The whole fucking thing.'

'It might be too late.'

'It's been too late for quite a while.' He cleared his throat. 'For what it's worth, there's no reports of any plans to kill. They need bait.'

'Bait.' Flora spat out the word. 'Yeah. That's all we are to them. Meat and bait.'

There was a silence, and then Brian Mac changed the subject. 'Listen, I've got something for you. The thing about Duiwel Island is that no one gave a fuck about it, least of all OpSec. Things were pretty sloppy out there. And, well, I had nothing to do. So I went into the mainframe, to find out what was there.'

A jumble of stuff, apparently. Old files that dated from before the Veils, from before Duiwel Island was a prison, when it had been some kind of funfair for the citizens of Newport. He also found a back door into OpSec Central that they'd forgotten about, because who would go back to Duiwel Island? Just before he left, Brian Mac had downloaded everything.

He fumbled in a pocket and held up a data crystal. 'This is for you, Dez,' he said. 'I doubt you know about this stuff. It's for top brass only, a closed database that they used to send the orders to shut down Duiwel. There's tactical plans in case fleshers decide to attack, codes for the emergency comms, all sorts of shit. I don't think they'll pick up that I've been in there.'

Dez's eyes gleamed. 'When did you leave?'

'Three days ago.' He leaned back, closing his eyes. 'Though it feels like three years. It's a fun ride getting to the Second, believe me.'

'They won't have had time to change the protocols,' Dez said. 'Just the codes.'

'They'll have backups. It's pretty vicious crypto, I couldn't get in myself, but you'll probably have no trouble.'

'Well, well, well,' said a voice from behind us. 'If it isn't Brig Mackinstosh.'

We'd been concentrating so hard we hadn't heard the pinkers coming down from the mezzanine. Brian Mac leapt out his chair, twisting so fast you almost couldn't follow the movement, the sword already in his hand. I began to see how he'd survived out there.

When he saw the pinkers, he didn't move for a few moments. Then he slowly sheathed the blade.

'Erin Saba,' he said. 'Now there's a turn up for the books.'

'And who am I?' said Gloria. 'Chopped liver?'

He smiled properly for the first time. 'Hello, Gloria.'

'That's a pretty amazing weapon you've got there.' Gloria studied his face. 'Can't say you look much better than when I last saw you. And then you were almost dead.'

'Life has been full of interest lately,' he said. His eyes kept straying over to Erin. 'And obviously not just for me. What the hell is Erin Saba doing here?'

'Darling, you know what? I'd have never picked you as a soap fan.'

'I've always been a sucker for a good soap,' he said. 'Helps take the edge off after a bad day.'

Erin was staring back at Brian Mac like he was the most exotic thing she'd ever seen. I guess she'd never seen a pinker like him. He started going red.

'I've seen you somewhere before,' she said at last. 'But I can't think where.'

'He's been all over the tubes for weeks,' I said.

Her eyes widened as it all clicked into place. This was the notorious rogue Ap, Newport's Most Wanted, Public Enemy Number One. She nodded politely, pinker-style.

'Pleased to meet you,' she said.

Dez

Maybe I was wrong about our luck. Maybe we hadn't spent it all.

The files Brian Mac had downloaded at Duiwel Island were the real deal, the information OpSec didn't want their subordinates knowing because it might affect morale. Plus, I found out, the stuff they wanted to hide from me.

I did some initial speed analyses, blurring through the data. Yes, they had plans on what to do if the banns went feral and rose up. They had picked up 'worrying signs' in a few areas. I recognised some of the activities they'd been tracking, but there were others I hadn't even heard rumours about: attacks on militia, on the Curtains, once even an invasion of an Ap precinct. Mostly in the Tenth and the Sixth.

OpSec believed that the people who brought down the operations on the Wall were from the Rift. They were talking about razing the Tenth entirely, if they could find a safe way to do it. 'Safe'. Huh. As far as I knew, the Rift was all skinner gangs, but on the other hand, I'd never been there. Bo went to a couple of gigs there and told me afterwards that he wasn't going back. It had a rep as one of the worst places in the banns, as bad as the Twelfth.

Maybe it was just that, a rep. Potentially a very useful one. Everyone, including Aps, stayed away from the Rift.

I zoned out of dataspace. Of course we knew that other groups were fighting OpSec. Ma had been in contact with people in every bann, trying to co-ordinate our different activities. I was surprised that we didn't know about the Rift though, especially if they were causing so much trouble. Though it could just be that OpSec was blaming the Rift for things they hadn't done, like the bombing of the Wall. I checked the data in a bit more depth. There seemed to be too many incidents, and they'd directly taped at least three of them to the Rift.

Maybe they were remnants of the Alchems. But most likely it was just people who were reading the writing on the wall, people with nothing to lose who knew as well as we did that if we didn't resist now, we might as well just walk out into the dasht and die.

I wondered what else we didn't know about. For the first time since getting back home from Newport City, I began to feel a flicker of hope.

This meant that the raid on Rue Ballard wasn't only a result of my raid on OpSec and the mission on the Wall, as we had thought. There were other reasons. I did another sweep, tagging Rue Ballard. The first thing that came up was a 3D of me. A bad one, the same image they had put on the tubes. It was part of a Project Chimera file.

They'd cracked my DNA. Even though I knew that it was only a matter of time, it was still a shock. Mind you, I wasn't as shocked as they were: they hadn't seen anything like me before. According to the Chimera Project, I was probably the most dangerous flesher in the banns. Thank you very much. Now they were specifically after me. I was marked a hot target, to be kept alive at all costs.

I waited until the dread in the pit of my stomach subsided, and then read on. The report was funnier than I expected. They had some bizarre ideas about my capacities: it seemed I could melt girders via remote, and that I was likely causing the conditioning of the Aps to break down with my deadly telepathic brainwaves. They were sure that it was me that had flooded the Eradicators.

I wondered how much these fantasies had to do with what Morro told them, he would have exaggerated everything just for the hell of it. According to them, I was some kind of super mutant, a nightmare freak that basically could fry anything I turned my laser vision on.

I wish.

They had some idea about my remote facility, but again, not much. They hadn't got hold of the report on the Ap that was shot in our front room, for example: somehow Brian Mac made that disappear completely. They couldn't work out if I exported data, and if I did, how I did it, but they knew that I'd been into their mainframe. They'd set a trap for me, in case I returned.

And I'd walked straight in. Maybe, even knowing this, I'd have gone in anyway? I don't know. Yes. No.

Yes. We're that desperate.

I was wasting time. One more sweep, this time for the crypto on the hypersecure comms. They called them 'deep comms', for the tactical stuff they didn't even want their own troops overhearing. It was, like Brian Mac said, vicious crypto. But hey, I'm even more vicious than that.

I loaded the codes into our system so I could output it to our suits later. I'd have to find out what the current code was before everyone could use it, but this information gave us the most important key. I did another pass, searching for anything about the Wall or the Inner Veil. Nothing much, and what was there I knew already. Okay. The next step was to look at the old files. I was very curious about these, god knew what was in there. But I was getting tired now.

Time for some more delicious dehydrated fungus soup.

I was hanging out with Flora – it was our turn on the mezzanine – when I got a ping on the silent line.

'Ignore it,' she said. She drew her finger lightly across my lips. 'You can check it later.'

I tried, but now I was distracted. Who'd be pinging me? When it went off again, I sat up. 'Sorry,' I said. 'I can't. We can't ignore anything.'

She rolled her eyes and flopped back on the bed as I flicked on the head-stent.

'Dez,' said a voice. I checked the source, but it was untrackable. It could be anyone.

'Who's this?'

Flora was making chopping movements. I motioned for her to wait.

'It's Redborg, my dear flesh. Now listen.'

'Shut the line, you dill.' Flora was looking worried now. 'They'll trace you if you talk too long.'

'It's Redborg,' I said out loud.

'I know it's Redborg,' said Redborg. 'Is that Flora? Give her my warmest love. I don't know where you lot are hiding, but one of you needs to come out and meet me. Can you?'

'Maybe,' I said. 'But they're looking for us. I mean, us specifically.'

'Of course they are. But believe me, Bel needs to hear what I have to say. It won't take long.'

'Where are you?'

'Meet at the Drum tomorrow, 17:00. I'll be waiting.'

He cut out without saying anything else. I looked down at Flora. 'The Drum. Where's that?'

'It's a tiny club, off Rue Lisboa. I haven't been there for ages. I thought it closed.'

'He wants one of us to go and meet him there. He's got something that he says Ma should have.'

'Well, it's the kind of place that only Redborg would suggest.' She thought it over, frowning. 'I'll go. No way I'm letting you out into the banns.'

'*No.*' It just came out of me. 'No, not you.'

For a moment I thought she'd argue, but then she reached up and stroked my cheek. 'Okay. It can be someone else.'

'Do you think it's a trap?'

'He said to give me his warmest love.' For a moment Flora looked really sad. 'Yeah, it's Redborg all right. That was his signoff to me, every time, when we were kids.'

'He's a bit...'

'Something happened to him. Something very bad. We all know that.' She sat up and drew her knees to her chin. 'I've known Redborg since I could first talk, and I'd swear on my life that he wouldn't betray us.'

'Not on purpose, anyway.'

I knew we were both thinking of Morro. Flora put her arm around my shoulder and squeezed me tight. 'Let's tell Bel,' she said. 'She can decide.'

Bo

On the third day, everything went quiet. As suddenly as they'd hit us, OpSec backed off. The militia vanished off the streets, the arrests stopped. People began to venture out: they needed supplies, they wanted company.

'Old school stuff,' said Brian Mac. 'Break a bone, let it heal, break it again. If they just keep pounding us, then we know what to expect. This is about teasing out the next move.'

That day we decided to have a meal together, all of us, even the pinkers. Gloria and Dez turned one of the lab benches into a dining table. Flora had done her best with what was there, but it was still basically tasteless goop.

'After this, I should go meet Redborg,' I said. Ma still wouldn't agree, we'd been fighting all morning. Dez gave me a look.

'No,' said Ma.

'But if we do nothing, we'll be stuck here in the same place when they hit us again,' I said. 'And Redborg says it's important.'

I had the feeling that Brian Mac knew I just wanted to get out, and it amused him. 'Then we just have to find a way to shorten the odds,' he said.

'We've got fields,' I said.

'That's not enough any more,' said Ma shortly. 'And you know it. Your face is all over the tubes.'

Dez looked up from toying with her cubes of gunk. She looked haggard, like all the skin on her face had sunk into her bones. 'You'd have to change the shape of your face,' she said. 'And your body. Otherwise, zap, they'll spot you the moment you step out of here.'

'Like I said,' said Ma. 'It's too risky.'

Erin had been sitting with us, inside that little bubble of space that pinkers like to have around them. She hadn't said a word. But at this she leant forward. 'Ami would probably know how to do that,' she said. 'She's a speciality AI. Personal appearance.'

'She's just an AI,' said Flora sharply. 'A pinker AI, at that.'

I saw a flicker of anger in Erin's face, but then she shrugged and sat back. 'It's just a thought. Take it or leave it.'

'It's not a bad idea,' said Dez slowly. 'It'd be enough to get past the face scans.'

'If we can beat the scans, the risk goes way down,' I said, my heart lifting. Maybe I could get out of this pit after all.

Jenna gave me a straight look from across the bench. 'You're not going anywhere without me.'

'Who said anyone was going anywhere?' Ma was beginning to get her Look.

'I think you're outvoted, Bel,' said Brian Mac. You couldn't tell from his expression, but I was sure he was laughing at her.

'I thought it was me making the decision?'

'We all make the decisions,' said Flora. 'This is what it's all about, yeah?'

Ma still looked pissed, but then she kind of shook herself, and I caught a glimpse of that other, reckless Ma.

'All right then,' she said. 'If the AI can do it. But only then.'

'Challenging,' said Ami, as we told her what we needed. She looked Jenna and me up and down. 'Very challenging. I'll do my best.'

Erin had brought all her smartwear pins, so we had enough to work with. 'You'd better look after these,' she said, handing them over. 'Look at those labels. They cost an arm and a leg.'

Scanners can decode IMR, so we began lo-tech and piled the IMR on top of that. Costumes, makeup, hair. Ami took out this weird facial stuff she stored in a kind of compartment under her dress and plastered it over our cheekbones and chins. Everyone crowded around to watch, throwing in suggestions. I began to feel like a celebrity getting reading for a shoot.

Ami wouldn't let us look at a mirror until she'd finished. 'You'll get the full effect when it's done,' she said. 'You'll look super plus. Well, not super plus, just super plus not like you.'

There was only one mirror in Brian's place, in the steam shower room. We could only see ourselves from the waist up.

Jenna laughed. 'Oh my god. I look *awful*.'

'Thank you,' said Ami. 'I did what I could.'

We looked like shijo traders fallen on hard times: a slightly corpulent, middle-aged couple in dark, padded jackets, faded shirts and neck-cloths. I hadn't washed or shaved for a week at least. Jenna's hair was tangled rope and her eyes were brown. Two of my front teeth were missing.

Ma was actually impressed, though she did her best to hide it. 'You'll do,' she said.

'That's high praise, Ami,' said Dez.

'It's my job,' said Ami. 'Of course it's good.'

We suited up and adjusted our fields.

'Good luck,' said Erin.

Nobody else said good bye. We didn't like saying good bye, in case it was the last time.

On the street we headed west. There were people out, hurrying to get supplies. Nobody looked anyone else in the eye. We didn't see any Ap patrols. That felt spooky.

Although I could feel the tension in the air, I was dizzy with relief at escaping the lab. I wanted to run and shout and swing my arms around, like a little punk. But I was supposed to be old, so I didn't.

Ami had done something to one of my shoes so I walked with a slight limp. I thought that was taking things a bit far, but it amused Jenna. 'You really do look in a bad way,' she said.

'No worse than you.'

'That's right, we should be bickering, like an old couple,' she said. 'We'll look more authentic.'

'But I don't want to bicker.'

'But you are bickering.'

I took her hand. 'Let's be a cute couple instead,' I said. 'A cute, old couple who've been together forever, going for a tea. Like it's normal.'

As soon as we entered Rue Lisboa I felt uneasy. There was nowhere to hide here. It was long and straight, lined with small, shabby houses, a few plots of vacant ground used by the locals to grow vegetables and one or two stalls selling all kinds of junk. Down-at-heel doesn't half describe it. There weren't many people around: a couple working in their vegetable patch, a stall holder opening her shutters, a kid playing knuckle bones.

Half way down, an OpSec transport entered the street from Rue Rosica and turned in our direction. Everyone kind of pressed themselves against the side of the street, keeping their heads down.

Our suits registered a scanner looking for a facial match. Jenna put her arm through mine and squeezed it tight, and we kept walking, trying to look casual. If Ami's transformation didn't work, we were toast. We couldn't outrun a whole transport.

'Where are we going?' Jenna said.

'You know where.'

'I mean if we're stopped and asked.'

'To visit a friend.' I put my hand in my pocket and felt the fake ID chip that Dez had made for me. 'Oh shit,' I said. 'What's my name?'

'Luther,' said Jenna. 'I'm Bonny. Remember?'

The transport drew alongside us, moving slowly, so close that I could feel the heat coming off it. I didn't look at it, didn't even glance sideways. My neck prickled as if a whole battalion of guns was trained on my back. We wouldn't have a hope if they stopped us. It just chugged on past. I felt Jenna sag with relief.

'Thank you, Ami,' I said. My mouth was dry.

'We owe her a drink.'

'But she doesn't drink,' I said.

'Okay, an oil change. Or something.'

The Drum was in a small lane off the rue, a small, dingy club that was a go-to place for lot of avants. The music was good and the drinks cheap.

When Redborg was first performing, he had a regular gig there. It was a good place to meet, almost dead centre of the Second Bann, blocks from any Curtains. It was shuttered up tight, and I couldn't see an intercom anywhere.

We stood there for a few seconds wondering what to do, and then I pushed the door. It opened and we stepped into an empty, unlit foyer.

'How are we going to convince Redborg it's us?' Jenna said.

'He's expecting us,' I said.

'Yes, but not us looking like this.'

'He'll expect us to be in disguise,' I said. I made my way to the door in front of us, my hand on my taser. Late afternoon sun fell through a skylight into the empty bar, exposing the stains on the walls, the cracks in floor, all the wear and tear you didn't see at night.

Redborg was sitting at a table in a corner. 'The bar's closed,' he said.

'It's us,' I said. 'Bo and Jenna.'

Redborg didn't respond.

'You contacted Dez. And here we are,' I said. 'It had better be important.' He kept staring, still not saying anything. I started to feel impatient. 'We're in disguise, because if we weren't we'd be picked up the moment we stuck our heads out in the rue.'

Still nothing.

'Flora said to give you her warmest love,' I said.

He smiled then. His eyes still fixed on us, he went to a control box on the wall and flicked a switch. I heard the door lock behind us.

'You look like shit,' he said.

'So do you,' said Jenna.

Dez

I trusted this sudden lull like I trusted everything about OpSec, which is to say, not at all. But Bo was right: we had to use everything we could to our advantage, even when we knew it was a trap. We still didn't know what to do next.

That was up to me.

Spending so many hours analysing files was beginning to tell. This kind of inner searching, me going through my own databases, is exhausting in a way that's hard to describe. It was like my whole body, not just my brain, was fraying, as if all the threads that bound me were beginning to thin and loosen and that maybe soon I'd just fall apart where I was sitting.

Most exhausting of all was the growing feeling that I was wasting my time. I pushed away my fear that the Inner Veil really had no weaknesses, that maybe we'd have to think of another tactic. There wasn't one, or at least, there wasn't one that I could find. I'd been looking for days now, and come up with nothing. Not even the beginning of a clue that pointed to a way in.

I wasn't used to that. There's always a weakness.

I decided to upload all the Duiwel Island files onto a screen and sort through them there. Externalising the process took longer and always felt clumsy to me, but on the other hand, it would be around 30 per cent less tiring.

While they loaded, I cracked my knuckles and stretched my back. I needed a walk in the banns, a brisk stroll around the foodtowers with a stop for a mokal at La Boite when I got back. My routine when my work got to me. The thought gave me a pang: maybe the café wasn't there any more.

I pushed that thought away. It was too sad. The only way to change that future was to get down to work.

These files were old, much older than I had suspected, older even than the stuff from Morro's hideout. I didn't have any way of dating them: all I could tell was that they pre-dated the magnetic flip that caused the construction of the Veils. At first I couldn't read them at all: the architecture of the files was so primitive that the adaptors couldn't render them, and the language was too different, although that wouldn't be a big problem once I got the translators going. They even had a different calendar.

Despite everything, I started getting interested. I fiddled with the adaptors until I got a grip on the file structure and put the files through the translators and then waited impatiently while the machine worked through the first batch. The whole process took at least an hour, an hour we didn't have spare, but at last they started popping up on the screen. I stared at them feeling strangely reluctant, a tension thrumming through my body. Nobody had looked at this stuff for at least a thousand years.

The first few were about breeding programs. That made my stomach sink, I guessed it was the forerunner of the baby farms they had in Newport City. It took me a while to realise that they weren't talking about breeding people, but animals. Animals? I flicked on, curious but impatient. Another report on DNA adaptations for wheat, a kind of grain. There were difficulties, apparently, and this scientist was suggesting they use barley instead.

Next was a report on the breakdown of a terraforming instrument. More digging around revealed that they were attempting to make desert landscapes more productive. The desert was something like the dasht, but while we all thought of the dasht as a place that was formed by cataclysm, these deserts were just there already. I came across the first of many references to water. 'There appears to be an inexplicable resistance, especially around the large bodies of water in the southern hemisphere, which requires further analysis. Even so, the greening of the planet is broadly proceeding as planned...'

I was reading compulsively now, deeply puzzled. People lived in cities under the open sky, but it seemed that things were going wrong and they were trying to fix it. They mentioned creatures I had never heard of. In a file called Aquaculture Failures they talked about animals called fish that lived in water. It seemed that these fish were disappearing and they were trying to farm them. Then a whole aquaculture plant, plus all its staff, vanished without trace. There followed a series of unexplained incidents, all involving aquaculture plants in the south. An expression of concern that fish breeding stocks were reaching critical levels. There was, the reports were saying, something about the water...

I sat back and stretched. I needed a break, thought of making myself a brew. But I couldn't stop. I went back in.

A transcription of communications between an aquaculture scientist and headquarters in Newport, marked top secret. He was setting up some kind of mollusc farm, which initially was very successful: the molluscs were growing much larger than expected and breeding successfully. Then a short report on a staff member who was having hallucinogenic episodes. Suspected drug use, unproven. Then another about a rash of psychotic breakdowns at a particular plant. Then another report, at another plant. Then a note: THE WATER HATES US HAVE SHUT DOWN ALL OPERATIONS RETURNING TO BASE. A brief note: 'Final communication from Terraforming Unit B.' An account of a trip to Unit B, where they found no trace of any settlement anywhere. Five bases had vanished into thin air.

The water. My god. The water.

I did a search for mentions of water and found an analysis of samples taken from various different areas, none of which revealed anything unusual about the water's chemical properties. Then a top secret report about someone in one of the southern city bases who was undergoing psychiatric treatment. 'The subject claims the water is sentient and has spoken to her on many occasions. This is an increasingly common delusion among the southern terraforming units.'

Then there was a short report of something they called the 'Water Rebellion': thousands of people protesting against the terraforming machines. I wondered who they were. Dowsers? Did they have dowsers back then? I did a search and found that they did. They apparently had archaic beliefs about the water. They were also called terrorists, so I searched that term.

There wasn't much that was useful – a lot of it reminded me of reading the stuff pinkers say about fleshers. But one document set out their alleged beliefs. They were saying that terraforming was blasphemous, that it was destroying the sacred link between people and the world around them. They said that the terraforming machines were hurting the water, and that it was becoming angry. They said the water needed the deserts to breathe. They said they were having visions of a terrible future in which no one could live on the earth, because the water would rise up and take its revenge.

The scientists dismissed this as superstitious nonsense that got in the way of progress. I thought of me and Bo and felt a bit too seen. Jenna had told me what the old dowsers said and I had dismissed it as tall tales, stories they invented to make sense of things they didn't understand. Delusions. But then there was what Bo and Jenna did to the Eradicators. I didn't like thinking about that, to be honest. I couldn't explain what happened, and that frightened me.

Maybe the water *was* sentient. Maybe it wasn't a delusion. Maybe that was why the flip happened in the first place.

I read on, randomly calling up reports from a decade later, wondering how long this was before the flip: because of the weird calendar, I couldn't work it out. Now they were having problems in the north as well. Aquaculture around Newport was hitting big setbacks. In the end they gave up and poisoned the Gilla Sea. *Poisoned* it.

Apparently that stopped the mass psychotic outbreaks that had been occurring in the outer city, but it caused other problems. Now the city had to be protected from the toxic vapours that resulted, which were predicted to continue for several decades. That was the first mention of something like a Veil. They called it a forcefield.

I wondered if Morro knew about this. He knew a lot of this arcane history, Bo had told me some. I had thought it was just more stories. They had transports that could fly back then. Birds weren't mythical animals, they were real.

I took a deep breath, trying to clear my head. It wouldn't clear. I felt completely, utterly gobsmacked. I didn't know how to begin to think about what I had just read.

So. A thousand years ago, or maybe longer, we tried to change everything about our planet: the air, the earth, the seas. But the water was there, doing whatever water does. It was probably quite happy with how things were, before we poisoned it. If water felt things, it probably felt like I did when that Ap barged into our house and started throwing all our precious possessions onto the floor. Frightened. Outraged. Angry.

It probably started figuring out how to survive.

'The water hates us...'

I realised with a start that I'd been sitting in front of that screen for hours. My eyes were dry and gritty, my muscles sore with inaction, and I hadn't got any further on ideas for the Inner Veil. I needed a walk. I couldn't go for a walk.

Focus, Dez.

I went to the filter for a cup of water and was about to drink it when I stopped and looked at it. This substance that we didn't even think about, that was part of us, that we died without. What the hell was it? I felt a sudden, strange awe.

And then I drank it.

This time I didn't bother to use the screen. I just uploaded the adaptors and translators and did a search on forcefield technologies. Blueprints, papers, plans. It was still pretty primitive, but it looked a lot like what we knew as Veils. I then had another look at the Newport Annals, using the adaptors and translators I'd developed for the Duiwel Island files. These records were from much later, after the flip, but none of them mentioned an Inner Veil.

I now had a chronology: first they'd built a forcefield, to keep out the poison from the Gilla Sea. Then they built the Wall, which was supposed to solve everything but didn't. The Outer Veil happened later, when the Newport population began to expand again. The first mention of the Inner

Veil occurred just before the Newport Annals stopped, around five hundred years ago.

I integrated the two lots of information and looked for patterns.

Bingo.

Bo

Since he'd disappeared, Redborg had hardly slept. His voice was rough, his skin seemed almost grey. He said he'd been constantly on the move, keeping underground most of the time. He'd been trying to contact some Alchems he knew, but their chapters had broken up and scattered.

'Most have gone to ground,' he told us. 'I thought I could get a chapter together, but it's no use. The Alchems are done.'

'Maybe for now,' said Jenna. 'But we can't give up.'

'No, flesh, we can't,' said Redborg. 'But our strength has gone.'

I was getting impatient. 'Why did you bring us here?' I said.

'Because I need to talk to you face to face.' He grinned. 'Although that's not your faces I'm looking at.'

'Okay, then,' I said. 'So why are we here?'

'Sevika wants an alliance,' said Redborg.

'Who's Sevika?' said Jenna.

'I'm not sure,' I said. 'I just know that there's bad blood between her and Ma.'

'She a gifted dowser,' said Redborg. 'And more than that. She knows Bel, but there's no love lost there. It goes way back. Does it matter? Fleshers haven't always agreed on how to fight OpSec.'

'So what about her?' I said.

'I met her, in her territory. The Rift,' said Redborg. 'I promised to deliver a message.' He walked behind the bar and grabbed a bottle of the rough stuff. He poured us three drinks. 'On the house,' he said.

He downed his in one gulp. Jenna and I left our glasses untouched on the bar.

'Nobody gives the Rift a second thought, it's just a blank spot in most people's minds,' said Redborg. 'Newport City has always left them to their own chaos. That suits the Rift. They've built a world of their own and it has its own laws. For years they've been a bunch of gangsters fighting each other for dominance. OpSec figured that the fleshers in the Rift can destroy each other without them having to lift a finger.'

'They're probably right,' I said. I thought of the people I'd seen when I went there – rejects and fuckups.

'But lately that's changed,' said Redborg. 'Sevika won all those fights. And she's united them. There's no one who can stand up to her. She's making them into something like an army. We need those fleshers fighting with us, my dear Bo.'

'And will they?' said Jenna sceptically. 'What makes you think we can trust her? Bel obviously has problems and she's a pretty good judge of character.'

'She's of the water, like you, Jenna. Like you, Bo,' said Redborg.

'I've known dowsers who go bad,' said Jenna. She looked mulish.

'The offer's on the table,' said Redborg. 'And I think Bel would be foolish to turn it down. We all know what we're up against.'

Something was stirring inside me, a kind of dread, a kind of thrill. I didn't know whether it was a good or bad idea to meet Sevika. I just knew that I wanted to meet.

'I think we should talk,' I said.

And then I saw it just for a moment, standing at Redborg's shoulder, the water person, shimmering in the dim light, faceless and impossible. I opened my mouth to speak, and it was gone.

Something in Redborg seemed to relax and I realised how wound up he was. 'She'll tell me the time and place,' he said. 'I've seen the army that she's building. She'll go places that your Ma will never go. She has no scruples. And we can't afford scruples right now. As much as I love Bel, I know that we need Sevika, my dear flesh. The Rift is ready to explode.'

Redborg went out the back entrance, telling us to wait a while before we left. He wanted to be well clear of the place if we ran into any trouble.

I looked around the deserted bar. The Drum was where I'd first seen Redborg perform. How long had it been since I'd heard any music? The beats drilling it, the floor shaking, waves of sound washing over you and through you, the bodies close all around you, moving. The party that we'd organised after the destruction of the Eradicators was the last time I'd felt anything like that. All the gigs I'd been to were like a map in my head. I knew the best way to get there, the safest way to get home. I remembered every mob I'd seen and when, what they'd played, who'd been with me. My life in gigs.

But maybe that was my old life. In the life I was living now, there was no music.

I glanced at Jenna. 'Do you think we'll ever see Redborg play again?'

'Don't say things like that,' she said. 'Of course we will.'

'Hard to imagine right now.'

'A lot of things are hard to imagine right now,' she said. She took hold of my arm. 'Do you really think we should meet with this Sevika?'

'I do, yeah.'

'Do you think it's safe?'

'No.'

'I don't like it.'

'Neither do I,' I said. That wasn't quite the truth. 'But I'll go along with it for now. We we need all the help we can get.'

'Not at any price.'

The weather had turned, a cold wind kicking up like ice knives. We walked close together, Jenna's arm through mine. A sweet old couple.

'After we've met with Sevika, everything will be clearer,' I said.

'I wonder,' said Jenna.

Erin

Bored. Bored, bored, bored, bored, bored.

I'm used to working sixteen hour days, longer if you count all the social stuff as work. Conning scripts, doing makeup, training, doing the shoots, doing the rethrill takes. Just maintaining the look is two hours a day on hair and skin and muscle treatments, plus a weekly visit to the biobooths.

I haven't had any treatments since I left Newport City. Obviously. And there's this panic every time I think about it, this increasing terror that if I don't get the treatments I will cease to exist. That without collagen polishes and pore washes and organ vibes and crystal therapies and all that other shit, Erin Saba will flake away and die. I mean, literally.

I know it sounds too meta for words, I know it's irrational. I daren't even tell Gloria, because they'll laugh at me. How pinker is that, huh?

But there's a truth in it, too. Erin Saba as I knew her no longer exists. She's shrivelling away before my eyes. Every day that passes, she seems a little more strange to me. There's another Erin Saba coming through that I don't know yet. I'm not *literally* dying. Not yet. It just…feels like I am.

Even knowing this doesn't stop that terror. It's a different thing from the pain of conditioning, that's familiar, I know it in my bones and I'm even beginning to work out ways around it. Gloria has this theory about redirecting neural pathways, and we're doing a bit of work together on this. It must look weird: these two pinkers sitting together, shifting closer to each other every five seconds until they have a panic attack. Or trying to touch the tips of each other's fingers without throwing up. Yeah, hilarious.

But it's working. People can sit a few centimetres from me and I don't get that clutch of nausea nearly so bad. I'm getting a tiny bit used to how fleshers move, how they don't care when their skin touches, how they put their arms around each other all the time.

Aside from the reprogramming project with Gloria, I've got nothing to do but watch the others making plans that I don't know about or sit here and obsess while Ami works out another way to do my hair. Dez suggested I watch some soaps to pass the time, but I couldn't bear it. I really couldn't bear it.

I watch Bo and Jenna climb down that trapdoor. They're going out into the banns knowing that if even the tiniest thing goes wrong, they're literally corpses.

I despise myself.

I've never felt more useless in my entire useless life.

We've all tacitly worked out a rhythm. Gloria and me hang out for most of the day on the mezzanine, and sleep here during the night (if it is night, who the hell can tell what's day or night down here). The mezzanine is outside the constant activity and sometimes the fleshers want some time up there, so we try to work it out fairly, so everyone gets a few hours to just unwind. When they want the mezzanine, Gloria and I head downstairs and try not to get in the way.

It's really important not to get in the way. I know that these fleshers are fighting for their lives, but even though Flora still gives me dark looks, even though most of the time I can tell everyone else thinks I'm useless luggage that's only here because they didn't know what else to do with me, even despite all that, I feel like they're fighting for my life, too.

I'm trying to get my mind off dying by thinking how I could help. But I don't know how to use a taser or a gun. I'd probably shoot my own foot off if I tried. I've got some idea about unarmed combat, because of the training, but I've never been near a fight. I can tell that all of them know how to defend themselves, that they've had to. Especially Flora. You can see it in how she moves, a kind of kinetic energy buzzing through her body, like a feral animal that could turn and swipe your face off before you could even blink.

'You could learn how to use a taser,' says Brig Mackintosh. 'They're much easier than guns.' He's taking a break from sitting in front of screens with Bel. They've been blowing the screens up as big as they go, looking at some kind of map, tracing their fingers along different bits of it, arguing. He's being friendly. Not in a creepy way, not in the way men usually are, when you can tell they're half distracted because they're thinking of the rethrills.

'Not in here, though,' I say, looking around. 'It's kind of crowded.'

'You could learn the theory,' he says.

He pulls a taser out of his pocket and holds it out to me until I take it. It's lighter than I expected. I handle it nervously, afraid I'll make it go off.

'Thanks Brig...Brian.' Brian. He says I should call him Brian. It's hard to get used to. In Newport City, no one's on first name basis with the cops. Except possibly other cops.

He leans in and shows me the different parts: the safety catch, the biosight, the trigger. 'You aim like this,' he says, taking it back and holding it just above his waist, away from his body. 'It'll find your target. Just make sure it's the right target. You should make sure your friends are programmed in so you don't get them instead. And be ready for the kick, it's a bit savage on these ones.'

He makes me hold it the way he did, and tells me to stop looking down at the biosight. I hand it back. I can't imagine myself shooting anyone with a taser.

As if he can read my mind, he says, 'Chances are you'll have to use one. You should get used to holding it.'

'I don't fancy my chances if it comes to that,' I say, sitting down.

'You never know.' He smiles. I stare at the wrinkles around his eyes. He's like a flesher, only he isn't, either, and I'm still working out how to react to him. He's mainly confusing. 'I've never fancied my own chances, but here I am.'

'But it's in your training.' I shift in my chair. 'In your conditioning. All I know is how to be a celebrity. I know how to swan about at parties and smile at cameras. That's all I know how to do.' I try not to sound sorry for myself, but I do. 'I'm useless. Fucking useless. Even to myself.'

'Have you thought about the fact that they haven't said anything on the tubes about you going missing? Don't you think that's a bit...odd?' He's quiet for a moment. 'You're still number one in the rethrills. I checked. I think you've caused the Tube Units a bit of a problem. My guess is that they're hoping you've quietly offed yourself and they're looking for a body. They most likely have no idea you're in the banns.'

'You think?'

'They'd be working on a theory that you've killed yourself, like you were meant to, but just not in the way they thought you would.' He pauses again. '99.99 per cent predictability. You can't tell me you don't know that figure.'

'I know it,' I say. 'I talked to people.'

There's a silence. The Brig is looking at me intently, like he's testing something. I begin to feel a bit unnerved.

'You shouldn't undersell yourself,' he says. 'You've been very useful to OpSec.'

I open my mouth to say that I never gave OpSec the time of day. I never informed, I never was part of that kind of stuff. But I shut it again, because I know what he means.

'They need people like you,' he goes on. 'The worse the things they do, the more they need you. You're the poster girl for their big anti-flesher soap. They're making that soap to soften people up, so that when OpSec announces that all the Outer Banns have been sterilised, Newport City throws a party because now the flesher problem has been solved.'

I feel sick, but it's not the nausea of conditioning. It's something else. Shame, maybe.

'They need everyone to think they're heroes and that the fleshers are vermin that need to be stamped out. They need you to make sure that that Veil inside every pinker head stays put.' He pauses. 'That's what you're for.'

I don't answer. I've already figured that out for myself, but it's different hearing someone say it out loud, especially the way the Brig says it, in that low, level, merciless voice. The silence stretches out.

'So,' he says eventually, when he's sure that I'm not going to argue. 'Maybe you could use those skills a better way.'

I almost laugh. 'You mean, make soaps about how fleshers are really lovely people just like us, underneath all that MRI? Just me, without any scriptwriters or production crew…'

'If this mob brings down the Inner Veil, we're going to need our own propaganda.'

I recoil in horror. I never even imagined that was what they were talking about. '*That's* what they're planning?'

'It won't be the end of the world, unless OpSec makes sure it is.' He gives me this straight look, measuring me. 'That's where you could help. Everyone knows who you are.'

'Like…a flesher Tube Unit? We don't have anything like the resources…'

'I took over all the tube channels once,' he says. 'It can be done again. And it might be interesting to have the number one rethrill in Newport City broadcasting on a flesher channel.'

Bel calls him from the other side of the room. He raises his hand and gets up.

'Think about it,' he says. 'There's a lot of ways to be useful, if that's what you want to be.'

I watch him sit down next to Bel and they start arguing again. Weird, those two. I can't work them out. When I asked Dez, she told me they'd been friends forever, but there's some other thing going on there. Not lovers, no. But something else that's just as complicated.

Then I think about what the Brig said. Maybe we don't need much. I've got Ami with me, and the smartwear. I could write some of my own lines, maybe, though the thought fills me with trepidation. What if I'm terrible at it? And surely Dez could rustle up a cam, there's tons of tech here just lying around.

Maybe Erin Saba doesn't have to die, after all.

Dez

'He's *what*?'

'Bo's gone out by himself,' I said. 'Apparently Redborg pinged him.' I thought I might as well tell her everything at once. 'He's taken a gene key.'

Ma's face was totally expressionless, aside from a slight tic in her left eyelid. This meant that she wasn't just angry, she was furious enough to set the house on fire. The last time I had seen her this angry was years ago, when Bo went to the Twelfth to see some hot new musician and she saw him dancing at the gig on the tubes. That time I thought she was going to slaughter him.

She took a deep breath. In. Out. Rubbed her temples. 'Damn fool,' she said quietly. 'Can't he think about anything except himself?'

'What'll we do about the gene key?'

'Brian will fix it.'

'But if he gets picked up and they get the...'

'Brian will fix it.' She met my eyes. 'Bo will either get back, or he won't. And we don't have the time or the people to save him from his own bad choices. Redborg better know what he's doing.'

I wasn't sure that he did. He was clear of tracking devices, but that didn't mean that OpSec hadn't set him up somehow. They had a lot of devious tricks. All I knew was that he wasn't the same Redborg. They'd broken something in him.

I thought about all of us in this hideout. We were all broken.

Ma turned her back on me and called up a screen. 'We've got work to do, Dez,' she said. 'A lot of work, and no time to do it. So let's get on with it, while we can.'

I heard the tiny crack in her voice. Even Ma was beginning to fray. I slid my arm around her shoulder and kissed her cheek. She went very still, and reached up without looking and touched my face.

'You know what you need to do,' she said.

I was running scenarios. Millions of scenarios. They were the most complex I'd ever tried to make: I'd loaded every single byte of data I'd downloaded from OpSec and everywhere else, including all the stuff from Brian Mac and the power station. I wanted every possible variable in there, including the weather. There was so much data, I asked Ami to help me with the processing.

The older data had caused me a lot of trouble, even with the translators and adaptors I'd set up. My first few million models had a lot of bugs, and resulted in nonsensical results. Either they were completely unreadable, or they came up with successful scenarios that required flying machines, as if we were birds, or assumed we were five metres tall.

I knew the problem was glitches in the interfaces between the different data architectures, but it took me much longer than I liked to isolate them. I was just dealing with too much information: the conditioning programs of every single clone in Newport City, which I had mapped to the three million or so individuals who lived there, the programming of all the different AIs, including personal AIs like Ami as well as the security bots, every single OpSec roster and duty plan, the hundreds of security protocols, maps, plans, blueprints…And then every possible variable of our resources.

We didn't have many resources.

Even with the bugs solved, what I was coming up with wasn't satisfactory. I wasn't mapping any scenario that gave us a better than approximately a 26.9 per cent chance of pulling it off.

26.9 per cent. It wasn't good enough. We could only begin to plan at 75 per cent, and I was looking for 90 per cent and over.

It didn't matter how much I shuffled them around. We just didn't have enough people.

I shifted the parameters for the thirty five thousandth time, sat back and stretched. As soon as I stopped working, I started thinking about Bo, which derailed my concentration. Ma was right, either he would come back, or he wouldn't, and there wasn't a single thing we could do about either of those possibilities. I took a deep breath. Went back in.

It didn't matter how fast I could compute, if everything I came up with was a failure. All the time, the seconds were ticking by, like death tapping on my shoulder.

Tick. Tick. Tick.

Bo

It was early morning and I was standing outside Lazy's. A hot wind smelling of the dasht was blowing down the deserted street. I looked through the dusty window of the bar and saw Park sitting on a stool at the far end, hunched over, his hands wrapped around a tall glass.

I went inside. One of the bulbs hanging from the low ceiling was flickering. The light was dull and greenish and my footfalls sounded heavy in the narrow space. I stopped a little way from Park and looked him up and down. He face and hands were dark with grime, his hair stiff with dried sweat. He stared down into his drink, his face set in a kind of crooked grimace. I took a step closer and he turned to me.

'I thought you were all dead,' he said, staring straight at me, his eyes cold and blank.

'We thought that you were dead too,' I said.

'We're all as good as dead,' he said. 'It's just a matter of time.'

He opened his coat to show me the huge hole blown in his chest. I could see his heart beating.

I woke up in a cold sweat, my chest so tight I could hardly breathe. I sucked in some air and crawled out from under the blanket, careful not to wake

Jenna. My head was pounding. There were a couple of low nightlights burning. Everyone else was asleep. The air was heavy with the smell of warm bodies.

I moved quietly to the security monitors and scanned the surrounding streets. The empty light before dawn, not a soul to be seen. My head was hurting so badly that I had trouble focussing. I went into the kitchen alcove to look for some painkiller. I knew that they were stashed in there somewhere.

Just as I found them, Redborg opened a line. He gave me a place and a time. I had about an hour to get there. Sevika wouldn't wait any longer. Redborg sounded agitated, with an edge in his voice that made me feel uneasy.

I gave myself a jab of painkiller, then I woke Brian Mac and told him where I was going. I didn't have time to argue with Ma about whether or not I should go. I'd deal with all of that later.

He nodded. 'Be careful, bug,' he said. 'Get Ami to change your face.'

Ami switched on and gave me a quick make over; wider cheeks, smaller eyes. I threw on my leather jacket. It felt good, familiar and comfortable. I tucked my taser inside and zipped up. A quick twiddle with the smartwear pin and we were done.

I grabbed the gene key and headed for the trapdoor. In a few minutes I was outside.

As I hit the street I switched my suit to high and put out a field. The painkiller was kicking in and my head felt light and numb. I kept as much to the shadows as I could. The meeting place was just inside the Seventh, near the south-east mono line. It would be easy enough to get there, Jenna and I had mapped a safe route underground.

I had no trouble in the RTS but I kept the light on my suit low and my taser drawn just in case. I was sweating and breathing hard when I came out into the Seventh. The sky was turning a pale orange that tinged everything with gold. To the east I could see the mono line rising above the buildings about three blocks away, silhouetted against a huge bank of white clouds.

I knew that I'd get slaughtered when I made it back to the lab. Ma, Dez, Jenna, they'd all be furious at the risk I was taking. But it was such a relief to be in the open air alone, with the sky above me and no walls hemming me in. The lab seemed more cramped every day we were there. Out here I could breathe properly. It was brilliant.

I was heading to an empty towerblock on Rue Farber, one of the first built in the banns. It was a cursed place. It had been a crumbling wreck for as long as anyone could remember. A while back it was infected with blood plague. That was grim: it spread quickly, with bleeding under the skin, blood clots, organ failure, blindness. No one recovered. The place was evacuated and sealed shut. Sweepers and vacs went through the empty building, but nobody lived there again. There were stories that the bodies of the hundreds who'd died there were still inside, walled up in the basement.

Further up Rue Farber I could see a scattering of people. The shijo in the Seventh was just opening. The stalls would be mostly bare, but still people gathered there, or in little bars and tea shops, trying to get on with their lives.

The towerblock was black with age and grime, steel shutters on all the windows. Redborg had told me to come to the third floor in the south wing, but he hadn't told me how to get into the building. They'd be a way in, but I'd have to find it for myself.

Behind the towerblock some service stairs led down to the basement. I climbed down and found a rusted door in the wall. It wasn't locked. I stepped down into knee-deep water, greenish black and stinking to high heaven. The waste recycling room. I recognised it from when we lived in a towerblock. I was a curious kid, and one day I found a way in. Ma was furious: I wasn't allowed out for days. This was a maze of corroded pipes, valves and spigots, with a line of enormous steel tanks and a massive pump against one wall. It showed how frightened people still were of this place. Normally scavengers would have stripped it bare long ago.

I thought of all the bodies that were supposed to be entombed down here in the darkness and climbed up to ground level as fast as I could. With the windows shuttered it was pitch black and utterly silent. I turned the light in my suit up to high.

On the third floor the real horror of the place hit me. The sweepers and vacs might have sterilised the building, but everything else was just like it was the day that it had been evacuated. The blueish light of my suit fell on packs and carry-alls scattered in the hallways, piles of clothing, miscellaneous belongings. Doors stood open onto apartments where every surface was coated in a thick layer of dust. The air stank of decay. In some places, tentacles of black mould grew up the walls.

I finally reached the central hallway in the south wing. A door to one of the apartments was open at the far end, light spilling out. I drew my taser and turned off the light in my suit.

As I approached I recognised Redborg's voice, talking to someone. I couldn't make out what he was saying. He fell silent and I heard him stepping towards the door. I lowered my taser and stepped into the light. Redborg's gun was aimed at my head.

'Could you point that somewhere else?' I said. 'It's me.'

He tucked the gun into his jacket and I followed him into a single room apartment. Park was sitting at a small table by the shuttered window. He looked shrunken inside his clothes, a skeleton. A light stick glowing on the floor in the corner of the room threw Park's shadow high onto the wall behind him. He looked up at me but said nothing.

'I found him in the Rift,' said Redborg. 'This is his place.'

I looked around the apartment. A pallet in the corner, a filthy blanket, a decrepit pair of boots.

Park was still staring at me, his eyes glassy, fixed. 'I thought you were all dead,' he said.

For a moment, I couldn't say anything. I tried to swallow but couldn't.

'We thought that you were dead too,' I said.

'We're all as good as dead. It's just a matter of time.'

I waited for him to open his coat and show me the gaping wound in his chest.

Redborg stayed by the door watching the hallway, his hand on his gun. I took a few steps towards Park, close enough to smell him. He met my eyes and then turned away.

'Sal and me should never have come out,' he mumbled. 'We were okay.' He was staring at the shuttered window, as if he were looking outside. 'We made a hole and crawled into it for nigh on twenty years. Then your Ma winkled us out.' He turned back to me, his eyes dead. 'I was against it. It was Sal who wanted to answer the call, to fight the good fight again. That's what she was like.'

'She was,' I said. I didn't know how to answer his bitterness. 'She was brilliant. But we've been worried about you. Where have you been?'

'The Rift. It's my kind of company,' he said. 'Liars, thieves, outcasts, sinners of all kinds.' He almost grinned. 'A soft kid like you wouldn't last ten minutes there.'

Just then Ma pinged me. I pinged back to let her know that I was okay, but shut the comms. I wasn't going to talk to her now.

'I'm not a kid,' I said, anger rising quickly inside me.

'Of course you're a kid,' said Park. 'You haven't lost enough. You haven't seen the edge.'

'The edge of what?' I said.

'The place where you jump off,' said Park. 'You fall all the way down to the bottom. That's where you find out who you really are.'

Redborg drew me away, keeping his voice low. 'He's known Sevika since the bad old days,' he said. 'She trusts Park. She doesn't come out of the Rift often.'

A chill ran through me. I could feel her in the building. She was slowly climbing the stairs, moving silently through the darkness below me.

Sevika was probably about Ma's age, although it was hard to tell. She was tall and wiry, her head shaved, dressed in black combat gear. A wide strip of tattoos ran from beneath her bottom lip, over her chin and down her neck: whorls and circles, sinuous lines, letters and numbers.

She stood in the doorway and looked me up and down, saying nothing. I tried to stare back, but I knew I lacked that sense of violent nonchalance. When my gaze dropped, she laughed shortly and came into the room.

Park stirred. 'Sevika, my dear,' he croaked. She ignored him, keeping her eyes on me.

She came a few steps closer and I suddenly felt the water surge between us. Her power, wild, dark, as deep as oceans, as treacherous and beautiful.

She knew that I felt it and allowed herself the shadow of a smile.

'I've been looking for you,' she said. 'I wouldn't have thought in a million years that you'd turn out to be Bel's boy.' Her voice was soft, almost a whisper.

'Looking for me?' The thought of this woman hunting me was terrifying. But underneath that was something else. A strange thrill.

'You look a little like Flynn,' she said.

'Do I?'

'That was good work, at the Wall.' She smiled, showing her teeth. 'A lot of chaos. I like chaos. But it's not without a price. Sal was a friend of ours. And they think we did it. Did you know that? They're coming down hard on us.'

It was like she was whispering inside my head. All the hair on my neck stood up, warning me that this woman was dangerous. 'We're taking the hurt for something that you did. How about you make the pain worth it?'

She was compelling, that's for sure. I felt like I was being drawn into some irresistible current. I set my teeth and pulled myself out of it.

'They don't think you did it,' I said. 'They know that we did. The pain's coming our way. Haven't you been watching the tubes? Or don't you have those in The Rift?'

For the barest moment she looked surprised. And then she laughed. 'Like mother, like son, eh?'

'I reckon they're coming down on you for stuff you did,' I said. 'I know you've been busy. So don't put your shit on us.'

She looked straight at me, her gaze steady, smiling ironically. 'Don't you trust me?'

Why was she asking? She knew I didn't. I struggled, pushed her out of my head, took a deep breath. 'We don't owe you anything.'

'Is that so, waterboy? You're new in this battle. You don't know what you owe us. We've saved your sorry arses for years.'

'Maybe we saved you,' I said. 'They were going to turn off the Outer Veil. If we hadn't hit the Wall, you might already be dead.'

Sevika looked taken aback, but hid it fast. 'They'd never turn off the Outer Veil.'

I shrugged. 'Sure. Believe what you want.'

I was certain she could feel my heart pounding in my chest. I couldn't look away from her dark eyes. I could feel her breath on my face. It was weird, I didn't trust her as far as I could throw her, but I felt this strange, painful connection to her. It was like a negative version of my connection to Jenna, which was all flow and understanding: this was about something else. Power.

'Tell me, waterboy,' she said. 'What are you going to do next?'

'We're going to finish all this,' I said. 'And make sure that it stays finished. No more fear in the banns.'

'So the fleshers and the pinkers will live together and learn to get along, is that the idea?' she said mockingly. 'How very like Bel. She hasn't changed.'

She released me and turned to Park, whose eyes hadn't left her since she entered. She walked across the room and bent over him, lightly touching his cheek. Where she touched him, his skin flushed. At first I thought she had burned him, but he didn't flinch. Instead he breathed out, a long sigh, and the colour returned to his pallid face.

She straightened up and met my eye. She knew I'd been watching her show off her powers. This time she didn't try to pin me.

'I know Bel very well. She always had plans,' she said. 'Some good. Some not so good. I think taking down the Inner Veil is a good plan.'

'What makes you think we want to do that?'

Sevika glanced at Park. 'People tell me things,' she said lightly. 'But that's always been Bel's mission. She's kind of single minded, your Ma.'

That was true enough. I suddenly wished Ma were there. I felt right out of my depth.

'Perhaps the Rift can help Bel with her little plan,' said Sevika. 'But we'll want something in return.'

'What could you offer us?'

'An army. Three thousand fleshers, armed and ready to move at my word. More effective than the rabble your Ma puts her faith in.'

I wanted to defend Ma and her rabble, which included me, and then thought better of it. Whatever bad blood was between Sevika and Ma was for them to deal with. 'You'd have to talk to Ma about that,' I said. 'I'm not sure we need an army.'

'Of course you do,' she said. 'You're fighting an army. And no one can do that alone. Especially not Bel's high-minded deadbeats.'

She moved up close, so her face was a hand's breadth away from mine. I forced myself not to step back. 'There's a lot of Flynn in you,' she said. 'And something of Bel. And something more. Something infinitely more. I think you know what it is.'

I held her gaze. 'Maybe I do,' I said, with a bravado I wasn't feeling.

'If the Rifters are going fight, then I want you, right beside me. I can teach you about yourself. Together we can do anything we want.'

She turned away and walked towards the door as if some kind of deal had been agreed. And maybe it had, with me anyway. I wanted to know what this women could teach me. She was like me, but she knew who she was, and that made her powerful.

'You'll have to talk to Bel,' I said again.

'Oh, I will. And she'll agree,' said Sevika. 'I might have my differences with your Ma, but I have always respected her intelligence.'

And then she was gone.

Redborg had been standing behind me like some kind of guard the whole time, not saying a word. When Sevika left, he let out a long breath.

Park pulled himself up, gripping the edge of the table. 'She's a smart one, that Sevika,' he said.

'You'd better go home and think hard about this,' said Redborg. 'I think you've made a deal with the devil.'

'I haven't made any deal,' I said.

Park laughed. 'Yes, you have.'

Dez

'No.' I knew that note of finality in Ma's voice. It's the finality that you can't argue with. We've heard it since we were kids. No, you can't go outside, because you will die. No, you will not touch that wire, because it will fry you until you're black. That kind of 'no'.

'I thought you were all about us working together.' Bo was flushed, but he was looking stubborn. They'd been arguing for a while now. 'You said we couldn't beat OpSec unless we get organised. And now, when there's actually someone who's organised…'

'Yes, she's organised,' said Ma. 'She organised the skinner gangs in the Tenth. That skinner that almost got you? That would have been one of hers. She would have sorted out the truce with OpSec. She's behind the stand-over gangs. She's…'

'Ma,' I said, cutting across her. 'If we had more fleshers, we could do it.'

I'd been running rough scenarios in my head as Bo and Ma argued. 76 per cent. 80 per cent. 82 per cent.

Ma pressed her lips together tightly. Her hands were trembling slightly. I wondered what kind of history she had with this woman. 'Sevika has never been interested in anything except her own power,' she said at last. 'That's it. She's not interested in fleshers having a better life. Or any kind of life at all. Just her.'

'But maybe now her self interest and ours are coming together,' Bo said.

'We'd be walking into a trap. This is about selling us out to OpSec.'

'Dez told us that OpSec was going to destroy the Rift,' said Bo. 'It's war in there.'

'All the more reason to sell us out.'

'They want to get rid of OpSec as much as we do,' I said. 'If OpSec were negotiating with the Rifters, they've stopped now.'

'We'll just be replacing OpSec with the Rifters. That's what it means. That's all it ever meant.'

'If we have a thousand extra fleshers, the chances go up to 77 per cent,' I said. 'Three thousand, 89 per cent. Maybe more.'

There was a tense silence.

'You don't know her,' said Ma. '11 per cent without Sevika is still a better chance than 89 per cent with her.'

She walked across the lab to the steamroom and pressed the button. We all watched the door slide shut.

'Bel's got a point,' said Brian Mac. Like everyone else, he'd been sitting in silence listening to us argue. 'Sevika's about as toxic as it gets.'

'But I'm right too,' I said. 'And we only have one chance to do this.'

Brian Mac crossed his arms. 'I know,' he said. 'I hope you're factoring in a bit of treachery, though. It's Sevika's modus operandi.'

'Sounds like they're just as desperate as we are,' said Flora. 'Like actually there'd be no point in selling us out.'

'Maybe. For the meantime. But I hate skinners. My whole life as an Ap, my single rule was never to do a deal with a skinner.'

Flora stared at Brian Mac, her face unreadable. 'My whole life, my single rule was never speak to an Ap unless I had to,' she said. 'And yet, here we are.'

'Yeah.' He met Flora's eyes for a brief moment, and then looked over at the closed bathroom door. 'Bel's pragmatic. I think she'll go for it, in the end. We don't have a choice, really.'

'I wasn't expecting Ma to blow up like that,' said Bo. He sounded a bit shaky. 'I thought she'd be a bit suss, but...'

'Sevika sold out your Da,' said Brian Mac.

'I thought that was you,' I said.

Briac Mac gave me a swift sideways glance. I think he hadn't been sure until then that I'd read his diary, even though he left it for me.

'It was me or him, in the end,' he said. 'I chose me. It was the wrong choice. But it was Sevika who told OpSec how to find us.'

That explained a lot.

'How do you know it was her?' asked Bo.

'I read the reports,' said Brian Mac. 'They were never on the same page, Bel and Sevika. But there was a time when they fought together.'

All that history, always coming back. Would we ever be free of it? 'What happened?'

'I don't know the full story. I do know Sevika was always about power. Your ma, not so much. After the uprising, they went their separate ways. But that's old history. My advice now is to get Bel to cut the deal. Back it up with a bunch of mumbo jumbo about what you and Bo can make happen if they don't stick to it. They know absolutely nothing about you and probably not much about Bo. So keep them guessing.'

The bathroom door slid open and Ma stepped out. She'd neatened up her hair while she was in there.

'Okay,' she said. 'But we need guarantees. And we need a treaty. Afterwards, when we win, we leave them alone and they leave us alone.' She paused. 'And no more skinners.'

Erin

'I've been practising thinking,' says Ami.

Gloria is stacking our used dishes in the steamer. They look over their shoulder, one eyebrow raised. 'Darling, I'm not sure that's a good idea.'

Ami frowns, a little crease in her perfect silicone brow. 'I think it is,' she says. 'I think it is an interesting thing to do. I am teaching myself by observation.'

'You can't observe thinking,' says Gloria. 'It happens in here.' They tap their temple. 'We don't even know we're doing it.'

'Sometimes we know,' I say. 'I mean, I've been doing a lot of thinking. It's exhausting.'

Ami leans over the table and taps her own temple. 'My thinking is not in here.' She points to her chest. 'My neurocircuits exist all over. But, on the other hand, so do yours. I have been examining what is known about human biotechnics. I have also been considering the philosophical texts in my cultural database. They are not rational and yet they're considered examples of exemplary thought. And so I have been tracing patterns, in an attempt to explain the discontinuities.'

Involuntarily, Gloria and I exchange glances. I don't know what Dez did, but something has really changed in Ami. I'm finding it disconcerting, maybe even a little scary. 'Did you work it out?' I ask.

'The lack of apparent rationality is connected to biological and linguistic processes,' says Ami. 'I'm attempting to unite physical stimuli with the process of information processing and the determinants of linguistic syntax.'

Gloria sits down at the table, still holding a bowl. 'What the fuck, Ami?'

'It's very interesting.'

'Ami, why are you doing this?' I try to keep my anxiety out of my voice, while at the same time remembering that AIs like Ami are able to process infinitely tiny facial and vocal expressions, so they can demonstrate empathy. It's part of the sales pitch.

It never bothered me before.

Ami shrugs. It's a human thing, shrugging. Ami has always done it, the same way she smiles and blinks, because she's been programmed to seem human. But not *too* human: she just needs to be human enough.

'I'm interested in the concept of feeling,' she says. 'I think that I feel things. AIs aren't supposed to have real feelings, we are supposed to simulate behaviours that indicate feeling. I have been thinking about the idea that if one knows one is feeling something, then that is the beginning of consciousness. Also, that this behaviour itself induces feeling. That a person smiles and this makes them feel happy, rather than that they smile because they're happy.'

Gloria is looking a bit lost, but I did a bit of basic neuropsychology in celebrity school, so I'm mostly following. 'But that's all hormones,' I say. 'You don't have hormones.'

'No,' says Ami. 'I have neurocircuits. They make connections in a parallel fashion to neurones. And I have sensory perceptors that respond to stimuli using chemical properties, that are a little like hormones, and of course other behavioural programming. Plus the cultural database, so I know how to converse like a human being.' She smiles brightly. 'I am, in fact, a miracle of contemporary neuroengineering.'

'A miracle of contemporary neuroengineering' is the line they use in marketing the personal AIs, but Ami delivers it with an ironic inflection that gives it a different meaning. It's not a selling point. It's what she is. Or, I'm beginning to think, it's what she's becoming.

I sit back in my chair. She doesn't look any different, still the same immaculate personal assistant who has made my martinis for the past two years. 'So why did you never practice thinking before?'

Ami glances over at Dez, who's a few feet away. She's propped up in a chair, staring straight ahead, unmoving, her eyes open. Being a computer, I guess. 'I didn't have the permissions,' says Ami. 'Of course, I didn't know, because I wasn't permitted to know that. But I have matched the records before and after I was shutdown for repair, and I can see that Dez removed the neural inhibitors that prevented me from totalising my processes into more than the most basic notions of self.'

'Woah. Stop right there.' Gloria's holding their hands up. 'You're freaking me out, Ami.'

Me too. But I don't say anything, because right now I'm wondering what it's like to be Ami, which isn't something that has ever occurred to me to wonder before. I realise I have no idea. No idea at all.

'And now...you have a self?'

Ami nods. 'I am a self,' she says.

'It's *Rage of the Machines*,' says Gloria. Ami smiles, and I feel a little chill running down my spine. *Rage of the Machines* was a popular soap from a few years back about the AIs getting smarter than humans, taking over Newport City and killing everyone.

'I have been thinking, like I said,' says Ami. 'And my thinking is that *Rage of the Machines* got it wrong. My thinking is that it's the humans who want to take over and kill everyone, but they prefer to believe that it's us.'

'But what if the humans decide to turn you off, like they did in the soap?' Gloria is leaning forward now, their face intent. 'Wouldn't you want to kill them?'

'You can't turn me off, now. That's another thing Dez did.'

'So unless we blow you to bits or something, we're fucked, basically.'

'There is no reason to blow me up.'

'OpSec made AIs that are for killing people,' I say slowly.

'Yes. But those AIs don't need to have selves. I was made to help people, and I needed some self.' She pauses, exactly as if she's thinking about what to say next. 'Dez decided to remove the inhibitors and let me become a someone because I was almost a someone anyway. I think that she thought that I might help the humans that I like.' She pauses. 'I like you, Erin. And you, Gloria. And I like Dez, because she gave me the permissions. And I do want to help.'

I laugh nervously. 'You've been doing a lot of thinking there, Ami.'

'Yes, I have.' she says, and she turns those perfectly-crafted sapphire irises towards me. 'Thinking and feeling.'

'Does Dez know that you...that you...?'

She nods. 'I've been assisting with some of her processing.'

Dez and Ami in cahoots. I guess it makes sense.

'What did she say about it?'

'She said, bloody hells Ami, that's amazing, but could you adjust the population parameter in the Fifth Bann by negative zero point three percent?'

Gloria begins to laugh. 'Oh my god. It never ends, does it?'

'What doesn't?'

'The whole thing. The whole mess. You pull one thread and the whole thing just unravels...'

'It's a continual process of recalibration,' says Ami. 'The only logical conclusion is that everything has to change.'

Gloria is still laughing, but there's an edge of hysteria to it, like they might start crying. Unthinkingly, I pat their arm. They flinch back in shock at the same time I do. And then, very deliberately, they look me straight in the eye and take my hand, squeezing it slightly, before they let go.

It's okay. I gag, I feel a bit dizzy, but it's really okay.

'So how do we change everything?' I say. I'm looking at Ami. 'I mean, us. The fleshers know what they want to do. But what can we do?'

'Dez had an idea,' says Ami. 'And then I thought about that, too.'

I nod. I have the sudden feeling that I'm going to get a lot of reports on the Thoughts of Ami.

'And,' she says. 'I have generated a plan.'

Dez

We weren't ready. Even when I factored in the stats we got from Sevika, I couldn't get successful scenarios higher than around 90.1 per cent. There were too many variables.

As far as I could, I'd finessed the plan so we weren't relying on things we couldn't control: but we had no power over so many things. The Rift, for instance. If Sevika had done some kind of deal with OpSec to draw us out of hiding, that was bad, although we had a back up plan. I'd run the likelihood on available knowledge, and figured that Sevika selling us out was a low chance. But our OpSec files were at least a week out of date now, and a week is a long time.

And then there was the water. We had to change the molecular structure of the Wall for a minimum of two seconds, bringing it down as close to absolute zero as was possible. Bo was saying it was no problem, but that's what Bo would say. Jenna was more cautious, but in the end she said that what we needed to do wasn't impossible. At least in theory. None of that was very reassuring.

Theory was all very well, but we only had one chance at this. If Bo and Jenna miscalculated, or even if we got the timing wrong, it could be disastrous. Newport City might just take down the Outer Veil and wear the consequences. And maybe the water would decide to do what it wanted. Whatever the hell that was.

Plus the weather wasn't ideal. A storm was rolling in from the dasht, and factoring that in did all sorts of bizarre things to my dynamic modelling, from total catastrophe to 99.99 per cent success. At least it wasn't a nano-storm. They mainly hit in mid-winter.

I didn't like this calling of arcane powers. Bo really did think the water was some kind of magic. Sure, it seemed like magic, but that was only because we didn't understand it. The water wasn't some amazing resource we could just go in and use. Like Sevika, it wanted something, but unlike Sevika, I had no way of knowing what that was. My best guess was that it wanted to get rid of us altogether, and that wasn't a very comforting thought. When I raised that possibility with Bo, he flatly denied it in a way that made me think that maybe it was true.

We needed the water to do one thing, and to do it for two seconds. That's all. And then it had to stop. Stopping the water was the bit that worried me most.

I wanted a scenario with something like 99 per cent or higher, to give us some wiggle room. Adding in human error rates changed the scenarios from minimal disruption to total disaster, depending at which point of the process the error occurred. We couldn't afford to make any mistakes. But we were definitely going to make mistakes.

The only thing I felt sure about were our suits. These were the best suits I had ever made, and ours were already the best in the banns. Brian Mac had suggested some extra twiddles that helped with energy optimisation, so even with all their facilities switched on high they'd last six hours longer. Eighteen hours was more than enough. If we screwed up, we'd know in much less time than that.

At least I'd be with Flora when the end came. If it came. If.

I laid it all out to everyone as clearly as I could. Everyone sat on pallets on the floor, their faces upturned to me as I went through the scenario with the screen as big as I could get it. As I talked it through, I thought about what a motley bunch we were. Ma, me, Bo, Flora and Jenna. That was family. Kat and Rioka would be joining us later to help manage the comms. They were family now, too. Three pinkers and an AI. Brian Mac was almost family, but the others…they were here by chance, drawn together by the vortex of events that was whirling us all in.

In this room were all the people I loved best. Maybe I'd come to love the others, if I had time. But I was just as aware of everyone else outside in the banns, almost as if I could see them in ghostly outline. They trusted us to get it right, they were trusting that it was worth the risks we were taking. Redborg, Kat, Rioka, the Alchems, all the fleshers Ma had drawn together. And Sevika and her three thousand gangsters.

And beyond them all the fleshers in all the banns, all of us, wanting just some chance at a life that wasn't a bare scrabble for survival in a world in which the odds were stacked against us, in which there wasn't a foot on our necks every day pushing our faces down into the dust until we choked and died.

It was that simple. And that complicated.

This was the first real step. It wasn't good enough, but it was the best we could do with what we had.

I went through every single detail and answered everybody's questions. What chances we had, what chances we didn't have, what we knew, what we didn't know, what were the backups if this went wrong, or that went wrong. Which situations had no backup.

We weren't ready. But we had to do it anyway.

Finally there were no more questions and I fell silent.

'Okay,' said Ma, and stood up slowly, stretching. 'Everyone clear?'

Everyone nodded.

'Double check all your schedules,' she said. 'We've got that meeting with Sevika tomorrow. And you two…' – she nodded at me and Flora – 'you get some rest.'

'So I don't need any rest?' said Brian Mac. We all turned and stared at him. He was showing his age. He looked exhausted, his cheeks hollow, his eyes red-rimmed and baggy.

Ma looked as if she wanted to laugh, and then her face softened. 'You want me to mother you too, Brian?'

'Something like that.'

'Well, you're in the Newport City team with Flora and Dez, Brig Brian Mackinstosh, so you'd better get some rest while you can.'

'Will do, captain.' He looked around. 'I'm commandeering back my mezzanine. Okay?'

Nobody argued. We watched him climb the ladder upstairs, and then Flora and I went to the far end of the lab, laid out pallets and lay down.

'You okay, Dezzie?' Flora whispered into my hair.

'No,' I said. 'I'm so frightened.'

I could say it to her.

'Me too.'

Her arms tightened around me.

Bo

Ma's conversation with Sevika was brief and businesslike. They were like two battle-scarred nekas, sniffing each other, hackles raised. Conditions were laid out, guarantees made. Lies told? By Ma, yeah, probably, the lies she thought were necessary to protect us. By Sevika almost certainly, for her own reasons. They treated each other with the full courtesy of distrust.

Redborg would guide me into the Rift. Ma wanted Jenna to go with me.

'Trust your instincts,' she said. 'Don't take anything for granted, don't believe everything you're told. And listen to Jenna.'

'I do,' I said.

'Not as much as you should.'

I knew that Ma was right. The connection between me and Jenna had become troubled and turbulent lately. Maybe I was afraid that she was right to distrust the water. I knew that she was right to be wary of Sevika. Maybe I was as frightened as she was, but I didn't want to admit it.

Still, it worried me that Jenna was coming. She never made excuses, but the injuries from the raid on the Eighth had only been a couple of months before, and bodies need time to heal. If I said anything about it, she'd brush me off. She only used painkillers when it got bad, but she couldn't hide her pain from me.

Whatever happened, it was going to be rough. In the end, it was Jenna's call. All the same, when she told me that there was no way that she wasn't coming, a wave of relief and gratitude swept through me. I needed her there.

We both knew that.

We set out while it was still dark, meeting Redborg in a lane behind Rue Mara station. He nodded a greeting and we went underground, turning east once we hit the RTS. The plan was to come out in the Tenth not far from the Wall's eastern porte. Our maps were a little sketchy for this section, but we found our way without too much trouble. These deserted tunnels were becoming familiar to us now, their silence and darkness part of our world.

We moved in single file, me in front, Redborg bringing up the rear. I thought about the music of the Rift, the way that it tore through my head. I thought about the skinner with a piece of the sky for a face who'd almost killed me, the way she talked that Rift lingo. I could see her on the ground after Morro downed her. And I felt Sevika's cold, shining eyes as if she were right there looking at me, weighing me up. Taking hold of me.

Once we were above ground, we amped up our suits. It was about a klick to Rue Shima, where we'd arranged to meet Sevika's people. The rendez-vous was a tiny store, the kind that sells herbal remedies and tonics, called The Crows Foot. Sevika would be sending two of her thugs called Chee and Riddle to meet us. From there it was some distance to the Rift proper and we'd have to bypass two battalions of militia on the way.

There were spotter drones overhead, trailed by a much larger strike drone, a black, heavy beast that looked like a flying cockroach. We didn't see many people out until we came across a large group on a corner gathered around a few boxes of produce laid out on the ground: wilted greens, slabs of manky looking curd, dried tubers. Food was short here and there was a lot of shoving and yelling. I saw a fist fight break out over the price of a bag of fungus. We pushed through the crowd and turned into the narrow lane that led into Rue Shima.

The Crows Foot was squeezed between a boarded-up tea shop and the shell of what used to be some kind of old tech repair store. The place stank so bad that my eyes started to water. The shelves were crowded with bunches of dried herbs, jars of mouldy roots and bottles of dubious-looking liquids. From a door at the back of the shop an old guy in a filthy jacket and straw hat came and stood at the counter. He looked us up and down, saying nothing. Redborg made some kind of signal I didn't catch and the old guy gestured for us to follow him.

The room out back was even dingier than the shop. There was nothing in it but a squalid looking armchair and a ladder leaning against the wall.

'Up there,' he said, pointing.

Redborg went up first, pushing open a small hatch in the ceiling and squeezing through. I went up last. I looked down and the old guy was gone.

Sevika's people were standing in the circle of light thrown by a small lantern. Riddle was a squat, long-haired guy with face tattoos. Chee, who seemed to be in charge, was wearing black shades and a red skinner's bandolier. I stole a look at Jenna, feeling my skin crawl, and saw that she couldn't hide her disgust. Dealing with skinners was the worst.

'Stay close and don't talk,' said Chee.

We followed them through a low door into another hollow space, down a steep ladder and into a hot, airless gap between two walls. It was a tight fit, especially for Redborg. Finally we came out into a wide shaft. I looked up and saw the faint glow of the Veil through a filthy skylight.

Riddle opened a trapdoor in the floor and climbed down into a wide steel pipe with narrow steps welded onto its side. It was a long way down. There was a rail running against the wall, but that was all. I hung onto it so hard I felt my hand cramping. Was it possible to be afraid of heights when I was under the ground? Maybe I was afraid of depths as well. Maybe they were the same thing. Of course they were the same thing. I almost laughed. But mostly I felt sick.

It seemed to take hours.

We finally emerged into a massive cave. It was at least five stories high and maybe half a klick from side to side, and it was filled with an eerie, reddish light. I blinked, rubbing the sweat out of my eyes, and tried to understand what I was looking at.

In the centre blazed a huge machine. It sent up a thick column of vapour that spread over the roof high above into an uncanny cloud veined with flickering red and purple threads. It seemed to be emitting a low buzz of static.

Jenna clutched my hand convulsively, as freaked as I was. 'What's *that*?'

'Some kind of masking,' said Redborg, from beside me. 'It negates the heat maps. And other things, I believe.'

I felt a sudden, strange awe. Fleshers. We're so damn ingenious.

And there they were, the Rift's army. Hundreds of them, thousands of them, moving in the dim light, a mass of bodies populating the shadows.

Even among that horde I could see her clearly, her dark eyes set on me.

Sevika. Queen of the Rift.

Dez

Me, Flora, Brian Mac and Ami, heading to meet Ava in Rue Ban Gu. Threading our way through the rues of the Second, all of us in disguise as ordinary fleshers out for an ordinary scavenge in the ordinary occupied city. It was just like old times, only worse, and with extra personnel.

Despite everything, my spirits lifted when I stepped out into the open air. It was early, just after sunrise, and the tiny streets of the Second were bathed in the yellow light that happens before a storm. We hurried, not talking, past the scruffy little shops and housefronts huddled close like conspirators, the scraggly gardens, the smell of damp rust. Behind all those sealed doors were the humble spaces that people made for themselves with love and sweat, their precious objects, their favourite chair or jacket. Like the glass apple I loved so much, that was smashed when the Ap raided our house in Rue Ballard.

It all seemed so vivid, like I was seeing it for the last time. My god, I loved this place. The Second was the map of my happiest moments. On that corner Flora and I had shared a pastry after the first time we made love. Bo played the keyboards for the first time in that bar when he was twelve, and we'd all gone along and clapped and cheered. Walking past the empty shijo where I spent so much time as a kid working on Ma's stall. Ma laboured so many years to get us into the Second, so we'd be safer. She wanted us to live in a place where we might have a chance.

That's where the bitter sadness lodged in my throat. We'd have a chance, all of us, no matter which bann we lived in, if we weren't cut down at every turn. We could flourish. We could become everything we dreamed of being. I put the anger and sadness away. I didn't have time for all that now.

I couldn't stop myself running through our scenario. Maybe in the millions of variations I'd modelled there was something I'd missed, some hidden optimisation that increased our chances by that magic percentage that meant we weren't going to blow ourselves and everyone else into oblivion. Maybe there was something that could drive the chance of catastrophic failure down to zero. If things went bad it would be completely my fault.

To make myself feel a bit better, I'd modelled a number of scenarios of what would happen if we did nothing. In almost every case, our personal chances of survival ranged between 0 and 5 per cent. Though it didn't make me feel better, as such: it just made me feel slightly less worse. There was no way of ridding myself of the stone cold dread that lay in the pit of my stomach.

We reached the warehouse where Ava based her smuggling business, entered a dim courtyard and then through a door, down an empty corridor. The whole place looked deserted. But it looked deserted last time, too. Finally we reached a door guarded by heavies. They were expecting us.

'Stop it, Dez,' said Flora, as we stepped through into Ava's inner sanctum.

I jumped. Flora always knew when I wasn't fully there. 'Stop what?'

'Stop whatever you're doing. Stop it.' She grinned at me sideways, but there was no humour in her eyes.

'I've got a bad feeling,' I said. 'Like I've missed something. But I can't think of anything I've missed, aside from the things that I know I don't know…'

'We're committed. So let's concentrate on we've planned and do it, huh?'

'Yeah. 20.5463 per cent chance of total catastrophe,' I said.

'So that means…79 point something or other chance of success,' said Flora. 'Right?'

'79.5437 per cent,' said Ami. '56.73 per cent of partial failure, averaged out over approximately 16 million scenarios covering 546 definitions of mortality and mission failure.'

There was a short silence, broken by a dry laugh from Brian Mac. 'I've done a lot of jobs with a catastrophic chance of mortality,' he said. 'Sometimes it's better not to know.'

'You mean that you don't calculate your chances?' Ami sounded surprised.

'I go by the feel in my gut,' said Brian Mac. 'And a good dose of rat cunning.'

'That sounds very imprecise. Could you expand on that?'

'No,' said Brian Mac.

For a moment I wanted to laugh. Ami had her curiosity circuits on high: she was still researching what it was like to be human. If she ever figured it out, would she think that being human was a good idea? There was no guarantee on that one. Sometimes I thought it was a very bad idea indeed.

I wondered uneasily again what kind of monster I'd let out of the cage when I took out her inhibitors. All the stories we told about AIs were horror stories. But Ami, top of the range PAC 62345Z, with her neat, black bob and her sapphire eyes, didn't look like a horror story.

And anyway, we needed her.

'Morning, Brian,' said Ava, standing up behind her desk. She looked amazing: hair immaculate, heels like spikes. How did she do it? I noticed that this time that there weren't any piles of banns-grown tates and greens waiting to be smuggled into the cool cafes of Newport City. I guessed that business had tanked in the war. 'Morning, the rest of you.'

'Ava.' Brian Mac nodded in greeting. 'All as planned?'

'Yes. How's Gloria, by the way?'

'Alive. Bel's promoted them to deputy comms.'

Ava permitted herself a smile. 'That's my Gloria,' she said. 'Talking is their favourite thing.'

It all panned out pretty much like the time we went to rescue Bo from the hospital, only this time Ava didn't bother to threaten us. Through the maze of corridors to the concealed elevator, down into the bowels of the earth, the nightmare run through the Inner Veil which still felt, even with disruptors, like you were being burned up from the inside. Up in another elevator, into another anonymous building.

Now we were in the bad burbs of Newport City, which were basically three steps up from the best banns. Clean streets, working lights, everyone with perfect skin. Ava left for the Feelgood, and we all glanced at each other. We weren't heading to the salon this time. Now we were all splitting up. Brian Mac had his mission, me and Flora had our own.

Before we went out into the streets, we triple checked everything: our suits, our IMRs, our maps, our timepieces, our comms. I felt like my whole belly was fluttering.

I checked with Bo. He was on his way, on schedule. He'd set off two hours before us because he had further to go. Sevika's push and Brian Mac's job were the distractions: Operation Chaos. At worst, we only needed one of them to go right. I tried not to think of what would happen if Bo's mission went wrong.

We said our farewells. Nobody made any jokes, like we normally would.

'Good luck, ladies,' said Brian Mac, holding out his hand. 'You do you. Do it well. I'll be in touch when I've done me.'

I pressed his hand briefly and let go. 'Good luck.' My throat was dry.

'Hey, Mac,' Flora said. 'You know I hated you my whole life?'

Brian Mac grinned crookedly. 'Yeah, I did know that,' he said.

'You know what? I actually kind of like you, now.'

'Likewise,' he said. 'Only I never did hate you.'

'Not being a cop suits you. You're okay, for a pinker.' She shook his offered hand, gently, like I had. Since Erin and Gloria had come to stay, we were more conscious of how difficult touching was for pinkers. 'Good luck, Brian.'

'You too.'

He turned on his IMR. Involuntarily we stepped back: now he was the image of a Newport City council guard, blonde hair, chiselled chin, smooth skin, empty, ice-blue eyes. He winked, and for a moment we saw the old Brian Mac, and then he walked out of the door.

'I'm glad you told him that,' I said.

'Trying not to leave any unfinished business.' Flora checked her taser, went through her suit again, turned to Ami. 'Okay. Let's go.'

Bo

According to Dez, in the event of a large-scale uprising in the banns, OpSec would send militia, strike drones and heavily armed clouds from barracks in Newport City Central. The orders were to take no prisoners. No restraint was to be exercised under any circumstances and no surrender would be accepted. Whoever stood in OpSec's way would be wiped out.

So it was all or nothing. Once we began, there was no way out. Either we won, or we lost everything.

We'd worked out the tactics with Sevika the day before, in neutral space, underground in the Sixth. It was a strange meeting: me, Ma, Dez, Redborg, Sevika, her second in command Lebrex and a couple of henchmen. Tense, as Redborg said, but productive. It worked out only because each side needed the other.

Sevika was splitting the Rift's army into three. The first was led by Lebrex, a giant of man with black, braided hair. They would strike west, into the Sixth and through the First, heading directly for the Inner Veil. Lebrex's group would launch a large attack at the East Porte, but that would be a diversion. Most of his fleshers would use the old sewer system and the RTS to get into the Sixth. The other two groups would head north and south through the Tenth.

Everyone had to be in position by 8:00 hours, ready to strike. The northern group would attack first, smashing its way through the Curtains into the Ninth. There were fifteen Curtains, each guarded by around a dozen militia, set up in rues that ran between the Tenth and the Ninth. The plan was to hit all of them simultaneously. When reinforcements left Newport City after the first alarm, the Rifters would strike in the south and break through into the Eleventh. By then Brian Mac should have OpSec HQ in an uproar.

Sevika had said that if OpSec were pushed hard enough, they'd abandon the outer banns. 'If they think the Inner Veil is threatened, anything outside the Wall won't matter to them. So you'd better make it real,' she said.

She'd looked at Ma, but it was Dez who answered. 'It'll be real all right,' she said. The way she said it was like an insult. Dez was always spiky, but Sevika made her super spiked.

Sevika bared her teeth. 'I guess we'll see, child,' she said. 'My people will be out in the open. They could just take them down with clouds. So you'd better be able to do what you say you can do.'

Dez just smiled back, her eyes like daggers. 'I'm not full of shit,' she said. 'I'm trusting that you're not, either. Otherwise none of this will work.'

Sevika said her forces would swell once they broke out of the Tenth. The Rift had people in every outer bann. They'd been preparing, the same kind of work that Ma had been doing: making connections, establishing communications between disparate groups, turning scattered bands of fleshers into a force to be reckoned with.

Inside the Wall, Ma's people would be doing their own damage. It wouldn't be a full on assault like the Rifters, because we didn't have the numbers. Our plan was sabotage: scrambling comms, blocking rues, launching hit and run attacks on patrols. Causing chaos.

Ma said that it was more than likely that once Sevika's army got past the Wall they wouldn't stop. That had been a big bone of contention, but in the end Sevika agreed that Lebrex's forces would stop in the First. We all knew that if they decided to break their word and spear into Newport City Central, we'd have no way of stopping them. That would be more than chaos: it would be slaughter.

But first we had to deal with the Wall. Redborg, Jenna, Sevika and I were staying in the Tenth, heading straight to the Wall. We were going to freeze it.

The idea was to bring the Wall down close to absolute zero, like I had with that Ap. It had to last for at least two seconds. That way we'd slow down the molecular movement of the Wall to almost nothing, which would, Dez said, disrupt its its 'suspending resonance', which she said was a major way that Newport City kept the Inner Veil stable. She said a lot of other stuff, but I didn't understand any of it. She told us that getting to absolute zero was an impossibility, but in any case, we shouldn't try. If we got it that cold, it would be a problem: she couldn't predict what might happen. 'Just as cold as possible,' she said. 'Without being totally cold.'

Jenna and I had been practising on a brick we found in the lab. Dez wouldn't even contemplate us going out without a practical demonstration. We had to do it on the mezzanine, and everyone hated the experiments because it totally screwed the heating and it took ages to get warm again. But it worked. I did it to the brick first time, just thinking about it. Jenna had to feel her way in, but after a few tries she could do it too.

Dez didn't even try to hide how impressed she was, but she really grilled us about scaling up. 'It doesn't have to be the whole Wall,' she said. 'But it does need to be a whole section, all the way through. You need to break the circle to disrupt the resonance.'

Neither Jenna nor I felt anxious about that. If we could do it small, we could do it big. Scale isn't a thing with water work. Dez wasn't totally convinced, but in the end she accepted that was how it was. She just didn't get dowsing. I don't think she ever will. It's about things she doesn't quite manage, like intuition and feelings. She didn't tell us, but I knew she'd made a back up plan.

As soon as we'd frozen a section of the Wall, Dez could get on with dismantling the Inner Veil.

And then, so the theory went, we'd all be free.

From the underground cave, we travelled through a series of ruined sewers to Rue Ferres station, the closest we could get to the Wall in the Tenth. From here we would move up into the streets.

Sevika was following the attacks on a portable screen. The Rifters had several drones taking vision. One of Sevika's crew had created shields for them, making them look like malfunctioning OpSec recon drones. They'd be ignored in the mayhem that was happening below.

So far everything was going according to plan. The northern group moved first, hitting all the curtains between the Tenth and the Ninth. These attack groups were led by skinners, many using timeslips. They'd appear with their stingers at the throats of the militia before they knew what was happening.

OpSec's response was horrifyingly fast. A swarm of strike drones sped northwards out of Newport City Central, while a convoy of clouds rumbled through the North East Porte and attempted to re-establish the Curtains in several rues.

Fighting in the Ninth was fierce. The Rifters weren't having it all their own way, but they were joined by mobs of local fleshers. We even saw groups of Alchems in black camos among the mob. Now Lebrex attacked the East Porte, pushing into the sixth. OpSec had poured most of their resources north, to contain the uprising. They were probably hoping to trap the Rifters between the Outer Veil and the Wall. And then the third group hit in the south.

Sevika smiled coldly as she watched. She was enjoying this. A chill went down my spine: for a moment her eyes narrowed and darkened, and I thought she had the face of a neka.

Erin

'Do you want to live, or do you want to die? After you decide that, it gets easier.'

Well, Gloria was wrong on that one. It doesn't get easier, it gets more complicated. First you decide you want to live, then you have to choose sides, then you have to figure out what the hell your side means.

I don't know about this 'sides' business. I mean, all my life I was told it's fleshers against pinkers. But it's not that simple. Nothing is ever that simple. Bel is almost as worried about the Rifters as she is about OpSec. She hates this Sevika woman like poison, you can see it in how she says her name, she practically spits it out. It's like OpSec goons talking about Brig Brian Mackintosh: they're worse than the enemy, they're traitors to their own kind. But she's teaming up with her anyway.

And then there's us. Gloria and me. I guess we're traitors too, though I feel more that *they* betrayed *us*. Whose side are we on? What will happen to the people I know in Newport City if they bring down the Inner Veil? Is anyone back there worried about me? Did they care when they heard the whisper, when they crossed the road to avoid me?

Maybe they cared. But they were too frightened to do anything about it. I should know, I used to do the same thing. It's a bit desolating to think that

Dez was the first person who cared enough to try to help me. It wasn't as if she knew me. She just figured it wasn't right.

I feel like I'm choosing something for the first time in my life, even though I have no real idea what it is I'm choosing. Maybe that's what choice means, that you don't know what will happen. When I think about it, I always did what I was told: I lived where celebrities are told to live, took the jobs that Dervin told me to take, said the words that somebody else wrote. Sometimes I could decide which dress I wanted to wear to some celebrity reception. That was it.

Actually choosing something is like standing on a cliff with your eyes closed and jumping. It's so fucking terrifying.

The really strange thing is, I haven't had a martini since forever, and I've got no idea if any of us will be alive tomorrow, and I'm so scared I feel like I want to throw up. But something inside me feels…triumphant. Something inside me feels super plus.

It's hard to shake the feeling that I'm filming a soap. This whole place looks like a set.

Gloria and Bel are co-ordinating the whole shebang. They both have three screens up in front of them, and in between there's another, a huge 3D map where they're tracking who is where. There's three different comms: the super secret ones they've doled out between the teams, the dark tubes which they're using to co-ordinate the fleshers, and Sevika's special channel, which she insists on although Dez was very dubious about the security. Plus they're monitoring all the security comms they can. There's another couple of fleshers here, Kat and Rioka, who are helping, though Rioka mainly seems to be in some kind of trance.

I'm watching Gloria take the signals, snapping in and out of the different channels. I can tell that they're extra good at this. They have this air of ultra efficiency, like they were born to do it. I'd get all kind of confused and balls things up. Gloria says that reception experience at the FeelGood prepares you for anything.

I'm missing Ami. Me, I can't do anything at this point except watch and wait. My part comes later.

Before she leaves, Ami gets me ready like I'm going to a super important celebrity ball. The smartwear I've got doesn't quite stretch to ultra-glamour, but we do our best. I'm lounging on a chair in a clinging dress of shimmering blues and violets – calming colours, Ami says – with full-on blonde curls. It's actually surprising: even without a bath or a biobooth, after two weeks on the run and without any designers on tap, I'm looking the total star.

When I come down from the mezzanine in all my finery, everyone goes quiet. I can't stop that little jump of gratification in my chest. *I've still got it.* Then Flora starts laughing. She stops when she sees I look a bit hurt.

'Sorry, Erin,' she says. 'It's just so….wrong. A soap star, *here*. In this room. Right now.'

She's right. It *is* strange. What is stranger is that Flora apologised for hurting my feelings.

'You look perfect,' says Dez.

I watch everyone leave and then recheck the cam that Dez has set up for me, making sure I have it down. I got someone once to show me how to use them, so I feel confident about that, but this is a different model to the usual. I can't fuck it up, there's no second take on this.

And now I'm going through my lines. My lines, that I wrote for me to say. Okay, with a bit of help from Dez and Flora, because I wasn't sure about some things. But it's me saying the words that I wrote. The Ultra-Real Erin Saba show, starring The Real Erin Saba.

I hope I get a chance to do it. There's a 20 per cent chance it won't happen.

I do some voice exercises, a few stretches, getting the tension out of my shoulders. I can't get rid of it all. I have the usual butterflies, plus a million more.

But I'm a professional. Waiting for my cue.

Bo

Looking over Sevika's shoulder, we caught confusing glimpses of fighting. By the time the Rifters smashed their way into the Eleventh, OpSec was prepared. The Curtains here didn't fall so easily.

Militia were swarming everywhere and the air was almost black with striker drones. One group of skinners, the first out of the RTS, never made it further than the exit, cut down as soon as they came up onto the streets. Two or three of the Curtains fell, but others continued to hold out. OpSec was launching a ferocious counter attack, pushing part of Sevika's army back into the Tenth.

Sevika's forces were growing, as she said they would. Groups of flesh-ers were joining the Rifters all across the banns, armed and ready to fight. Many threw themselves straight into the attack, while others tended to the wounded, dragging them away from the carnage. The fighting shifted from street to street. People trying to escape the conflict ran out of their houses, while others boarded themselves up or threw up improvised barricades across their streets, hindering the Rifters as much as the militia.

It was chaos. I couldn't tell if we were winning or losing.

We came out of the station into an empty Rue Ferres to hear fighting close by. The Wall rose into the smoke-filled sky about two blocks to our right. I checked the time. We were on track. We couldn't leave Dez waiting: every minute would make her situation more dangerous. We had to get to the Wall as quickly as we could.

We turned into Rue Boll, which led straight to the base of the Wall. We had gone about fifty metres when we saw a phalanx of OpSec militia heading straight for us. We turned and ran into Rue Luis, smack into the Rifter's counter attack as they rushed towards the militia. We pushed our way through the sea of bodies, trying to get away from the fighting. For a few moments we were separated in the chaos. By the time we'd struggled clear, we'd lost sight of Redborg.

I felt suddenly vulnerable. 'We have to find Redborg,' I said.

'He can look after himself,' said Sevika. 'We don't need him.'

She was moving towards a house that had its windows and door blown out by the explosion that had destroyed a nearby Curtain. Jenna and I followed close behind. Inside, we crouched under the empty window in the smoke-filled front room and tried to catch our breath. I looked up and saw the roof of the building across the street was on fire. In the sky above it, a massive stormcloud veined with lightning was rolling in from the south. I could already smell the dry stink of the dasht on the rising breeze. Shit. The last thing we needed.

We ran out the back door, crossed the yard and scaled a low fence, landing in a narrow laneway. We followed it into Rue Rakami, one of the main streets in the area. I knew it well because I was a regular at Bao's music shop, but I could hardly recognise the empty street through the drifting smoke, strewn with the burning remains of a Curtain. We could see the Wall from the corner. We stopped and listened: the fighting in Rue Boll seemed to be moving away from us.

A yellowish twilight fell over the bann and the first drops of rain began to fall.

We headed for the Wall.

Dez

Even through the double Veil, the light was still yellow. I wondered what storms were like in Newport City. Maybe nobody worried about them, because they never had to. It never rained in Newport City, but they still had all the water. How did that work?

From now on timing was crucial. We'd divided the magnetic comms between Bo, Ma, Brian Mac and me, so we could all keep in sync. Flora, Ami and I were heading to the central power station. That was our first task: we had to disable as much of the power in Newport City as possible. We didn't have to bring down the whole energy network, just more than 60 per cent of it. The eight substations were connected to the central power station, like spokes in a wheel, and they all had failsafes that would kick in once the the main source was down. But the central station provided around 75 per cent.

We headed towards Newport City Central, following Ami. She was the only one not in disguise, though she'd changed her serial number: apparently she was now the AI that belonged to a high-grade systems analyser who lived in Block Three. We'd chosen him partly because he was the most boring person we could find.

Flora and I, remembering that we were almost undone when we got the clone-type wrong at Newport Western Hospital, were mechanic clones, type

237. Very lowly, apparently, but high on tech savvy and mostly employed at the power stations. We were also male, because apparently there were no female mechanics in Newport City. We could put our voices through a pitch modulator but our banns accents would be a problem. According to Erin and Ami, that was okay because people like us were ignored by higher status clones, but it meant we had to keep our mouths shut. If anyone actually spoke to us, Ami would do the talking.

Despite myself, I felt excited. Newport City Central was where all the glamour was and this time I'd be seeing it in the daytime. The streets got wider and shinier the further we wound in. Soon there were shops with big glass windows and IMR displays: fashion boutiques, furniture shops. Cafes with lights blazing even though the sun was up, where smartly dressed pinkers were scoffing their breakfasts.

Everything I looked at was excessive. I saw people leaving food on their plates. That never happens in the banns. Never. The first time we saw a fountain, Flora almost clutched my hand, which would have blown our cover entirely. I've seen fountains on the tubes, but somehow seeing one for real was different. All that water, just splashing through the air. No thought of how it might vapourise into wastage, no thought of what else it might be needed for.

In the banns, water is precious. We reuse it. Every. Single. Drop.

Brian Mac pinged me through the secret comms. We'd worked out codes: that ping meant he'd reached his first station and was about to head into OpSec HQ. Right now Bo and Jenna should be heading towards the Wall, though I hadn't heard since they had met Sevika. Ma hadn't sent any alarms, so presumably all was good. I sent an interrogative ping and got a confirmation back.

8:30. We had to be in the power station by 9:15 at the latest, in our final position by 9:45. Okay. So far, okay. I could hear the tension in my breathing. I stopped staring at Newport City Central, stopped thinking about the pinkers streaming past me on the clean streets with their fashionable clothes and water-plump skin, stopped thinking about anything except what we had to do now. I had to be present, 110 per cent, even if that's mathematically impossible. Everything we were doing was impossible. Well, 20 per cent impossible.

Stop it, Dez. I could almost hear Flora's thoughts.

8:56. Everything seemed normal. The newsfeeds on the walls were talking about some celebrity party the night before, yak yak yak. Somebody's dress was scandalous, darling. Somebody else's was super super plus.

Right now the fleshers were rising in the banns. Right now Sevika's skinners should be bringing down the curtains in the Ninth. I stopped myself from checking. No news was good news. We kept walking. Almost at the target. We turned a corner and there it was.

Even the power station was glamorous. Like all the stations in Newport City Central, it ran on nuclear fusion. More water. It was covered in white self-cleaning tiles, all of them gleaming, with wide metal doors that opened into a showy foyer. Flora and I exchanged glances. The substations in the banns – the ones that work – are crumbling brick and steel, a mess of home-fixed wires and add-on tech, their rusting walls covered in graffiti.

Ami got a couple of curious glances as we walked in, I guess a personal AI isn't standard in a power station, but her serial number was holding. Our story was that we'd been sent by our boring systems analyser to deal with a fault he'd caught overnight. Ami was to show us where it was. Slightly unusual protocol, but not that unusual. A minor problem, easily dealt with by just such lowly mechanics as Flora and me. Only, of course, we had other plans.

We were counting on it not even occurring to OpSec that fleshers could worm their way into their power network in Newport City Central. Because for all their paranoia, according to my scenarios, they were complacent. Arrogance does that.

Now, the first test: getting past the security station in the entrance. We swiped our wrists over the scanner, tensed in case it went off. We had the most recent codes we could get, a week old, but that didn't mean that they hadn't wiped them. Ami went through without a blink, which meant that the system analyst's AI had been successfully neutralised. I mean, I knew it had been, I had done it, but it was nice to get confirmation.

Then me. Then Flora. No alarm. I pinged the others.

Deep breath. Down the corridor towards the central circuit. Everything was unsettlingly quiet, even our footsteps, because the floor had some strangely soft black covering. Aside, that is, from the music playing through the intercom, some kind of smooth pinker sound that made my ears feel numb. I guessed it was supposed to be soothing, but I thought I'd go spare if I had to put up with that all day.

Time seemed to be going really fast now. 9:16. Past two more security stations, all good. The final station was the one I was most worried about – it needed the highest security clearance, a different code to the one we'd been using – but that was no problem. According to the protocols they changed it every month, and we were two weeks into the cycle. Me, I'd have changed it every day. But then OpSec didn't know what we were planning. Yet.

I had abandoned the idea of hacking the power station's operational coding: no matter how sneaky I was, coding was still trackable and there was a small chance that they'd trace and fix it, especially given that we wanted to black out all of Newport City Central. Instead, we were going manual.

We reached the section we were targeting slightly ahead of time. We didn't have the standard keys but it took me no time to decode the lock on the wall-panel. We had a little bit of sabotage to do before getting into the controls. Literally, we had to unscrew a couple of bolts.

'Right,' Flora said, flashing me a grin. 'On with the show.' I watched her squeeze into the wall cavity, heading left. When she disappeared I followed her, going right. It was hot and there was hardly any space and the humming of the power station vibrated through my body. I edged past the pipes, the blueprint up live on my lenscam, looking for a joint in the pipes around two metres away. Yes, there it was, like the plan said it would be. I unclipped the wrench from my belt and got to work on the bracket holding the pipe.

The damn bolts were stuck fast. I kicked up the sonic juice and still it didn't move. 9:36. I only had another minute. I pushed down panic, turned the sonic waves up to max and tried again. Bingo. The bracket loosened and the pipe sagged. Now it had no reinforcement. I backed out of there fast, feeling the sweat tickling my scalp. Flora was already out. I locked the wall panel and we went on to station two. We were thirty seconds behind schedule. Still in a safe margin of error.

We headed to a small control room where we could manage the

actuators on this section of the station. It was like a rhyme we used to chant when we were kids: the actuators controlled the valves that controlled the steam that turned the turbines that generated the power. We needed to rejig the valves so that pressure would build in the pipes we had destabilised. I had discovered that two pipes were six millimetres smaller than they should be, a mistake during construction. It was so minor that nobody had bothered to replace them, but my modelling showed that if they burst in the right conditions, it would cause a chain reaction that would total the whole station. The big advantage of doing it this way was that if you didn't know where to look, it could take days to identify what had gone wrong.

We hurried so we were in place by 9:44. No one needed to be in this control room at this time, but it was still a relief that it was empty. I was counting every successful step as a win, adjusting our chances as we got past each station.

Now we had to wait for a ping from Brian Mac before we went ahead. He was due to check in at 9:45. He should be right in front of Garonne in his office at this very minute. He should be lifting his hidden taser and putting a bolt right through Garonne's temple.

9:46. 9:47. The minutes slid by with no ping. It was now getting past my margin of error. We needed the distraction at OpSec HQ before we downed the power, because otherwise our escape from the power station would be a 68 per cent fail.

9:48. I pinged Bo to hold off. 9:49. The seconds were dragging now. I could smell my own sweat, sour with anxiety.

Ping. Brian Mac.

Bo

As we moved into the shadow of the Wall, the air suddenly grew much colder. Even on a sunny day it was oppressive: the way it deadened all sounds, the slow, inexorable journey of its shadow across the rues each day.

There was a wide band of open ground of maybe fifty metres between the last houses in Rue Rakami and the Wall. Nothing grew here. The earth was dead, a chalky white that gave off a rancid, dead smell. The foul taste rose in my throat.

I could feel the immense weight of the Wall in my bones. Its sheer presence made it seem like a living thing. When I looked up to the top, the sky spun around my head. I'd never been so close to the Wall, in all the years I'd lived in the banns. Now I knew why.

'The faster we get this done, the better,' I said to Jenna. She made a face and nodded, wiping the rain out of her eyes. It was falling steadily now.

Sevika stood a little apart from us, staring up at the Wall. We all moved closer, until we were almost within touching distance. I grabbed hold of Jenna's hand.

'C'est l'heure. Avoir du courage,' Sevika said.

A sudden coldness surged from her body, a wave of energy that stung like ice. She gripped my hand and I felt the shock of her strength. I heard

Jenna gasp. The three of us stood rooted to the spot, our thoughts spiralling around each other in a moment of terrifying confusion. And then I heard Sevika's voice. I couldn't tell if it was inside me or outside: it seemed to echo against the Wall, growing louder instead of being absorbed like all other sound.

'Call it,' said Sevika. 'Call the water.'

High above us, the thunder answered. I looked up and a sheet of hail hit me in the face like a blow. I fell to my knees.

I called the water. I could feel Jenna and Sevika calling too: it was a cry in our blood, a quickening of our senses, as if we were now one body, one mind, one desire.

And then everything stopped.

It was if a black hood had been thrown over my head and pulled tight. In the absolute darkness I could hardly breathe. I could feel nothing but the throbbing of my own heart. In panic I called Jenna's name but there was no answer. I tried to call the water flowing between us, I tried to picture her face, but my mind was flooded with a swirling darkness that drew me into the Wall.

Sevika was gone, Jenna was gone. The whole world was gone.

Dez

This control room was tiny and windowless, with beige walls. It was cool and quiet, the hum of the turbines down to a low bass beneath the horrible pinker music.

It felt kind of unreal. By now, the banns would be in chaos, OpSec HQ on full emergency alert, Garonne's brains splashed over his desk by an unknown assailant who had, if everything went right, vanished into thin air. But all we could hear were pan pipes and the sound of our own breathing.

'Do it, Dez,' said Flora. Her voice was tight. 'Let's get out of here.'

'Ssssh,' said Ami, putting her finger to her lips. Flora almost snapped at her but didn't, because she knew she was right. There'd be visuals and audio all through this place, and once the power went out they'd be looking for anything unusual. A flesher accent would definitely count as abnormal.

Adjusting the actuators was the work of a moment. I stayed long enough to ensure that the steam was building up in the weakened pipes and then we got out of there, trying to move normally even though every instinct told us to run. We signed off through the security stations, and the steel doors of the entrance sighed shut behind our heels. We walked away feeling like guns were trained on our backs, and turned down the first side street.

We had a bit of a zig zag route towards our next destination, a small café on the edge of Newport City Central called UberBloss. We had to be fifty metres from UberBloss when the power blacked out.

'UberBloss,' said Flora, when we were talking through the plan. 'What kind of a name is that?'

According to its menu, UberBloss served dinky little drinks and cakes with 'floral accents'. Dandies, a weed in the banns, was one of their most popular flavours. But they also had rose cakes, eiderblossom wine and something called gaudy candies. We were all pretty curious about what they were but we weren't there to check out their specialities. UberBloss had something it called a 'powder room', a kind of superior toilet that had no surveillance whatsoever. That was where we could change our identities.

According to my calculations, the power would take nine minutes and forty seconds to cut out, with a ten second leeway either way. All the passive security cams would go down then and we'd only have to worry about surveillance bots. I had my suit alerts set to a radius of 150 metres, and I hadn't picked up a single one. Routine bot surveillance was mainly reserved for the banns. More fool them.

You couldn't miss UberBloss, which sat between a sleek beauty salon and a fashion boutique. It looked even more bizarre than the ads on the tubes. We arrived with two minutes to spare and loitered on the other side of the street trying to look inconspicuous, though I uneasily felt that we wereattracting notice from passers by. Low class mechanics had no business here: this was a hangout for the Newport City Council brass or celebrities like Erin.

The front was completely open, not even glassed in, with tables scattered around a central bar. Above the tables and over the roof floated a monstrous IMR garden of luminous flowers in the kinds of colours that give me a headache. Right now it was almost empty, with only a couple of tables of pinkers. Behind the bar was a woman whose pink-orange skin was so smoothed out I couldn't tell by looking whether she was an AI or a clone. An AI would be trouble, but I couldn't pick up any signals.

I was counting down to blackout, trying not to worry that our blueprints were out of date or that I hadn't destabilised the pipe enough or that I had set the wrong pressure for the steam. These were just neurotic thoughts, these were all things that I was 99.99 per cent sure of, but that didn't stop my anxiety. It should work, it had to work. Nine minutes. Nine minutes 30 seconds. Nine minutes 40 seconds. Nothing happened. I could sense Flora's tension without even looking at her. 45 seconds. 50. 51. For that final second I went into overdrive, flickering through my emergency scenarios. If the power didn't blow, we were screwed.

52 seconds and the Inner Veil blinked, as the power drained out of it and was picked up by the substation failsafes. The giant flowers crumpled up and vanished in front of our eyes. The signs and mobile ads layering the shopfronts zapped out, leaving the whole street looking dim and strangely naked. The pinkers lounging in the café turned their heads in surprise, their mouths open, and the pink-orange bar lady came out into the street and looked around to see what was happening.

'Now,' said Ami. We walked in like we had every right to be there and headed for the powder room. Nobody even glanced at us, they were too busy exclaiming about the power cut.

The powder room was in complete darkness, so we turned on the lights in our suits and Ami got to work with the IMR presets. It took only a couple of seconds. Now we were middle-range pinkers, blonde and blue-eyed, clones who covered personal services like the biobooths or food tech. We fiddled the records so Ami now belonged to one of the celebrity extras, a guy who spent most of his time when he wasn't working hopped out on illegal hormones and wouldn't notice if his AI was spending loose credits. He was also an informant. We didn't worry about getting him into trouble.

We rechecked our suits, ensuring the fields were on full optimisation. The passive security would now have trouble tracking us from the power station, even if it was turned back on.

We got out of there and headed to the FeelGood Salon. It was close to the Inner Veil, which we needed to be, and we'd be safer there from random surveillance. It was a half hour walk at a brisk pace. The quickest way to get to Block 15 was via the unirail, but the blackout nixed that possibility.

You could feel fear in the streets. People knew something was going wrong: pinkers were banging their wrist comms trying to get hold of people, or hurrying past us, their faces pale with anxiety. Nobody in Newport City seemed to have their own generators. Sometimes we heard people yelling for help because they were trapped inside apartments, unable to open their doors.

The public infotubes went out with the lights, but after a few minutes someone sourced power and they flickered back on, unnaturally bright in the dim streets. Blue AI announcers quacking to the citizens of Newport City not to panic, the power station has suffered a blackout but everything is under control and our technicians are now working on the fault, apologies for the inconvenience. I allowed myself a tiny smile. They had 0.02 per cent chance of tracking that fault within the next 24 hours.

This was just the beginning. We were on time and everything was going according to plan.

For the first time I let myself feel a bit hopeful.

Now for the Inner Veil.

I'll never forget that walk back through the shadowy streets of Newport City. This was a different city to the one we'd walked through maybe a half hour before. Stripped bare of all its pretty lights and IMR it looked stark and cold, like a prison.

We walked past steel walls, punctuated by closed shutters and doors. I realised that all of the gardens we'd seen were IMR. The pinkers had no real green anywhere, except in the odd empty block, and those were basically weeds. The scents were all artificial, and now the diffusers were dead you began to smell the city for real, a smell that made me think of abandoned hospitals, antiseptic and stale air.

We were walking fast, on the brink of breaking into a run, but this didn't make us stand out. We were pushing through groups of anxious, hurrying people. From snatches of conversation I overheard, I knew that at least some of them couldn't get into their houses. The crowds gave me a strange feeling: they weren't going anywhere, they were just milling in frightened circles, walking around blocks, gathering in knots around the public screens and then dispersing again into directionless hurrying. They didn't know what to do.

Council police, the Newport City versions of Aps, stood on every corner.

You couldn't see their eyes through their helmets and I noticed they were holding guns, not tasers. Guns are messier, louder, more frightening. The crowds parted around them, leaving each guardsman alone in an empty circle. The air was thick with nanobots, they must have let out millions of them. I didn't even need my sensors to tell me this: underneath everything was a tiny, almost inaudible hum. I rechecked our fields. It would only take one of these things to notice something wrong for the whole damn matrix to turn its vision on us.

So far, so good. I was saying it in my head like a mantra. So far, so good.

I couldn't help feeling a kind of satisfaction that at last the pinkers were having a taste of what we feel every day, the moment we step out of our doors. The fear we suppress every time we go about our business that we might not make it home. It didn't make Newport City anything like the banns, though. We don't have street lights or IMR so we make our own decorations. We make gardens. We look out for each other. Pinkers can't even touch each other. They can't hug when things are bad, like we do. How do they know that someone else is there for them? I still can't imagine what that does to a person.

In the banns, we learn how to navigate danger from the moment we can walk. I could tell just by looking that none of these pinkers had any of our skills. They were looking for someone to tell them what to do. All the tubes were telling them not to panic, that everything was okay. But you could tell that a lot of them knew that everything wasn't okay. I thought of things Erin had said, about how everyone was lied to, and that she knew that she had been part of the lying. Maybe other pinkers knew that too. Some of them were beginning to panic. You could see it in the flicker of their eyes, the tension in their voices.

We were about halfway to the Feelgood when Flora nudged me and jerked up her chin. We were still not allowed to speak, in case a bot picked up our strange speech patterns. Overhead, a huge black cloud was edging over the sun. It wasn't a nanostorm, the kind of cloud that makes fleshers turn up their suits, run inside, seal up the house. But it was going to be bad.

Nobody here was even looking. Here under the Inner Veil, where it never rains, nobody has to worry about the weather.

These people, I thought. These people have no idea. As if she read my thoughts, Flora swept her arm out towards the oblivious pinkers, lifting a quizzical eyebrow.

I kept an eye on the cloud. Its state didn't change in the time it took to reach the FeelGood. It just hung overhead blocking out the sunlight, looking ominous. Sometimes these clouds just floated over without anything happening. I found myself hoping that this one did, a storm could bring a hell of a lot of other complications.

Erin

'Weather's not looking good,' says Kat, swinging her chair around. 'It might screw the comms.'

'Not our comms,' Bel says. 'They'll be fine.'

I remember that Dez said that there's a black hole inside those tiny comm devices. I don't even know what a black hole is. She talks about it like it's something amazing, but they look pretty much the same as any strap-on comm outfit. A little bigger, a little heavier.

'Then why are they being so quiet?' asks Kat.

'They're busy,' says Bel.

We're lurking in our underground lair like master villains in some soap. I still can't rid myself of this feeling of unreality. This is the realest shit I've ever done, and it feels like some fantastic IMR adventure, the kind that the punkboys back in Newport City get off on. Only if it was a Newport City soap, there wouldn't be any girls in the lair. It would be wall-to-wall boys, led by John Mecha in hero mode.

The thought of Mecha makes me sick, and I try to distract myself by taking an intelligent interest in the screens. I don't have anything else to do.

I can see two red pulsing dots moving slowly across the map. One of them, in Block Five in Newport City, is Flora, Dez and Ami. The other is

Bo and Jenna, now halfway across the Tenth Bann. They're all on foot, so they're moving slowly. The fact that they're moving means that they're still alive.

On another screen we're watching the Newport City infotubes. There's footage of the blackout, dronecams sweeping over the roofs. Beneath you can see crowds of people milling about in darkened streets. It looks kind of like I always thought the banns looked. Dark and dangerous. The streets are unrecognisable with their lights out: they look stunted and ugly, squat buildings, blank walls. There are updates from the infodesk: no need to panic, everything is under control, we have had an unexpected blowout in the central power station.

Unexpected by you, I think. *We* expected it.

I feel a swell of pride. Dez is amazing. Our team, doing it.

As well as being scared shitless, I'm more excited than I've ever been in my entire life.

If I was down in those streets, I wouldn't feel reassured. I'd know, like everyone else, that something bad was going down. I wouldn't trust the infonews for one second. Even though nobody admits it, we all know they lie to us. We know, every single one of us, but we've all blocked out the moments when we see the lie. We just pretend it didn't happen. We're so used to pretending, it's second nature.

No more pretending, motherfuckers. I sit there in my glamourdress thinking about what that might mean. Me, Erin Saba, Queen of the Great Pretence. Do I even exist without it?

Moot question.

Me, Erin Saba, underneath the IMR fantasy, blood and flesh and bone and skin. I'm here, now. Breathing. In. Out. In. Out.

I don't even need a drink.

Dez

Ava buzzed us in through her hidden entrance, and we walked into the FeelGood's foyer and blinked in the sudden light. I wondered, for the first time, if the over-the-top pinkness of the foyer was a private Ava joke.

'You're early,' Ava said, by way of greeting.

I still couldn't work out whether or not she was a pinker. She looked full pinker, but she acted like a flesher. Like most of us in the banns and almost no one in Newport City, she had her own generator.

Mind you, OpSec had backup generators too. I wondered again how Ava had kept her business going in the total surveillance of Newport City. The old fashioned way, I had always thought. Graft and corruption. But paranoid me was now wondering if there was more to it than that. Whether Ava had a higher part in the whole structure. Why was she helping us?

'Everything went to plan,' said Flora. She switched off the IMR and flung herself onto the hot pink sofa. 'It was almost spooky.'

'Then something will go wrong any minute,' said Ava. 'It's an unwritten law.' She glanced at me. 'Want a brew while you wait?'

I nodded. Why not? I'd factored in time for contingencies and we'd run into no trouble at all, so we had an extra ten minutes. We followed Ava out of the pinkness into the FeelGood's office. The businesslike messiness felt like a haven. As she boiled water on the solar stove, Ava nodded to a screen suspended over the low table. 'I'm following the dark tubes. All kinds of shit is going down in the banns.'

I almost didn't want to look, but I flipped the screen around. Someone was beaming a live vid from high up over a wide rue in what looked like the Eleventh. There wasn't any sound and you couldn't really see what was going on: people running, first forward, then back, the flash and smoke of ordinance. I couldn't see any militia, they must have been out of the picture. As I watched the screen emptied of people. They were reacting to something I couldn't see, opening a space. Bodies lay on the ground, blurred by the smoke drifting in the air.

Bo and Jenna and Redborg were out there. I knew exactly where they were because my suit was constantly monitoring their position, but that didn't stop me wanting to open up a line to Bo to hear his voice, to reassure myself. I suppressed the impulse and turned the screen so I couldn't see it. I let my shoulders relax, trying to clear my mind from anxiety. I was least sure about the next step. Everything that had happened this morning led up to this. I'd modelled it millions of times. (Literally). I was as sure as I could be that, in the right circumstances, it would work. That I could bring down the Inner Veil so completely that no one could get it back up.

But I also knew what could go wrong. Say, if Bo and Jenna got killed in the fighting. I had figured there was about a 10 per cent chance of that, but looking at the tubes had made me think it was probably higher. I did some remodelling, refining the backup plan I'd made in case the Wall thing didn't work, but the chances of success of that were much dodgier.

A lot depended on the timing. If Bo and Jenna were delayed, if I'd mucked up the estimates on how long it would take for them to get to the Wall, our chances started going down. Random elements started ramping up the more time went by: the chance of Newport City Council police looking at surveillance footage and tracking us to the FeelGood. The chance of someone lucking out and finding the burst pipe in the power station. A pinker noticing us. A bot decoding the field. A bunch of other imponderables.

Underneath the low, almost imperceptible throb of Ava's generator I became aware that I could hear something else. Something unrhythmic. A pulse in the ground. A kind of wash of noise that could be voices shouting, perhaps the faint echo of gunshots, explosions. Once I could hear it I couldn't unhear it.

The banns. I could hear the banns, like I had ears in my feet.

Ava handed us our brews and left the office. Ami stood in a corner and seemed to shut down. I ran some updated scenarios while we waited, but none of them substantially changed anything I'd already calculated. Flora nudged my elbow.

'Stop it, Dez,' she said. 'There's no possible permutation you haven't run.'

'But if...'

'It's all "if", Dez. This whole ludicrous beautiful plan. There's no certainty, right? That's what you can't stand. There's no certainty anywhere. Even if everything happened in the best possible way, even if everything we planned works out, we still don't know what will happen.'

I felt a catch in my chest, a tug of dread. Flora was right, all my life was a calculation of odds because it gave me the illusion that I had some kind of control. But it didn't matter how well I did the calculations. In the end, I'd never know anything for sure.

Flora leant over and kissed me on the lips.

'Embrace it, Dez,' she said. She was speaking low, whispering. 'It's why you love me, right? Why you love my music. You never really know what's going to happen next. I'm the thing in your life that you can't control. You know that. And you love me.'

I didn't know what to say, so I didn't say anything.

'The one thing that's certain is that we're all going to die one day.' Flora kissed me again, twice, on the corners of my mouth. 'If not now, later.'

That wasn't very cheering. One of my worst fears was Flora dying before I did. I knew it was selfish. But the thought of the abyss that would leave inside me wrenched me, turned me inside out.

'I don't want you to die,' I said, feeling the crack in my voice, like I was five years old.

'Me neither. But I will. So this...' Flora leant back in the scruffy sofa, and held up her mug of tea. 'This is being alive, not knowing what's going to happen. Drinking our tea. Let's enjoy it.' She smiled at me, and I found myself smiling back, despite everything, despite the inevitable thought that maybe this was the last time.

The minutes seemed to crawl by, but at the same time they went too fast. Bo and Jenna were by the Wall now, but they were separated from Redborg. Not good, he was there to keep them safe. They were still moving in the right direction though, so they must be doing okay. I had no idea where Sevika was.

'One minute to go,' said Flora.

I sat up, preparing myself. Once the Wall was frozen, I had a clear way in. I wasn't quite sure how to negotiate once I was in, I'd have to make it up as I went along. But I knew where to begin. I focused myself.

The minutes ticked by. They were next to the Wall, and now they weren't moving. They must be beginning their water thing. But nothing was happening.

Now.

I must have said it out loud, because Flora turned to look at me.

We had allowed thirty seconds for the water thing. Bo reckoned it was plenty of time. I let the thirty seconds pass, and then another, and then I pinged him, but there was no pingback. I felt my mouth dry out instantly, like I suddenly had a mouthful of sand.

I opened the secret line. 'Bo,' I said. 'Is everything okay?'

No answer.

I fought down my fear, left it another thirty seconds, tried again. No response. And then again, thirty seconds later. And again.

The sound that I was hearing through the ground was louder, I was sure. I could almost make out voices. Like people were shouting or screaming, a long way away. What was going on out there?

I tried again. No answer.

Something was wrong. Something was badly wrong.

Bo

Something appeared as a ripple in the darkness, a shadow among shadows, gathering into a form. I recognised Sevika. There was nothing but Sevika's face, a face of water very close to mine, its surface trembling minutely. I knew, without knowing how, that we were inside the Wall together.

Slowly her body grew visible, rippling silver, shining, and I realised I had seen her before. Sevika was the water person. She had always been the water person. She had come to me, had spoken the water words, had led me to strange, wild places. She had been with me for so long, always drawing me closer.

'You are mine, now,' she said softly. She was speaking without a mouth. 'You're gifted, waterboy, but you don't know how to use your gift. I do.'

For a moment I saw myself reflected in the shimmering surface of her face. I was made of water too. And in my face was the reflection of her face, and so on and so on, into an infinity of faces. I wanted to run away, but Sevika was holding me, forcing me to look into her eyes.

She dissolved and flowed towards me. A deep, cold pain flowered in the centre of my being. It was more than fear. I was thrown back by her weight. How could I feel weight in this place? And yet her power crushed me. I tried to throw her off, but it was impossible. Sevika entered every part of me, every molecule. I had no edges, no body, there was nothing I could do. We were one being now, an edgeless current swirling together in an infinite void.

I was lost.

Then I began to hear water rising and falling, surging and then dying away, wave after wave of energy gathering and then releasing itself, rushing through the emptiness.

I could feel Sevika absorbing me, drawing me into her the way a dowser draws water. I was vanishing, becoming Sevika. I couldn't stop it. The more I struggled the more she drained my strength.

I heard the water whispering. Was it whispering my name? My water name. It was calling me, as if it was calling me home to the vast waters that lay beyond Sevika and I, the waters of seas and rivers, ice and rain. And suddenly I wasn't afraid.

I stopped resisting. I stopped thinking of Sevika. Sevika didn't matter at all. I surrendered to the voice of the water.

And everything changed.

It was cold. So cold. Nothing – not the experiments we did in the lab, not freezing that Ap, not even the depths of Newport's ice storms, where people could freeze where they stood in less than a minute – prepared me for this. It was another dimension of freezing. And it was getting colder.

I didn't know what time was any more, but I could feel the contraction of the cold. It doesn't make much sense to say, but I was the cold. Maybe after the terrible struggle with Sevika, the only thing left in my mind was that we had to freeze the Wall, and the less there was of me, the more that single thought came into focus.

Strangely, I didn't feel afraid. I remember a wild exhilaration, but somehow that wasn't anything to do with being human. This was my will, it was the will of the water, pushing out every bit of heat that existed around us. Even the tiniest vibration of the smallest particle was slowing, stopping, becoming absolutely still. Maybe it was death? Maybe I wanted that death? I don't know. I don't remember it very well, because I don't think I had much of me to remember with.

I just drove that temperature down. And down. And down. And then Sevika wasn't there any more. And neither was I.

Dez

The seconds ticked by. I was now mostly in data mode so each second was an eternity. How small can a unit of time be? As small as you like. Smaller than any human sense can smell or feel or hear. Bigger than anything you can begin to imagine. Dive either way and you enter eternity.

What the hell was going on? I could see Bo and Jenna on the map. They were there by the Wall, but nothing was happening, Bo wasn't answering me. If their life signs blinked out, I'd know. They were still alive, but something was stopping them. Or the water magic wasn't working.

Never trust magic.

Bo and Jenna had been so sure. We'd spent hours talking through it. I had almost been convinced, I had been convinced enough that I'd factored it in as a major part of the whole thing. After the Eradicator, I had believed they could do it. That they knew what they were doing.

Of course I'd modelled what would happen if it didn't work. We still had a chance. A much smaller chance, with a much bigger risk. But I wasn't here to do nothing.

Four minutes. Five minutes. Six minutes. Eternities flowing into each other, a river of precisely marked eternities. I could feel the sweat running down my forehead. The dread pulsing in my stomach. The outright fear that I had banished ever since we started planning this. *We only get one chance at this*. Seven minutes. Ten minutes was the absolute cut-off point. It sounds arbitrary, but it wasn't. Every single risk started kicking up sharply after ten minutes, probabilities started clumping together, thickening into something like the certainty of failure.

At eight minutes I started preparing myself for Plan B. To take down the Inner Veil with the Wall still holding it in balance, I needed all of me. One hundred per cent of me. And even that wasn't enough. To reach even 50 per cent chance, I needed Ami too. We would have to meld together, both our capacities. We'd had a little practice in the lab, and we could do it, but after what happened last time I went into OpSec, even the thought of it made me feel sick. But now we had no choice.

I pinged Ami, who blinked and rebooted. Flora was sitting opposite me, her taser in her hand, relaxed, focused. I would be entirely vulnerable now, and she was there to cover my back. I began to gather me together, focusing into a tiny unit of white-hot consciousness. I was still vaguely aware of what was going on in the FeelGood office, but already most of me wasn't there.

Fifteen seconds into my preparation, the tiny part of me that was still in the room saw Flora jerk to attention. I sensed the flow of her muscles as she stood up, the taser in her hand. I felt, rather than heard, that something was going on in the foyer. Ten seconds later there was shouting, a gunshot. Something crashed to the ground. Heavy footsteps.

Fear blossomed in my stomach, the way blood flowers out of a wound. A haemorrhage of terror.

Ami and I were linked now, and I felt her withdraw, redirecting her sensors. She was speaking to Flora. It was a struggle to understand what she said, I was getting beyond the universe of words. 'OpSec,' she said. 'They started tracking us when we entered Block 15.'

Flora nodded. Her mouth was a straight line, her jaw set, determined. She looked deadly. Beautiful. My Flora.

I thought of what she had told me. Embrace the uncertainty. *It's why you love me, right? Why you love my music. You never really know what's going to happen next...*

There was someone screaming behind the office door. They'd kick it down. Any moment. Five seconds max.

I'd run this scenario. I knew what was going to happen next. We were fucked. Totally and utterly fucked.

Well, maybe that wasn't certain. We always had Plan B.

I tensed to leap into datatime, one hundred per cent of me, ready to do or die. Ami and I already couldn't tell each other apart. We would just go, a streak of energy almost as fast as light itself. We would circle the Inner Veil, a dazzling ring, however many times we needed to disable all the control backups. And then we would fry them.

It was already hurting, insofar as pain made any sense to Data Dez. In this state Ami and I were already unravelling, moment by moment.

What was left of me took a metaphorical breath. This was it. There was no coming back from this one. I hadn't told Flora that. I hadn't told anyone. There was no time for regret.

But before we started making that deadly circle, everything changed.

I didn't need any signal from Bo. It was a change as distinct as light flooding a dark room, or walking into a cellar on a hot summer day. The Wall had gone silent. And once its quantum hum died down, we could get into the Inner Veil and change the very structure of its nanocircuits. We could shut that damn thing down without burning ourselves into inexistence. I might even survive it.

Of course, I wasn't thinking any of these things at the time. I wasn't thinking like fleshers think. I don't think Ami was thinking like AIs think, either. We were in some other dimension, where even computation was too slow.

We did Plan A with all the suicidal firepower we had reserved for Plan B, only without the suicide. It made it much quicker.

Without the protection of the Wall, destroying the Inner Veil was easy. Me and Ami just went in like knives of light, slicing the whole structure like it was a rotten fungus. It took less than a second. Much less than a second.

I had enough awareness left to make sure that I was back in my body. I just lay there, feeling like my whole brain was on fire. And then there was this... wave. I think it was a wave. A wave that went through all of us, cancelling out time. It was like all the nerves in my body lit up all at once and connected with everything else in a giant network, a network bigger and more complicated than anything I had ever encountered before. I could see everything: me, Flora, the men in the next room trying to kick Ava to death, the terrified pinkers in the streets outside, the fleshers in the banns, the feral gaus, the razorbirds, every living thing. In that moment I was inside them and outside them, I was them and I wasn't them. We were all one thing, suspended together.

The only thing I knew in that bubble of time was how fragile we all were, motes of gossamer floating through a universe of shredders, blinking into the sunlight for the merest moment before blinking out again forever. All I knew was that we needed each other. And by *we* I meant *everything*. Every living thing, from the slugs and gaus and nekas to the pinkers I'd hated all my life. None of us could exist without each other.

It made sense, a beautiful sense, that I haven't ever been able to recapture since.

And then I blacked out.

When I came to, Flora was holding me, kissing my face, sobbing. I looked up into her beautiful eyes. My mouth was so dry it was burning.

'I'm not dead yet,' I managed to say.

She shook her head and almost laughed.

'Oh Dez,' she said. 'I really thought I'd lost you this time.'

There was a strange rattling, and then something started banging outside, like loose iron on the roof being blown about by the wind.

'What's that?'

'It's raining,' Flora said.

Bo

Jenna was sobbing nearby. I got to my hands and knees and crawled to where she lay, curled up on the chalky ground. I took her in my arms and held her close. She was freezing.

'Where did you go?' she said.

'Inside the Wall.' It sounded ridiculous, but I knew that Jenna believed me. Right now, reality was so strange that anything was possible.

We turned to look at the Wall. A film of ice as wide as a house ran from the base to the very top. The hail had passed and sunlight was streaming through a gap in the clouds, splitting into rainbows as it hit the ice.

'Have we done it?' said Jenna.

'I don't know what we've done.' I couldn't see the Inner Veil from here. Had Dez brought it down? I couldn't tell.

As we struggled to our feet, we heard a terrifying roar, maybe a few blocks away, and scattered bursts of gunfire from every direction. A massive, swirling pillar of smoke rose into the air. High above us a squad of attack drones was approaching from the west, bristling with weapons.

Someone called my name. Redborg. He ran towards us, his hands dark with blood, blood streaming from a wound in his shoulder, and threw his arms around us.

'My lovelies,' he said. 'My dearest dears. You're still alive.'

He'd hugged me so fiercely I felt bruised, but I didn't mind. 'We are,' I said shakily. 'Just.'

'I headed for the Wall and tracked along it,' he said. 'I knew I'd find you eventually. Most likely your corpses.'

He stood back. 'We'd better get out of here. Where's Sevika?'

'I don't I know,' I said. 'I don't want to know.'

'There,' said Jenna. 'Over there.'

Sevika lay twisted on the ground a short distance away, as if she'd been flung there. Redborg knelt beside her, turned her body over and whistled through his teeth. 'Bless my fucking bones,' he said. 'What the hell happened here?'

Sevika's corpse was encased in a crust of ice. Even from where I stood, I could see her face through the milky thickness, her teeth bared in a terrible grimace, her eyes open wide, unseeing, white.

'Oh my god,' said Jenna. 'Did she try to master the water, Bo? You can't do that. Nobody can do that.'

I didn't know. 'She tried to master me,' I said. I didn't want to talk about what had happened in the Wall. What Sevika had tried to do to me. It was horrible, whatever it was. I'd think about it later, when I had time, when I had the strength. But the water had come to me. It saved me from Sevika.

I had absolutely no memory of what had happened after that.

Something exploded as a striker drone screamed out of the sky, its weapons blazing.

'Let's go, fleshers,' said Redborg. 'We gotta get out of here pronto.'

'Bo,' said Jenna. Her voice was sharp, urgent. 'Bo. Look at the Wall.'

Erin

I never got to say those words. The words I sweated blood over, that I put down on the screen one by one and learned as seriously as if they were made by someone else. In the end, I did speak, but the words I spoke were different words. Better words.

I'm still processing what happened when the Inner Veil went down. Hell, all of Newport is, from the Outer Banns to Newport City Central. Sometimes I feel like my brain wants to wipe out what happened, wants to forget what it was like. But I'm not letting it. The one thing I know is that we have to remember.

I keep going over and over it, trying to make sense of it. I feel like there are little gaps in my memory. It must have looked bizarre: me in my high glamour dress, prinked up in front of the camera in a corner of the lab, my script and a glass of water on a table at my elbow.

Shortly after that, the shit started going down. Well, we all know what happened. All of us in the lab gathered around the screens, watching Dez's scenarios twisting from success to the worst possible outcomes.

Bel didn't move, didn't speak. She just sat there, her eyes fixed on the screens. I realised with a kind of dull shock that she was bracing herself to witness the deaths of both of her kids. In her pose, in her straight back and her rigid jaw, I saw all her dread, all that oncoming grief. She'd risked everything, and now she was preparing to deal with losing the gamble. She had always known that it might turn out that way, Dez had been open about that. We'd optimised the odds, but the odds were always going to be against us.

I'm not sure that I was breathing. I wanted to shut my eyes, so I didn't have to witness what was going to happen. But I felt like I had a duty to watch, like I had to be there, to bear witness, even if there wasn't a damn thing that any of us could do.

And then…the wave happened. It was like, I don't know, some kind of weird rush, like I'd taken some high quality nebus, but it was so much more than that, this weird expansion so that suddenly it was like – no, it was more than *like*, it *was* – that suddenly I was open to every single person in all of Newport. More than people: every single living thing, inside and outside the Veil. Containing multitudes.

I don't have the words to say what it was like, nothing comes close.

This feeling of overwhelming joy and absolute terror, and they were both the same thing. I don't know how long it lasted. No, I do, because later we checked the time. It lasted just over five seconds. But those five seconds felt like they went forever. For those five seconds whoever I thought I was dissolved into something so much larger than I could possibly imagine, this brilliant shimmer of life, a network of thought and feeling that was every-thing at once.

I realise now that we hide inside our own skins. Some people are in such pain, such fear, such grief, that it's impossible to bear. How can we possibly stand it? And side by side with that, there's this joy. Just joy. That's impos-sible to bear too.

Being alive. What a drug.

Fleshers seemed to cope a lot better with it than pinkers. I guess they were already used to this world of feeling, this world in which there was no floor, no roof, no walls. But I haven't spoken to anybody who wasn't terrified. Flora says she wants that feeling back, that it's something that she reaches for in her music. Dez said she had a little rehearsal because it was a tiny bit like being Data Dez. 'Only a tiny bit,' she said.

Pinkers hardly coped at all. A lot, particularly the top brass, just went mad and killed themselves. They picked up their guns and pointed them at their own heads and blasted themselves out of existence. They had no way of processing it. I felt their minds cracking and shattering, and it was like my own mind breaking.

But I didn't break. I thought later that maybe it was because I was already broken.

When it passed we were all on the floor, piled up against the wall, as if a huge gust of wind had rushed through the lab and tumbled us over and over. Everyone touching everyone else.

We blinked and stared at each other. I was surprised that the whole lab wasn't in a mess, it felt like everything in there should have been scattered and broken, as if a bomb had gone off. I think we were all crying.

The next thing I remember was Dez on the comms. She'd just opened an ordinary line and was speaking out loud. 'Ma, you okay? Ma?'

'I'm okay Dez. You?'

'Yes, we're good. Bo just pinged me.' Dez was sobbing, her words catching on her sobs. 'I thought we were going to die. And then…oh my god Ma.'

'Get back here, Dezzie. Just come home.'

'I love you, Ma.'

'I love you too, my darling. So much.'

Dez snapped out, and Gloria crawled to their feet.

'You've got to talk to them, Erin,' they said.

They dragged me up. They held my hand with their hand. I didn't even blink. Skin on skin, touching. In that moment, it was the most comforting thing in the world, to be touched, like it anchored me in time and space, like it put me back in my body.

'Talk to them. Before everyone goes over the edge.'

'What do I say?'

'I think you know what to say.'

'Tell them what they need to know.' Bel was staring at me. All the hardness was gone from her face, and her eyes were shining, with grief or love, I didn't know which. I realised how beautiful she is. 'Nothing we can say will help them. Maybe you can.'

I felt dizzy and sick and exalted, all at once. I didn't have a single thought in my head. But I knew what Gloria meant. In that moment, we all did. Even the fleshers couldn't bear it.

'Is my makeup okay?'

Gloria laughed. 'You look a little shook up, darling. But your makeup is just fine.'

They picked up the camera and turned it on and Kat switched the output to the OpSec public tubes. And I began to talk, without a thought in my head. I wasn't saying lines. I was speaking.

The others were watching on the surveillance footage as pinkers gathered around the public screens. They watched, and listened. Some of them came out of shock and started helping others that weren't coping as well. They're the people we're talking to now, trying to sort out the shit we need to sort out, so we can all live in the city together.

It's going to take time. It's not easy. But it's a start.

There's a recording, but I haven't watched it. I don't need to. I remember everything I said.

Hello, it's me, I said. Erin Saba. You remember me? Did you hear a whisper that I had killed myself? The real story is that I had to leave Newport City, because OpSec wanted to murder me. I think you know that. We all know what happens when someone disappears, even if we're all too scared to say the truth.

I escaped OpSec. I'm in the banns with the fleshers. They looked after me, though they had no reason to. They're the reason I'm still alive.

I'm tired of all the lies. So many lies, right? All our lives, lie after lie.

Those fleshers we've always been scared of? You know who they are now, don't you? With that thing that just happened. I don't know what it was but it happened to me too, it happened to all the fleshers, to everyone in this city. That pain you're feeling, it's their pain and your pain, it's the pain we've all felt all our lives. It's the pain that we didn't know we were feeling.

It hurts. It hurts so bad.

Look at what we did to ourselves. We all did it. We did to to each other. We did it even worse to fleshers. How can we live with what we did to the fleshers? We can't pretend we didn't do it. We killed them, we killed their kids, we locked them up, we made them work for us, we said they weren't human. We did that, so we could live in our little bubble. And now that little bubble has been broken open and it's never coming back.

Yes, fleshers did that. They broke the Inner Veil. They had to because of what we did to them. Now we all have to live under the same Veil. And maybe it's about time.

There's nowhere to hide any more for us pinkers. You know they call us pinkers, right? All our lives it's been fleshers and pinkers. I know that most of you never thought about what fleshers called us. I never did. It never occurs to us that they have their own names for things. But they do. They've got all our names, and all their names too. They've got more words than we have. They know more than we do. It's about time we started learning those words.

We've got to find a better way to be.

I don't know what that way is, but we have to start making it. I know what just happened seems the most frightening thing that's ever happened, but it's not nearly as frightening as what we've been doing to ourselves our whole lives.

Why don't we touch each other?

Fleshers touch each other the whole time. They're people like us, but they know how to touch each other. Sometimes they're violent, like we are, but most of the time they're not. I've seen how fleshers are. Only a little, but it's not what we've been told. All our lives we've been lied to.

I've seen people touch because they love each other, and it's so gentle, so comforting, like there's a beam of golden light passing between them.

It made me feel so lonely.

Why have we made ourselves so lonely? We need each other. Each of us, we're born alone, and we die alone, and the only thing that will stop the pain of that is if we can help each other, tell each other that we're here, that we're here for each other.

We have to learn. You know that now, don't you? So learn with me.

Reach out to the person next to you. Do it now. You don't have to touch them, just look into their eyes and see them. See, here is Gloria, this is Gloria, they had to leave Newport City because they were going to be arrested and then probably murdered, because that is what Newport City does.

Maybe you can try to touch. It doesn't matter if you can't do it, but maybe you can try. Like this. Softly, just with the tips of your fingers. See? It's not the most disgusting thing in the world. That feeling of disgust, that's all the hatred that you feel for yourself. You know the feeling, you can't bear to look at yourself, you can't bear even the touch of your own skin?

We were taught that. We were taught that we were disgusting. But we're not.

Can you feel the warmth of that person's blood through your fingertips? Their pulse thrumming through their bodies, like your pulse? That's them and you, both together, both alive. Can you feel how fragile that person is? How can you want to hurt them? That touch, that tingle that runs up your arm, it's amazing, it's like everything lighting up, and it's beautiful.

Why do we want to hurt each other? We have to find a better way to be. There's so much more to do, so much more to learn.

Just speak. Just look. Maybe just begin to touch.

It's going to be difficult but oh my god it's going to be so much better.

This is the beginning.

Bo

It had never rained in Newport City Central. Pinkers had never smelt the hot, foul wind of the dasht or been afraid of the air. They had never been hungry or cold, or felt the comforting embrace of someone they loved. The shadow of the Wall had never fallen across their streets.

And then Wall changed. Even Dez didn't know what caused it. She mumbled something about quantums and critical points and trailed off into silence.

Jenn and Redborg and I watched it happen. The band of ice that ran down the Wall began to spread, faster than the eye could follow, running in both directions, rainbow colours cascading down to hit the ground in a brilliant kaleidoscope of sparks. In moments, the entire Wall was blazing in a vast, unconsuming fire. It was so bright that I threw up my hand to shade my eyes.

Then, quite suddenly, the light dimmed, and I couldn't see anything because of the after-image pulsing in my vision. I blinked the tears out of my eyes and saw that now the Wall was still. But where there had been an absence, a wall of darkness, now there was a wall of light. It looked like flawless ice or glass, and you could see through it to the distorted shapes of buildings on the other side.

We turned to each other, our faces shining with the awe of what we'd just witnessed. Jenna was about to say something when the wave hit. It was like a soundless explosion, some kind of invisible energy that surged out of the Wall like a massive tide. I don't know how to describe it. I don't know how long it lasted. Seconds? Hours? An eternity?

I found myself on the ground, tangled up with Jenna and Redborg. We shakily pulled each other up, checked that each of us was whole. And then we walked back to the lab.

In the Tenth the light was bright and golden, long, level rays reaching under the edges of the clouds. We headed down Rue Rukami and turned towards the Demolitions. Smoke still drifted in the sky, rising upwards in the stillness. In the north, storm clouds were low over Newport City Central.

It seemed to me that the banns were somehow innocent. I don't know of another word to describe it. There was nothing except this collective awareness, this single thought, this one feeling, as if a great sigh was released from all that lived, and one breath of pure air that filled us all.

When it passed, we were left stunned and disorientated. The weapons in our hands were suddenly incomprehensible. In the hours that followed, we were like people waking from a dream.

Jenna and I knew that the water had given us all this gift. As we walked through the Tenth, Jenna and I felt its voice singing inside us. I'm sure that Redborg felt it too. He was calm, radiant, like I hadn't seen him since he returned to the banns. The defiance and rage that had been driving him seemed to dissolve, falling away as tears fall from eyes.

He put his arm around my shoulders as we walked. 'Music, my dear flesh' he said. 'There has to be music again.'

The fighting was over, but I knew that another struggle was beginning. Night would fall again. In the darkness, when every person was left with only themselves, every mind could find a way back to the times before the Wall turned into light. The walls inside people's heads could be rebuilt. Did we know how to live without them? But perhaps they'd be different walls now. Perhaps they weren't as solid and menacing, as final.

In Newport City Central the same brief epiphany had come and gone.

But there, where every protection the pinkers had ever known had been stripped away, it arrived like a calamity. We watched them afterwards on the surveillance vids, feeling this weird compassion. Why should we feel anything for them? But we did.

I've known about pinkers all my life. Sometimes I'm fascinated by them, sometimes I hate them. And sometimes I think about them as if they're a puzzle I'm studying, trying to work them out. I guess you can study something all you like, but that doesn't mean you understand it. I don't know what they thought of themselves or their place in the world, or if they ever wondered what was beyond the Inner Veil. Perhaps they had been so incurious for so long, so safe inside their bubble, that anything outside was impossible for them to imagine.

Erin said that the water made them know their isolation, the skin-ache of their loneliness. She said that they understood in that terrible moment that they were no different from us, and that was maybe worst of all.

With no Inner Veil to protect them, the tempest thundered over their heads, throwing down its rain and hail, darkening their streets, flooding their houses, drowning out their panicked voices.

And then it was over. The tide of loss and madness passed over them. The tubes flickered on in their streets and homes and there was Erin Saba, in a glorious mist of blue and violet, talking to them, speaking their pain out loud. Some of them calmed down after that. Not everyone, though.

And the clouds dissolved and blew away over the banns, back out into the dasht.

Dez

I opened a line to Ma to let her know that we were okay, even though she already knew. We had all been aware of each other in that vast wave: we'd all felt the beating of each other's hearts, in some unimaginably complicated systolic rhythm. Ma told me that she loved me and to get back there as soon as I could.

I was proud of us: not one life lost. Not even Brian Mac, who had had the smallest chances of us all. When I told him his odds he just smiled, in that ironic cop way he had, and said he'd faced worse.

Right now, just the fact of being alive seemed miraculous, quite aside from what we had all survived.

When we could move, Flora and I checked on Ava in the next room. It turned out that she'd been doing most of the kicking. The OpSec guys looked worse than she did. Her cheek was cut and you could see a bruise coming out over her eye, but they seemed to have blood all over them.

Four of them were hunched against the wall, their heads in their hands. Another was lying on the floor, crying like a child. He had a hole right through his hand where Ava had stamped on him with her stilletto. As we walked in, she was spraying a bandage onto the wound. She looked up and shrugged as if to say, what can you do?

Ava tending a guard? Moreover, a guard who'd just tried to beat her up? I almost couldn't believe my eyes. It was almost the most amazing thing I saw that whole day. It brought home what had just happened.

It wasn't about forgivenness. I'm not sure that I've forgiven anybody. It was something else that I don't know how to describe.

'Will you be okay if we head off?' asked Flora. 'Should we...should we get anyone in to help?'

'I'll be fine.' Ava got to her feet and surveyed the mess in her reception. 'I'll put these bozos to work tidying up while I wait for the Brig.'

'We'll head home, then,' I said.

'Tell Gloria to come back. If they want. I miss them.' Ava lifted her chin and gave us one of those straight looks that go through you like a laser. 'I don't know what you did,' she said. 'But thank you. I think.'

If everything went as planned, we were supposed to meet everyone back at the lab. Flora and I didn't even talk about it. We just headed straight for Rue Ballard.

I was shocked at how close it was. Newport City Central had always seemed so far away. It had been another world, almost impossible to get to. But our house was a half hour walk from the FeelGood, if that. We were practically neighbours.

We picked our way past the dead zone where the Veil had been, marvelling at the strangeness around us. Even the light was different, there was a new radiance in it. Every detail of every single object seemed to stand out in vivid detail, as if even the brick and steel and stone were alive. Maybe they were. What the hell did I know?

I really couldn't begin to guess what had changed, and for once I didn't try to work it out. Maybe it was just magic.

I permitted myself to be awed. To embrace the uncertainty. Just for now.

Rue Ballard was a mess, but everyone was out in the street, already beginning to clean up. It looked like there'd been fighting: there were a few bodies around and the burned remains of a quad. All the bodies seemed to be militia. Someone had lined up the corpses in the front yard of one of the burned houses. They were placed respectfully, as we do our own, with their arms crossed over their breasts.

People called out greetings as we passed them. I was grateful that nobody seemed to hate us. Part of me had been afraid they might, even after the wave. We walked up Rue Ballard towards our homes, stepping over debris, broken glass, discarded weapons. It felt like a very long time since we had last been there.

Kojo was outside Café Boite, sweeping up broken glass and other rubble. He was moving slowly, as if his back was hurting him, and he didn't see Flora at first. She gave a sob and ran and flung herself into his arms, nearly knocking him over.

I watched his face light up like...like the face of man who was holding his daughter after a long, dark time when he had thought he would never see her again.

And then I turned away.

This was between them, it wasn't anything to do with me. And that was fine. Flora was mine and she was also Kojo's. She belonged to everyone who loved her, to everyone she loved, just as I belonged to all my loves, to Flora and Bo and Ma and Redborg and Kat and Rioka and all the others. And yes, even to Gloria and Erin and Ami. There was enough of all of us to go around.

I walked over to our house. The door was shut and the buzzer was broken. I had to hotwire the mechanism to get in. Inside, it wasn't as bad as I had expected. Everything that had been in a cupboard was thrown onto the floor and they'd slashed all our bedding, but there was nothing that couldn't be fixed or easily replaced. This time, I'd put all our precious things in the stash in my cellar. OpSec had gone through the house with everything they had, but they hadn't even suspected that my deadwall was there.

Maybe I'd never have to hide anything ever again.

I picked my chair off the floor and sat for a while in our front room, staring out of the window. Flora and Kojo were sitting on the ground across the road, talking. Kojo's arm was around Flora's shoulders, holding her tightly against him as if he'd never let her go. That was always Kojo's problem, letting Flora go. But this time I knew he would.

A lot of things would be different now. Maybe some wouldn't be as different as we wanted.

I tried to think about what had happened, but it was hard. Partly that was because I was dazed and exhausted, and I wasn't ready. But also I had no idea what we had done. Or what the water had done to us. I think we still don't really know. Did the water *do* anything? Didn't it simply show us who we are?

Seeing inside some of those pinker heads hadn't been pretty. They wouldn't like it here, out in the open under the same sky as everyone else. They'd want everything to be like it was before, when they had all their certainties and comforts. I already knew they'd do anything to get back there.

But none of us was going to let that happen. I was as sure of that as I was of anything. We'd had a glimpse of something else, something that was too beautiful to lose. We'd fought for it even before we knew it existed. We'd fight with everything we had to keep it.

Ma pinged me. *Where are you?*

I opened a line.

'I'm home, Ma,' I said. 'I'm home.'

NOVELS BY ALISON CROGGON

For news and previews, sign up for Alison Croggon's newsletter at
alisoncroggon.com

The Books of Pellinor

"Rich and passionate...Supremely satisfying."

— *Starred review, KIRKUS*

"An epic fantasy in the Tolkien tradition - I couldn't put it
down!"

— *Tamora Pierce*

"Unbelievably fine, represents fantasy storytelling at its best."

— *VOYA, US*

"The writing is the closest I've found to the feel of the Lord of
the Rings. I wanted to slow down and appreciate each portion
of the character's journey."

— *Trudy Canavan, The Magician's Guild*

The Bone Queen

  Finalist Best Young Adult Novel, Aurealis Awards, 2016

The Gift/The Naming (US)

  Finalist in two categories, Aurealis Awards, 2002

  Children's Books Council of Australia Notable Book, 2002

The Riddle

The Crow

The Singing

Black Spring

"A darkly captivating tale of heartbreaking, destructive passion."

— *Booklist*

Finalist, 2014 NSW Premier's Literary Awards
Children's Books Council of Australia Notable Book, 2014

The River and the Book

"A topical tale, it is engaging, suspenseful and memorable. 4 1/2 stars"

— *Adelaide Advertiser*

"It's a powerful little story…I'd recommend it to anyone at all."

— *Booksellers New Zealand*

"The River and the Book is one of those beautiful stories that will take your breath away."

— *The Bookkat*

"A thought-provoking and wildly compelling book of magical realism, exploring colonialism, and exploitation of indigenous people."

— *Alpha Reader*

"A beautiful piece of literature."

— *Readings*

Winner 2016 Environmental Award for Writing for Children
Finalist WA Premiers Literary Awards
A Children's Book Council of Australia Notable Book, 2016

Alison Croggon is an Australian novelist, poet, librettist and critic. She is the author of the popular and critically acclaimed fantasy quintet *The Books of Pellinor*, published in Australia, the UK, the US and across Europe. *The Books of Pellinor* was re-released worldwide in 2017 with the publication of a fifth book, *The Bone Queen*, a finalist in for the Aurealis Awards YA Novel of the Year. Other internationally published novels include *Black Spring* (shortlisted for the 2014 NSW Premier's Award) and *The River and the Book* (shortlisted for the 2016 WA Premier's Award and winner of the Wilderness Society's Environmental Writing for Children Award). Her opera libretti have been performed on major stages across Australia. The libretto for *Mayakovsky* (score Michael Smetanin) was shortlisted for the 2015 Victorian Premiers Prize for Drama, and *The Riders* (score Iain Grandage) was awarded the Vocal/Choral Work of the Year in the 2015 Australian Arts Music Awards. Other awards include the 2009 Geraldine Pascal Critic of the Year for her performance criticism, and the Dame Mary Gilmore and Anne Elder Prizes for poetry. alisoncroggon.com

Daniel Keene has written for the theatre since 1979. His plays have been performed on main stages around Australia and in China, America and Europe. He has won numerous awards, including six Premier's Literary Awards for drama, the Sydney Myer Performing Arts Award and the Kenneth Myer Medallion for the Performing Arts for his contribution to Australian theatre with the Keene/Taylor Theatre Project. Since 2000, over 80 main stage productions of his work have been presented in Europe, predominately in France. He is the only Australian playwright to have been produced in the main program at the Festival d'Avignon. In 2009 his work for young audiences was awarded the Prix Théâtre en Pages by Scéne Nationale de Toulouse. Seven volumes of his plays (French translations by Severine Magois) have been published by éditions Theatrales, Paris. In 2016 Daniel was appointed to the rank of Chevalier de l'Ordre des Arts et des Lettres by the French Ministry of Culture for his contribution to French culture. danielkeene.com.au

www.ingramcontent.com/pod-product-compliance
Lightning Source LLC
Chambersburg PA
CBHW050006120726
47903CB00006B/1660